A DIFFERENT KIND OF FIRE

A Novel

Suanne Schafer

JACKSON COUNTY LIBRARY SERVICES
MEDFORD OREGON 97501

Published by Waldorf Publishing
2140 Hall Johnson Road
#102-345
Grapevine, Texas 76051
www.WaldorfPublishing.com

A Different Kind of Fire

ISBN: 978-1-64136-865-0
Library of Congress Control Number: 2018933242

Disclaimer

This is a work of fiction. Names, characters, businesses, places, events and incidents are either the products of the author's imagination or used in a fictitious manner. Any resemblance to actual persons, living or dead, or actual events is purely coincidental.

The town of Truly, Texas is an amalgam of countless small towns scattered across the Llano Estacado.

For the sake of verisimilitude, certain historical figures have been incorporated into *A Different Kind of Fire*, but their actions and interactions with the artist Ruby Schmidt are derived purely from the author's imagination.

Victoria Woodhull ran for President of the United States in 1892, but her visit to Philadelphia imaginary.

The following people from Pennsylvania Academy of the Fine Arts (PAFA):

Edward Hornor Coats, the tenth president of PAFA

Thomas Anschutz, professor

Thomas Eakins, professor at PAFA and the Art Students' League

From *Buffalo Bill's Wild West and Congress of Rough Riders of the World*

Colonel William F. Cody

Nate Salsbury

Frank O'Donnell

North Texas Normal College and Teachers Training Institute (now the University of North Texas) was founded as a nonsectarian, coeducational, private teachers college in 1890.

Acknowledgments

Endless thanks to all those people who contributed to the writing of Ruby's story, especially:

The Stanford University Creative Writing Certificate Program and the dedicated professors who took me under their collective wings: Sarah Braunstein, Helena Echlin, Joshua Mohr, Angela Pneuman, Stacey Swann, and Wendy Tokunaga.

San Antonio Romance Authors, *SARA*, the members of which critiqued many drafts.

Women's Fiction Writers Association, *WFWA*, members LaDonna Ockinga and Martha Sessums who also provided valuable critiques.

My beta readers from the Stanford Program, Michael Hardesty and Kristine Mietzner, who were most generous with their time and the quality of their critiques.

My editor, Caroline Tolley, who polished my words.

My friends, Kathleen Heer and Linda Carr, as well as the medical assistants and patients at Texas MedClinic who urged me on.

Table of Contents

Chapter One
Acceptance

Truly, Texas, March 1891

Ruby latched the chicken-yard gate behind her and waited for the hens' cackling to settle. If anyone tried to sneak up on her, the birds would squawk an alarm. Certain she was alone, she pulled a scrap of paper from her pocket and read it again. Molly, her best friend, had sent the note by way of a passing cowhand five days ago. Since then Ruby had read the two words—*It's here*—so many times the edges of the paper had feathered and Molly's red wax seal had fallen off. It was the reply to clandestine correspondence Ruby had sent months before. It could change her life.

Ruby had been to town with her father just the week before, so her turn would not roll around again for three long weeks. Trusting one of her siblings, especially that sly Beryl, to pick it up without tattling to their folks, was unthinkable.

When Ruby asked to take her sister's place in the wagon, the little snot had flat refused. Bartering continued for days with the deal consummated only this morning while doing breakfast dishes together.

Beryl whined a hard bargain. "I want the brooch Granny gave you for Christmas—"

Ruby couldn't believe that she, a grown woman of eighteen, was reduced to negotiating with a nine-year-old. She rolled her eyes but gave a reluctant nod.

"—and a month's worth of dinner dishes."

"Fine." Ruby blew out a breath hot with exasperation. From the triumphant expression on Beryl's face, Ruby had been played for a sucker. Under her breath she muttered her father's term for his daughters when they didn't live up to his expectations, "Hellion child."

Now, beside her father in the buckboard, half-listening to his mumblings about what he needed in town, Ruby envisioned the changes *it* could make in her life.

"Sixteen penny nails, two-by-fours, poultry wire. You got your mother's shopping list, girl?"

"Yes, sir." Ruby's heavy gloves didn't prevent her fingers from worrying the bottom button on her winter coat until it dangled by a thread. One more twirl snapped the fiber, spiraling the bit of bone to the floorboard. She grabbed for it, but it tumbled into the rutted road, buried forever beneath red West Texas dust. To keep from losing another, she sat on her hands. The closer they got to town, the more her heart felt like a kernel of popcorn ready to explode.

Groceries—Ranch Supplies—Dry Goods—Clothing. From its perch above Statler's Mercantile, the hand-painted sign knocked a wind-blown greeting against the eaves. Pa pulled the buckboard adjacent to the storefront. Before he could set the brake, Ruby kicked off the buffalo robe protecting her from the cold blue norther that had blown in. Without waiting to be helped down, she jumped from the seat, her skirt flaring so high frigid air lassoed her knees. She ignored his "Are you ever going to behave like a proper young—" and dashed into the store.

Inside, her gaze darted into every corner of the store, making sure Molly was alone. "Where is it?"

"Don't I even get a hello?" From her station behind the dark oak counter, the middle Statler girl grinned and waggled her feather duster in greeting.

"Hello, Molly," Ruby sassed, wondering how her friend could be so calm on such a momentous occasion. "Happy now? Where is it?"

Molly put aside the duster and carefully wiped her hands before pulling several items from a cubbyhole.

Ruby jiggled on her feet at her friend's deliberate pace.

Most items Molly returned to their place, but one—a fat ivory envelope—she waved high in the air, tormenting her friend.

With one hand Ruby pushed off the counter, stretching for the letter with the other. As her fingers closed on the paper, Molly jerked it away.

"You wretch." Movement out the front window caught Ruby's eye. She tugged Molly's arm down. "Here comes my pa."

The smile snapped off Molly's face as quickly as a mousetrap closing. She thrust the envelope toward Ruby who stashed it in her coat pocket and extracted her mother's shopping list.

The store door creaked open to admit her father. "Any mail, Ruby?"

"No, sir." She tucked her hand back into her pocket, pressing the letter against her thigh.

Mr. Statler, his arms filled with boxes, stepped out of the stock room. "Howdy, Hermann. Anything I can help you with?"

"Put whatever the girl needs on my account, Jack. I'll pick her up when I'm done at the lumber yard."

Ruby ran a finger down her mother's checklist but was too excited to focus. The spidery handwriting became a tangled, illegible web as *ten pounds of flour* moseyed into *five pounds of cornmeal* and *backstrap molasses* poured onto *one card of small white buttons.*

Unable to calm herself enough to fill the order, while Ruby waited for her pa to leave, she studied her friend. Despite performing her usual duties of stocking shelves and cleaning the store, Molly's white cuffs remained pristine and not a strand of hair escaped the flaxen braids crowning her head. With a sigh, Ruby removed her bonnet, tried in vain to pat her hair into place then brushed off her clothing. Wind-blown and gritty, Ruby looked like she'd rolled into town on a tumbleweed.

After an interminable conversation about the upcoming town hall meeting and the quarter-inch of rain the town had gotten the week before—things that weren't nearly as important as Ruby's letter—Ruby's pa drove off and Mr. Statler returned to the back room.

Molly whirled around the counter to join Ruby. "Open it."

After a final survey ensured they were truly alone, Ruby pulled the envelope from her pocket, slid a finger beneath its seal, and removed the letter. Her hands trembled too much for her to decipher the words, she thrust the page at her friend. "I can't bear the suspense. Read it to me, please."

Perched on a stool, Molly unfolded the page with excessive care. As she read, she shook her head periodically.

Ruby paced the width of the store, her skirts swirling at each turn, preparing for disappointment.

At last Molly looked up, her face pinched in disappointment.

Ruby slumped. "I knew I wouldn't get in."

The letter flapping in her hand, Molly jumped off her stool, hopped up and down then hugged her friend. "But you did. You got in."

"You fiend!" Ruby snatched the page and read aloud.

"Dear Miss Schmidt, Congratulations…" Astonished, she sank to her knees on the pine floor. "I got in. I really did."

"Your parents are going to pitch a hissy fit."

"Oh, Lordy, not just my folks. What's Bismarck going to say?"

* * * *

Ruby slopped the hogs and gathered the eggs. The barn thermometer read forty-four degrees, almost balmy after that cold snap. The wan sun on her cheeks made her long for freedom from coats, shawls, and gloves. The scent of the earth awakening hovered in the air. A green stubble of new growth peeked through the thatch of last year's grasses. Soon wine cups and primroses would carpet the plains. On horseback she could better appreciate the changes in the landscape and—she bounced with excitement—a gallop would be a good excuse to visit Bismarck and tell him her news.

Coupling her second-best shirtwaist with a split riding skirt, Ruby dressed for a call on her betrothed, then swiped a brush through her curls, lamenting their wildness. Damnation. No matter how many hairpins she used, those corkscrews escaped. A glance in the small mirror above her bureau told her she was presentable enough. After all, she didn't want him to think this a premeditated occasion. With a deep exhale, she tucked the letter in her coat pocket, gave it a pat, and headed to the barn. Ladybug, her quarter horse mare, danced in the corral eager to lope toward Stonecrop Ranch.

She had to talk to Bismarck. Her news affected his life as well. She already knew how he felt. She could only think of one way to change his mind, one way to convince him to let her go, one way to prove her love.

* * * *

From atop her horse, Ruby memorized the image of

Bismarck shoeing a horse, its hoof trapped between his thighs. His voice calm, his hands soothing, he led the animal to believe its desires and his were identical. The whole county envied his way with livestock.

Ruby sighed, wondering how he would feel knowing their desires were no longer the same. "Bismarck!"

Over the rhythmic clang of his hammer, he didn't hear her.

She pitched her voice higher, louder. "Biz!"

When he lifted his head, sunlight spilled beneath the brim of his hat, illuminating his welcoming smile. He spread his legs to release the horse's hoof, dropped the rounding hammer, and slowly stretched his tall frame.

Ruby slid out of her saddle, her boots stirring up dust as her feet hit the ground. She ran toward him, towing her mare by the reins with one hand while extracting the letter from her pocket with the other. The crisp page crackled as she shook it under his nose.

"Settle down before you spook my horse." He grabbed her wrist in play.

The letter flew from her hand and fluttered across the corral like a chicken after a grasshopper. "Lordy. Look what you've done. Catch it before it blows away."

The errant paper zigzagged across the barnyard, Bismarck giving chase. As he stretched to capture it, the wind whisked it away. He muttered a cuss word under his breath and redoubled his speed.

"Hurry, Biz."

A dust devil swirled before him, spiraling the letter out of his reach. "Damn."

Ruby, fearing her mail lost forever, joined the pursuit. She could simply tell Bismarck her news, but that letter was proof someone thought she had potential.

In a sudden reversal, the twisting wind lost power and deposited the paper ten feet from Bismarck. With a lunge, he captured the page and returned it to her with a courtly flourish. "My lady."

Giving eager little hops, she shoved the post back toward him. "Read it. I got in. I got in."

He opened the letter and read aloud. "Dear Miss Schmidt, congratulations on your acceptance to the Pennsylvania Academy of the Fine Arts. We recognize the commitment entailed in learning and developing as an artist by association with a worthy institution…." He scrubbed his hand across his unshaven chin. "Why'd I build this house if you're going to leave?"

"We talked about this before I applied."

"You already went to college for a year in North Texas. Weren't that enough?"

"Texas Normal College was for my teaching certificate. My folks made me do it, so it doesn't count. You said this would be all right."

"I never said I'd be happy about it." Bismarck crumpled the letter and crushed it back into her hand. "We had this same talk six months ago. Nothing's changed. I thought we were getting hitched this fall. Instead you want to take off again."

The accusation in his voice struck her like a rattlesnake. With a huff, she turned her back on him. "It's just for a year. We have the rest of our lives to be together." She smoothed the wrinkles in her precious paper. "You didn't think I'd get in."

Behind her, Bismarck clasped her shoulders, clenching then relaxing his fingers, as if he couldn't decide whether to hold her tight or let her go. "I knew you'd get in." He brushed her nape, four delicate kisses beneath the rasping of his stubble. One hand loosened her hair from its knot on her neck, his thick calluses snagging the fine strands. "But I hoped you wouldn't."

"Please, Biz." She half-turned toward him. "Haven't you ever needed to try something new?"

"I've never wanted to be anywhere but right here, doing what I'm doing." He released her and turned in a slow circle looking at the plains. "It's beautiful out there. Never the same one minute to the next." He spread his right arm wide, indicating Pole Cat Draw and the distant escarpment. "If you think you can tie this down in a picture, you're as bad as those damned fellers using barbed wire to tame this land."

She tugged his hand around her waist, pulling him close. Together they gazed at the only landscape either had ever known. "I love Texas, too. But I have to know if I'm cut out to be an artist. I'll be back."

"Will you?" His gaze pierced her.

She pointed to the house he had built for her. "That's our home. I love you. I'll come back. I promise." Eager to prove her affection, she kissed him in a way she never had before.

His arms corralled her.

The intensity of his return kiss made her sway.

Bismarck plucked the reins from her fingers and looped the leather straps over the fence rail behind her. His hands fumbled with the buttons of her coat then slipped beneath, encircling her waist, pulling her close. He kissed her hard. By the time they paused for breath, he was shaking. "Whew. Another smooch like that, no telling what I'd do."

In reckless reply, she drew his hand to her bosom.

He inhaled sharply as he cupped her breast for the first time.

She encouraged him, pressing his hand more firmly against her chest then moving his fingers to her buttons. The tiny discs on her shirtwaist confounded his hands, so with deliberate movements, she unfastened the mother-of-pearl buttons for him, pausing between each making sure he still watched.

His gaze never strayed from her fingers fluttering along her buttons. Suspended mere inches from her chest, his hand awaited the opening of her blouse.

Heat, ready to break into a boil, simmered beneath Ruby's clothing. She closed her eyes as the last button popped free from its buttonhole.

Bismarck slipped one hand inside her clothes and wriggled between the multiple layers of her undergarments, chilly rough fingers on warm smooth skin. With the other hand, he drew her against the length of his body.

"Oh." She opened her eyes, surprised the universe had not altered its course with his touch. The house was so very far away. If they walked all the way there, she might change her mind. With her arms wrapped around his neck, her body entwined about his, she nodded toward the barn.

Bismarck grinned and carried her to the stable, giving her a hand up the ladder to the hayloft where he unfurled a horse blanket for them to lie on.

The rough wooden walls broke the wind, but fingers of cold seeped through. Brr-r-r. It was colder inside than out. Between shivers, Ruby thought longingly of Bismarck's bed. But he had been outdoors since dawn and would have banked the fire, so the house would be little warmer than the barn.

She struggled with her clothing. Now that she had decided to love him, she needed to remove the split skirt but worried how much more to take off. If she removed everything, she'd freeze. At length, she slid off only her culottes and shirtwaist. Uncertain if her fingers shook from cold or nerves, she folded her clothes and placed them to use as a pillow. Clad in her undergarments, she felt naked and covered her chest with her arms. She attempted an elegant descent to the blanket, but without the assistance of her hands, she landed with a thud, sending dust whirling through the air.

"You all right?" Bismarck's lips twitched at her graceless landing, but he didn't laugh.

She gave a sheepish shrug.

"We can stop—"

Ruby shook her head.

"Then let me look at you."

She leaned back on her elbows letting him see her while she studied him. Though she was well-covered by her chemise, corset, corset cover, and flannel pantalets, his gaze stripped her completely.

Bismarck stood above her, unbuttoned his trousers and shucked them halfway to his boots. When he unfastened his red union suit and withdrew his—Ruby dared not even think the word—she realized that every man she had ever drawn had been misconceived. The flat plackets she had placed on pants did not acknowledge what lay beneath. A ranch girl, Ruby had seen the male parts of bulls and stallions. Never had she dreamed men would be so similar yet so different. Having changed her little brother's diapers, she knew the anatomy—in theory. Reality was so much more.

Somehow, she summoned the courage to reach for him. "I want to sketch you. Naked. I need to draw you—draw this." With one finger, she traced his length.

He sucked in a breath. "Later, honey."

His skin was so soft there, more soft than his lips, yet so hard.

He trembled at her touch.

She stroked him again, smiling at her power.

Pulling another horse blanket and her coat over them, Bismarck stretched out beside her.

Soon his mouth and hands had her so enthralled she no longer thought of art. The fabric separating them became tinder catching fire.

Ruby loosened the two middle buttons of his long-handled underwear then ran her hands beneath, tracing the map of his chest and abdomen as far south and north and east and west as she could reach, discovering the crinkly texture of his hair, the undulations of his muscles, the peaks of his nipples, and the indentation of his bellybutton.

His rough fingers invaded the slit in the fabric of her split-crotch undergarments.

She gasped.

Bismarck moved half atop of her. Harsh and irregular, his breath left billows of steam in the air between them.

His weight pressed her into the hay, squeezing the breath from her. "If we don't quit now, Ruby Louise, I won't be able to stop."

The tingle between her legs begged for his touch. She couldn't stop him now if she wanted to. His face, so familiar, held a tautness she'd never seen. Her trembling fingers unfastened the remaining buttons of his undergarment and pulled him closer.

Spreading the gap in her pantalets wider, he lay over her, nudging himself inside.

Pain lanced through her as he penetrated. She clenched her teeth to suppress a whimper of discomfort, but her body recoiled and remained tense.

He stopped. "I don't want to hurt you."

Above her, he held himself still, remaining immobile so long she became aware of the world beyond them. Grass stems prickled her skin through the horse blanket. Bits of straw and motes of dust danced on beams of afternoon sunlight. Whistles of wind wheezed through cracks in the barn walls.

At last he said, "You ready?"

"Yes." She closed her eyes.

Slowly, slowly, he filled her. "Sweet Jesus."

At the sound, she opened her eyes.

He seemed almost in agony, his eyes shuttered, his face intent. His whisper floated, a cloud of steam suspended in the air between them.

With a moan, Ruby closed her eyes again, shutting out everything but the new sensation of Bismarck between her thighs. The smells of the barn receded, over-ridden by the scent of man and desire. She wanted more. Her need grew so fierce, she lifted her hips to meet his.

Encouraged, Bismarck moved faster, deeper. After a dozen strokes, he collapsed on her with a cry.

As he withdrew, Ruby wondered if that was all there was. Horses took longer to accomplish the act.

Afterwards, they snuggled together, arms and legs tightly entwined. He stroked her thigh. Goosebumps re-erupted as soon as his warmth passed.

"If you're carrying my child, I won't let you go."

Ruby's eyes widened. "You did this on purpose—to keep me here."

"Little one, I tried real hard to be good." He laughed as he chucked her under the chin. "You were dead set on some loving."

"I got tired of being all proper when we're together." She scooted closer, kissed him then laid her head on his chest. "At the quilting bee, I overheard Ma and the other ladies talking. It only hurts the first time. Then the more you do it, the better it gets."

"I reckon so. Practice does make perfect, I hear."

His laugh rumbled low where her ear lay against his body.

She sat up, turning to look at him. Stray daylight sliced through a crack in the barn wall, highlighting his twinkling eyes and burnishing his brown hair with a golden glow. The reflection of his union suit outlined his jaw with red.

He nuzzled her breast and came up making a face. "I hate flannel. All that fuzz sticks to my tongue."

Her hand followed the lines of his body to where his maleness peeked from his long johns. She stroked him, delighting in his immediate response. This time the deed took much longer, accompanied by a wondrous feeling rising to heaven before falling into an abyss. "Lordy. I never thought it'd be like this."

Bismarck raised himself on an elbow and studied her. "Me, neither. I swear you make more sweet sounds than a little song bird." He left her for a moment. When he returned, he cleaned her gently, his bandana icy cold from the water from the horse trough, before wiping himself.

She shivered. "You sorry we didn't wait?"

"I'll never regret loving you, Ruby Louise." Her parents used her full name as evidence of their disapproval. When Bismarck called her that, the words were a caress.

"Do you think we sinned?"

He winked. "We jumped the gun a bit. Once we're married, I'm sure God will look the other way."

She slipped from the blanket and reached for her clothing. When her attire was in order, she pulled the pins from her hair and combed it with her fingers. Her hair was always such a riot her ma wouldn't suspect anything—as long as Ruby removed every sprig of hay.

Bismarck grabbed her hand, pulling her back. "Don't

go, Ruby. Don't go."

"I have to." With a twist of her hands, she piled her curls on her head, restraining them with hairpins. "It's almost dinner time. Ma will be worried I've been gone so long."

"You know what I mean." His tone carried the plaintive timbre of a coyote's distant wail.

Nearly undone, she kissed him hard and long. Moments later, her voice dreamy, she said, "I love you. I'll come back. I promise. And when I do, I'll be a famous artist."

Chapter Two
A Real Artist

The Schmidt parlor was hushed except for the faint slither of embroidery thread sliding through taut fabric, the click of knitting needles as they dove in and out of yarn, and the swish of pages being turned. The soft glow of the kerosene lamps and the flickering fire illuminated the space. Ruby hated to break the evening's peace, but she'd postponed telling her parents about the letter for a week. Further waiting would not make her task any easier. She took a deep breath and plunged ahead.

"I want to be a painter." Her voice cracked the silence like the pickaxe her pa had slammed into the frozen stock pond last week.

Her sisters, Pearl and Beryl, perched like bookends on a velvet camel-backed settee, lifted startled eyes from their stitchery. Nearby, her brother Jasper's tin soldiers clattered to the ground as if pounded by cannon shot. Pa jerked his head from his dime novel about Kit Carson. Four pairs of curious eyes rotated toward her. Only Ma kept her gaze on her knitting.

Feeling like a chunk of beef had taken root halfway down her gullet, Ruby swallowed repeatedly. "I want to study art back East."

Her pa slowed the ambling gait of his mule-eared rocker. "Just when did you arrive at that conclusion, young lady?"

"Several months ago." She pulled the letter from her apron pocket. "I applied to the Pennsylvania Academy of the Fine Arts—and I was accepted."

"Give me that." Her pa snatched the page from her hand, read it, and shook his head. "You went behind our backs? You're not setting a good example for your sisters, girl. You're not too old for me to tan your hide."

Ruby flattened the smile that threatened to break through. Though strict, her pa had never struck his wife or children, yet his gruffness always left her with the impression she never lived up to his expectations. Somehow she was too outspoken for her pa and not nearly lady-like enough for her ma.

"Where does Bismarck fit into this nonsense?"

"We talked about it. It's all right with him."

"Really? You spoke to him before you cleared matters with us?" Eyebrows crunched together, her father set down his book, tamped tobacco into the bowl of his pipe, lit a match, and puffed a couple of times. "Beef prices are down. With the drought, your ma and I can't afford to send you so far away."

"I'll use Gran's legacy."

"Those funds were intended for your future."

"My education is my future."

"You're mighty young to be heading so far from home."

Another excuse from her pa. He just didn't want her to go.

Her mother lifted her head. "Pearl, put some music on the Victrola, please." She bent her neck again and picked up the next loop of yarn. "According to *The Presbyterian Review*, Lake Forest College is building a new art institute. You could live with my sister Josie in Chicago. She's close enough to the college you could walk to classes. She'd love to have you."

Ruby rolled her eyes. Living with old maid Aunt Josephine would be too cruel a fate, far more confining than being at home. "But the Academy is the oldest art school in America. It's the best place to study."

"You already do lovely watercolors." Ma clicked her knitting needles for emphasis.

"I loathe painting piddly landscapes and flowers. I want to paint *Life*. There's no one to study under in Truly, no place in all of Texas to even look at paintings."

"Be patient. Texas is in its infancy. I read that some Fort Worth society ladies are organizing a library and museum."

"As often as I'd get to go, Fort Worth might as well be back East." Ruby sniffed. "I want an honest to goodness art school."

"You already went off for your teaching certificate." Pa spoke around the pipe stem clamped in his mouth.

"Only because you and Ma made me." Ruby refrained from saying she first learned of art schools at the Texas Normal College and Teacher Training Institute, and her professors there had encouraged her to apply.

Her mother said, "We were only considering your future. If anything happens to Bismarck, you'll need to support yourself and your children."

"We're not even married yet, Ma." Ruby let out a breath fraught with aggravation. "I need to go. I'll just die—"

Like an old dragon, her father drew on his pipe and let out a few puffs of smoke. "What you *need* is to marry and start a family. Let Bismarck work that restlessness out of you."

Quickly, Ruby lowered her gaze to hide her burning cheeks.

Ma's eyes widened as she peered at her husband over

her spectacles. "Now, Hermann—"

His glare silenced her. "Your ma and I will discuss this, young lady, but don't get your hopes up."

"I'll run away, just like Ma did." She shot a defiant look at her pa.

"Hellion child." With a dark glower, he snapped his book shut. "The subject is closed."

* * * *

When Ruby had applied to the Academy, she had enclosed her portfolio, watercolors done on Sunday afternoons under her ma's supervision. Her mother deemed the images ladylike, but Ruby considered them dull. When she headed to school, she wanted to show her true capabilities. Through the spring, she painted feverishly, determined to present work more in keeping with her own vision. She sketched West Texas landscapes and portraits of the ranch hands—anything but flower vases and English cottages. The bleached cow skull lying on her bed served as her current inspiration. Once the bony calvarium took its place on her sketch, she lightly penciled a copperhead wandering through the eyeless sockets, an insolent *S* snaked over the paper. Across the upper third of her watercolor, she placed a wash of venomous green in a sky that presaged a tornado. With her brush she began pulling its wet edge toward the horizon.

"Ruby?" Her mother's voice trailed up from the kitchen, interrupting Ruby's work.

"Coming." Within seconds, though, she lost herself in painting and forgot about her mother.

A bellow broke her concentration.

"Ruby Louise Schmidt!"

She flinched at the tone. "Yes, Pa."

"Your ma called you some time ago." His brusque voice resounded from the bottom of the steps leading to her attic room.

Ruby glanced at her work. If she stopped now, the painting would never be right, but she dared not ignore her father. With a sigh, she rinsed her brush in a Mason jar of water, placed it on the table, and tromped down the stairs. "Yes, ma'am. What do you need?"

"Beryl could have used some help hanging the sheets, but I did it myself. Nearly burnt lunch, though, finishing up your chores."

"What were you up to?" her pa said. "Painting?"

Ruby gave a guilty nod.

"I don't care what you're doing, girl, when your ma or I say jump, you better ask how high." He forced a huge brush into her hand. "Since you're so fired up about painting, get started on the front door."

* * * *

June 1891

Seated at the kitchen table, Ruby mindlessly sorted pinto beans. Her fingers slowed as her thoughts wandered to Bismarck and what they'd done. In her usual rash manner, she'd never considered the consequences of her actions. She'd intended to lie with him once to prove her love before heading to school. Never had she dreamed the act would be so pleasurable they would do it—she cringed—over and over in the past several months. A baby would surely interfere with her plans. She must not lie with Bismarck again. But neither could she deny him. She licked her lips, recalling the taste of his kisses. Oh, Lordy. She snatched her thoughts back to the task at hand, and with a sweep of her fingers, the legumes skittered across the oak tabletop before dropping into the cast iron pot with a clatter.

At her mother's deep sigh, Ruby glanced behind her. Her ma was washing dishes at the sink. The day had just begun, and already she looked tired.

Her ma returned the last plate to its assigned spot then wiped her chapped hands on the apron that protected her rounded belly, her eleventh pregnancy with only four living children to show for her efforts. Loose curls dangled damply on her temples. She tucked them behind her ears then joined her daughter at the table, settling heavily into a chair with another sigh. "Sweetie, I want to talk to you."

Unsure if mothers could tell by looking that their daughters had been with a man, Ruby paid intense attention to the beans, picking out imaginary stones.

"Are you quite certain you want to go away to school?"

Safe. Ruby relaxed. "Yes, ma'am. More than anything."

"Your pa thinks this is all my fault." Her mother sighed again. "Because I raised my gaggle of girls as ladies instead of ranch wives and, of course, you inherited your rebellious streak from *me*." Her mother stifled a giggle. "Your pa's still got all his."

Ruby laughed. "I'm sorry, Ma. But I have to find out if I was meant to be an artist."

"You're so young—"

"You were younger when you followed Pa out here."

"And far more foolish." She stroked her belly. "My father brought a young cattleman home to dinner one night, and I wanted your pa the minute I laid eyes on him. With no more thought than that"—she snapped her fingers—"I decided the life of a Chicago socialite was not for me. I don't regret marrying him, but…"

"But what?"

"Only seventeen and all starry-eyed, I ran away and followed him to Texas. I didn't know how hard life would be here. Wild Indians. The loneliness. The incessant wind. The dust storms. I had no inkling what happened between a man and a woman. How babies were made. What it would be like to lose child after child...." Her ma rubbed her belly again and sniffled.

"Ma—" Ruby reached over and patted her mother's hand.

"Frankly, I'd be pleased if you found an easier life. I'll talk to your pa. In our twenty years together, we've made many sacrifices for each other—and for our children." She sighed. "I do believe Bismarck feels as strongly about you. He's a fine young man. Someday he'll make a good husband and father." She rested her hand on Ruby's, stilling the sliding of beans across the table. "Fly for now, but come home and plant your feet into good, solid Texas soil."

-21-

Chapter Three
Leaving Home

August 1891

Light-headed and sweaty, Ruby slowly pirouetted, allowing her kneeling mother to check the pinned hem of a new winter coat.

"It'll do." Her mother, one hand on her pregnant belly, awkwardly pushed herself to a stand. "Philadelphia's climate can't be that different from Chicago's." Her lips pursed in thought. "You'll need plenty of warm clothing"—she cleared her throat delicately—"flannel unmentionables, an extra quilt or two."

Under her ma's supervision, Ruby packed and repacked a steamer trunk and portmanteau with dresses, her coat, and linens along with her paints and portfolio.

At last, Pa loaded Ruby's baggage into the family wagon to drive her to Truly where she would catch the Texas and Pacific Railroad to Philadelphia. Ruby turned and watched the Schmidt homestead fade into the horizon, until only the flashing of sunlight on the windmill vanes remained, signaling the end of her old life.

In late August, the plains were so hot not even grasshoppers chirped. Red dust spiraled like flames above the wagon. Licking her dry lips, Ruby hoped summers in Philadelphia would not be so oppressive and that her mouth would not be perpetually full of grit.

At the train station, after Pa helped the two women out of the buckboard, her mother smoothed her skirt over a flat belly. Another baby lost before it was due. Her mother still seemed downcast by the stillbirth, and now her oldest daughter was leaving, too. Ruby closed her eyes, momentarily considering staying home to help her mother, but with the whistle of the train her excitement surged.

From the mercantile down the street, Molly came to see Ruby off, excited because of her part in helping Ruby escape Truly. Half the town was there, including that snooty Hortense Hammond. Ruby couldn't figure out why that woman had appeared unless it was to make sure Ruby actually left town. Hortense would set her cap at Bismarck the moment the train rolled out of the station.

The whistle blew a long plaintive moan. Everyone important was present—except Bismarck. He had promised to see her off, but perhaps he was so angry he wasn't coming. Anxious, she scanned the horizon for a dust cloud indicating her beau's arrival. Nothing.

"All aboard!" the conductor sang out.

The whistle blew a final blast.

Still no Bismarck.

Ruby's ma gave one last warning about talking to strangers.

Her gruff father said, "I'm still not sold on you heading back East. You need anything, send a telegram." He patted her arm as he slipped her five twenty-dollar bills. "For emergencies."

"Thank you." Ruby pecked him on the cheek. "This is important to me, Pa. I have to do this."

"I reckon. Your ma says it's best you have our blessing rather than run away from home like she did. Pert near worried her folks to death." He grunted. "I only agreed to this nonsense to ease her mind."

At last Bismarck galloped up, sending dust flying up Main Street.

Frantically Ruby waved to him, fearful the train would pull away before he reached her. "Biz!"

After tying his horse to the railing, he joined her family. Her mother pulled her father aside in an awkward shuffle so Bismarck might kiss Ruby goodbye.

She grasped her betrothed's arm. "You're late."

"Sick foal. Had a hard time getting away."

Lordy. His longing gaze made her wish they were alone in the barn. She couldn't kiss him like *that* here, but she sure wanted to.

Bismarck planted a chaste smooch on Ruby's cheek. "I wish you had the same fire for me as you have for painting." His deep voice grumbled in her ear.

"I do, Biz. It's just a different kind of fire."

Hands encircling her waist, he lifted her on board, fingers and eyes lingering. "I'll be waiting. Someday I will marry you, Ruby Louise."

* * * *

When the fluttering lace of her mother's handkerchief and the slow wave of Bismarck's hat became lost in the steam of the engine, Ruby turned from the window and looked around the passenger car. Strangers, all men, surrounded her. Though not shy, she had been well brought-up. If a cowman caught her eye, she bobbed her head and quickly lowered her gaze in an attempt to appear neither snobbish nor friendly enough to encourage liberties.

Once Truly was lost in the distance, Ruby gazed at an unseen landscape while gripping her reticule so tightly its glass beads imprinted on her palms. Maybe she should get off in Big Spring and turn around.

With acreage from both families and the legacy from her maternal grandmother, Ruby and Bismarck could marry immediately and settle into their five-room frame house with its tall-hipped roof, large windows to capture breezes, and a kitchen sink that faced the rising sun. With the help of his brothers, Bismarck had built the home, hauling the water by wagon from the natural spring in the Truly hills. Later, he dug a well by hand, climbing in and out on a rope, using dynamite to blast the limestone. He had labored for their future, on top of his usual ranch work, while she attended college.

Raised to ranch life, hard work did not bother Ruby. She loved the land as much as Bismarck did, but painting enraptured her. Deep in her soul, she knew she had talent. As far back as she could remember, at every free moment, she had drawn pictures. During times paper was scarce, she traced images in the dust with a stick, lamenting the interminable wind that blew them away. When she sketched, she felt as free as Bismarck's mustangs. If not allowed to become a painter, she would shrivel up inside. But leaving Bismarck had been harder than she thought possible. At the break in his voice when he said goodbye, only her white-knuckled grip on the handrail kept her from falling into his arms. She could turn around. She could go back. It wasn't too late.

The clacking of wheels on train tracks set the pace of her swirling thoughts. Yes. No. Stay. Go. The train's whistle announced the stop in Big Spring. Ruby stood, preparing to get off the train, still not certain if she was coming or going, but thinking she should at least stretch her legs. As she descended, she noticed a careworn woman waiting on the platform. Not much older than Ruby herself, the woman was pregnant, had a toddler slung on one hip, and her fingers enclosed another child's hand.

Ruby closed her eyes. That was her future if she returned

home. She got back on the train and announced her final decision with a determined stomp of her foot, loud enough that the men around her looked up in surprise. After an apologetic shrug, she returned to her thoughts. She would stick with her original plan. Bismarck had agreed to wait a year. If her studies didn't work out, she could always return home. Things would still be the same. Nothing ever changed in Truly.

* * * *

At last, the train screeched to a halt at Broad Street Station in Philadelphia on a rail line perched two stories in the air. Ruby exhaled in relief at ending her journey. With a slap against her thigh, she shook the dust off her Panama hat and adjusted its ribbons and silk flower before applying it to her head. She hoisted her carpetbag, stuffed with the sweater she was knitting, books, her toiletries and a tartan lap robe then stared out the door, frozen in place.

Before her, Broad Street Station churned with more people than she'd seen in her entire life. Hawkers and newsboys shouted above the grumbling of trains on iron rails.

Behind her, someone plowed into her, nearly sending her tumbling to the platform below. Recovering her footing, she resolutely straightened her shoulders and disembarked. After days in a swaying railroad car, her knees wobbled. Several minutes later, having regained her land legs, she retrieved her steamer trunk and portmanteau.

Ruby stepped out of the station, followed by a porter hauling her baggage. The air, blackened with smoke from the steam-powered locomotives, smelled of horse manure and refuse. Tall buildings narrowed the sky to a claustrophobic strip of dirty blue through which no sunlight penetrated. Black lines crisscrossed overhead, the wires of electrical streetlights draped from post to post. Massive wagons carried farm produce and coal. Horse-drawn buses clattered down tracks. Horseshoes rang against cobblestones. Trolley bells clanged. Bicycle horns bugled. Newspaper boys shouted. Dogs barked. People swirled around her, closer and closer.

Overwhelmed, she dashed back into the station, clapping her hands over her ears and squeezing her eyes tight to shut out the chaos.

"Hey, miss, you coming or going?" Her porter followed her, towing her baggage back into the terminal. "Make up your mind."

Realizing she was no safer inside, Ruby resigned herself to returning outdoors and hailed a cab on Broad Street.

The driver hopped from his station high in the back of his cab, placed her trunks beneath his seat and strapped them in place. Once he tossed in her carpetbag, he gave her a hand up.

Her heartbeat slowed with her escape from the clamor of the depot.

"Where to, Miss?"

His accent was so strange it took her a moment to figure out his words. She removed a slip of paper from her purse and read it to him.

"That's in North Philly, not far from here."

Minutes later, the cab wound through the city, past a curious mixture of fine old homes, factories, and row houses, then stopped before a gate with a sign reading *Mrs. Wheelwright's Boarding Home for Christian Ladies*. The Academy had recommended the furnished room house as proper living quarters for young women. Another student, Willow Wycke, would dwell there, too. Ruby's mother had urged her to live where she might have a companion when walking to and from classes, saying, "There's safety in numbers, Ruby

Louise."

She alighted from the carriage and walked through the gate in a wrought iron fence that surrounded a rose-filled yard. A white front door and creamy marble steps highlighted Mrs. Wheelwright's three-story red brick home.

A portly woman, as stolid and austere as the facade of her house, answered Ruby's knock and introduced herself as Mrs. Amelie Wheelwright. Her beady eyes, submerged in round cheeks, matched her black bombazine dress. The proprietress welcomed her new tenant. Then she ordered the cabbie to follow with the baggage and, leaning heavily on the handrail, led the way upstairs.

Ruby trailed after her landlady, pitying the man hauling her trunks up two flights of steep steps.

Once he delivered her belongings, the cab driver stood in the doorway, shifting from foot to foot, hand outstretched.

Ruby realized he was waiting for a tip. Unsure of how much to give him, she removed a quarter from her purse and held it toward him.

A quick bob of his head covered his sly grin as he pocketed the coin.

"Give the girl fifteen cents change," her landlady said.

He shrugged and returned two coins before walking away.

Mrs. Wheelwright extended her own hand. "The room, three meals a day, and laundry is six dollars a week."

Once Ruby handed over the appropriate sum, the proprietress waddled down the hallway.

Ruby glanced around her new home. Tucked between two much larger rooms and down the hall from the water closet, her space measured barely ten feet square. She wondered if it had been a nursery or dressing room. Never mind. As she would be in school, she would spend little time there.

Beneath tired wallpaper decorated with cabbage roses, a mahogany bureau with a speckled mirror presided over a single bed. A needlepoint footstool accompanied a worn but cozy armchair. Ruby waited until Mrs. Wheelwright's plodding footsteps were well down the stairs before giving several childish bounces on the bed and chair and pronouncing them comfortable.

Once she placed her personal belongings in the tiny closet and slid her paintings under the bed, she felt quite at home—until bedtime. When she removed her quilt from her steamer trunk, with one finger she traced the nine-patch design composed of squares of her father's faded chambray work shirts alternating with squares from her sisters' baby clothes. So many tiny flowers. So many shades of blue. All painstakingly stitched together by her mother's work-worn hands.

Chapter Four
A True Life

Eager to explore the Academy, Ruby skipped there the next morning. She reined in her eagerness, not wanting to appear a foolish schoolgirl. Red and black brickwork patterns graced the magnificent façade of the Academy. Terra cotta statuary, floral designs, and stone tracery surrounded a large Gothic window. Above, a bas-relief frieze depicted famous artists. She'd never seen such elaborate ornamentation on a building.

She entered through a two-story arch, gaping in awe at the decorative tiled floors, a spectacular staircase with banisters of bronze and mahogany, walls studded with golden rosettes, and a blue ceiling spangled with silver stars. How easy to learn art here where beauty dwelled.

In the student store, she received the list of supplies for her first class, *Drawing from the Cast.* She purchased Venetian charcoal, paper, and fixative, and for a modest additional cost, she chose a portfolio instead of a drawing board. Carefully she counted $3.72 from her reticule before placing the majority of the items in her new locker, rented for a dollar a year, keeping only pencils, an eraser, and a sketchbook for immediate use.

She climbed the grand stairs to the second floor galleries. The largest painting Ruby had ever seen dominated the landing. Beneath it, a gold plaque read *Dead Man restored to*

Life by touching the Bones of the Prophet Elisha, Washington Allston (1779-1843).

An entire wall of her room at the boarding house could not hold the image. Scarlet accents swirled through a pyramid of figures. At its peak, Allston had placed a Roman centurion's gleaming gold armor, and at its base, the dead man's white shroud.

As Ruby moved through the galleries, she understood why the Academy's art collections were considered the most valuable in America. Briefly she worshipped before each picture, moving close enough to study the translucent layers of colors and shifting her head to catch the play of light across individual brush strokes. Her fingers itched to hold a paintbrush, and she rubbed her fingers together to soothe their prickling.

On the Cherry Street side of the Academy, Ruby wandered into galleries containing paintings and casts of sculptures. Rooms lit by skylights contained furnishings for drapery painting and life drawing classes. She inhaled deeply. Pungent odors of turpentine and linseed oil mixed with paint permeated the building. Black fingerprints from charcoal dusted the doorjambs.

A stout, middle-aged woman watched over the door to the Antiquities Room. She beckoned to Ruby. "Come on in, dearie. It's Thursday, Ladies' Day. No men allowed."

Glad she happened to come when the galleries were open to women artists, Ruby entered, her heart thumping with anticipation. Inside a dozen women, uniformed in dark smocks, stood before easels and sketched. All her life, she had seemed singular in her desire to study art. She was no longer alone. The urge to whisper hello to her fellow painters rose within her, but the silence in the room was so profound she found herself unable to speak.

The Nike of Samothrace caught her eye, a sculpture she'd only seen in art books at the library of the Texas Normal College. Carved by an ancient Greek sculptor, the figure of the goddess Nike commemorated a victory at sea. Wings unfurled behind her, she descended from the heavens to land on the prow of a warship, struggling to maintain her balance against the combined forces of ship, air, and water. The wind whipped her garments behind her like sheets snapping in a Texas breeze. The goddess's missing head and arms did not diminish her grandeur—nor did knowing she was a reproduction of the statue in the Louvre.

Compelled to touch the graceful wings and the undulating rhythm of the robes, Ruby skimmed one hand sensuously over the plaster, finding it hard, cool, smooth, yet delicately textured at the feathers. The *Nike* celebrated Ruby's own triumph in being in Philadelphia.

Next Ruby stood before a copy of Michelangelo's *David*. From loving Bismarck, she knew what lay beneath the fig leaf and longed to pry away the ludicrous covering and sketch the Biblical hero in all his glory.

She wandered around the cast room, her lips clamped together to control her desire to exclaim over every statue, bust, or bas-relief. She hesitated before taking out her sketchbook, afraid the other artists would intuit she was a mere amateur. Beginning her academic career by sketching the *Nike* or *David* would surely be too audacious, so she chose a plaster cast of a woman's hand. As she drew and redrew the long chalky fingers from different angles, the natural light from the skylights faded unobtrusively from warm gold to mercury silver. Suddenly, the brilliance of midday blazed again from overhead. Startled, she looked up.

The guardian of the galleries noted her dazed expression. "It's just our new electrical lights, dearie."

Once the Academy closed, Ruby returned to the boarding house, spinning in giddy circles, oblivious to peoples' stares. She was intoxicated, as drunk as old Joe Greer, the town ne'er-do-well, when he stumbled from the Dark Horse saloon back home. Art everywhere! More than she had seen in her entire life. The Academy exceeded her dreams. Too delirious with joy to pay attention to where she was going, Ruby wandered into the path of an omnibus. The driver clanged its bell in frantic warning. She jumped to the sidewalk, narrowly escaping being struck by the electrical conveyance.

Back at Mrs. Wheelwright's, she wrote her family and Bismarck describing her adventures. Enthusiastic words flew from her pen:

> *My dearest Biz,*
> *My New Life began today! I walked into the Academy and immediately knew I had answered my Calling. Before that moment, I had not truly lived. Art will give my life meaning and purpose from here on...*

* * * *

Friday was Men's Day at the Academy, so Ruby explored the city, walking the streets around the boarding house and the school, her head spinning at the bustle of downtown. Omnibuses, pulled by dray horses similar to those Bismarck's father bred, ran along tracks and carried most of the city's workers to and from their jobs. Her nerves jangled by the constant bustle, she ducked into Leary's Used Book Store on South Ninth to escape into quiet. She lost herself among the second-hand books before purchasing a forty-year-old copy of Winkelmann's *History of Ancient Art*, Howard Pyle's *The Merry Adventures of Robin Hood* for her brother Jasper, and a guide to the landmarks of Philadelphia.

That evening Mrs. Wheelwright introduced Ruby to her fellow boarders, most of whom were teachers at the new Central High School. When Ruby mentioned she had a teaching certificate, they were astonished that she'd chosen the unseemly discipline of art instead of education. Over the meal, they reveled in school gossip, sharing anecdotes of their colleagues and students, excluding Ruby from their chatter.

After Sunday dinner, still fatigued from her travels, Ruby needed a nap, but not wanting to get off on the wrong foot with her formidable landlady, she attended the Bible reading instead.

In the parlor, ladies sat on upholstered settees and straight high-backed chairs, embroidering or knitting, and sipping tea as another young lady droned from the Good Book. "Who can find a virtuous woman? For her price is far above rubies…"

Ruby knew that particular verse, Proverbs 31:10, by heart. Pa had chosen her name from that passage. She would have preferred to be called Venezia, India, or some exotic locale visited by Miss Nellie Bly during her circumnavigation of the globe last year. She and her sisters had eagerly awaited the arrival of each newspaper detailing Nellie's trip from departure through triumphant return to New Jersey seventy-two days, six hours, eleven minutes and fourteen seconds after leaving Hoboken. A mere woman had beaten the fictitious time of Phileas Fogg in Jules Verne's *Around the World in Eighty Days*.

She jerked her thoughts from foreign lands and focused on the Bible passage. Her knitting slowed, barely keeping pace with the reader's soporific hum. Certain Mrs. Wheelwright would think drowsiness sinful during readings of the

Good Book, Ruby sucked a yawn back into her throat.

The young lady reading stopped abruptly.

Startled, Ruby turned her gaze to the front door as a tall, thin woman stepped into the parlor. Her clothing was expensive but somber. She appeared several years older than Ruby. A harsh bun, pulled tightly against the back of her head, imprisoned her brown hair. This disregard of fashion set her apart. Ruby patted her own luxuriant chignon and dangling tendrils. Since drawings of the Gibson Girl had appeared in *Life* magazine a year earlier, Ruby—and nearly every other young woman in America—had adopted the hairdo.

Mrs. Wheelwright rose then grasped the newcomer's arm. "Girls, this is Miss Wycke." She turned to Ruby. "Miss Schmidt, as you will be students together at the Academy, I have given you adjacent rooms."

Ruby grinned and wiggled her fingers in greeting.

At the sight of Ruby, Miss Wycke's mouth gaped. She stared, eyes fixed on Ruby's face as though she was some ungodly creature.

Taken back, Ruby lowered her hand and ran her tongue over her teeth, wondering if she had a speck of food lodged between her teeth.

Their landlady waited for Miss Wycke to be seated. "Now that we are all together, I shall review my rules. I maintain a Christian home for ladies. Unless ill, you are expected to attend church.

"Profanity, alcohol, and tobacco are not permitted.

"Sunday through Thursday evenings, the front door is locked at nine. Friday and Saturday nights it remains open until ten.

"Meals are served at six, noon and six. Boxed lunches are provided for those unable to return for the noon meal.

"Laundry of clothing is done on Tuesday. Linens on

Thursdays. Saturday and Wednesday nights, I provide hot water for bathing.

"Should I learn of any impropriety either within or without this house, you will be asked to leave." Her penetrating eyes sought each boarder in turn.

Ruby felt she was under particular scrutiny for misbehavior. Though her own mother had never discerned that her daughter had lain with Bismarck, Ruby lowered her eyes under Mrs. Wheelwright's gaze, convinced that her landlady knew.

Through the remainder of the Bible reading, Ruby surreptitiously tapped her feet beneath her skirt. The instant the Holy Book was closed and women began adjourning to their various rooms, she leapt up and caught the new woman's arm. "Miss Wycke?"

The woman tensed, jerked away then stared at Ruby's lips.

Uncomfortable beneath the other's gaze, Ruby again ran her tongue over her teeth, wondering if she'd missed a bit of cabbage. Finally she said, "I'm Ruby Louise Schmidt, from Truly, Texas."

At last, Miss Wycke looked Ruby in the eye. In an arid voice, she said, "I can tell."

"My accent gives me away, doesn't it?" Ruby emphasized her drawl by stretching her vowels to a comical length.

"Your cadence is quite provincial, Miss Schmidt. I am Willow Anne Wycke."

"It's nice to meet a fellow artist. Have you been to the Academy yet? I've never seen so much art." In her excitement, words tumbled from Ruby's mouth.

Miss Wycke's mouth formed a tight moue. "Excuse me." She whirled and strode away.

With a surprised blink, Ruby stopped her prattling. Miss

Wycke had flat-out snubbed her, just like that snooty Hortense Hammond back home.

Chapter Five
Pennsylvania Academy of the Fine Arts

Too excited to sleep, Ruby waited in the dark for her alarm to signal the start of her first official day at the Academy. At half-past five, she dressed in the faint light of dawn and dashed to the dining room.

So far, Mrs. Wheelwright's dinners had been miserly, and Ruby was starving. She wolfed down biscuits, scrapple, and eggs. Her lunch, tied in a blue bandana, consisted of two slices of bread, an apple, a fried chicken leg, and a boiled egg. Modest, but it would keep her until dinner.

After breakfast, Ruby gathered her lunch and ran up the stairs to fetch her book satchel, portfolio, reticule, and parasol. She locked her door then paused. Perhaps she had misinterpreted the young lady's actions yesterday. After a moment's hesitation, she walked the fifteen steps down the hallway and tapped on the door. "Miss Wycke, would you care to walk to class together?"

"My carriage will be here shortly." The closed door muffled Miss Wycke's reply.

Ruby couldn't believe the other woman was taking a cab to the Academy. The school was no more than ten blocks away. So much for safety in numbers.

Turning east, Ruby walked quickly to class. Her portfolio banged her left leg. Her reticule and umbrella rapped against the opposite knee. By the time she arrived at the

Academy, her arms had grown heavy. She dashed up the stairs to the school, thinking tomorrow she would simply tuck a few coins into her pocket and leave the purse and umbrella at home.

An orientation, which included both men and women, occupied the first morning. Ruby sat in a prime front-row seat. The remainder of the room filled rapidly. Miss Wycke rushed in late and was forced to stand against the wall.

Edward Hornor Coats, the tenth president of the Academy, introduced himself and the faculty and welcomed the students.

Professor Thomas Anshutz spoke next, filling in details. "When you walked through those doors, you entered an Academy established to provide the finest in art education. Our education of women exceeds the more liberal ateliers in Europe. In 1812, the Academy began teaching drawing from live models. Ladies gained admission in 1844, though they studied in segregated classes to protect their more delicate sensibilities." Mr. Anshutz droned on about the history of the Academy. "For two years, scholars, both men and women, learn the fundamentals of drawing, painting, sculpture, and printmaking, followed by two years of independent study."

Four years? Bismarck had only agreed to one. For a moment Ruby felt panicky. She'd worry about that later. At least she had this year.

"Our anatomy studies remain the most comprehensive of any modern art academy. Following a tradition that dates from the Renaissance, our students dissect human and animal cadavers in exercises equal to those of medical schools. In fact, these studies are supervised by William Keen, M.D., Professor of Clinical Surgery at Jefferson Medical College."

Ruby gulped and slid down in her seat, her mind occupied with thoughts of anatomy classes. Back home, she'd cleaned her share of farm animals and game, but a human? She envisioned dissecting a person, particularly their privates. Her face heated. Surely women would not be required to dissect those.

Anshutz stopped his pacing near Ruby and tapped her shoulder with his wooden pointer.

With a start, she abruptly sat up and returned her attention to his lecture.

"We will tour the Academy then move to the galleries for tea and an opportunity for you to meet your professors. The ladies will be excused at that point to return tomorrow at eight sharp to begin their classes. The gentlemen shall embark immediately upon their studies."

Ruby sighed. Another obstruction to beginning her training. But it was only one day. She could wait that long.

* * * *

On the first of many mornings spent in the Antiquities Room, Ruby arrived early and claimed space near the front of the room. Like the other women, their shirtwaists buttoned to their chins, she donned a dark smock with a gathered bodice and roomy pockets before setting up her easel. A droplet of sweat trickled between her shoulder blades, tickling her. She opened a window to let air into the stuffy room. The breeze brought gritty coal dust and the clatter of traffic from Broad Street below, accompanied by odors of sewage and horse droppings so vile she jerked down the sash.

Anshutz cleared his throat preparatory to his lecture. "The study of casts from the Antiquities is an integral part of our program, allowing students to sketch without the movement inherent in dealing with a live model." The professor spoke at length about drawing. "Art is based on knowledge, and knowledge on facts, but an artist must put aside facts that interfere with the full rendering of the new truth and use only those which translate it. I urge you to develop your own."

Under his watchful gaze, the dozen women sketched and re-sketched, starting with simple spheres and pyramids. Each work was submitted for approval before being permitted access to the next item in the hierarchy of casts, ranging from hands and faces to busts to full-sized sculptures such as the *Nike of Samothrace* Ruby had seen on her first day in the Academy.

Before dismissing the class, Anshutz said, "Bring your portfolios to our next class. I shall review them to determine where each of you stands in your education."

* * * *

With her leather case leaning against one calf, Ruby perched on a wooden stool, one foot tapping, waiting her opportunity to display her work. So far, the others had shown vases of flowers, gardens filled with roses, and insipid portraits of children. Ruby had similar watercolors, ones her mother forced her to produce, but determined to prove her mettle, Ruby hadn't brought them today.

When her turn arrived, she placed her most recent paintings across the blackboard. A cow skull set among prickly pear blossoms, an arid landscape where nothing broke the horizon but a lone mesquite, and, last, Bismarck riding a bronco at the peak of its buck, dust flying all around, the two so precisely balanced they merged into a single organism.

When the whispers started, Ruby knew she'd gotten her fellow students as riled as a nest of hornets.

After a long tense silence, Anshutz said, "Very interesting, Miss Schmidt. Next?"

Ruby groaned mentally as the remaining women reprised the ever-popular ladylike themes of babies and flowers. At last the class ended.

Anshutz tapped Ruby's shoulder as she packed to leave.

"Miss Schmidt, may I have a word, please?"

"Yes, sir." She waited aside while he spoke with another student. Though she sculpted her face in a carefully neutral expression, she shoved her hands in her pockets of her smock fearing her tightly clenched fists would reveal her taut nerves.

"Take out your paintings."

Ruby swallowed, unballed her pocketed hands then complied, carefully setting each image against the chalkboard.

Anshutz studied each carefully, his face so stern Ruby expected to hear, "You have no talent. Go home."

Instead, he shook his head. "You lack training, but the aptitude is there. Your composition, your sense of color are excellent. However, your subject matter—"

"I paint nothing but what I see at home every day—"

"What you paint is unladylike. Men have a sacred duty to protect women and children, sheltering them from the savageries of life. In turn, women nurture their husbands and offspring in a warm, loving home. Your artwork does not lie within the realm of womanly art."

Ruby bit her tongue to squelch her reply. He would undoubtedly think her impertinent, and it was too early in the term to antagonize a professor. She dipped her head and muttered, "Yes, sir."

Disappointed in his critique, Ruby stowed her paintings. Apparently only men were to discover their own truths. She'd never imagined that men and women should paint differently. Societal convention might strangle her hopes of becoming a real artist. She wanted the training, so she would present one oeuvre to the Academy while secretly painting in her own style. Hardly what she had dreamed of when she left Truly.

* * * *

As she walked home from church one invigorating fall afternoon, Ruby encountered a demonstration in Logan Square. Ladies, dressed in suffragette-white, waved placards exclaiming FREE LOVE in bold letters. Men, leaning out the windows of nearby buildings, whistled and yelled taunts. A row of policemen prevented on-lookers from storming a platform filled with male and female orators.

Curious, Ruby stood on the top step of a building, pressing herself against the bricks to avoid the maelstrom while she listened to the speeches.

At the podium, a petite woman, clothed in dove gray, spoke. "I take this opportunity to introduce Mrs. Victoria Woodhull, who has returned from England to seek the Presidency of the United States." She clapped enthusiastically.

Mrs. Woodhull, garbed in somber purple, moved to the rostrum. Her serious demeanor belied the brilliance of her personality. Melodious, yet defiant, her voice rang out over the multitude. "Yes! I am a Free Lover. A woman has the right to control her own body, to refuse her husband if she desires. She has the right to remain unmarried, to bear children outside of wedlock, to love whom she chooses when she chooses. The state has no right to interfere with a woman's—"

A ripe tomato struck Mrs. Woodhull on the chest, splattering her peplumed jacket. She raised her voice above the catcalls and jeers and continued, "—right to self-determination." An egg narrowly missed her eye, its yellow yolk trickling down her cheek. Policemen whisked her off stage and down a narrow alleyway. The speakers remaining on the dais swiftly followed.

With one accord, the crowd surged onto the makeshift stage. With a loud creak, the wooden platform collapsed. People stumbled, crying out as others fell atop them.

More officers arrived, these on horseback, encircling the throng, trying to keep the peace. Demonstrators dropped their placards—now preferring anonymity to free political expression—and stole away.

Ruby cautiously worked her way through the mob. As she rounded a corner, panicked picketers plowed into her, knocking her over in their attempts to evade the police. Fearing she would be trampled, she struggled to regain her feet.

Two women, their arms filled with pamphlets, broke from a half-run to assist her. They dropped their booklets and hoisted her upright. "Best get out of here." They melted into the crowd without waiting for her thanks.

Before Ruby could follow their example, a mounted policeman approached her, a scowl on his face.

She glanced at the pamphlets at her feet. She looked guilty. The policeman would assume she was a demonstrator. She should have gone straight home. Wildly she peered one way then the other, seeking a quick escape. Her arrest was imminent. Damnation. Mrs. Wheelwright would condemn Ruby for sure.

Two men swung their fists at each other, capturing the policeman's attention. "Move along, young lady." He dug his heels into his horse's flanks and rode past her.

With a sigh of relief, she stuffed a pamphlet in her pocket and raced away, weaving in and out of the crowd.

Safe—if breathless—in her own room, she studied the brochure. The front comprised a political endorsement:

Victoria Woodhull
for
President of the United States of America 1892
Sponsored by the
National Woman Suffragists' Nominating Convention

> *...Coercion should not exist within a mar-*
> *riage...A woman has a right to refuse her husband*
> *should she not wish to bear a child...A woman has*
> *the inalienable and natural right to love whom she*
> *chooses for as long as she wishes, whether that*
> *person be male or female...*

Ruby wondered what the words meant. Bismarck had not forced himself on her. She had chosen him as clearly as he had her. Nor did she believe her father pressured her mother into bearing children. She did not understand why two women—or two men, for that matter—would ever choose to be partners. Confusing her further, the struggle for Free Love was tied somehow to the battle for women's rights, especially the right to vote. She was uncertain where these movements intersected or how they affected her.

* * * *

With the advent of cold weather, Ruby's classmates succumbed to illness. Often half her class was absent, but she remained blessedly healthy. Newspaper articles warned of Russian influenza or *Le Grippe,* a syndrome with a high fever accompanied by great prostration, loss of appetite, muscular aches, and severe respiratory symptoms. First recorded in St. Petersburg in 1889, the epidemic had spread worldwide.

Perched on her stool in the studio, Ruby watched Miss Wycke enter, late as usual. She didn't look well. Despite herself, Ruby kept a concerned eye on the other woman. Halfway through their studio session, Miss Wycke's cheeks paled. Shaking like a leaf in a tornado, she grabbed for her easel for support. The wooden frame crashed to the floor. Her eyes rolled upward. She toppled over in a dead faint.

The blonde student next to Miss Wycke did nothing but

fan the stricken woman with her sketchpad. Other women gathered around but were equally useless.

Exasperated at their incompetence, Ruby shoved them aside and felt Miss Wycke's face. She burned with fever. After rubbing Miss Wycke's hands briskly without results, Ruby placed a few swift slaps on the woman's cheeks. No response. Society ladies frequently carried smelling salts in the event of a swoon, so Ruby upended the woman's reticule and searched its contents, finding a tiny silver-stoppered vial. She opened it carefully. A trail of vapor rose toward her nostrils. She jerked her head back. Her nose began to run. Her watering eyes squeezed shut against the noxious fumes. Smelling salts, all right. Carefully she wafted the vial several inches from Miss Wycke's face.

Her eyelids fluttered. She moaned and gradually recovered her color.

"Hail a cab." Ruby pointed first at one student, then another. "And you—get her coat and portfolio."

When the hackney arrived, she asked Miss Wycke, "Can you stand?"

When she nodded, Ruby and the fair-haired girl half-carried Miss Wycke downstairs and into the carriage while another woman carried their art supplies and portfolios.

At the boarding home Ruby, with Mrs. Wheelwright's help, managed to get Miss Wycke up the stairs to her room.

Curious, Ruby looked around. Easily twice the size of hers, the room held a grand bed with a velvet coverlet, a settee and two plush chairs adorned with needlepoint pillows. Ruby's room must once have been a closet, converted so her landlady might bring in a few extra dollars.

"I'll send the housemaid to fetch the doctor and to telegraph the family of their daughter's illness." Mrs. Wheelwright moved toward the stairs.

Undressing Miss Wycke like a child, Ruby removed the woman's shawl, coat, blouse, corset, its cover, and camisole. She rummaged through the bureau and found a flannel nightgown, which for modesty's sake, she pulled over Miss Wycke's head before releasing the drawstrings of the various lower undergarments and dropping them to the floor. "Can you finish alone?"

Swaying slightly, Miss Wycke stared blankly at the mirror.

As the woman was clearly incapable of caring for herself, Ruby removed the other woman's hairpins, letting her fever-damp locks tumble free. A few quick strokes with a brush then she braided and tied the hair with a ribbon. She jerked down the coverlet and fluffed the pillows. "Hop in bed. Get warm."

After tucking Miss Wycke beneath the covers, Ruby placed her hand on the doorknob to return her room.

"Don't leave me. Please?" Willow begged.

"I'll be right back."

In her cubbyhole, Ruby peeled off her coat and tucked her portfolio under her bed before taking a minute to wash paint and charcoal from her fingers.

A faint knock sounded on their shared wall, followed by a plaintive "Are you ever returning, Miss Schmidt?"

"Coming." Ruby pulled the extra quilt from the foot of her bed and walked down the hall. There she encountered Mrs. Wheelwright who advised her the physician would arrive at his earliest convenience, but due to the volume of house calls he was obliged to make, Miss Wycke would likely have a long wait.

When Ruby entered Miss Wycke's room, shaking chills wracked the other woman's slender frame. The woman's pulse fluttered rapidly at her neck, and her breathing was shallow and rapid.

Ruby added another blanket to the pile covering Miss Wycke. Filling a blue and white washbasin with tepid water, Ruby sponged Miss Wycke's face to reduce her temperature.

When the woman's breathing slowed, Ruby felt Miss Wycke's forehead again and was relieved to find it cooler. The chills had passed. The high fever had broken. Ruby tugged the blanket and feather comforter to Miss Wycke's chin then settled on the settee, wondering how long she would have to wait before the physician arrived.

Well after dark, the doctor rushed in, his face gray with fatigue.

"Influenza." He held up a brown bottle. "Give her two teaspoons of this every four hours for fever." When he warned Mrs. Wheelwright about contagion, the two decided that Ruby, who had already been exposed, would care for Miss Wycke until her family came from West Chester to take her home.

Ruby awakened in an unfamiliar place. After a moment, she remembered she was in Miss Wycke's room. She rose, wrapped her quilt about her, and looked outside. She blinked at the cold white light reflecting from the heavy snow that blanketed the city. The sun, a silver circle hanging in a gray sky, barely pierced the clouds. It was well past noon. Nearby, Miss Wycke's breathing was slow and regular. Both women, after being up and down all night, had slept the morning away.

Soon, Miss Wycke's older brother and mother arrived. The family made rapid introductions and thanked first Mrs. Wheelwright, then Ruby, for caring for their invalid. With Miss Wycke heavily bundled against the weather and with heated bricks at her feet, they whisked her away in their brougham.

Chapter Six
Antioch Farm

December 1891

After her last class before winter break, Ruby swirled her shawl tightly around her shoulders and marched up Broad Street. Snowflakes glittered in the golden glow of the streetlights. Evergreen wreaths decorated doors in anticipation of Christmas. People rushed past her, trying to reach home before the weather worsened. She shivered and raised her umbrella.

As Ruby walked, lights—both gas and electrical—illuminated families sharing meals. Envious of the folks in those cozy houses, she trudged to her boarding house. With two weeks off for the holidays, traveling ten days to spend but four with her family seemed pointless, so she chose to remain in Philadelphia. Her fellow boarders departed to holiday with their families, leaving Ruby alone with her landlady until the New Year. Though several invited her to their homes, Ruby hated to intrude. Mrs. Wheelwright spent Christmas Day with her family—and didn't issue an invitation. The cook, feeling sorry for Ruby, left a covered plate for her in the kitchen.

Ruby had mailed gifts to her family, and she received a large box in return. On Christmas morning, she started to unwrap them but stopped. If she opened them now, a long empty day loomed. Better to save them. Finally, in late afternoon, she carefully undid each box. Sniffling, she tried on the mittens knitted by her sisters and the wool shawl embroidered by her mother. She paraded before her mirror thinking how dashing she would appear when school started again. She chuckled at Jasper's gift. He'd sent her butter-scotch hard candy—his favorite—while her pa had enclosed twenty dollars.

Several days after Christmas, Ruby knitted in her room. If the weather wasn't so cold, she'd explore the city rather than count the cabbage roses on the wallpaper.

A tentative knock sounded at her door. Before she could get to her feet, a more solid rat-tat-tat followed. She couldn't imagine who it could be. The Academy was closed. Most of Mrs. Wheelwright's lodgers were away for the holidays. Having endured a forlorn vacation, Ruby answered the door with alacrity, hoping to chat with someone. She recoiled at seeing her visitor.

"Am I disturbing you?" Miss Wycke's smile couldn't decide if Ruby was worth coming to life for. "I wanted to thank you for caring for me."

"Have you fully recovered, Miss Wycke?"

"Please, call me Willow. I must confess I'm still quite weak. But better, thank you."

Fearing rejection, Ruby hesitated before asking, "Would you care to come in, Miss…Willow?"

Willow nodded. "Not for long, though. My brother waits downstairs."

Ruby sat on the bed, ceding her sole chair to her visitor.

The two women chatted a moment before Willow, after a diffident glance at Ruby, said, "Miss Schmidt, would you care to spend New Year's with my family? Unless you've made other arrangements?"

Ruby hesitated. She had no plans but was unsure she

wanted to holiday with strangers.

"Oh, you must. Please? Allow me to express my gratitude for your attentions"—Willow glanced down at her jittery fingers—"especially since I've treated you so poorly."

At the contrite expression on Willow's face, Ruby capitulated.

For the first time, a genuine smile graced the young lady's face, turning her almost attractive.

Quickly throwing a few days' clothing into her portmanteau, Ruby followed Willow, racing down the stairs, eager to escape Philadelphia and spend a few days in the country.

At the curb, Mr. Woodrow Wycke, Willow's older brother first helped his sister into the carriage. As he guided Ruby's ascent, his hand and eyes lingered. "Miss Schmidt, it is a pleasure to see you again—and under more pleasant circumstances than our first encounter."

* * * *

Relieved to be out of the dinginess of Philadelphia, Ruby enjoyed the twenty-six mile trip through the Brandywine River Valley to West Chester. Cows burrowed their noses through melting snow searching for grass. A pastoral landscape but quite without the openness of the Texas plains.

At a sign that read *Antioch Farm*, Mr. Wycke followed a curved road drive to an elegant white Greek Revival home, a jewel perched on a low hill. "Our grandfather patterned it after President Jefferson's Monticello."

Four pillars supported a portico that framed a broad door with leaded glass windows. As the carriage approached, servants dashed through the slush on the drive to retrieve Ruby's luggage.

Inside, Mr. Wycke passed Ruby's coat to the butler. "While Willow and the servants get your belongings situated, perhaps you'd accompany me on a tour of the house?"

Tucking her hand into the angle of his elbow, he drew her between the double staircases into a parlor where ancestral paintings and landscapes hung from the egg-and-dart crown molding, enlivening buttercream-colored walls. Casual groups of chairs and settees dotted the room. A large mirror reflected a grand piano. A graceful, stylish room. Next came a library and the elder Mr. Wycke's office.

Overwhelmed by viewing the ground floor, Ruby was relieved when Mr. Wycke led her to what became her favorite place in the manor. Situated under the cupola, the room could only be reached by stairs so narrow she had to crush her skirts tightly about her thighs. The sparsely furnished room might have illustrated Andrea Palladio's *The Four Books of Architecture*. Beneath a magnificent domed ceiling with a round skylight at its apex, six bulls-eye windows looked across the valley. At last, she could see for miles, and a brass telescope on a tripod provided infinite detail of the panorama. She could spend hours here watching light play across the vista.

Upstairs, in the family's private area, the simplicity of the Greek Revival furnishings of the ground floor gave way to the excessive ornamentation currently in vogue. The heavy draperies and elaborate furnishings piled one atop another made Ruby long for the clarity of the ground floor.

Once Mr. Wycke escorted Ruby to her room, she collapsed on a tufted upholstered chair and studied her surroundings. Another elegant space, though furnished with a heavy hand. A four-poster bed, draped with a canopy, sat so high that she'd need the provided step stool to climb into bed.

Ruby reviewed her tour of the Wyckes' grand home. Her guide, home from university for the holidays, had been charming, polite, and quite attentive, far more entranced with her than she could ever be with him. Compared to Bismarck, Mr. Wycke held no appeal.

* * * *

In the parlor, the two younger women waited for Mrs. Wycke to join them for luncheon. Already Willow had told tales of her outspoken mother's commitment to political and social causes. The older woman seemed quite different from Ruby's own ma. The longer the girls waited, the more anxious Ruby grew and the faster her foot tapped beneath her skirts.

"You'll simply adore Mamá," Willow reassured her. "She's from an old Abolitionist family. Quite the radical. She's even been arrested."

Jailed? Now Ruby was even more nervous.

A woman in the soignée plumage of a dove rested a hand on Willow's shoulder. "And you were taken into custody alongside me, darling," Mrs. Wycke proudly said as she perched on the loveseat near her daughter .

Ruby shot a shocked glance at Willow then returned her gaze to Mrs. Wycke. The violets on her hat echoed the lavender ribbon on her snowy collar. Unlike her child, she was quite petite. Her personality outshone her plainness.

"Fortunately, your papá bailed us out before the afternoon was over. The jail was intolerable. Absolutely filthy. Head lice. Body odors. Women of ill repute." She shivered then looked Ruby over from the pheasant feather in her hat to the buttons on her shoes. "How do you do, Miss Schmidt? Woodrow was right. You are quite adorable."

Caught off balance, Ruby tweaked her lips into a half-smile. "Thank you."

Mrs. Wycke said, "I've just returned from a meeting of the National Woman Suffrage Association. We're merging with the American Women Suffrage Association. I'm on the committee orchestrating the union. Miss Schmidt, what is your opinion of the female vote?"

"I-I-I've never thought about it."

"You should consider it—and seriously. We ladies will vote. It's inevitable. We have emancipated the Negro. We females will be freed from bondage next. I'll leave you a pamphlet, my dear." Mrs. Wycke gave Ruby's hand a motherly pat.

"Mamá would give you a booklet on voluntary motherhood as well, but they were confiscated under the Comstock laws as being obscene." Willow rolled her eyes.

"Can you believe such abuse of power? Ridiculous!" the older woman said.

Ruby could not imagine what voluntary motherhood might be. She had never considered that women might have a choice about carrying a child. The radical statements triggered memories of the Free Love rally and the realization that Mrs. Wycke had been the woman who introduced Victoria Woodhull.

As the ladies lingered after their luncheon, Ruby grew even more intimidated by the intensely civic-minded Mrs. Wycke with her assertions that, as women were no different from men, females should be entitled to the same social, political, economic, and religious rights.

"I must return to my suffrage work." Mrs. Wycke stood with a swish of her skirts and kissed her daughter's cheek. Then she extended her hand to Ruby. "My dear Miss Schmidt, you must spend Easter with us as well. Willie hasn't had a close friend in a good while. She talks about you constantly. We would be most delighted to have you visit anytime."

Taken back for the second time in minutes, Ruby nodded, not knowing what else to do. Willow had ignored her until two days ago, yet her mother thought they were dear friends.

* * * *

Ruby ate silently at the most elegant dinner table she'd ever seen. Early in Ruby's life, her mother had used fancy table settings but, when she realized that cowhands and good china were incompatible, she'd resorted to tinware. Ruby mimicked Willow's choices of the three glasses, three forks, three spoons and other utensils and somehow survived the meal without dribbling her soup on the snowy tablecloth.

Finally, having exhausted current events as topics of conversation, the elder Mr. Wycke engaged Ruby on a subject she could safely discuss. "Miss Schmidt, how large is your family's ranch?"

"Ten thousand acres."

Mr. Wycke's bushy eyebrows shook hands above his nose. Ruby could almost see his mental calculations.

"Perhaps your father and I should discuss going into business together." He nodded sagely. "We could market both beef and milk in Philadelphia."

"Our ranch is not as big as it sounds. In West Texas, we figure twenty acres per cow—if it's been a wet year. And we run beef, not milkers, because they consume less grass."

"How do you get them to market?"

"Before the railroad came, we drove cattle overland in huge cattle drives. Now we herd them the seventeen miles to Truly where they're loaded onto a train bound for the Fort Worth stockyard."

"We?"

"If it's only a few head, my sisters and I help Pa so the cowhands don't lose a day's work."

"If you're doing a man's job, Miss Schmidt"—over her wineglass Mrs. Wycke looked archly at Ruby—"you should be permitted to the right to vote. And paid a man's wage."

"Yes, ma'am," Ruby said, though she did not know a ranch girl one who had ever been rewarded for helping her family.

"Later we can discuss voluntary motherhood. Women should not be forced to have children they do not desire."

Mr. Wycke cleared his throat. "Elizabeth, my dear." His voice held the tiniest admonition. "Might we limit our conversation to subjects appropriate for dining?"

As the meal neared completion, Mr. Wycke said, "Woodrow, shall we retire to the library for cigars?"

The young man took Ruby's hand. "I'll join you shortly, Father. Allow me to escort the ladies to the parlor and entertain them at the piano. Miss Schmidt, do you play?"

* * * *

With the New Year, the two art students returned to the boarding house. Though Ruby and the other woman had spent several days in each other's company, Willow seemed reluctant to separate. "Would you care to see my portfolio? Works I didn't present in class?"

"Yes, please." Ruby, despite their time together, hadn't had an opportunity to study her new friend's work.

Willow led Ruby to her room and opened a black leather case. As she displayed her paintings, her passion for art illuminated her face. A rosy glow enlivened her cheeks. The upturn of her mouth softened the angles of her face and rendered her quite beautiful.

Most of Willow's paintings were still-lifes, portraits, and landscapes of Antioch Farm. Willow, Ruby thought—like herself—was a good, but not yet great painter, with a natural talent that needed training.

Grasping Willow's hand, Ruby tugged Willow to her room. "I'll show you my work." From her steamer trunk, she removed her paintings and sketches.

Ruby flipped through images of cowmen, Indians, wild animals, and the austere Texas landscape. One she snatched before Willow saw it and stowed it beneath her quilt.

"What are you hiding?" Willow laughed and pulled out the concealed image. After a quick glance at it, she snapped her eyes shut. "You do sketch the most unusual things, Miss Schmidt."

"It's my fiancé, Bismarck." Ruby's face burned with embarrassment. "I drew him from memory." Damnation. She had opened her mouth before she thought and admitted seeing Bismarck naked before their wedding. Willow would be appalled and would never speak to Ruby again.

"I should be shocked." Willow's face bloomed a lush rose-red. She opened her eyes, her gaze remaining fixed on Ruby's detailed pen and ink sketch of her betrothed's most intimate parts. "Instead I am envious. At the Academy, we shall study the nude. At least you have an idea of what to expect. I was quite clueless—until now." She tittered nervously, still staring at Bismarck.

Ruby jerked the sketch from her friend's hand and tucked it in the very bottom of her trunk.

* * * *

Over the ensuing weeks, Ruby's friendship with Willow grew. Taller than Ruby by several inches, Willow was slight and boyish, always wearing a sparrow's drab plumage. But, when discussing art, her pale fingers fluttered in delicate wing-like motions, giving her stillness sudden animation, eloquent gestures impossible to reproduce on paper before they vanished. Willow's most marvelous feature, her brown eyes, sparkled against dewy skin. Ruby wondered why she had thought the other woman plain.

On Ruby's bed, they sat side-by-side, an art book balanced over their thighs. Chilled, Ruby placed her shawl across her back.

Next to her, Willow shivered.

"Shall we share?" As Ruby arranged the wool over their touching shoulders, she inhaled the delightful scent of lavender, geraniums and cloves emanating from her friend.

Bound by fabric and art, the women conversed late into the night, their subjects ranging from chiaroscuro to gouache, from Renaissance artists to those infamous French impressionists.

"I was born with the need to paint." Willow's hands quivered in her excitement. "Sometimes when light strikes a person's face or a flower weeps in the rain, I'm driven to capture it on paper."

"Me, too. At night before I sleep, colors appear in the darkness and align themselves into fantastic images. The gnarled hands of an old cowhand, the calligraphy of the sun tracing the clouds, the curve of my sister's cheek…" Ruby trailed off.

Willow patted Ruby's hand. "Have you been away from your family before?"

"Long enough to get my teaching certificate. But the college was near home, and I visited frequently. Sometimes when I think on how far away my family is and how dreadfully long it will be before I see them again, I get rather weepy."

"My parents dumped me in a finishing school in Paris for years." Bitterness tinged Willow's voice.

"Were you lonely?"

"At first. Until I made a special friend." Willow's face softened in recollection.

"I have a dear friend at home, too. Molly Statler. We've known each other since grade school."

Willow gazed at Ruby a long moment. "We shall simply

declare ourselves sisters. From now on, I shall be your Willie and you my Ruby."

The newly-born siblings chattered through the night. At length, Ruby and Willow yawned simultaneously. Their arms entangled as they stretched. Willow lowered her arm and draped it over Ruby's shoulders.

Ruby leaned on her friend's shoulder, feeling the pulse at the other woman's neck against the top of her head. In truth, Willow seemed more her sister than any of Ruby's own family. She was filled with a sensual longing for communion with the woman who shared her vision, her heart, her soul.

The two women sat in affable silence, growing sleepier by the minute, yet unwilling to part.

Willow's dry lips brushed Ruby's forehead. "I should return to my room."

Ruby escorted her friend the few steps to the door.

Willow drew Ruby into an embrace. "As sisters, we shall encourage each other. Our devotion to art—and each other—will be as strong as marriage vows. Our ambition shall not lie dormant. We shall become artists."

Ruby kissed Willow's cheek. "The true journey of our lives begins now. We will travel it together. Pleasant dreams, sweetest sister, dearest friend."

Chapter Seven
A Bit More Time

February 1892

Ruby sat on a stool before her easel with Willow to her left. On Ruby's right, Ira Wheatley paced as he worked. Like her, he was a redhead, though more carrot than blond, and so large in frame she'd found him intimidating when they first met. She wondered how his enormous hands could manipulate a brush, much less create the delicate lines of engravings. His work captured bizarre unposed moments, making her wonder what happened immediately before or after the scene. The week before he had shown her etchings of everyday life in the tenements of Philadelphia. One depicted a woman in a nightgown holding a kerosene lamp and looking down at a man in a bed.

"Is she a wife? Perhaps caring for an ill husband?" Warmth raced up Ruby's face as she posed another possibility. "Or a soiled dove who's forgotten which man remains in her bed?"

"A soiled dove?" Wheatley smirked.

Embarrassed, Ruby averted her eyes. "You know, a lady of...of...ill repute."

He shook his head at her euphemism, smiled enigmatically, and refused to clarify his artwork. "It is what it is, Red."

"You fiend!" She'd swatted him with her paintbrush.

Now, she sensed Wheatley's frequent, prolonged gaze. Irritated, she turned to confront him. "Quit staring."

Hearing whispering, Anshutz walked toward her as if to shush her. Instead, he stopped at Wheatley's easel. "Is there a reason you're not working on today's assignment?"

Ruby, along with the rest of the class turned, stared, and held their collective breaths waiting to see what happened.

"I finished the bust." Wheatley lifted the sketch he was working on and revealed he had indeed completed his drawing.

One of Anshutz's famous *harrumphs* of disapproval erupted as he looked at Wheatley's drawing from the cast. He made several swipes with his charcoal before he flipped back to the top drawing and appraised it. "Hmm. Well done. However, the Committee on Instruction feels your fellow class members are not appropriate subjects, particularly if sketched without their consent."

Wheatley scribbled his name across the bottom of his drawing before tossing it at Ruby. "Here, Red." He slammed his portfolio shut and stormed out of the classroom.

Ruby looked at the drawing. Her irritation faded. Surely she was not as lovely as Wheatley envisioned her. He had rendered her face and body in charcoal but had used red ochre for her hair. In his sketch her shoulders were bare. Her cheeks burnt as she wondered if, in his mind, he had removed the rest of her clothing.

Mr. Anshutz moved toward Ruby. "You may wish to keep that. I suspect Mr. Wheatley's drawings may fetch a pretty penny one day." Then he made numerous bold corrections on Ruby's work. "Do it again. You must not *think* the lines, Miss Schmidt, you must *feel* them."

She had thought her drawing good. Her smugness evaporated with his criticism. Anshutz was worse than her father.

Nothing she painted would ever please her professor. She stood abruptly. Her stool clattered to the floor. Holding back tears, she dashed from the room.

In her retreat, she ran by Willow. Her friend grabbed Ruby's hand, tugging her back.

Ruby broke free.

When Willow tried to follow her, Anshutz said, "Remain here, Miss Wycke. She must develop a thicker skin, or she'll never survive as an artist."

* * * *

Sunday afternoon, after Mrs. Wheelwright's Bible studies, Ruby returned to her room. In her chair, with light from the window falling over her shoulder, her feet propped on the footstool, she re-devoured long news-filled pages from her mother and Molly before replying. No word from Bismarck this week or last. Though she corresponded with him on a regular basis, he replied erratically. Perhaps, being a fellow, he did not grasp how much his letters meant to her. She shook her head. He had no excuse. Her pa, the toughest man she knew, wrote every week, if only a scribbled line at the end of her mother's letters. All Ruby needed from her beloved was a paragraph—even a sentence—to say he thought of her. Every day, she pretended his last letter had just arrived and read it again. With each reading her disappointment grew.

> *Dear Ruby,*
> *Nokoni and I set cedar posts and strung barbed wire around the house and barn. Shot the coyote that's been plaguing the henhouse. Bought another dozen sitters. Stopped work on our house until you get back and decide what you want.*
> *Molly says to tell you hello. She misses you.*

Yours,
Bismarck

As taciturn on paper as in life, he put down sparse details of the ranch but nary an emotion. She didn't care about the fence dividing her future home from the plains. Nor about Nokoni, Bismarck's half-Comanche hired hand. Nor Bismarck's mention of Molly. Ruby's friend wrote regular newsy letters enlivened by local gossip.

Ruby wanted words of love from the man she planned to marry. For as long as she could remember, he had been part of her life, her first memory of anyone outside her family. Over the years he had played with her, teased her, idolized her, protected her, but above all loved her. They had an uncanny ability to communicate without words, but surely he could not expect her to fathom his thoughts across two thousand miles.

She envisioned his rough hands, awkwardly holding a pencil, chewing one end as he plotted what to write. In school for only a few weeks at a time, his education came mostly from his mother on winter nights after his chores. He read well, enjoyed books, and could cipher enough to keep track of ranch expenses but was never at ease writing.

Though she had graduated from high school, he had not. She had been eight, he ten, on his last day of formal education. The other boys were shooting marbles on the playground when he sidled up behind her and sliced off the tip of her braid with his pocketknife. She whirled, kicked him in the shin, and stuck her tongue out at him. He dashed off, waving his token with glee. She gave chase. He hid behind the stairs on the far side of the school building and caught her as she raced by, planting a swift kiss on her cheek.

"Someday I'll marry you, Ruby Louise."

She believed him. She'd never met anyone as single-minded as Bismarck. Once he set a goal, he accomplished it. He had their whole life planned. A skilled horseman, he would raise championship horses. They would wed and start a family.

* * * *

May 1892

Ruby made the momentous decision to remain at the Academy another year. Determined not to change her plans, she paid her tuition in advance. She hated withdrawing the hundred dollars from her bank account, but by doing so, she removed the temptation to go home. Her first year had been spent settling into her new environment. Months passed before her ache for the prairie subsided. Her friendship with Willow had blossomed into a true sisterhood, a union of artists of differing styles but similar inclinations. Ruby had a small circle of friends, all comfortable enough to give each other honest criticism. Though she remained trapped between doing the art she desired and that which the school expected, new techniques gave her paintings a professional polish. She improved daily, making progress in her journey to becoming a painter.

She dropped into her chair to write her weekly letters home then immediately stood, needing something firm to write on. After she placed a sketchpad on her lap to serve as a desk, she hopped up again and grabbed more paper. Then it occurred to her that she might run out of ink. So, with an eyedropper, she filled her fountain pen and sat for the fourth time. Nothing to do now but take pen in hand and write. She'd postponed informing her parents and her betrothed of her decision until she could delay no longer. After much gnawing of her fingernails and many false starts, she composed a letter to Bismarck.

> *My darling Bismarck,*
>
> *I have decided to stay in Philadelphia another year. How can I describe the joy of working with fellow artists? Though I hesitate to promote myself, I am holding my own with painters with far more training. Stopping my studies now would be a travesty.*
>
> *I know you will understand. I miss you. I beg your patience—and forgiveness. I love you and promise to return to you.*
>
> *Your loving little bird,*
> *Ruby Louise*

Those last words would remind him of what they had done in the barn and give him hope. Her own memories of lying with him still thrilled her. Though she was grateful she had not conceived during those secret couplings, she hoped to carry Bismarck's child someday, but not until she'd finished her training.

Her thoughts wandered back to the second time Bismarck had declared his love. He was fourteen, living in a one-room shack at a line camp miles from home, sleeping on a rickety rope-bottomed bed on a mattress stuffed with cornhusks, minding cattle with no companion other than his old sheepdog and a quarter horse. His sister Lillian saddled up every morning and dropped off hard-fried eggs, beans, biscuits or cornbread, sausage, whatever leftovers his mother could spare.

One warm spring afternoon Ruby stole away from her tasks and rode Ladybug to visit him. When he wasn't near the shack, she grew concerned and searched for him, riding in a slow spiral, calling his name until she grew hoarse.

At last, alerted by the sheepdog's frantic barking, she found Bismarck crawling through the sagebrush. She flung herself from her horse. "What happened?"

"Rattlesnake. Horse shied. Threw me and took off. Snake bit me." Stranded, he had hobbled toward home as venom marched inexorably through his flesh.

Ruby jerked up his pants leg. Above his shoe, his calf had swollen to twice its usual size, the skin blackened. If only he'd had on boots. But his parents would only buy him cheap brogans. Bile hit the back of her throat. She couldn't—wouldn't—allow herself to get sick. Bismarck needed her strength. She tugged at the boy, trying to lift him.

Half-crazed with pain, he was too far gone to help her.

Time slowed. Every cloud of red dust she stirred up hung in the air like the Devil's breath. Her muscles strained to move Bismarck's dead weight. She moved her pony as near to Bismarck as she could and somehow got the boy to his feet. As she struggled to get him on the horse, Ladybug skittered away. Bismarck's knees buckled. He slid down Ruby's legs. Damnation. She grabbed the reins, jerked her horse back in place, and hefted Bismarck again. And failed over and over until her entire body ached from the effort. He grew weaker with each attempt. She hated to leave him. He might be dead when she came back, and she couldn't bear the thought of him dying alone. "Biz, wake up." She slapped him. "Help me. Otherwise, damn it, I'll leave you here."

To this day, she remained unsure how she got him on her horse, if the strength she found came from deep within or from somewhere Above. She swung up behind him. Closer to her home than his, she galloped for the ranch on the longest ride of her life, leaping the fence and riding right onto the front porch, screaming for her ma.

The house blazed into turmoil. Bismarck's pa galloped to

San Angelo, returning a day later with the only physician in the area. Ruby peeked around the door, watching the doctor, eavesdropping on Bismarck's prognosis. Under the old quack's supervision, Bismarck's swollen limb was propped high on pillows, cold compresses applied, and whiskey or laudanum poured down his throat for pain. The doctor pronounced the boy too ill to move, so he remained, lingering near death, at the Schmidt house for days.

Hilda, Bismarck's mother, came and spent as much time as she could spare from caring for five other children. Josef, his father, came every evening.

Ruby snuck into the sickroom between chores, relieving her ma and his from sick duty. At first playing nursemaid had been fun. As he recovered, he was no longer sweet and appreciative. Bored and restless, he tormented her by yanking her braids and making her read western dime novels aloud. She played with him as best she could with him confined to bed. Biz always wanted to be the sheriff and rescue a fair lady, oblivious to the fact that a damsel had rescued him. He dragged Ruby next to him on the bed and, for the first time, kissed her on the mouth, expecting her to be grateful for his slobbering. "I'll never marry unless I marry you, Ruby Louise."

She swallowed hard, recalling his words, wondering if she had done the right thing by staying in Philadelphia. Though she considered going home for the summer, Mrs. Wheelwright would not guarantee Ruby's room unless she paid the entire three months' rent in advance. Otherwise, Ruby would have to vacate her room and either put her belongings in storage or ship them home and back. Those fees, plus the round trip train fare, represented a substantial sum, more than a woman of limited funds might afford. Her father might help her but, as he had been dead set against art school, he would place untenable conditions on his aid. She determined to make it on her own. Though homesick, logically, she was better off paying for her education and waiting another year to return to Truly. If she pinched every penny, she could reserve the majority of Gran's legacy for her future with Bismarck. Besides, if she went home, leaving Bismarck again would be too difficult to bear.

A week passed, then another. Four weeks without a word from him. Ruby's sister, Pearl, wrote of her engagement to Willem Buskirk. Ma, in an accompanying letter, expressed regret over not seeing her daughter for another year and pointed out that Ruby, too, was engaged and that perhaps her errant daughter should come home before Bismarck grew weary of waiting.

Irritated, Ruby blew out a huff of air. Though her mother had been content to marry young and raise a family, Ruby had the rest of her life to settle down. She needed more time for her studies.

Chapter Eight
A Dangerous Man

May 1892

A sharp rap on her door interrupted Ruby while she mended the torn hem of her skirt. At the sudden sound she stabbed herself with the needle. Damnation. She mumbled "Yes?" as she bit the tip of her finger to staunch the bleeding.

"Miss Schmidt?" Mrs. Wheelwright sounded wheezy from climbing the stairs.

Ruby, clad only in her shirtwaist and petticoats, yanked the partially repaired garment over her head before cracking the door. "Yes, ma'am?"

Her landlady sucked in several hoarse breaths. "You have a gentleman caller."

"Who?" Ruby reviewed the men she knew, unable to think of anyone who might come calling.

"Didn't give a name. Looks dangerous, though."

Ruby couldn't imagine who the visitor downstairs might be. Since she had moved into Mrs. Wheelwright's, no man had ever called on her. Ira Wheatley and Fred Ames were the only gentlemen who might visit, but she saw them nearly every day. And neither of them could remotely be seen as menacing. The young Mr. Wycke was away at college. Everyone else was either back home or wouldn't dream of calling on her.

"I'll be right down."

Her landlady's heavy tread retreated.

With a glance at her dangling hem, Ruby realized she must change into something more presentable. Quickly, she donned a green striped skirt with black passementerie braid and inspected herself in the mirror. Lacking time to tame her riotous hair, she contented herself with pinching her cheeks and nibbling her lips to heighten their color, then fastened the top two buttons of her high-necked blouse, smoothed her skirt, then skipped pell-mell down the hall. Just before reaching the last flight of stairs, she slowed, took a deep breath, raised her chin, and began a ladylike descent even her righteous landlady could not fault.

Halfway down the steps, the faintest whiff of a familiar scent stopped her. Man, horse, hay, Texas—all rolled into one. She shook her head, certain her imagination was at play, and continued down the staircase.

Mrs. Wheelwright came from the kitchen, wiping her hands on her apron, meeting Ruby in the antechamber. "You took your sweet time." Her gaze raked Ruby up and down, checking for inappropriate attire before fixing a malevolent glare on her. "You know the rules. No men except in the parlor—with a chaperone."

"Yes, ma'am." Ruby's mouth turned to cotton. She was not sure she could speak with anyone, much less a gentleman caller, with Mrs. Wheelwright present. Her formidable landlady would regard as immoral anything other than the most tedious of small talk. Ruby and Willow only discussed art in their rooms, in case their conversation veered toward that most scandalous of topics—the nude. For about the millionth time since moving in with Mrs. Wheelwright, Ruby thought perhaps Aunt Josie wouldn't have been so bad after all. But at Wake Forest College, she'd have never met Willow.

The older woman nudged Ruby. "Don't keep him waiting, girlie. It's my time you're wasting as well. I'll be there in a minute. Be on your best behavior."

"Yes, ma'am." Ruby squelched the urge to curtsey.

She stepped to the parlor and peered through the door. A tall man faced the window, staring beyond the heavy lace draperies. Her breath hitched in her chest. Though she could not see his face, his form was unmistakable. She had not dreamt the scent in the stairwell. As she entered the room, her toe snagged the rug. She tripped.

Before she recovered, the man turned to face her, his eyes twinkling at her ungainly entrance.

Unable to tear her gaze from his, Ruby stumbled again before regaining her balance. She inhaled deeply as she looked him over.

His left hand held his Stetson. The right he clenched into a fist several times before wiping the palm on his coat, revealing the holster strapped to his right thigh. Big, broad-shouldered, and clothed in black, he did appear dangerous, but he was gentleness personified.

Lordy, Lordy, Lordy. He had not written but came to her instead. She gave a cry of delight.

In four steps, he crossed the room and swept her into his arms.

Ruby's lips met his in joyous reunion. Heavens, how she had missed him. The sweet taste of his mouth. His quiet strength. His enveloping warmth. The way their hearts thudded against each other's chest when they embraced.

Their kiss lasted forever but not nearly long enough. Then Bismarck held her, simply held her, his face buried in her hair as her tears inked his black broadcloth coat.

She mumbled into his chest. "I can't believe you're here."

"I've come to take you home, Ruby Louise."

Shocked, she pulled back. Her heart had sung at her first sight of him. Now, she didn't know whether to kiss him or strangle him. How dare he show up unannounced and declare he was taking her home.

"Miss Schmidt!"

At Mrs. Wheelwright's outraged voice, Ruby and Bismarck parted.

"Who might you be, sir?" the proprietress demanded from the doorway.

Ruby faced the older woman. "Mrs. Wheelwright, may I present my fiancé, Mr. Bismarck Behrens of Texas. Mr. Behrens, Mrs. Amelie Wheelwright, my landlady."

"How do you do, ma'am? Pleased to meet you." He extended a hand.

Ladies should not indiscriminately shake hands with gentlemen, so the always-proper doyenne did not accept his hand. Instead, with an abrupt swish of black bombazine, she deposited herself in the middle of the settee, the only place in the room where two people might sit side by side. She gathered her yarn and set to work, her glance flashing between her knitting needles and the couple.

"Won't you take a seat?" Ruby led Bismarck as far as possible from their chaperone.

He looked at the dainty chair as if fearing it might collapse beneath him before perching on its flowery edge. He brushed his fingers through his hair then thumbed the brim of his Stetson with both hands, looking less comfortable sitting than he had standing.

Ruby set his hat on a table and chose a neighboring chair, determined to avoid further faux pas in front of her landlady. For now, Ruby chose to ignore Bismarck's first pronouncement. They could discuss things later in private.

Still shaken, her words tumbled out, her voice pitched too high and edged with panic. "How was your trip? Why are you here? How's your family? Nokoni? The horses?" She took a quavery breath.

"Whoa." He held his hand palm out. "Slow down."

Ruby stopped her chatter.

He ran his hand over his face several times then came abruptly to the point. "I got your letter."

Ruby tensed, fearing his next remarks.

"I've come to take you home."

"Oh, Biz." She placed a hand on his arm.

A prompt "Ahem" from the direction of the settee warned Ruby of her impropriety.

She jerked her hand away. "Perhaps you might escort me on a walk through the neighborhood, Mr. Behrens?"

With an audible sigh of relief, Bismarck concurred.

"Please give me a moment to get my purse." Ruby handed him his hat then smiled, a promise she would not leave him forever in the clutches of the dragon lady.

Minutes later, with a summer shawl draped over her shoulders, the chain of her reticule wrapped around one wrist, and a parasol held in the opposite hand, Ruby descended the stairs. Rather more elegantly this time, she entered the parlor.

Mrs. Wheelwright glared most ungraciously at the couple while wielding her knitting needles like dueling swords.

"I'm quite ready now, Mr. Behrens."

At Ruby's voice, he stepped forward, moving ahead of her to open the front door and allow her through. After her clumsy entrance earlier, he probably feared she'd trip over her own skirt. Her flounces swished by him. He took her arm and helped her down the steps.

Halfway down the block and well out of sight of the

ferocious proprietress, Ruby erupted in giggles. "Oh, Biz. I'm sorry. My landlady is an absolute tyrant."

"How do you stand living there?" He clutched his throat dramatically and gasped. "I swear the jail in Truly lets in more light and air."

She sighed. A sudden vision of her hometown, surrounded by wide-open prairies, brought a wave of homesickness. "I open my window from time to time and take great breaths. Mrs. Wheelwright knows within seconds and hollers for me to close up before 'ill humors' penetrate."

* * * *

Ruby led Bismarck west on Callowhill toward Logan Square, proudly demonstrating how well she had settled into Philadelphia. "This street was named after William Penn's second wife, and those strange little buildings are row houses." She indicated the tightly packed red-brick homes, one room wide, joined by common side walls. Identical facades with identical doors above identical creamy marble steps. Identical lone windows on the first floor with identical pairs of windows on the stories above. No yards. No trees. An occasional flower box was the only concession to nature.

"How do folks live jammed together? I couldn't stand someone breathing down my neck all the time." Bismarck worked a finger beneath his collar to loosen it. "And the noise. I cain't hear myself think."

"At first, I felt the same way. I don't mind so much now."

A promenade along the banks of the Schuylkill would give them a modicum of privacy, so she led him along West River Road to where they could watch the river and its waterworks.

Bismarck stopped and shook his head in amazement. "I've never seen that much water before." He pointed to young men pulling the oars of sculls. "Enough water for folks to play in."

"If you think this river is big, we can walk along the Delaware tomorrow."

For the most part, they strolled in silence, getting used to being near each other again. Bismarck had come a long way to say words Ruby did not wish to hear. Once he had loved her because she was independent, but when she did something bold, he didn't like it. She feared hurting him yet equally feared denying her own ambition. If only he'd written. A letter would have been easier. In response she would have composed tender words to let him down gently. But with the man she had loved her entire life here in person, she'd find it difficult to refuse him.

Bismarck rolled his neck as they walked and fidgeted again with his collar, finally loosening his tie and top button. "How can you live this way? All closed in? You cain't see the whole sky. Or the far horizon. You cain't see what's really there for all the stuff that's in the way."

"You get used to it after a while."

"I wouldn't. Not ever."

He would never adapt. She knew that. His true north lay with the land. He needed the emptiness of the wide-open spaces, the wind, his horses. His whole life, he had never wanted anything else.

Her training as an artist demanded this sacrifice from them both. After a year in Philadelphia, she still felt trapped within the city's narrow canyons. If she told Bismarck that, he'd definitely want to take her home.

Being unable to see the sunrise and sunset disconnected her from time. Dawn and dusk had always been her favorite times of day. She missed those treasured moments of quiet solitude when the sun first peeked over the edge of the world marking the fresh start of a new day. Hours later, fiery sunsets followed, tempered by the cool indigo of night and the knowledge the last chore was done, rest awaited, and the day had been good.

Bismarck wiped his face with his bandana, leaving black streaks across his cheeks. "At least Texas has clean dirt. Philadelphia is filthy. Stinks worse than a pigsty."

She wrinkled her nose. "I've even gotten used to that." Leaning closer, she took his handkerchief and rubbed away the grit. The fabric snagged on several days' growth of beard. "You didn't shave."

The muscles in his jaw twitched at her touch. "Came straight from the train station. Couldn't wait to see you." He pulled her hand to his face, rubbing his nose against her fingers, inhaling her then tasting her.

Her hand lingered on his cheek then followed the lines of his face toward his chin and upwards to caress his mouth. "I like it." When he bent to kiss her, his stubble rasped her face. "It tells me you're really here."

The heat of his breath skittered across her cheek. Sliding her hands around his neck, she stepped into his arms. The intensity of his kisses made her sway. After a year apart, she wanted him. Badly. She stepped closer, pressing her entire body against his. Their kiss deepened. She moaned softly.

At the sound, Bismarck broke their contact.

Disappointed, she whispered, "Sorry."

He tilted her chin with his hand. "Don't be, little one." His hand trembled. "It's been too long, and you're too tempting." With a glint in his eyes, he added, "I cain't make you sing on the sidewalk, little bird."

Glancing at the sky, she said, "It's late. We should head back."

As they walked, her awareness of Bismarck grew. His kiss had left her tingly. Her hand tucked in his arm served as a lightning rod for the tension arcing between their bodies.

Finally he broke the silence. "Ruby, I'm starved. All I've had for days is bad railroad food."

If she could not feed one hunger, she could feed another. "The men at school go to Haeberle's Saloon on Twelfth Street. It's the only place I know of."

At the tavern, they threaded their way through a crowd of working men, dirty with black dust and smelling of sweat, eating before returning to rooming houses after long shifts at coal yards and factories.

Seated on long benches at communal tables, Ruby and Bismarck faced each other. Still uncertain if he meant to take her back to Truly, she studied his face for clues.

He removed his Stetson and placed it on their table. His eyes were serious, his eyebrows drawn straight, two dark slashes. Near his hairline, where covered by his hat, his skin was pale. Below, sun-exposed areas were mesquite brown.

"How's your family?" She tried to restart the stalled conversation. "Molly wrote that her sister Clara was engaged to your brother, Christoff."

"They got hitched in April."

"She didn't mention that." Ruby frowned. "I thought the wedding was this month."

"I reckon Chris has less patience than I do." He winked. "Heck, I was half-scared the babe would pop out before they got their I do's said."

Ruby's mouth gaped. "Oh, my. I had no idea."

"They jumped the gun a little, just like we did." Bismarck stroked her fingers with his. "Your hands are smooth. Pale. City girl hands."

His thick calluses scratched her skin. She removed her hands and rubbed her fingers together. He was right. After months without ranch work, her hands had softened.

Philadelphia was changing her in unexpected ways. Her only callus was where she held her paintbrush.

She kept her gaze on her fingers while her thoughts raced. Bismarck's earlier comments made her wonder if he was running out of patience, if he was ready to marry and start a family immediately. At nineteen, she had at least twenty years of childbearing ahead of her. She couldn't imagine being like her mother, spending half her life pregnant and the other half mourning the loss of another baby. Her mother still grieved over her most recent miscarriage, the baby she'd lost just before Ruby came to Philadelphia. Maybe, after another year of school, Ruby would be ready to settle down.

"Ruby Louise—" He reached for her again.

A voice behind him snarled insolently. "Who we got here? Buffalo Bill?"

From behind Bismarck, a brawny hand, filthy with coal dust, grabbed the snowy hat.

The table rattled as Bismarck whirled and slammed an elbow into the perpetrator's gut, leaving him gasping for air.

The bench screeched against the slate floor as Bismarck stood. Conversation stopped.

Inches taller and broader in the shoulders than the thief, Bismarck lifted his hat from the man's greasy head and brushed off the dirty fingerprints. "Much obliged to you for returning my Stetson." His soft drawl carried like a shout through the now-silent restaurant.

A group of men rose to champion the local thug.

"You fellers keep your seats. Don't get all riled up over a five dollar hat."

A few men backed away.

"He's a crack shot—" The words burst from Ruby, hoping to intimidate anyone not already discouraged by Bismarck's size.

"Hush, Ruby."

Most of the men retreated, but one behind her snorted in derision.

She stood and whirled to face him, advancing toward him, jabbing her finger at him, determined these city folks see her Texan as tough. "He can shoot the tail off a jackrabbit at fifty yards."

"Enough!" Bismarck's voice was firm, controlled. "Kindly take my arm. We're leaving. There won't be any problems, will there, gentlemen?" Bismarck replaced his hat, swept aside the front of his coat, exposing his Colt, and backed out the door pushing her behind him as he went.

Ruby peeked around his shoulder. Half a dozen men forced their way through the saloon door, following the couple.

Bismarck drew his pistol. "You fellers stay right there."

The men in front stopped cold. Those in the rear tripped over them, tumbling into a pile of tangled limbs.

Ruby gasped, realizing the factory workers were all unarmed. Folks didn't carry firearms here like they did back home. Bismarck had the upper hand all along.

Bismarck held Ruby's arm and strode rapidly in and out of crowds, hustling her several blocks away. After a glance around ensured the ruffians hadn't followed, he slowed to a less conspicuous pace and loosened his grip on her elbow.

Without his support, she stumbled on the uneven cobblestones.

Just before she pitched forward, he caught her and pulled her upright. "You all right?"

She nodded. As she regained her equilibrium, she stepped nearer him, needing his strength after their narrow escape.

"How often do you go there?" he said.

"Haeberle's? Never. The men from school say it's a family restaurant. I assumed it would be safe."

"You're not gallivanting around?"

She came to an abrupt stop. "What are you implying? I'm a demure little church mouse."

He snorted.

"I came to Philadelphia to paint. That's all I do." Ruby blew out a huff of air. "Mrs. Wheelwright is worse than Pa. We girls can't get away with anything."

"Philadelphia's not safe. I've been in town less than a day and already drawn my pistol and nearly knocked the block off a child."

Alarmed, she peered at Bismarck's tense face.

His hand trembled as he adjusted his collar for the dozenth time. "At the train station, someone tried to pick my pocket. I turned around, ready to punch someone. Turned out to be a boy." He shook his head. "A little boy. Not more than six or seven."

Ruby gasped. "What did you do?"

At her outraged expression, he snickered. "I grabbed the little runt by the seat of his britches, dumped him in the waste bin, and reclaimed my wallet. He looked so scrawny, I was scared he'd go hungry"—he shook his head—"so I paid him a dollar for the honor of picking my pocket." He released her arm and looked around. "Philadelphia is dangerous. No place for a woman. I worry about you being here alone."

"It's not bad once you get used to it. Nothing's ever happened to me."

He took his hat off, twirling the brim around with both hands. "The Truly jail has sat empty so long the sheriff stores grain in it." His concerned gaze wandered across her face. "I don't belong here. Neither do you."

They walked a few blocks to a small restaurant that

appeared more costly but where hooligans were unlikely to accost them. While they ate, she tried to persuade Bismarck she needed to remain at the Academy longer. "Tomorrow I'll take you there. You won't believe the art. I'll introduce you to Willow, Ira Wheatley, and Fred Ames. It took most of last year to get settled. Now I'm making real progress, but I need more time for my studies."

His expression darkened.

"Twelve months, Biz. That's all I'm asking for." She missed him—and Texas—too much to live in Philadelphia forever. "It'll pass before we know it."

The water in their glasses trembled as he jabbed his finger against the table in time with his words. "You said the same thing last year. And the year before."

"But my folks made me go to Texas Normal. That wasn't my choice."

"Don't make no difference. Another twelve months makes three years without you being my wife. My patience has worn mighty thin." He reached over the table and dug his fingers into her arms, giving her a tiny shake. "A fence cain't be built with one post. I need you. Come back with me."

She shook her head.

His face tightened. "Why cain't you see it, Ruby Louise? You're trying to be something you're not."

She recoiled. He'd pronounced her full name in the same tone her father used when he was angry. The two words no longer held the promise she was his alone. Bismarck didn't believe in her talent. He never had. The only real disagreements they'd had came before she left for teachers' college, before she applied to the Academy, and again when she was accepted. This was their fourth dance around the same issue, and they remained at an impasse. Her heart shattered. They belonged together yet could not overcome this obstacle.

In silence, they walked to her rooming house. Bismarck opened the front gate and escorted her up the slate walkway to the porch.

"You were born to be a horseman. As much as you need to ride, I need to paint." She searched his face, seeking some sign he understood. Not finding it, she gave his arm a desperate squeeze. "You're keeping me from becoming what I was meant to be."

He crossed his arms over his chest, shutting her out.

She blinked back tears. This was it. The end. Ruby ran inside. She pressed her forehead against the wooden door and looked out at Bismarck.

Mrs. Wheelwright came behind her and patted her on the back. "I told you he was dangerous, girlie."

Ruby peered through window at her beloved. The lace curtain fluttered in time with her shaking shoulders, but she suppressed her sobs. She wouldn't cry. Not here. Not with Mrs. Wheelwright looking on.

Head down, he remained on the slate path in the netherworld between house and street for an eternity. His hat dangled from one hand as he ran the other through chestnut hair. With an abrupt motion, he clapped his Stetson on his head, wheeled, and strode away, leaving Philadelphia, leaving her, but taking his pride.

Ruby dashed outside but couldn't bring herself to call his name. If he turned, if he even glanced back, she would fly to him.

Halfway down the block, he hesitated, rubbed clenched fists against his thighs, but did not look back. The irregular cobblestones accentuated his bowlegged gait and his snakebite limp as he disappeared.

Never had Ruby thought he would leave. She believed that he would turn back, that he would give her the time she needed. They would spend the rest of their lives together. He left her because she wanted to be something beyond a ranch wife. With a cry of despair, she ran upstairs, slamming her door behind her. The close atmosphere of her little room stifled her. At the window, she struggled with the sash lift. With an ear-splitting squeal, the bottom pane flew upward, rattling the glass alarmingly. She leaned out, sucking in deep gulps of air.

A moment later, a screech climbed the stairs. "Miss Schmidt!"

Dutifully Ruby lowered the window, but left it cracked. With her chin resting on the sill, she inhaled air devoid of the scent of her home and her man.

Later that evening, when Ruby confided what had occurred between herself and Bismarck, Willow said, "I applaud your strength of will. And mourn with you over the loss of your love. Truthfully, though, I admit to some joy at not losing my sister." She patted Ruby's shoulder and passed her a handkerchief. She paused for a long moment. "He will wait, if his affection is genuine, no matter what he says."

Chapter Nine
A Child's Hand

July 1892

Sunday afternoons remained Ruby's letter-writing day. At first, after completing her weekly letter to her parents, she wrote Bismarck, hoping her letters might bridge the chasm between them. He had neither verbally dissolved their engagement before he left nor written to officially release her from their betrothal. His rare replies were terse and noncommittal. She wondered if she should take the initiative and break things off, but she could not write the words that would end a love that had endured since childhood.

In her most recent correspondence, Molly Statler wrote that, at the town celebration following the Fourth of July parade, Bismarck outbid everyone in Truly for Hortense Hammond's basket at the picnic auction and, though he had danced with every unmarried woman present, he had twirled Hortense around a scandalous three times.

Ruby fumed. Any other woman would be preferable to that mean old Hortense. Disheartened, Ruby spaced her letters further apart. Certain he could write more often if he chose to, she once waited four entire weeks before setting her pen to paper, hoping he would realize he was being punished.

Ruby's mother, in her weekly missive, chastised her eldest for not corresponding better with her fiancé.

My Sweetest Daughter,
When Bismarck advised us he was going to
Philadelphia to bring you home, I had hoped to see
you by now.
Judging from the boy's eyes, things did not
go well between you two, and I am most sorry for
that. He claimed you when he was three and you
were barely toddling. With the grimiest little hands
I'd ever seen, he touched your red curls, saying
"Mine." From that day forward, he believed you
were truly his...

Guilt-ridden for neglecting Bismarck, Ruby wrote.

My darling Bismarck,
Philadelphia has been cold and cloudy, damp
and dreary for weeks on end. Blue sky broke
through today for a brief moment, and I imagined
your kind eyes. Your forgiving eyes.
I beg your patience with me. I miss you—and
Texas. Please write soon...

* * * *

With the new school year, Ruby moved to the interme-
diate level of drawing where she sketched portraits and figures from live models, studied costume, drapery, perspective
and modeling with clay. She also passed many afternoons in
a dark lecture hall viewing lantern slides of artworks, learning to recognize the works of Botticelli, Raphael, Titian and
dozens of other artists. Like other ladies, she brought her
knitting to class, and soft clicks from the needles tucked under their desks punctuated the professors' lectures.

"Take your seats quickly." From the front of the room,
Professor Anshutz snapped his fingers in irritation as Ruby

and Willow slipped into the studio, a few minutes late for their first day of life-drawing class. Their classmates had claimed the prime territory near the model, so Willow and Ruby garnered less desirable spots. The skylights spilled a gray morning light into the room, bouncing off white walls and providing soft-edged shadows. She placed her sketch-pad on an easel and selected a charcoal stick. While Ruby was uneasy about sketching a nude model, she knew Willow was petrified.

Anshutz glowered at the two women but continued his talk on ideal human proportions. He sketched as he talked, covering the blackboard with a drawing. "You see here *The Vitruvian Man* by Maestro Leonardo da Vinci, a male figure in two superimposed positions, simultaneously inscribed in a circle and a square." Anshutz scribbled on the board. "The length of the outspread arms is equal to the height of a man, etc. Commit these proportions to memory. Remember, you can't put clothing on a model until you understand the anatomy beneath."

Willow whispered, "At least you've seen the front end of a man before."

"Only Bismarck." Ruby flushed at the thought that Willow—thanks to Ruby's sketch—had seen him, too.

"Do you think a man or a woman will pose first?"

Ruby shrugged. With little experience sketching the nude, she would find either a challenge, both in maintaining her equanimity and in the drawing itself.

Mr. Anshutz wound down his talk, and their subject stepped out, a man wrapped in a heavy robe.

"Think he'll undress?" Ruby said.

"I wonder what he's wearing beneath?" Willow's voice shook as much as the hand that held her charcoal. She tittered nervously.

The professor faced a tall shelf laden with props, selecting an object for their model to hold. Hearing the giggle, he whirled, a human skull held in his right hand, his eyes unerringly finding the culprit and transfixing Willow with a disapproving glower.

Ruby stared at the model, afraid to watch, afraid not to.

After an audacious wink directed at Ruby, the man disrobed. Holding the robe over his particulars, he sat on a stool then dropped the garment to the floor.

Ruby blinked in astonishment then poked Willow in the shoulder. Except for a loincloth, the man was naked. Tough looking, coarsely muscular, with crude tattoos of ships on his arms, he must be a sailor or stevedore from the Philadelphia Shipyard making extra money sitting for their class.

Anshutz posed the man, seating him with his right elbow resting on his right thigh, arm outstretched, peering at the skull he held before him. Ruby and Willow, in sub-optimal positions due to their later arrival, were privy only to the broad triangle of his back, the bones of his spine, and the curve of his buttocks moving into a strong right thigh.

"I thought Hamlet wore clothes." Willow smothered another nervous giggle.

Soon sketching commanded Ruby's full attention. Absorbed in her drawing, she didn't have time to talk. Her fingers placed faint, uncertain streaks of charcoal in a rough sketch she would later darken and fill with details.

Beside her, equally engrossed, Willow grew silent.

The professor paced the room, peering over students' shoulders, *hmming* if an image met his approval, *harrumphing* if it did not. Swift currents of exultation or shame swept through the gallery depending on which monosyllable one's work inspired. Ruby sensed Anshutz standing behind her. Nervously she anticipated his grumpy expression of disapproval. She sketched a tenuous line, rubbed it away with her left thumb, drew and erased it again and again, until charcoal dust covered her hand. She remained unable to capture the curve of the model's right flank where it tapered in, then out over his hipbone. That bone connected to the symphysis pubis where his—visions of Bismarck flew before her eyes. She took a shuddering breath.

A hand clenched her waist.

Ruby stiffened and closed her eyes tightly. Surely the hand did not belong to Anshutz. Her stuffy professor would never touch a female student. In fact, according to Wheatley, he had orchestrated the dismissal of the infamous Thomas Eakins from the Academy. When a female student asked Eakins about the movement of the pelvis, he invited her to his office, disrobed, and gave her a personal anatomy lesson. Those actions, along with his removal of a loincloth from a male model during a women's life-drawing class in 1886, brought his swift termination from the Academy.

A hand covered hers and lifted it toward her easel.

She swallowed, terrified to open her eyes and confirm that the professor indeed held her. Probably in his forties, he was positively ancient.

Above the sudden buzz of whispers whirling around her, a man's voice—not Professor Anschutz's—sounded in Ruby's ear. "If I may?"

Startled, Ruby snapped her eyes open to find elegant fingers with smooth olive skin, not the knobby knuckles of Mr. Anshutz. A heavy signet ring with a blood-red cabochon rested on one finger. The hand guided hers in redrawing the line she had failed to capture, catching it in one swift sensuous stroke.

She jerked her hand away. With a swift pivot, she faced the intruder. "How dare you!" Her chin dropped as her vision registered the most handsome man she had ever seen.

With startling blue eyes, he looked down at her, laughed, and brought her hand to his mouth, his lips feathering across her fingers, his breath scalding the top of her hand. "Francesco d'Este at your service, *signorina*." Unfashionably long black curls bounced against her hand. "I could tell you were struggling."

"I was not. I simply couldn't make up my mind."

He laughed. "So you were struggling."

"I'd have gotten it eventually." She forced confidence into her voice. In spite of his charm, Ruby grew irritated. Just because he was a man he thought he had the right to interfere—and he wasn't even her professor, just another student she'd seen around the Academy. She looked about for Anshutz, but he was at the front of the room helping another student.

D'Este nodded toward the sketch of the *Vitruvian Man* on the blackboard. "I've seen the original in the *Gallerie dell'Accademia* in Venice. There, it doesn't wear a fig leaf." He flashed a mischievous smile.

"Ruby, it's women only today." Willow jerked her chin toward Anshutz. "You're going to get into trouble."

"You better leave." Ruby urged d'Este away with a flutter of her hands.

"I had to meet the woman with such glorious hair." He lifted a strand that had tumbled to her forehead and tucked it in place. "Only Titian could capture its color."

Murmuring increased from the ladies near Ruby.

Mr. d'Este was quite forward, positively the most brazen man she had ever met, but somehow irresistible. His voice was as smooth as satin. Foreign words, an exotic spice she could almost taste, sprinkled his speech. She hid a smile behind her charcoaled fingers. As her thumb deposited a streak of black grit across her cheek, she immediately regretted her action,

"*Se mi permette, signorina?* With your permission?" He extracted a handkerchief from his pocket. With languid motions, he wiped the discoloration from her face and each of her digits, holding her hand far longer than proper before kissing it again. "And what name belongs with such a lovely *signorina?*"

Ruby flushed.

"Ruby!" Willow's anxious whisper was more urgent.

"Miss Schmidt!" From across the room, her angry professor called out, "Please ask your gentleman caller to leave the classroom."

She turned toward her professor. "But I don't even know him."

Anshutz strode in the direction of the interloper and, realizing who the gentleman was, shook his head as if dealing with a recalcitrant child. "Mr. d'Este, I should have known. You know the rules—women only on Tuesdays, Thursdays, and Saturdays. Come back on your designated days."

"*Va bene.* I'm leaving." D'Este laughed. As he exited the studio, he stuck his head back through the door long enough to say, "Miss Schmidt, I'm taking you to lunch after your lesson. *Ciao, bella.*"

At the end of class, Willow and Ruby put away their portfolios.

"What are you going to do about Mr. d'Este?" Willow said.

"Ignore him. We brought lunches today anyway."

"But he compared you to a Titian painting, and he's a masterpiece himself."

"He does have nice eyes. However, he thinks far too highly of himself. And I am betrothed." At least she might

still be. Bismarck had not terminated their engagement—
yet. Perhaps he thought walking away from her was enough
to end their relationship.

Though Ruby and Willow ate their lunch sprawled over
the front steps where Mr. d'Este would be sure to trip over
them, he never appeared.

"Willie, as a certain gentleman thinks too little of me to
keep an appointment, I shall no longer concern myself with
him. In the future, I shall not succumb to his charms."

* * * *

"I can't do this." Willow held a dead chicken with two
fingers, keeping it far from her pristine artist's smock, her
face reflecting her disgust.

"I can kill, pluck, and clean a bird in six minutes flat."
Ruby whipped the fowl from Willow's hands and laid it on
their table. They sketched the entire bird.

"Now the wings." Ruby stretched out one wing as if in
flight and drew a detail. Willow followed her lead. Once they
finished those sketches, Ruby showed Willow how to pluck
the feathers to reveal the goose-bumpy skin beneath. Last,
like a surgeon, Ruby used a scalpel and forceps to delicately
lift the epithelium and uncover muscles for more sketches.

Day after day, Ruby worked beside Willow in a classroom where drawers held fossils, bones, and seashells for
drawing practice. The fragile skeleton of a child's hand, the
joints formed by wires, was wrapped in cotton and stored
in a wooden box. Finely textured, like marble an ancient
Greek might have carved, only the hardest lead pencil with
the sharpest point could capture the intricacy of those tiny
bones.

Along with other students, Ruby dissected a horse and
drew from casts made from anatomical specimens. A *manik-
in*, a physicians' aid much like a giant paper doll, allowed

students two-dimensional views of the human body. Color plates were overlaid with cutouts, each lifted in turn to reveal successive layers of anatomy. Male and female genitalia were hidden behind locked compartments but never opened for the women to peruse.

In life drawing classes and in anatomical dissections, women weren't allowed to view male sexual organs. Ruby remembered Bismarck, proud and erect, and wondered how men appeared in death. When female students at last had a chance to dissect a male cadaver, Ruby was astonished to find that the male parts had been removed. She found the senseless mutilation more damaging to her psyche than the sight of the male organs would have been.

* * * *

"Hey, Red," Wheatley called from across the upstairs gallery. "We're going to Eakins' lecture this afternoon. Want to come?"

Ruby hesitated, knowing she needed to work on her entry for the school's annual exhibition, but Eakins' classes, whether he spoke on perspective, anatomy, or locomotion, were always informative. She'd considered attending classes at the Art Students' League of Philadelphia, but the tuition was fifty dollars for eight months. Attendance at both schools was beyond her budget. Because the Academy had such a good reputation, she chose to stay, despite its shortcomings and her run-ins with the conservative Professor Anshutz.

"Come on." Wheatley beckoned, urging her compliance. "He's speaking on the human form."

"Very well, I'll meet you there after this class."

The moment class finished, Ruby dashed to the lecture at the Art Students' League. Out-of-breath, she opened the door to find a nude Wheatley posing for Fred Ames, Franklin Louis Schenck, Charles Bregler, and several other men.

What did she expect? The Art Students' League of Philadelphia was formed for the study of painting and sculpture based on the study of the nude human figure.

"Oh my." She banged her satchel and portfolio on the doorjamb in her hasty retreat.

"It's all right, Red. Come on in." Wheatley's voice followed her.

Eyes shut, she timidly reopened the door. "I didn't mean to interrupt."

"I'm decent now."

She opened her eyes and peeked in.

Wheatley had covered his groin with a skimpy cloth.

"Join us, Miss Schmidt?" said Eakins.

Ruby looked around. She was the only woman present, but she refused to allow her own prudery to prevent her studying the full male form.

With one hand on Wheatley's shoulder, Eakins continued his lecture, demonstrating the movement of muscles by twisting the younger man's back from side to side. "As he turns to the right, the muscles on the right contract and those on the left lengthen. The spinous processes curve to the right as well, and the right ribs become more prominent. Visualize the anatomy before you drape clothing on a model's body. Only then will you achieve satisfactory results."

Ruby whisked her sketchpad from her portfolio and, within minutes, became engrossed in her work.

As his students sketched, Eakins moved around the room offering advice and occasionally pointing his camera at the artists.

Later, when she showed the sketches to Willow, Ruby realized Wheatley's drape had slipped away, revealing him in his entirety. She had not noticed but simply sketched what she saw. She laughed. "It simply proves we women are not driven to carnal behavior by the sight of manly parts."

Art students frequently posed for each other. One day Ruby would have to return the favor. The question remained whether she could remove her clothes and let a bunch of men stare at her. Perhaps they would be as dispassionate as she had been while sketching Wheatley.

Chapter Ten
New Love

September 1892

Engrossed in her work, Ruby turned from her canvas to reload her palette.

A hand jiggled her shoulder. "Ruby?"

Dazed, Ruby shook her head then realized where she was.

"You were lost in painting, my dear. I called your name three times, but you were oblivious." Willow laughed as she stroked Ruby's cheek. "You skipped lunch. Had nothing to drink. Sometimes I almost believed you stopped breathing. Nothing existed except your palette and canvas."

A glance outside told Ruby the sky had darkened. She'd painted the day away. When she'd begun classical Venetian oil painting at the Academy, she had discovered her true medium. Though the Old Masters' technique was slow—and patience had never been among Ruby's virtues—the technique fascinated her, from the methodical preparation of the fabric with gesso, the transfer of her refined drawing to the canvas, the application of the neutral-toned *imprimatura*, the *grisaille* underpainting, and the luminous depth of color achieved through the precise placement of layer upon layer of pigment that transformed white fabric into a painting.

"Lordy, where'd the time go?" She'd lost herself in the painstaking addition of minute details to her canvas. She set her paints aside and, after a luxurious stretch, covered her work with a sheet. Her stomach grumbled. "We should hurry. Mrs. Wheelwright won't hold dinner. And I'm famished."

* * * *

As she spent most of every day with Willow, Ruby grew closer to the other woman than to her own kin, as close as the sisters they imagined themselves to be. They traded views on art and critiqued each other's works. Ruby's siblings did not share her fascination with images. They had only a rudimentary knowledge of painting and no wish to learn further.

When Ruby and Willow studied ancient Greek temples in art history class, they carried their watercolor boxes to the Philadelphia Waterworks with its Doric columns, pavilions, and elaborate balustrades. Side by side, they sketched the flowing water at dawn when golden mists transformed the buildings into ghostly temples to pagan gods and again at sunset when sculls scuttled like black long-legged water bugs across orange water, their wakes forming lavender ripples endlessly intersecting, splitting the reflections of clouds into mosaics, before dying out in the dark boulders at the shore.

If they walked far enough in Fairmount Park, they escaped into a pastoral world of dappled forests footed by ferns, the air laden with the rustic scent of leaf mold. Though relieved at being away from the tight confines of city streets, Ruby still felt hemmed in by the green glade. "Home is nothing like this. I've never seen such tall trees, so much water, so many shades of green. Texas is flat. Really flat. Hot. Brown. Hostile." Momentarily, she became lost in reminiscence. "But with an austere beauty of its own."

"You still miss it?"

"Oh, yes." A deep yearning rose in Ruby, one she thought long suppressed.

"Are there really half-naked, wild savages?"

Ruby shook her head at Willow's naive ideas about the West. "The last of those have been confined to Indian Territory. The only one I know is Nokoni, and he wears—"

Willow's glance flickered to something beyond Ruby's shoulder. "Quick. Hide here." She grabbed Ruby's arm and ducked behind a tree.

Peering around the trunk, Ruby's gaze tracked Willow's extended finger as it pointed toward the Schuylkill.

Along the shore, half a dozen naked young men played unselfconsciously. Their laughter rumbled up the embankment to the two women. Sunlight gilded male bodies. As they wrestled and flung one another into the water, their muscles flexed and contracted and their pale skin contrasted with burnt umber rocks. They emerged, river gods rising from the primordium, fluid sluicing over white arms and whiter legs, dripping off their curls, the tips of their noses, their fingers, and other protrusions.

Ruby sighed. "We should be allowed to paint men like that, Willie. After all, they paint us *au naturel.*"

"Eakins once said that a female nude is the most beautiful thing in the world—"

"—except for the naked man." Ruby finished the quote.

"I would argue we women are the more lovely of the sexes." Willow ran a finger across Ruby's shoulder.

With a mischievous grin, Ruby ducked from beneath Willow's hand, pulled a sketchpad from her satchel, sank to the leafy ground, and began drawing. "Get busy, Willie. Let's sketch them before they leave."

Twenty minutes later, the men dressed and climbed the bank of the Schuylkill.

Ruby shoved her drawings deep in her bag and tugged at Willow's hand. "Hurry, before they catch us." She and

Willow raced away, smothering their laughter.

* * * *

Now a frequent guest at the Wyckes' farm, Ruby usually visited Friday evening until Sunday afternoon when she and Willow returned to Mrs. Wheelwright's. Other than an occasional appearance at fund-raisers for the Wyckes' various charities and political functions and appearing "at home" when ladies came to call, the two women had few duties and lolled away the days.

Ruby was unaccustomed to such indolence. Her mother had insured her girls were capable of managing a household and, until the birth of a lone son broke up a string of daughters and miscarriages, her pa insisted his daughters learn ranching. They could rope and ride, wield branding irons, build fences, round up cattle, castrate and doctor animals, and fire a gun if needed.

Other than choosing a husband from the choices presented by her father, Willow had no responsibilities at all.

One morning, the young Mr. Wycke interrupted Ruby and Willow as they painted amongst the flowers. "Miss Schmidt, permit me to guide you through the gardens. My sister is far too busy painting to devote sufficient attention to you."

With an imploring glance, Ruby sought Willow's help.

Her friend shrugged helplessly, unable or unwilling to deter her older sibling.

Without waiting for Ruby's consent, Mr. Wycke tucked her hand into the crook of his elbow and led her through the vegetable and herb gardens, the orchard, and finally the elaborate rose garden. The grounds were extensive and well-manicured, commensurate with the family's wealth. The young Mr. Wycke would inherit a vast farm and an immense fortune. His future wife would benefit from the family's social prominence. Despite this knowledge, Ruby remained uninterested. She couldn't understand why he pursued her, a Texas nobody, and was unsure how to discourage him without insulting the Wyckes.

They passed beneath an arbor crowned by climbing roses as he led her to an ornate gazebo surrounded by lush flowerbeds and an oval of closely cropped grass and seated Ruby on a bench inside.

"Thank you, Mr. Wycke."

"I believe we've known each other long enough to dispense with formalities. Please, call me Woodrow."

"Very well." She fought to control her grimace. Moving to a first-name basis would encourage his attentions, but she couldn't gracefully avoid it. "Then you must call me Ruby."

"Do you enjoy poetry, Miss…Ruby?"

She nodded.

"Permit me to entertain you then." He pulled a tiny volume from his pocket. In stentorian tones, he intoned the words of Miss Emily Dickinson.

Before he could butcher another lovely poem, Ruby leapt up. "I should return to Willie. We must pack up our paints before going indoors."

Woodrow returned Ruby to his sister's side. "Shall I see you at luncheon? Perhaps we might sit together?"

"I fear I would bore you with conversation about my betrothed." A bee buzzed past her head, drawn by her too-sweet smile.

* * * *

Though Ruby and Willow hoped to escape to Ruby's room after lunch, Mrs. Wycke waylaid them. "Would you girls kindly accompany me to the library?"

Once she closed the pocket doors and leather-bound volumes were their only companions, Mrs. Wycke seated

Ruby and Willow on a settee and pulled a chair for herself before them.

"Girls, I've had this discussion with Woodrow. I shall repeat it when little Henry is of an appropriate age."

From her pocket, she removed two tins of sewing needles and placed them in her lap. She flicked her tongue over her lips and began uncertainly. "Marriage...as it is currently defined, gives a husband...legal ownership...of his wife's body. He may take her as he wants, with or without her consent. A woman should have control of her own self, a right inseparable from her very existence."

Willow blinked. "Mamá!"

Ruby, her cheeks burning, glanced at Mrs. Wycke.

Mrs. Wycke's wedding ring clanked against the tins as her fingers jiggled nervously. "Women are just as intelligent, just as capable, as men. Constant pregnancies keep us from achieving our own lofty goals. Men have no such impediment, do they?"

"No, Mamá."

Judging from the warmth flaming over Ruby, her face and neck must be as scarlet as Willow's cheeks.

"You may rightfully say no to any man, including your husband, to avoid an unwanted child." Mrs. Wycke's eyes blazed with a zealot's fire. "Having said that, should you find—as I have found with my darling Mr. Wycke—a most uncommon bond, you may not wish to say no."

Though her words had been hesitant at first, they came now at full gallop. "A healthy woman has as much passion as any man and can be as attracted to a man as he to her. Our learned Mr. Whitman says in his *Leaves of Grass*: 'Without shame the man I like knows and avows the deliciousness of his sex, Without shame the woman I like knows and avows hers.'"

She pried off the lid of a tin and extracted, not needles, but a translucent cylinder which she pinched between two fingers and held at arm's length, her eyes squeezed closed. "I wish you both to avoid pregnancy until you are prepared in heart, mind, and soul to care for a child. These"—she wiggled the cylinder slightly in the air—"are called *condoms*. Thanks to Mr. Comstock's antiquated obscenity laws, they may no longer be ordered by mail. But a gentleman should know where to purchase them. I believe they are available in most apothecaries." She opened her eyes, replaced the condom in the needle case, and handed each young woman a tin. "A man must place one on his part...on his...on his manhood...before he..." She swallowed hard then finished in a rush, "...before he commits the deed."

Ruby wondered if her ma realized a woman might avoid pregnancy. If so, she had chosen childbirth, though the state led to her many stillbirths.

With a delicate cough, Mrs. Wycke continued. "In addition, there are ways of attaining the satisfaction of your mutual desires that do not involve the risk of bearing a child. I shall leave you and your husbands to discover what can be done with...fingers...mouths...and other... orifices."

Ruby thought of Bismarck and their explorations of each other, and her face heated violently as new images flooded her brain.

With a few final words of warning, Mrs. Wycke wound up her talk. "Choose your spouses well, my dears. Marry men like my dear Mr. Wycke, a 'suffrage husband' who believes not only in women's political equality but in a woman's rights in the bedroom." She clapped her hands together, clearly congratulating herself on a job well done, then shooed the younger women from the library.

That evening, Willow slipped into Ruby's room after

preparing for bed. "I do hope Mamá's little chat didn't offend you."

"She is rather forthright." Ruby laughed as she dropped on her bed. "Ma lost a baby just before I left. Her eleventh confinement in twenty years, and she's lost all but four." Ruby shook her head. "I should hate spending half my life with child. How can a woman care for a clutch of chicks and still paint?" At the same time, the thought of a babe or two was not unappealing. She could see herself with a small family, children widely spaced to allow her time to breathe.

"And *housewife*! What an odious word. First, foremost, always, my waking thought, from the moment I was conceived, has been my desire to be an artist." Willow hugged Ruby. "I shan't have children. I shall give birth to paintings. Ruby, my dearest sister, we shall love each other. Our offspring will be our art, and we shall be more fruitful than any male artist."

* * * *

While in West Chester, the budding artists wandered Antioch Farm, pulling their easels and paints behind them in a wooden wagon, borrowed from little Henry. The Brandywine River splashed musical accompaniment to the sonorous hum of bumblebees. Ruby was painting Willow wearing a white muslin dress sprigged with flowers. With her face relaxed and dappled by sunlight, the young lady was quite striking.

As Ruby worked, warm highlights from the sun slid into blues and violets. In the west, dark clouds cloaked the sky. The sky turned blackened, signaling a change in weather. Distant thunder growled through thickening air. She directed Willow's gaze toward the roiling horizon. "We should head back. In Texas, this wind would herald a tornado."

"Let's sketch the storm first. We won't melt if we get a

little wet." Willow broke her pose, stood, and grabbed her brushes.

"But our paintings might be ruined."

"So what?" Willow whirled her easel toward the oncoming clouds. "Let's see who produces the best picture before the storm arrives."

"I accept your challenge." Ruby saluted her competitor with a paintbrush and began placing an image on paper.

With the sudden arrival of cold, hard raindrops, the women stuffed their paintings in their portfolios and ran for shelter, their belongings umbrellaed above their heads to protect their hair. Amid giggles, they dragged Henry's wagon behind them through sodden grasses. Halfway to the house, the rain worsened.

"Leave the wagon, Willie. It's slowing us down."

The girls raced in earnest the rest of the way. Laughing, they tromped up the stairs. Willow draped her arm around Ruby and pulled her close. On the portico, arms around each other, they contemplated the storm.

"What a magnificent tempest." A gust of wind gave Ruby a sudden chill. She shivered.

"Let's warm you up." Willow rubbed Ruby's arms briskly before tousling her hair, sending fine droplets scattering across the porch. "Your curls are bejeweled with a thousand rubies."

They traipsed inside. A maid followed them, wiping up the water that dripped from their clothing as they dashed upstairs. In Willow's room, before they even considered changing garments, the women inspected their sketches for water damage and laid them out to dry.

"Our works are so different. Were we looking at the same storm?"

"Those swirls"—Ruby indicated the trees in Willow's

painting—"capture the wind whipping through the leaves."
She giggled. "And those blots made by raindrops give a certain verisimilitude."

Willow laughed. "You painted a maelstrom as harsh as the Great Flood."

Ruby shivered.

"Get out of your wet clothes." Willow unbuttoned Ruby's dress and tugged at the sleeves.

Ruby balked at removing her clothing and covered her chest with her arms. No one had seen her completely naked since she was a child. Not her sisters. Not Bismarck. Not even herself. The tiny mirror above her chest of drawers at home was not conducive to viewing her entire body. If she lifted her nightgown, stood on tiptoes, and turned this way and that, she could glimpse her breasts, though never both at the same time. Other than what she saw with her own eyes as she bathed, her back, bottom, and full length remained a mystery.

"Don't be ridiculous. You'll catch your death," Willow scolded.

Incapable of halting Willow's fingers, Ruby watched as they unfastened buttons, loosened corset laces, and untied drawstrings of petticoats and pantalets.

With a few final tugs, Willow peeled Ruby's clothing from damp skin, leaving her nude.

Ruby tightened her arms over her chest to hide herself as Willow seated her before a mahogany vanity topped by a large mirror.

Willow swept up the sodden items. She disappeared into the adjoining bath chamber and returned with a stack of thick Turkish cloths. After unpinning Ruby's hair and wrapping it in a towel, she enthusiastically began polishing Ruby's skin to a rosy pink.

Delighting in the luxurious sensation of Willow buffing her with the rough fabric and the resultant warmth flowing over her body, Ruby closed her eyes. Swathed in towels, she relaxed as Willow dried her hair then brushed it out with sensuous strokes. Warm and cozy, Ruby wanted nothing more than to curl up in her friend's arms.

"You are beautiful, my dear. Fiery hair. Luminous skin. Let me see you." Willow unwrapped the towels and dropped them to the floor. She stepped behind Ruby and trailed her fingers the length of Ruby's back before tightening on her hip bones.

The anterior superior iliac spines. From nowhere, the scientific words popped into Ruby's head. Thinking in anatomical terms seemed preferable to considering how close Willow's hands were to her private areas. But she could not deny the goosebumps popping up everywhere Willow touched.

But Willow simply held Ruby, neither advancing or retreating. Eventually, Ruby leaned back into Willow's arms, hoping to be further enveloped. Instead, Ruby's newly warmed skin contacted wet clothing. She jumped forward in surprise and spun to face her friend.

"Willie, your teeth are chattering. Your turn." Ruby stripped Willow and burnished her skin to a glow.

She hung Willow's sodden clothing in the bath then returned to the bedroom.

"Come." Willow, pulling Ruby with her, stood before the vanity mirror. "Look. We resemble *Gabrielle d'Estrées et une de ses soeurs*."

Ruby knew the painting to which Willow referred. Painted by an unknown sixteenth-century artist, it depicted Gabrielle d'Estrées, mistress of King Henry IV of France, and her sister, in a bathtub. Gabrielle held Henry's coronation ring as her sister pinched Gabrielle's right nipple. The painting served as a birth announcement for her first child with Henry.

Ruby agreed with the similarity though Gabrielle's hair was smooth and controlled while her own hair frizzed from the dampness.

Still gazing in the mirror, one arm entwined around Willow's waist, Ruby nestled her head against her friend's neck. There, a steady, if rapid, pulse reassured her. Ruby found it easier to look at their reflection than at Willow. Ruby could almost convince herself she gazed at a canvas rather than the mirror image of herself with a naked woman.

The sensation of being within the canvas of *Gabrielle d'Estrées* was enhanced when Willow delicately caught Ruby's nipple between her fingers.

Ruby glanced down. A tiny gasp escaped as her nipple hardened.

Willow laughed softly and squeezed a little tighter.

A tingle flew from Ruby's breast to between her legs as though those parts were somehow connected. She stood stock-still, afraid to move. Afraid those fingers would leave her nipple. Afraid they would not find the other breast. Afraid the fingers would not wander to the quivering place below, the place only Bismarck had touched.

Willow stepped behind Ruby. As lightly as a paintbrush, her lips burned Ruby's neck with kisses as her fingers strummed Ruby's nipples.

Bismarck. Ruby must remember him. She was betrothed to him. Lusting for a woman could send her to hell. Enough damage had been done to her soul when she lay with Bismarck before marriage. Her thoughts tumbling, Ruby jerked from Willow's hands. Hot and shimmery all over, she trembled. "I'm cold. Let's dress."

* * * *

That evening, as they chatted and readied themselves for bed, Willow said, "As the Academy will not allow us women to draw the complete nude, we should pose for each other."

"We already sketch each other."

"Not without clothing. How else can we learn the entire female form?" Willow glanced at Ruby then lowered her gaze. "You've sketched Wheatley and Ames. Have you posed for them?"

"No. They haven't asked me."

Despite her initial misgivings, when drawing a naked man, Ruby had never experienced the prurience social conventions—and her own preconceived notions—had led her to expect. Drawing the male nude had been no different than sketching a still life.

At the Art Students' League while in male company, she'd sketched a female nude. The young woman had not objected to revealing her body but hid her face behind a veil so she could not be identified. She supposed, if Wheatley and Ames asked, she could sit for them.

"Don't you wish to draw me?" Willow said.

"Of course, but—"

"But what?"

Ruby's voice hitched, unable to voice either her fear or her attraction. Finally, she shrugged.

Willow persisted. "Perhaps it would be easier if we practiced—just the two of us— before we unclothe before others."

Still uncomfortable from the earlier events, Ruby hesitated but ultimately gave in. Willow was right. Surely it would be easier to disrobe before one person, especially one she knew well, rather than a dozen. And the day was coming when her male friends would expect her to model for them.

Willow produced a scarlet kimono from her closet. Ruby donned it then Willow positioned her before the fireplace. The slippery silk glistened in the firelight, reflecting the colors of the flames.

Though Willow had seen her unclothed, Ruby was relieved that her friend permitted her some covering. Cool silk slithered across Ruby's skin as Willow arranged the fabric in artful folds until satisfied with her composition. Aware that only the sheerest of cloth separated her body from her friend's hands, Ruby grew damp between the legs as she wondered how her body would feel if Willow caressed her with silk instead of rough Turkish towels.

As Willow adjusted the kimono, her fingers grazed Ruby's breast. Seconds later, she repeated the motion. Ruby peeked downward. Her right nipple sprang to life, clearly visible beneath the thin silk.

For the third time Willow touched her. This time her hand lingered.

The caresses were deliberate.

When Willow's soft, sweet kisses, dry as talc, greeted Ruby's cheek, she replied with tender pecks while inhaling Willow's familiar smell of lavender and geranium from the bottle of *English Fern* on her bureau.

Emboldened, Willow's lips moved to Ruby's mouth, placing moist, urgent kisses, her tongue skating across the crack between Ruby's lips. "Open to me, my love."

Ruby hesitated. Once she opened her mouth, Willow's tongue slipped in. Ruby moaned with pleasure as their tongues danced.

Willow broke away, a flush across her face. She adjusted the kimono again. Her hands didn't linger, rather she behaved as though Ruby's skin was too hot to touch. Leaving Ruby with a leg and a shoulder bare, Willow sat on the bed, sketchpad before her. "Turn towards me a little."

Ruby complied. The silk slipped partway off her shoulder exposing her breast. The cool temperature and the glide of the cloth across her skin made her nipple as taut as it had been earlier with Willow's touch.

Ruby's left side, facing the fire, grew toasty. Her right, facing Willow, was chilled. Goosebumps set up quick residence on Ruby's bare flesh. A new edginess rose in her body.

From across the room, Willow's voice was barely audible. "A bit more."

As Ruby turned, the kimono crept down her side, exposing most of her body to Willow's gaze. Warmth flooded Ruby's cheeks. Unable to meet Willow's eyes, Ruby looked down.

"Don't hide your face. Look at me."

Ruby raised her head.

Something flashed between them and hung in the air a long moment.

Ruby licked her lips, tasting the remnants of Willow's kisses.

Willow caught her breath. "Perfect. Don't move." She gave a breathy exhale.

When Willow showed her the pastel drawing, Ruby could not believe she looked so beautiful. Her untamed curls made her seem as wanton as she felt. Mouth open, lips moist, she appeared to be waiting for a kiss. The chiaroscuro from the fire led Ruby's eye from her blazing hair across a rounded rosy breast to a bared leg, beneath which crimson silk pooled like blood.

Chapter Eleven
Women of Pleasure

The following evening, Ruby and Willow retired to the library. There, they found Woodrow reading. At their entrance, he glanced up. The lamplight heightened his blush as he tucked a small volume behind his back.

"What are you hiding?" Willow teased.

"Nothing at all." He rose and took Ruby's hand. "How nice to see you again. As always, you are quite lovely."

At his interest, Ruby's face warmed. Compared to Bismarck, he was effete. Though her relationship with her beau was tenuous, she still could not take Woodrow seriously. Quite simply she was not attracted to him; indeed, she felt a near-antipathy. Thus she did not deem it necessary to bat her lashes, smile insipidly, or provide the flirtatious responses with which certain available young women indicated their interest in certain available young men. So far, her tactics had not discouraged Woodrow in the least.

The next morning, Woodrow didn't appear at breakfast.

"My brother slept late. Let's take advantage of his somnolence," Willow said as she pulled Ruby into the parlor. "Hush." She placed a finger over her mouth as she tiptoed across the room to the window seat.

Willow removed the cushion and lifted an underlying board. "This is Woody's secret hiding place." She withdrew a book, rotating it to read its title. "*Fanny Hill: The Memoirs of a Woman of Pleasure*." Willow tittered nervously as she slipped the novel in her pocket. "Now we know why Woody was so secretive about what he was reading. I knew he was up to something."

Minutes later, Ruby followed Willow from the house, heading for the Brandywine River, again borrowing Henry's wagon to haul their easels and paints. When they tired of painting, the two young women spread a plaid blanket over the grass, stretched out, their heads together, and read *Fanny Hill* aloud.

"Heavens!" Ruby exclaimed, her eyes wide, as they finished the first chapter. "Shh, someone will hear."

"We're in a meadow. No one else is around."

"But we shouldn't be reading this, Willie. It's positively scandalous."

"I know, but it's delicious." Willow laughed. "No wonder Woody found it fascinating." Her eyebrows bounced toward her hairline. "You're enjoying every word as much as I am."

"Yes, but I shouldn't." Eyes wide, Ruby took the book and turned the page. "No one writes books like this for women. Men have all the fun."

* * * *

Clad in her nightgown, Ruby answered a faint tap on her door. "Yes?"

Willow pushed her way in. "Shall we continue the naughty adventures of Miss Fanny Hill?" She threw herself on Ruby's bed and patted the space beside her. "Come sit with me."

Dramatically Willow read the part where Fanny described Charles covering her breasts with kisses and the flames thus aroused.

Ruby grew as tremulous as she had when Bismarck

touched her.

As Willow read, her fingers grazed Ruby's breast. Clearly visible beneath her thin nightdress, Ruby's right nipple leapt to life. Willow continued to read and stroke, her fingers tugging the nipple into an aching point. When Ruby arched her back, Willow dropped the book and set her teasing tongue and teeth to the other nipple. Willow gave a soft laugh. "Mamá did say the use of hands and mouths was acceptable."

Previously content with kisses, the now-emboldened women explored each other's breasts with mouths and fingers and dared to touch the other's lowermost curls.

A delicious tension rose between Ruby's thighs, intensified by the delightful sensation of fingers fondling her breasts. In time, a joyous fluttering occurred. She cried out. Only Bismarck had aroused such feelings in her before.

"Hush, we must be silent." Willow quieted Ruby with a kiss. Moments later, she muffled the sound of her own release against Ruby's chest.

Sated, they fell asleep in each others' arms.

Long before dawn, Ruby awakened, her head cushioned by Willow's breast. The linens dangled off the bed. Her nightgown and Willow's were unbuttoned, skewed well above their waists. Willow's fair skin glowed in the predawn light. The dark patch of hair between her long legs blended into the shadows of the white linens. Memories of every word, every kiss every touch replayed in Ruby's mind.

Desire.

Desire filled her.

Desire like she had for Bismarck, only different. What she felt for him was sharp, hard, earthy, primitive—and fraught with the risk of pregnancy. She loved the sensation of him filling her. What she felt for Willow was soft, easy, ethereal, intellectual—and safe from pregnancy. She loved the sense of two equals becoming one.

She wondered how—and why—she and Willow had waited so long. She awakened Willow with gentle kisses. Half-asleep, they loved again then slept.

Ruby next awakened in the harsh light of morning. The night's activities flew into her mind. She had sinned. They had sinned. Their sin was abhorrent to God and humanity. With a rough shake, she roused Willow. "Go before someone finds us." She couldn't keep the brusqueness from her voice.

Willow looked bewildered but kissed Ruby's disheveled curls.

Ruby jerked her head away and jumped out of bed.

Willow slipped from beneath the sheets and trailed one hand across Ruby's cheek. "Are you angry? Do you regret what we did? Do you regret…us?"

Ruby tugged her gown to her ankles, buttoned it to her chin, and donned a robe. She picked up her brush and began flailing her hair. "I don't know…"

"I'm so sorry, my dear…I never meant…" Willow ran from the room.

Ruby, miserable and out of sorts, was unable to fall back asleep. Also unsuccessful at reading, she stared out the window into the distance seeking reassurance from within that their behavior was not aberrant.

Hours later, a gentle rap sounded on her door, followed by a soft "Ruby? Are you coming down for dinner?"

"I'm not feeling well." Her stomach grumbled as Willow's footsteps faded down the hall.

Back home, Reverend Magruder called it fornication when men and women performed sinful acts together. When he had shouted that word in church, followed by a slam of his Bible against the pulpit, the sound reverberated from the rafters, awakening those who dared doze off, making them think they had been called to Judgment Day.

Ruby wondered if a term existed to describe what two women did together. Her thoughts careened between how being with Willow had been wrong yet how right it seemed. Ultimately, she acknowledged her attraction to the other woman and knew it had begun the moment they first spoke about art. She found immense fulfillment in their friendship, a growing evolution of conjoined consciousnesses impossible to describe. Though denied for months, the longing had grown daily until a physical consummation was inevitable.

Bismarck, oh, Bismarck. She could not imagine life without him. Since childhood they had known they were to be married. Though she felt abandoned by him, he remained a profound part of her.

Frustrated, Ruby shook her head. She was in a desperate plight, hopelessly in love with two people. Willow was her sister in art while Bismarck represented everything she loved about the West. Somehow, if she could magically mix the woman's artistic temperament with the man's bond to the land, she'd have her ideal lover. These days, her fiancé seemed out of reach. She could only be certain of Willow's love.

After a knock on Ruby's door, Willow entered, carrying a small tray laden with tea and petite sandwiches. "You must be hungry, my love."

Ruby nodded then lowered her gaze.

Willow set the platter on the dresser before clasping Ruby's hands. "You seem rather discomfited by what happened last night."

"What we did was wrong. It did not seem so last night, but in the light of day—"

"We have done naught but love one another. There can

be no sin in that." Willow unbuttoned Ruby's shirtwaist.

Ruby stayed Willow's hands. "I know you have not been with a man, but have you loved another woman?"

Willow's face reddened. "That special friend at boarding school in Paris."

"Did you have feelings for her?"

"I suppose, such feelings as a sixteen-year-old girl can have. But I loved you from the moment I saw you."

"That first day? In Mrs. Wheelwright's parlor?" Involuntarily Ruby ran her tongue over her teeth, remembering their awkward introduction. "From the way you stared at me, I thought I had food caught in my teeth."

Willow gave a low laugh. "I couldn't tear my eyes from your mouth, imagining your kisses. I feared being near you. Feared I would kiss you. Feared your rejection." After unlacing the stays and tugging the corset cover and underlying corset over Ruby's head, Willow fingered Ruby's breasts through the camisole. "God, you ignite a fire within me no one else has."

In truth, rather than sinning, she and Willow had found heaven together. Ruby sighed with resignation. God had not punished her for lying with Bismarck. She prayed he would overlook this indiscretion as well.

* * * *

After class Ruby and a group of students stood on the steps of the Academy as Wheatley vented his frustrations. "Eakins is right. The Academy's regular models are coarse and flabby."

"Hard to get inspired by fat old whores, isn't it?" Fred Ames agreed.

"Indeed! The same few over and over. Never a young, beautiful woman."

Ruby raised an eyebrow. "Or a handsome man."

"They think us incapable of controlling our carnal urges." Ames snorted in derision. "At least at the Art Students' League, the basis of study is the nude human figure in its entirety."

Wheatley added, "Fred and I rented a loft above a photography studio on Chestnut Street. Not far from the Academy or the Art Students' League. Won't you join us, Ruby?"

With due consideration of the additional expense versus the benefits—more space than her cubbyhole of a room, more privacy than her workspace at the Academy, and above all, more freedom from Anshutz' overly-critical eyes—she agreed. And persuaded Willow to join as well.

As the men carried easels, a scarred table, mismatched chairs, and stools up three flights of steep stairs, Ruby supervised, ensuring a pleasing arrangement of their second-hand furnishings. "Put my easel over there." She pointed to one corner. "The bed against that wall."

Wheatley groaned. "Red, you're worse than my mother."

She stuck out her tongue. "Without proper direction, you men would leave this place a shambles for months."

Wheatley built simple shelves to hold supplies and props and manufactured a modeling stand, a small platform to elevate their subjects, which he covered with a scrap of well-worn rug. Junk-shop draperies and old canvases from the shipyard, swagged overhead, served as backdrops. The artists hung paintings floor to ceiling, salon-style. The rickety bed provided a haven should they work themselves to exhaustion. The two men, with several comrades, hauled Wheatley's heavy printmaking press upstairs.

Carefully arranging her quarter of the space, Ruby turned her easel at an angle to the window so her shadow would not interfere with the light playing across her canvas. A mahogany gate-leg table found on the street provided a spot for her palette while nails in the plaster held her coat and artist's smock. Thumbtacks pinned sketches to the wall. To speak with Willow, Ruby had only to poke her head around her painting.

Ready to work, Ruby placed a pristine canvas on her easel and loaded her palette with lead white, cadmium yellow and orange, vermilion, light red, burnt sienna, permanent blue, Van Dyke brown, and black. Eakins had advised his students that, if they wanted their work to endure, to avoid the new synthetic colors made from anilines.

Weeks passed. Ruby and Willow wore a path in the floor walking back and forth to encourage and critique each other. Though circumspect in public, when the men were not around, the two women freely made use of the bed. Behind locked doors, they explored each other. Ruby bought a sketchbook in which they recorded their own taut nipples, curly-haired *montes pubis*, and rounded buttocks.

Thanks to Wheatley's outgoing personality and Willow's radical acquaintances, the new studio quickly became a meeting place for Academy students, local artists, and bohemians. Most evenings, equal parts tobacco smoke and intellectual conversation filled the air. Wine and spirits flowed. Gatherings featured life drawing—of each other if no other model was available—plus rather boisterous socializing, readings from Walt Whitman and Émile Zola. Wheatley preferred John Rushkin, thinking the English critic and patron of the arts, draftsman, artist, social thinker, and philanthropist, a modern Renaissance man. Talk ranged widely. Art. Politics. Sex. School gossip. Stories abounded of the quasi-legendary Thomas Eakins, a former teacher at the Academy, who was forced to resign after stripping the loincloth from a male model in a ladies' life drawing class. And how conservative the Academy became after his dismissal.

"As long as a work stimulates aesthetic or emotional—rather than erotic—feelings, it should not be labeled pornography."

Ruby's mind flashed to her own sensual adventures with Willow.

"And nothing we have done at the Art Students' League or in this studio is remotely erotic." Wheatley wound up his current rant by taking a swig of wine.

Perhaps due to the influence of alcohol plus her progressive mother, Willow sparkled on these occasions, pushing conversation to radical ideas, the Free Love movement, and women's rights.

Ruby tired of the chatter and returned to her canvas, muttering, "Cow patties. Most of what they talk about is plain old cow patties." She could not understand how Willow and her friends got so involved in these discussions that they neglected their vocations.

* * * *

One Sunday afternoon, while Ruby worked alone at the studio, Wheatley entered. "Is Miss Wycke here?"

"She's home for the weekend. I expect she'll arrive by dinnertime."

"I brought this for her mother." He unwrapped an etching plate from its brown paper covering. "The cover for her newest suffrage booklet."

"You support women voting?"

He bobbed his head. "Don't you?"

"Mrs. Wycke is attempting to convert me." Ruby touched the etching plate, feeling the slight tooth where the metal had been raised by incising. "I wish I could do this."

"I'll teach you."

She smiled. "Thank you. I'd like that."

Wheatley stood at her easel to see her current work, a

mid-sized canvas of a woman stooped by the weight of water buckets she carried to a garden wilting under a white-hot Texas sky. "It's like a Pissarro but hard-edged rather than impressionistic." He stepped back a few feet and let out an explosive breath. "Where do you come up with these things?"

Ruby parroted a line from Anshutz. "The only possible source for true art is an artist's own experience, gained through direct observation of one's subjects."

"You certainly captured the harshness of her life. Your work challenges current ideas of acceptable women's art." He stared at the image then pointed to a rattlesnake curled near the woman's foot. "Somewhere in your work, danger always hides."

"Life is like that. Just when you think you have your problems conquered—" Ruby snapped her fingers.

Wheatley laughed. "You paint like a man, Red. Nothing pretty or maudlin for you."

"Damnation, Ira. Only a man would consider those words a compliment. I am a painter—period—not a woman painter." She stabbed her brush in the air. "You men think you own the field of painting, and art should be judged solely by male criteria. Unfortunately, most women have been taken in by your arrogance. I have not. Why, simply because I am female, must I paint insipid mothers holding smiling children? Or vases over-filled with flowers? Or brooks babbling before cottages?"

"Now you sound like Mrs. Wycke." Wheatley laughed.

Ruby gave him a sidelong glance. He was right. The radical Mrs. Wycke was rubbing off on her. Women were capable of producing true art, and their repertoire should not be restricted to "ladylike" subjects.

* * * *

Most nights Ruby slept in Willow's room at Mrs.

Wheelwright's, tightly wound around her lover. Should Mrs. Wheelwright catch Ruby in the hallway, she could say she was visiting the water closet. Willow, if caught going in the opposite direction, would have no such excuse. As Willow's room was the most removed from the other boarders, should the two women cry out in passion, they were unlikely to be heard.

Ruby tiptoed on bare feet over the meadow of flowers that covered the faded carpet. She had learned each creak of the wooden floor and avoided the musical spots. Clad in a filmy muslin nightgown, she became a spirit haunting the distance between her door and Willow's. Tonight, longing to be with Willow, her thoughts danced ahead of her feet. A plank complained loudly at her step. Ruby halted, listening. The night sounds of the house eddied around her. Someone snored. She smiled. She needn't worry about that sleeper. Seconds later, a bed groaned as someone rolled over. Frozen, Ruby awaited discovery.

Down the hall, Willow held the door open, her face etched with concern. "Hurry," she mouthed.

Ruby shook her head. An eon later, when certain no one had roused, she lifted her foot, planted it silently on the rug before her, and continued her journey. She slipped into Willow's room and fell into her lover's arms. Safe. Ruby breathed with relief. Perhaps the unusually damp weather made the board swell enough to moan with her weight. Next time, she must avoid that bit of squeaky flooring.

Willow cut short their embrace and soundlessly eased the door closed.

Behind the locked door, their fingers painted each other's curves. Ruby delighted in the sensation of her buttocks being traced by Willow's fingers and her own hands stroking Willow's nipples, brown and hard as hazelnuts.

Chapter Twelve
In Flagrante Delicto

Antioch Farm

"What are we going to do about your brother?" Ruby asked Willow as they lay in bed.

"I don't know." Willow. "He's so over-bearing."

"Not to mention pompous."

Woodrow often intruded on the women's painting sessions at Antioch Farm, enticing Ruby to join him. Though he'd done no more than steal a kiss, he apparently thought himself lord of the castle—and Ruby his by *droit de seigneur*.

Willow gave an exasperated huff. "Just like Papá, Woody is used to getting what he wants. We must be on constant guard to keep our secret."

"I told him I'm engaged, but…"

"Keep telling him that. If he believes you are betrothed, he won't suspect we're lovers."

Ruby nodded. She ran her fingers down Willow's arm. "I can't even bear to rest my hand on his."

"Endure, my love. We'll figure something out." Willow clutched Ruby's arm. "Are you still engaged to Bismarck?"

Torn between her two loves, Ruby's stomach roiled. "I don't know. I might be. I suspect we've been pledged to each other so long, neither of us has the gumption to break away."

"Do you love him?" Willow's voice became plaintive. "Or me?"

"I love you both. That's the problem."

"Who do you desire the most?"

Ruby sighed. "Both of you. Please don't make me choose."

"What are we to do?"

Ruby's shoulders couldn't decide whether to shrug or not.

"Someday, you'll have to choose…"

* * * *

To regain their privacy and to keep Woodrow from playing court to Ruby, the two women painted in a little glen beside the Brandywine. Enclosed by greenery, the isolated spot served as both studio and boudoir. Isolated, she and Willow splashed in the river like the swimmers they'd seen on the Schuylkill, their bodies bare, worshipping pagan goddesses, sketching each other. In the seclusion, they no longer loved in silence but gave voice to their passion and discovered, as Mrs. Wycke had intimated, what wonders might be wrought with fingers and mouths.

On a quilt beneath the trees, Ruby lay completely naked. She glanced around. Butterflies danced in the air. Bees hummed. Birds sang. The wind's delightful breath teased her nipples. She pushed Willow downwards until her head burrowed between Ruby's thighs. In ecstasy, her fingers and toes dug into the quilt.

In the distance, a horse snuffled. Ruby tensed. She propped on her elbows and looked about. The sound came from afar. Nothing disturbed the peace where she lay with Willow. Ruby's muscles slackened, and she sank back onto the fabric.

Minutes later, a flock of birds took off with raucous chatter. Ruby opened her eyes. Doves streaked across the sky. She held her breath. Frogs resumed their croaking.

Birds reprised their song. Again, she gave herself completely to Willow.

Ruby, her body arched to the sun, closed her eyes against its brilliance, the red glow behind her eyelids replicating the warmth between her legs. Gradually, the buzzing of insects and the whispering of grasses faded. All sensation became seated between her thighs. Her own moans joined the birdsongs. She pulled Willow's long hair over her abdomen and breasts and rubbed her skin with its silk, the long locks encasing her as softly as a spider web. As she cried out in release, a whish and a loud whack sounded above her.

Willow's scream reverberated through the glen.

Ruby snapped her eyes open.

Silhouetted against the sun, Woodrow stood above them. His raised hand gripped his riding crop. He threw Willow onto her back and struck again and again, raising red welts on her breasts and abdomen.

"Hussies! Clothe yourselves." Wild in his aim, Woodrow struck both women indiscriminately.

Dodging blows, Ruby and Willow struggled to rise.

He shoved his sister aside.

"Woodrow! Stop!" Willow placed herself before Ruby. "Don't you dare strike her again!"

"Neither God nor Man would fault the beating of women engaged in such vile acts."

Willow lunged for the riding crop, grabbing it with both hands.

Woodrow jerked the whip free, lifting his sister off the ground with his effort.

She tumbled against him. "Will not God fault you, brother? You are no Quaker today."

Either the force of her body or the weight of her words broke the momentum of his attack. He again lifted his arm to strike his sister but stayed his blow though he shook with anger. He averted his eyes. "Cover yourselves."

When the women were decent, he commanded Willow to walk home.

"Get up." He flung Ruby to his saddle before mounting behind her. Though he had to reach around her to hold the reins, he leaned backward at an awkward angle as if he feared contamination by her sin. They rode in relentless silence to the train station.

Too stunned and angry to cry, Ruby edged forward as far as the saddle would permit. His arms around her rubbed the wounds he'd made. Her physical discomfort heightened her emotional distress. How naïve she and Willow were to have thought they'd not be discovered.

At the West Chester station, Woodrow dismounted and reached to help her from the horse.

She scowled at him, dodged his hands, and slid down alone.

Before she could walk away, he squeezed her chin with one hand and glared at her. "Once, Miss Schmidt, I had thought to ask for your hand. I would gain an attractive wife and Willow a friend and sister. How cruelly you repay the kindness my family has shown you."

Ruby did not reply, though she thought how poorly he treated his sister.

He snatched her wrist and dragged her toward the ticket window.

Woodrow paid Ruby's fare, then assisted her onto the train, his tight grip on her elbow indicating he feared her escape.

"Your belongings will be delivered to you at Mrs. Wheelwright's. You will never see my sister again." He doffed his hat and stomped away. He walked a few yards, then turned back and addressed Ruby through the train window. "I pray God will guide you and my sister back to the Kingdom of the Lord."

* * * *

By the time the train arrived in Philadelphia, Ruby could scarcely move. Rather than walk, she took a cab, sitting stiffly to prevent her stays from rubbing her injuries. Never before had a hand been laid upon her. In her room, she removed her clothing and washed. She felt dirty, not from loving Willow, but from Woodrow's vile touch. Her reflection in the mirror revealed a dozen lashings, red, raised, and fevered, cross-hatching her body from thighs to breasts.

Naked, she lay across her bed, cool compresses on her burning skin. At length, she pulled the pillow over her head. She prayed for Willow but refused to ask forgiveness for her hatred of Woodrow.

Several days later, Ruby returned from morning classes at the Academy to find a wagon before the boarding house. She raced inside. Woodrow had indeed sent her belongings from the Wyckes' farm—they had been tossed in a pile before her door. Sounds came from Willow's room. Ruby rushed past her own door and knocked on Willow's. "Willie!"

No answer.

She rapped harder.

The door opened with a heavy thud against the wall. The butler from Antioch Farm blocked the opening with his body.

"May I speak with Miss Wycke, please?" Ruby edged from side to side, trying to peer into the room.

Behind the servant, Willow's personal maid packed clothing into open trunks.

The butler danced back and forth to obscure her view. "No." His voice was clipped and authoritative.

"Is she here?"

"No."

"Where is she? What have they done with her?"

"Be gone, girl. She is not your concern."

At the stern glare in his eyes, Ruby retreated.

An hour later, the hall floor creaked, Willow's door slammed. The butler cursed at the maid as they hauled Willow's belongings down the stairs.

Ruby rushed into the now-empty room, praying they had not found the sketchbook. Reaching beneath the mattress, her fingers searched desperately for the volume. It had to be there. She felt under all sides of the bed. Nothing. She stripped the linens from the bed and raised the foot of the mattress. Nothing. At the head of the bed, she lifted the heavy mattress. The book was truly gone. As she lowered the cushion, an irregularity in the shadow between the slats and the bedrail caught her eye. She looked closer. Relieved, she wiggled the sketchbook free, tucked it in her pocket, and returned to her room. One last time she viewed the intimate portraits she and Willow had drawn of each other—so much love captured in each image—before hiding it in the false bottom of her trunk.

* * * *

Two weeks passed without a word from Willow, time enough for Ruby's bruises to heal but not her heart. Her daily letters went unanswered. She resolved to learn what had happened to her lover. On a wet morning, she rose early and caught the train to West Chester. With the rain, the only carriage remaining for hire was an open wagon. She raised her umbrella and endured the drizzle on the ride to the Wyckes' home. The closer she drew to Antioch Farm, the more the weather dampened her bleak mood. Anxiously she twisted her fingers in her skirts, wondering whether she would find

Willow unharmed

"Wait for me, please?" she said as the cabbie helped her down.

Beneath the portico, she tapped timidly on the leaded glass door. When there was no response, she gathered her courage and knocked loudly.

A face, distorted by the bevels of the glass, appeared. A long moment passed, during which Ruby became more frantic, before the door opened.

"Yes?" A young maid raised a haughty eyebrow as she answered the door.

Ruby placed her hand on the doorjamb, seeking support for her shaking knees. "May I speak with Miss Wycke, please?"

"The Wyckes are away."

"I must speak with her. When will she return?"

The maid's eyes widened as footsteps thundered behind her. She glanced back then abruptly slammed the door in Ruby's face.

Voices intertwined behind the closed door, too low for Ruby to understand. Hesitantly, she knocked again.

The tight-lipped butler reopened the door. "The Wycke family is unavailable. You are not welcome here. Do not come again."

Disheartened, Ruby felt near tears. She wouldn't cry here, not in front of that infernal butler. She returned to her cab, and the driver gave her a hand up. Heaviness settled in her heart. She slumped in her seat. Fearing Willow lost forever, she pulled her handkerchief from her pocket and dabbed at the accumulating moisture.

The cabbie shook the reins above the horse's back. The wagon jerked forward along the broad circular drive.

"Wait, Ruby!"

A woman's cries, coming from behind, startled Ruby. She whirled to see what was happening.

Chapter Thirteen
Torn Asunder

"Stop!" Ruby ordered the cabbie.

On the portico, Willow struggled in the butler's arms. "Let me go!" With a final jerk, she pulled free and raced towards the carriage.

"Halt here." Ruby placed her hand on the cabbie's shoulder to stay him. Willow would be at the cab before they could circle back for her. "But be ready to fly off."

"Wait, Ruby! Please."

As Willow ran to Ruby, her morning dress and dainty slippers left a trail through the raindrops sparkling in the grass.

Ruby stood, ready to grab her friend and whisk her into the vehicle.

Willow reached the cab, her hands clutching convulsively at Ruby. "Take me with you."

With all her might Ruby hauled her in. She turned to the cabbie. "Go, quickly!"

The cabbie whipped the horse to a trot.

As they neared West Chester, hooves clattered behind them. A rider galloped alongside the cab. "Pull over. Pull over, I say."

"Never!" Willow screamed at her brother.

Woodrow rode beyond the carriage and reined to a stop. "Halt immediately." He whisked a pistol from his waistband

and pointed it at the cabby's head.

The driver immediately reined to a standstill and raised his hands in surrender. "D-d-don't shoot."

Woodrow moved his horse to Willow's side of the wagon. "Darling sister," his voice held the contempt most humans reserved for slugs and leeches, "I can't permit you to run away."

"Leave me be."

"Don't be absurd. Return home. Now."

"No." Willow lifted her chin defiantly.

"Father will disinherit you. You'll be penniless." Woodrow leveled his pistol at her breast. "I'll shoot you before allowing your continued liaison with this—this abomination." With a glare, he shifted his aim toward Ruby. "Though I would prefer to see her dead."

Willow's fair skin lost all color. With a glance at Ruby, she stepped toward her brother and prepared to descend from the carriage.

Ruby grabbed her hand. "Willie, no! He's too cowardly to fire." She leaned forward and shook the cabbie's shoulder. "Drive off, please. Hurry!" In her own ears, her voice sounded high-pitched and frightened.

The driver held the wagon in place.

"Move!" Ruby shoved him aside, grabbed his whip, and stretched for the reins.

Woodrow fired.

A whistle sounded past Ruby's ear. At the sudden noise, the horse startled and skittered. The carriage lurched. Ruby lost her balance. She fell back, striking her shoulder against the seat.

Willow shrieked in alarm and turned to Ruby, snatching at her desperately. "Are you injured?"

"Get out now, sister. I won't miss the bitch next time."

Woodrow's hard voice cracked the quiet country air. "It will be justifiable homicide."

Ruby reached for her lover. "Don't listen to him."

Willow swatted away Ruby's hand and moved toward her brother.

"Get up here." He wrapped one arm around his sister and lifted her to his saddle.

Turning to Ruby a last time, Willow said, "Farewell. I shall love you always."

"Drive on!" Woodrow ordered Ruby's cabbie. He slapped his riding crop against his own horse's hindquarters.

The crack of the driver's whip over the horse's back sounded as loudly as the report of Woodrow's pistol. Ruby's wails echoed from the nearby green hills as her wagon rode one way, and Woodrow galloped off with his sister in the other.

* * * *

Ruby had lost hope of ever hearing from Willow again when a letter arrived, hastily scrawled on stationery from the Plaza Hotel, Central Park, New York City. Her own tears stained the paper as her fingers traced the watermarks Willow's tears had made.

> *My Beloved,*
> *Papá and Woodrow hold me captive as punishment for our love. To ensure I do not slip away to you, they brought me to New York. I remain under constant surveillance. Papá is determined I shall marry, willingly or not. We depart December first for an extended tour of the Continent where he plans to foist me off on the first unsuspecting soul.*
> *I fear there is no hope for our lives together. I return you to Bismarck and hope you find happi-*

ness with him. Abroad, I pray I find a 'suffrage husband' who will indulge my art and not insist upon children.

My heart breaks that I cannot see you, hold your dear hand, feel your curls on my cheek, and kiss you tenderly in that most sacred place once more.

Your loving,
Willie

The letter plunged Ruby further into despair. She tried to paint, but the classrooms and studio she had shared with Willow held too many memories. Their bonds had grown so deep neither had cultivated friendships with other women. Their female classmates preferred to be safely ensconced in parlors and gardens, the provinces of the females of the species, rather than wandering the city and painting its sights as Ruby and Willow had done. Ruby's reputation for "unladylike" art isolated her further from her classmates.

One school day, she stepped outside to eat her lunch. When she returned to her easel, a book sat on her stool. As she leafed through it, she realized it was a novel, similar to *Fanny Hill*, with the pornographic parts heavily underlined. Her temper flared, warming her face. She blew out a hot huff of air, snapped the book closed, and looked around. The women in the class studiously avoided her gaze. If they had given her the volume, they were not as innocent as they protested. They were just plain mean, as mean as Hortense Hammond back home.

* * * *

Willow's absence shaded the already-gray Philadelphia. To release her restless energy, Ruby walked the city. Gray weather, gray buildings, gray everything compounded her

ither of them was worth crying over. Once
about choosing between them, now deserted
adjust to her new destiny—a solitary life.
to allow her friend to think she did not care
to wish her the best, Ruby composed a letter.

rling Willie,
ice in your happy news and pray God
nd Walter joy. As a wedding gift, I shall
wo something special.
cent work has given me fits of discontent.
to chuck it in the fire and return home.
ked en plein air, attempting to recapture
he energy we once shared but still am not
to my satisfaction. I find it quite mad-

letter she found more difficult to answer.
terse. No feelings expressed at all. As she
ern the true state of his emotions, she post-

Willow had been artistic soul mates. That be-
ong, Ruby did not find other women attrac-
Willow had married, their love seemed a fol-
n impossible. At the same time, Ruby could
r attraction to Bismarck or truthfully express
above all others. She found herself unable to
at being abandoned—and furious, if she ad-
emotion—Ruby, when not in class, painted
dio. Months later, Ruby found herself walk-
canvas to talk to a woman no longer there and
w much she missed Willow. She returned to

bleak mood, and the winter seemed longer, gloomier, and dingier than the year before. The narrow streets trapped her. Coal dust turned the snow dingy and filled her mouth with dark grit. She missed the limitless sky and open range of Texas—which made her miss Bismarck as well.

"Every artist goes through times when they can't produce." Wheatley, complaining about his own dry spell, assumed she suffered from the same malady. "Keep painting, even if you don't like your work. You'll eventually come out the other side."

She considered going home but, anticipating more time with Willow, had paid tuition for a third year and couldn't justify the expense. Besides, she had already written her family and beau that she would remain in Philadelphia. Slow to respond at best, Bismarck's silence stretched for eons after Ruby's announcement. They now corresponded so rarely, there was no rush to return to Truly. When Ruby wrote Molly Statler inquiring about Bismarck, her friend had little to say.

When I ask Bismarck about you, he never replies. He grunts and thinks of something he needs, invariably all the way across the store. I have to interrupt our conversation to find it. I suppose that's his way of changing the subject...

On the other hand, Willow wrote Ruby weekly, but her letters arrived irregularly, newsy dispatches mailed in bunches when she could bypass her family's guard. Each post detailed her European journey so clearly Ruby could visualize every painting and sculpture her friend saw. Many letters arrived from London and Paris. A sole dispatch from Rome was followed by an abrupt cessation.

As the silence from her lovers lengthened, Ruby worried

about them both. Willow she pardoned on grounds of erratic mail from abroad. But Bismarck, as far as she was concerned, had no excuse. With America connected by railroads, letters traversed the continent in mere days. After a silence of over two months, in which Ruby imagined every calamity which might have befallen Willow and invented every slight Bismarck might deliver, a package from Willow and a letter from Bismarck arrived the same day. She opened his first.

> *Ruby,*
> *I cain't honestly say I'm pleased with your news about staying back East. But I ain't surprised neither.*
> *Nokoni took off for weeks and left me running the place alone. About wore myself to a frazzle. He came back with a sweet young bride. She's real hard-working, took over the cooking and cleaning, leaving us fellers doing men's work. I put them in our attic until he and I can build them a place of their own.*

Ruby whimpered as she finished his note. It was too short to be termed a letter. Bismarck hadn't broken off their engagement but had written to let her know she was no longer needed. Another woman—even if temporarily and in the attic—was living in the house he had built for her. He was still unhappy about her staying in Philadelphia. The future they had planned long ago seemed as unlikely as her love for Willow.

Ruby tore open the box from Willow. Dozens of prints of art works were stacked inside. At the bottom, as though her lover had hidden it, lay a brief letter.

> *My dearest Rul*
> *Forgive me, m*
> *friend for weeks, bu*
> *ing news. I have m*
> *photographer and g*
> *In the Louvre,*
> *at a painting ana*
> *arms. He quite swep*
> *We delight in a*
> *ery exhibition and r*
> *Walter and I stole a*
> *for our vows. Mama*
> *prived of an elabora*
> *Tomorrow we a*
> *moon.*
> *Yours always,*
> *Willie*
> *(Mrs. Walter E*

> *P.S. After seein*
> *d'Este was quite co*
> *hair you truly are la*

Ruby crushed the let
across the room. The tw
would someday marry B
preferred art to any ma
Willow's whirlwind mar
marriage with a woman.
barked on a marriage of
And if a true affection, w
vows of eternal love had

Though feeling unde
up their letters, smooth

Damnation. N
she had frette
by both, she'c

Unwillin,
deeply enoug

> *My c*
> *I re,*
> *grant yot*
> *paint you*
> *My r*
> *I am rea*
> *I have we*
> *outdoors*
> *succeedi*
> *dening...*

Bismarck
His words we
could not dis
poned her rep

Ruby an
lief was so s
tive. Now tha
ly, their reuni
neither deny
she loved him
write him at a

Miserabl
mitted her tru
alone in the s
ing around he
realized just b

her side of the room, shoulders sagging.

Woodrow had never retrieved Willow's belongings. Her easel, pigments, and paintings remained, a memorial to her art, to their friendship, untouched except once when Ruby borrowed some cadmium scarlet. As she squirted the color from its metal tube, the brilliant pigment brought memories of the red kimono and their first lovemaking.

Their friends assumed Willow had undertaken a grand tour of Europe to further her education, and Ruby was loathe to reveal the truth.

To keep from dwelling on her sorrow, Ruby attended lectures at the University of Pennsylvania given by Eadweard Muybridge on the "Science of Animal Locomotion." Fascinated by his stop-motion photography of animals and humans moving, she spent the phenomenal sum of five dollars for a copy of his book, *Animal Locomotion: an Electro-Photographic Investigation of Connective Phases of Animal Movements*. She justified the expense knowing it would prove a resource she'd use the rest of her life.

She relentlessly pushed forward with her work, painting constantly, capturing scenes from memory of horses galloping across the relentless Texas plains, using Muybridge's images as a reference. She realized she'd conquered her dark spell when, in her opinion, her art surpassed Frederick Remington's. Locked in the past, his paintings depicted a violent environment laden with conflict. Her images surpassed his in anatomic accuracy and conjured a new vision of the West, men and women building lives in a tough land.

* * * *

When Wheatley asked her to pose for him, Ruby hesitated but consented. They had been friends long enough she knew no sexual undertones lay beneath his request. Most days only she and Wheatley painted in the studio, so the session would be private. Recently Ames had taken issue with the Academy's rigid stance on nudity and had broken with the institution. Instead he took up with Eakins at the Art Students' League.

On the appointed afternoon, Ruby arrived early and paced nervously while Wheatley placed a stool on the modeling stand.

"You sure you want to do this, Red?"

"Certainly." After all, it was only fair to reciprocate. Hesitating momentarily, she stepped behind a curtain, briskly removed her clothing then wrapped herself in a robe. She thought of disguising her face with a veil but instead hid everything but her chin beneath a large flowery chapeau. She didn't quite have the gumption to reveal herself completely.

"Take your time, Red. Let me know when you're ready."

After a deep breath, she stepped beyond the drapery and seated herself.

Wheatley stayed behind his easel, chatting with her, yet maintaining a professional distance.

Gradually she grew more comfortable. Her pitter-pattering heart calmed. Her heated cheeks returned to normal. Willow had been right. Having exposed herself once, Ruby found the second time easier. She and Wheatley chatted as he sketched her, and she let the robe drop partway, then all the way. Eventually, she relaxed enough to remove the hat. No more false modesty for her.

* * * *

The streetlights extinguished as Ruby arrived at the studio. From her window, the early morning moon posed above the canyon of city buildings. She gazed at it, creamy against the watery gray sky, wishing she could lasso it and pull it to earth, hold it in her hands. Its soft flesh would feel like Willow's breast. Ruby roused herself from her reverie and began setting up for the day. As morning blossomed, the February light grew intense, excellent for painting; strong winds and rain the day before had lifted the diaphanous gray that habitually shrouded Philadelphia. She could work all day in peace.

Weeks of damp weather stirred Ruby's longing for home. She loathed the City of Brotherly Love. Though she walked daily, she never found a place where she could see into infinity as she could on the plains. In Texas, the world had stretched before her if she stepped outside, and, invariably, her heart would soar.

Again and again, she considered returning home but refused to waste her tuition by leaving halfway through the year. Besides, Bismarck scarcely wrote anymore. Most likely she had no one to go home to. She started letter after letter to him but destroyed them all. Afraid of rejection, she was too proud to ask if he still cared.

Some days Ruby faced the hard fact that, with Willow married and Bismarck half way across the continent, she was utterly alone. Other days, Ruby knew, if Willow suddenly returned from Europe, married or not, they would resume their affair. Just as surely, she knew if Bismarck magically appeared, she would fall into his arms. Unable to reconcile the war within herself, her emotions ricocheted.

In those moments before sleep, she envisioned her two lovers as pure colors wrapping themselves around her. With both, she became complete—a palette laden with every conceivable color. Willow brought vibrant blues, streaked with ice and violet, cool, intellectual, embodying their cerebral *affaire de cœur*. Brown with strands of fire and green, Bismarck epitomized their corporeal relationship, grounded in Texas earth.

Chapter Fourteen
The Stillbirth

Spring 1893

Despite her ambiguous feelings toward her fiancé, Ruby began a new canvas for the Academy's annual art exhibition, her largest yet, inspired by a Sunday afternoon several years earlier when a subdued Bismarck had called on her, dropping limply into a chair on her parents' front porch.

"Anything wrong?" She handed him a cup of coffee and a monolithic slab of pound cake.

He reared back on the legs of the mule-eared chair, resting his head against the wall. "I'm plumb wore out. Up all night delivering a stillborn filly. Nearly lost the mare, too." Overcome, he choked up, rubbing his forehead with his hand to hide his emotion.

Ruby knew he'd envisioned the foal, the product of his favorite mare and a wild mustang with an indomitable spirit, as the key to their future, the first in a string of fine horses.

"Oh, Biz." She leaned down and drew his head against her breast and stroked his hair. He lifted her hand to his mouth and kissed it before pulling her into his lap. They held each other until he could speak again.

Ruby wanted to capture that mixture of sadness, fatigue, and momentary defeat in a painting she planned to entitle *The Stillbirth*. After sketching for weeks, she realized her original idea of showing Bismarck as she remembered him, on the front porch in broad daylight, lacked drama. The scene should be painted as it happened. In her final version, the barn was lit by a lone kerosene lantern. An exhausted Bismarck sat on a milking stool, his hands clasped behind his head, leaning against the barn wall. He was shirtless, one red suspender sliding off his shoulder. Sweat, blood, and birthing fluids soaked the denim pants that clad the long legs stretched before him. The body of the foal lay at his feet. Behind him, barely visible in the dark, the mare hung her head, the barn cat licked its paws, and the cock perched on the door to the horse stall.

Ruby turned her easel toward the morning light, refreshed her palette, and poured turpentine and linseed oil into tiny tins before loading her brush with pigment. Soon painting transported her to that holy place where the outside world ceased to exist.

Wheatley and Ames came in later, but she kept working, letting the men's conversation float around her as hazily as their cigarette smoke. Close to noon, footsteps bounded up the stairs. She ignored the interruption.

"*Ciao, tutti.* Hello, Ira, Fred. I heard you'd rented a studio."

Intrigued, she peeked around her easel. Spying the capricious Mr. d'Este, the man who promised her lunch then disappeared, Ruby rolled her eyes.

He turned, surveying the studio.

Before she could duck behind her canvas, he strode toward her. "Ah, Miss Schmidt, the girl with the titian hair."

Wheatley interrupted d'Este's progress. "Where've you been, Frank?"

He turned back to the men.

Ruby retreated behind her painting. Curious as to where the Italian gentleman had been, she occasionally peeked around her canvas as she eavesdropped on the conversation.

"New York. The Art Students League. I couldn't escape old Eakins even there—he's on the Board of Directors. Then in October, I went on to Chicago, for the dedication of the World's Columbian Exposition. I met Saint-Gaudens there, the artistic advisor for the Fair. Charming fellow."

"So the prodigal son returns?"

"For now." D'Este gave a diffident shrug.

"Where are you staying?"

"I've taken a room at the Art Club."

Ames whistled. "Not too shabby."

"Show me what you scoundrels have been painting."

Wheatley and Ames brought out their canvases. A critique session ensued in which she was totally ignored. While Ruby might "paint like a man," she clearly was not manly enough to be included.

Ruby peeked around her canvas. "Cow patties. That's all you men talk about."

"*Cow patties?*" Wheatley snorted. "Do you mean *bullshit?*"

"Yes." Her face heated with embarrassment. "But ladies don't say such things."

The three men's laughter echoed off the studio walls.

Following a rousing discussion, they left Ruby alone in the studio and headed to Haeberle's Saloon to eat lunch and soothe their dry throats. The saloon had the added advantage of allowing Wheatley to court his Nan, who served as a barmaid there.

Ruby opened the windows to clear the smoke and hot air. She poured herself a glass of water and sat before her painting, taking harsh stock of it while eating her lunch. Somehow, she'd captured Bismarck's deep sadness at the loss of the foal. Juice from her apple dribbled down her chin.

She wiped her face, remembering how moist her mouth had become with Bismarck's kisses. She wondered if her letter had made him as sad as when he lost the foal. Perhaps he was relieved she stayed, leaving him free to marry someone else. She ran through the few single women in Truly, imagining Bismarck married to Molly Statler, Eloise, or even Hortense. Unlike her, they had no pluck, he once said. Maybe now he considered her independence less attractive as it was keeping them apart. Perhaps he preferred more docile women now. Even someone as despicable as Hortense.

Ruby hated to ask her sisters if Bismarck was courting someone else. They were too young to pay much attention to couples aligning and realigning themselves. Working at the mercantile, Molly was privy to every scrap of gossip in town, but even she had been unable to give a definitive answer. She simply reported that at town celebrations, no one in particular had caught Bismarck's eye, though he danced with all the ladies.

Ruby threw the apple core across the room with such force it shattered against the wall. With a sigh, she cleaned up her mess. Blinking back tears, she picked up her brush and began painting, taking solace in the repetitive placement of minute golden highlights on tiny bits of hay. She would be a painter. A damned fine painter. As she worked, her breathing slowed. Her shoulders relaxed. Eventually, she entered the space deep inside herself, where nothing existed except her brush and canvas. She was unsure what to call this place. Bliss? Ecstacy? Rapture?

A single set of feet clomped up the stairs. A loud rap sounded as the door creaked open. Damnation. Another interruption. Her calm evaporated. Irritated, she stuck her head around her easel to see who it was.

"Ah, *bella*, you are still here?" D'Este's smile said he'd

known she'd be here—alone—and had returned for that reason. He moved around her easel, stared at her painting, and whistled. "*Incredibile*. Miss Schmidt, it's like an old Master, *come un Caravaggio*."

"You exaggerate, Mr. d'Este, but thank you. It's for the exhibition."

"*Per piacere*, call me Frank." He stroked his well-trimmed goatee with his thumb and forefinger. "You'll have problems with the critics. Your chiaroscuro is superb but the subject matter *indecoroso*. Once they find a woman has painted it—*un scandolo*."

Ruby groaned. "I know. But I don't want to be Mary Cassatt and paint mothers and babies. Or do society portraits like Cecilia Beaux."

"What do you wish to paint?"

"This." Her brush vaguely indicated her painting, but her voice was firm. "*Life*. At least life as I know it. The Census Bureau declared the Frontier closed in 1890, but Texas is still wild. We struggle daily for survival. It's not pretty, but it is beautiful."

"*Brava!*" He applauded. "Who's the man?"

She hesitated. "My fiancé, Bismarck."

D'Este backed away and stared hard at the painting. "You have made love with him?"

"You, sir, are most impertinent!" Ruby's cheeks burned with mortification.

"If you have made love with him, you know what goes here." A devil's grin flashed over his face as he pointed at Bismarck's pants. "Yet you have emasculated him."

"I started to paint it, but—" Her cheeks flamed red hot.

"You were afraid, *bella*? If you are going to *fare un casino*—to make a scandal—you might as well make a big one."

In spite of herself, she laughed.

"Mr. Eakins once divested himself of his clothing to show a female student the function of the human pelvis." D'Este moved his hands to the placket of his trousers. "If you have never seen a male, I would be happy to provide you the same service."

"That won't be necessary." For the third time in minutes, Ruby's cheeks heated.

He laughed and changed the subject. "Fred and Ira said Miss Wycke is in Europe, leaving space here for another person. Would you object if I joined your group?"

She pursed her lips. If he could afford the Art Club, Mr. d'Este could certainly pay the rent here. "Five dollars a month, in advance." She nodded her head toward Willow's corner. "That's your section. Clean up after yourself. I may be the only woman, but I am not the maid."

D'Este withdrew silver dollars from his pocket and counted them into her hand. He pulled a lock of hair from her chignon, twining it around his finger. "Wheatley calls you *Red*, but I prefer *Tiziana*. Perhaps you'll pose for me?"

She shook her head and danced away from him. "It wouldn't be proper."

He followed her. "False modesty is the greatest enemy to painting the figure. How can it be improper to observe Nature's most beautiful works?" One hand lifted her skirt to her knees. "Would you condemn me to merely imagining what lies beneath your petticoats?"

"In case you haven't noticed, I'm working." She evaded him again, tugging her rumpled skirt from his hand and smoothing it.

"Pardon my intrusion. We will give your *sposo* his manhood now?" D'Este trapped her between his hands and spun her to face her canvas. One hand he left clasped about her waist while the other grasped the hand that held her paintbrush.

Her laugh caught in her throat as she slipped out of his grasp. "Yes. But I'm capable of doing so without your assistance." With a few subtle touches of paint, Bismarck's pants assumed his underlying form.

"That belongs to a child." D'Este grabbed her glass of water and upended it on himself. "His trousers are wet; one should see *everything*. Make him a real man. Remember, old Eakins says that the clothing must reflect the anatomy beneath."

As Ruby stared at him, her cheeks blazing hot again, her eyes unable to leave his pelvis. He was right. One could see everything. Dipping her brush toward her palette, she picked up a bit of cobalt, a dot of zinc white, and a smidgeon of bravado. With a touch of the bristles to the canvas, Bismarck grew bigger than Mr. d'Este.

Ruby stepped back and squinted her eyes, staring dispassionately at her painting. D'Este was right. Bismarck was manly. Strong. Perfect.

"*Brava!*" D'Este put his arm around her waist again, pulling her toward him, kissing the side of her neck. "*Perfetto!*"

A thrill surged through Ruby. She evaded his arms, trying to discern whether her response was to her own painting, d'Este's reaction to the image, or her body's arousal by his kiss.

He took the brush from her hand and laid it on the table. With one arm around her waist, he steered her to the stairs and helped her into her coat. "I owe you a meal."

Over dinner, Valentino told Ruby, "You must submit your painting under a false name."

"You mean lie?"

"When the judges and critics learn a woman did your painting, they will be outraged and dismiss it entirely."

* * * *

Ruby removed Willow's belongings the next day, shedding a few tears as she cleared space for Mr. d'Este—Frank. He might replace Willow in the studio but would never supplant her in Ruby's heart.

Ruby continued with her classes at the Academy but spent less time there. Anshutz irritated her with his constant nitpicking. After classes, she painted in the studio above Albion's photography studio. Most days she worked in solitude until late afternoon when the men dragged in, bleary-eyed but boisterous. They painted through the night, but Ruby left early, unwilling to walk home alone in the dark and needing to reach the boarding house before Mrs. Wheelwright locked the door.

One day, Ruby entered the studio and found d'Este asleep on the tumbledown bed, his black curls disheveled. The rope supports creaked as he rolled from his side to his stomach, his unbuttoned shirt partially revealing his chest.

Dozens of wadded up papers lay strewn about the room. She stooped to gather them but stepped over them instead. After all, she thought with a huff, she had warned him she was not the studio maid. Curiosity overcame her, though, and she picked up one crushed ball. Smoothing the paper against the table edge, taking care to not smear the charcoal, she flattened the drawing. The image startled her. As she retrieved the others, she repeated the process, studying the crumpled sketches. Soon she held dozens of images, each her own likeness. Some comprised only a few quick lines, others rendered with exquisite detail. She chose her favorite, slipped it between her drawings, re-wadded the remainder, and tossed them to the floor.

Before starting her work, she stood a few moments, watching d'Este's chest move with every breath, the occasional twitch of his limbs. With a deep sigh, he turned on his back, clutching the pillow in his arms like a lover.

If he could sketch her, she had the right to draw him. In case he awakened suddenly, she half-hid behind her painting as she filled several pages.

He groaned. The bed moaned in response. His eyes fluttered. He yawned.

Quickly tucking her drawings beneath her palette, Ruby retreated completely behind her easel. A moment later, she stuck her head around her canvas to greet him but held her words, watching him. He pulled his suspenders off his shoulders and removed his shirt, revealing the muscles in his back, the smooth even tone of his skin, the trim waistline. When he ducked his head beneath the faucet at the sink in the rear of the studio, the sight of his bottom tightening his trousers stole her breath. All too soon, he lifted his head, blindly reaching for a towel. Water dripped down his back, coalescing into the valleys between his muscles and trickling down his spine, disappearing in the waist of his pants.

"*Dio*! It's too bright in here." As he dried himself, the rag muffled the mutterings of his awakening.

"Feeling a tad under the weather?" Ruby decided to announce her presence rather than wait to be discovered.

Startled, he turned to face her. "*Tiziana*, how long have you been here?"

"Long enough." She grinned and looked down, suddenly embarrassed.

With a stretch and a yawn, still shirtless and drying himself, he walked around her painting and gazed at it. "You're making progress. Quite good. Wheatley is correct. You paint like a man."

She gave him a look poisoned by rattlesnake venom.

He clutched his heart, feigning a deathblow. "Would

you rather I said you painted like a woman?"

"Can't I paint like myself?"

Facing her, a blasé expression on his face, he unbuttoned his trousers, slipped on his shirt and tucked the tails into his pants.

Ruby's face heated. She turned away. His overt sexuality disturbed her. Every time she saw him, she spent their entire encounter blushing.

"I thought you'd seen it all before, *bella*."

He had the gall to laugh at her discomfort! Her face grew hotter yet, the warmth spreading around her neck and down her chest, stopping below her bellybutton.

"Where were you last night? I needed you." He stooped to pick up a crumpled ball and smoothed it. With one hand, he held the paper near her face, comparing the image with reality. "Your face torments me." A sweep of his hand encompassed all the sketches on the floor. "None of these are right." He moved so close his breath stirred her hair. A droplet of water from his wet hair dripped down her shirtwaist as he kissed the back of her neck.

She tensed.

"I want to paint you as more than a woman. I want to create a goddess."

The heat of his lips faded as the cold water slithered down one shoulder blade. For the second time, she found herself aroused. Mr. d'Este was entirely too charming for his own good—or hers. Quickly she stepped away.

"I can't paint you unless you sit for me." He reached for her. "You've posed for Wheatley. Why not me?" Abruptly he released her then walked across the room and pulled something from a shelf. "I have a gift for you."

Intrigued, she ventured around her canvas to see what he'd brought.

With a flourish, he waved a small paper bag beneath her nose. The scents of sugar, butter, and nuts wafted toward her. He opened the sack to reveal tiny hemispheres glued together with chocolate at their equators. With his fingers, he lifted one to her lips.

Just before he slid the delicacy into her mouth, she said, "What are they?"

"*Baci di dama.* Ladies' kisses. From the Italian market."

Blood rushed to her cheeks—again—but she giggled. "They're delicious."

His hand caressed her ear, her cheek, then slipped lower to stroke her lower lip. "Your kisses would be just as delectable."

"You, Mr. d'Este, are trying to seduce me."

"Is it working?" His voice was eager, hopeful.

"Of course not!" With a laugh, she backed away. "I am already betrothed." Perhaps the wee white lie would save her, though it had not worked particularly well with Woodrow Wycke.

D'Este followed her. "I only want you to pose for me. Be my goddess. My muse."

"With your charm, Mr. d'Este, I'm certain you can persuade almost any woman to sit for you; however, I have too much work to do to bother with such nonsense." While posing for Wheatley, there had been no undercurrent of attraction. Being nude in d'Este's presence would leave her far too vulnerable.

Every day for weeks, Ruby rushed from class to the studio where she painted alone. D'Este arrived later, bringing her treasures from the Italian market. Some days he enticed her with cheeses and fruit, sometimes sausages or wondrous paper-thin slices of *prosciutto*, most often sweets.

"Try these." He popped a tidbit into her mouth and

another in his own. "They taste as good as you do."

She closed her eyes in awe as she savored the divine flavors. "What are they?"

"*Tette de venere*. Venus's nipples."

Ruby blinked. Another delicacy with a titillating name. "You, sir, are incorrigible." Her face burned yet again.

"*Sono il suo schiavo*. I am a slave to your love."

* * * *

Under Ruby's supervision, d'Este and Wheatley transported her painting *The Stillbirth* to the Academy's exhibit hall where they submitted it under the name R. L. Carter, her own initials combined with her mother's maiden name.

At the opening, Ruby along with dozens of artists swirled around potential patrons. The art critic from the *Inquirer*, a gaunt, hawk-nosed aesthete, accompanied by others of his ilk, stopped before every painting. They glanced at each other and, almost in unison, sauntered on after well-timed shrugs, condescending sniffs, admiring nods, one or two rare words of acclamation, and the inevitable scribbling in notebooks. At *The Stillbirth*, a sudden silence was followed by an explosion of chatter and prolonged writing before the group proceeded to the next painting.

Ruby, who had been discreetly lagging behind the reviewers, wondered what their reactions meant. At least she could interpret Anshutz's *harrumphs* and *hmms*.

* * * *

The following afternoon, Ruby met Fred and Ira at the studio to read their reviews together. Though Ruby had submitted work to the Academy's annual art exhibition, this was the first time her work had been accepted. Though ecstatic at the honor, the niggling thought persisted that her work had been shown simply because no feminine name was attached to it.

To her surprise, d'Este appeared though he had not placed paintings in the exhibit. As always, he projected an attitude of good breeding overlaid with slight boredom and languor.

The loft was cold and dusky. Even flipping the light switch did not discourage the gloom of a spring day that looked backward to the worst of winter.

"I'll go first," Wheatley volunteered. "Get it over with." He cleared his throat then intoned in an affected, high-pitched nasal voice, "The dark works of Mr. Ira Wheatley and Mr. Frederick Ames are abhorrent to this critic. Prostitutes, drunks, crowded tenements and other prurient subjects are scarcely the appropriate subject matter of true art. How much more pleasing are the paintings of...blah...blah...blah." Wheatley snorted as he handed the newspaper to Ruby.

With an anxious wave of her hand, she demurred. "Read them to me. I can't bear the suspense."

"You sure?"

She nodded.

He cleared his throat and began to read. "Student artists frequently jog along copying their teachers. *The Stillbirth*, produced by a Mr. R. L. Carter, a painter previously unknown to us, is such a work. An obvious attempt at duplicating the horror of Mr. Thomas Eakins' painting, *The Clinic of Dr. Gross*, the image contains so much blood it resembles a battlefield. Artistic ideals cannot be taught. Either one is an artist or not. Mr. Carter merely parrots technique and does not aspire to grandeur in his art. It is difficult to understand why anyone would waste such exquisite skill on trash."

Ruby blanched then tried to swallow her dismay. She hadn't expected such a vehement reaction.

"What the hell does Ziegler know about art anyway?"

Wheatley fumed. "You caused quite a stir, Red. There's more." He picked up the *Philadelphia Press*. "*The Stillbirth* is strong and virile, one of the most powerful, realistic, and fascinating pictures in this exhibition. The chiaroscuro and drapery are exquisite; however, one must condemn its public display where the tender eyes of a woman may be forced to look upon it."

"What about the tender eyes of the woman who painted it?" Ames laughed, tossing the *Inquirer* across the room. "After those tongue lashings, the sweet oblivion of alcohol calls."

The men traipsed down the stairs, heading to Haeberle's where Wheatley could flirt with Nan as she served their beer.

Once they were gone, Ruby picked up the newspapers and read the articles herself. Her first reviews were devastating—except that single line that described her work as *virile*, as though only a male could accomplish such a painting. Her work was good. She knew it. Wheatley wouldn't lie to her. Even d'Este, who had seen great art all over Europe, thought it good. Though she did not know him well, she doubted he would fabricate responses to her paintings.

Chapter Fifteen
Rejection

Two weeks later, as Ruby began the endless climb to the fourth floor, Albion, the photographer, called "Miss Schmidt! A letter came for a Mr. R. L. Carter. Is he one of the young men sharing your studio?"

Puzzled, she hesitated a moment before recalling that she was R. L. Carter. "Yes. Thanks. I'll take it." She backtracked for the envelope he held out.

Once in the workspace, she nodded an absent hello to Wheatley as she used a pallet knife to lift the seal. She skimmed it quickly then read it again in disbelief. "Gracious! The University of Pennsylvania Veterinary School wishes to purchase *The Stillbirth*." Delighted, she twirled around the room, her wide skirt brushing easels and furniture indiscriminately.

"Congratulations, Red. I suppose it'll be their version of *The Gross Clinic*. How much are they offering?"

"Seventy-five dollars."

Wheatley whistled. "Not bad. You should let us men deliver the painting."

"Why?"

He rolled his eyes. "For the same reason we told you to submit it under an assumed name."

"My painting is not a bastard child. I wish to acknowledge it."

Wheatley shook his head at her obstinacy. "You'll regret it, Red."

Ruby replied by letter she would be happy to sell the image. By return mail, an appointment was arranged to exchange the painting for a check when the exhibition finished.

Ignoring Wheatley's advice, on the appointed day, she arrived twenty minutes early at the veterinary school at 36th and Pine Street. The picture, crated in a heavy wooden box, remained downstairs in a wagon. For three-quarters of an hour, Ruby waited in a cubicle. Finally a secretary led Ruby to the office of the president.

For several moments, she stood uncertainly as he ignored her, continuing to write at his desk. Finally, she said, "Dr. Zenker? I'm R. L. Carter. Here about the painting?"

He glanced up.

She extended her hand to shake his, but he dismissed it with an arrogant wave.

"I was expecting a Mr. Carter. You're a little slip of a girl."

"Nonetheless, I am R. L. Carter. I assure you I painted *The Stillbirth*."

"It's an indecent subject for a woman."

"How ironic a woman might endure a stillbirth yet be unable to paint one." Ruby bit her tongue before another such unladylike outburst escaped.

Dr. Zenker gaped like a beached fish. His cigar fell from his mouth onto his desk. He rose, shoved the tobacco back between his lips, and paced the floor trailing a cloud of smoke. "We cannot purchase the painting under these circumstances. Had we realized you were female, we would never have offered to buy the picture. You perpetuated a fraud on the art academy and on this institution."

"The image is the same no matter who painted it." Ruby

raised her chin and glared at him. "I'm not leaving until you honor the contract implied in your letter."

Cigar in hand, Zenker jabbed her repeatedly in the chest with his third finger. "Miss Carter, any contract is invalidated by your deceit. Unless you wish to add arrest to the list of your indecent behaviors, I advise you to take your leave."

She defiantly stood her ground until the smell of his cigar scorching her linen and lace jabot wafted upwards to her nostrils. With a last irate look, she backed away.

* * * *

Ruby stormed up the stairs to her studio, furious at her rejection. She was out several dollars for the boxing and transport of the canvas, had nothing to show for months of labor, and needed a new blouse. With Wheatley's claw hammer, she pried the nails from the crate, unpacked the painting, and leaned it against the wall. Damnation. It was a strong image. There was nothing wrong with it.

One by one, she lined up her drawings, sketches, and canvases in a row, studying each dispassionately. Her most hideous floral watercolors, she rejected outright and ripped to shreds, sending snow flying through the studio. The red-tailed hawk snatching a rabbit from the prairie grasses was quite good. Tough, realistic, vibrant, it was not as finely detailed as an Audubon, but the flurry of feathers and fur was intended to convey speed and power, not the ornithological details of a taxidermy specimen.

She kept her portraits of Ames, Wheatley, and two of Willow. They were decent. Her best canvases were those of home: Bismarck, other cowhands, livestock, wide-open plains, cold blue northers, fierce thunderstorms, and days when the sky lay white-hot above the earth. Every painting of home hinted of danger, the reality of a wilderness not fully conquered. Vultures circled overhead, a white-hot sun bleached a skeleton, a rattlesnake lay coiled beneath the hooves of a bucking bronco, cowhands drove cattle on a trail drive while rustlers, partly hidden by swirling dust, watched from a ridge.

As Ruby viewed the paintings she had done to satisfy Anshutz and other teachers, the ones that met their demands but didn't reflect her inner self, self-loathing consumed her. She had come to Philadelphia to study art but had not remained faithful to her own vision. Only her images of home demonstrated true inspiration. With a cry, she stabbed the first portrait through the heart with a palette knife and slashed the canvas with a violent *X*.

Someone pinioned her arms to her sides.

"Let me go!" She struggled to see who it was.

D'Este held her tightly against his body. "What are you doing?"

She jerked free. "Destroying craven images."

"Because some *cazzo* gave you a bad review?"

"No, because they're not *me*." She burst into tears, stabbing blindly at another rejected canvas.

D'Este restrained her again. "*Bella*, you're trembling." He pulled her to the bed, enveloped her in his arms, stroking her until her tears ebbed and she stopped shaking. "Tell me what happened."

Amid sobs and hiccoughs, she spilled the tale of her rejection.

"Wheatley was right, you know." He touched the moisture from her face with his handkerchief. "You should have let one of us men collect the money."

"But I wanted people to know"—she poked herself in the chest, fresh tears rising—"I painted it."

D'Este kissed the threatening storm from her eyes. "Wheatley and I warned you there'd be a scandal."

"The recognition would have been nice—and the money."

"Never destroy paintings, *cara*. Sell those you can unload. Paint over anything else—even Rembrandt did that."

"The object of art is not to produce sellable pictures. It is to save yourself."

He laughed. "You are a romantic, *Tiziana*, if you believe that."

He kissed her then, on the mouth, his lips scorching hers. His hands moved all over her, touching places they shouldn't. Softer than any man's had a right to be, his fingers were all too familiar with the workings of women's clothing. And it had been so long since she'd been touched.

Before she realized it, he'd opened her shirtwaist and pulled it from her skirt, kissing her shoulders as he bared new territory. The cool air raised goosebumps on her arms as he peeled the blouse from her. When he loosened her corset, she sucked in a tremulous breath as her breasts sprang free. Item by item, her clothing vanished until she wore only her chemise, petticoats, and pantalets. She covered her chest with her hands.

One by one, d'Este pried her fingers away, sucking on each, before removing her chemise. His mouth found her nipple, and a smooth hand meandered under her petticoats, feathering across her thighs until discovering the entrance in her pantalets.

Surprised, Ruby glanced up. Across the room, Bismarck stared at her from her painting. She pushed d'Este away then covered her face with her hands to avoid her fiancé's gaze.

D'Este twisted his torso to see what she had been looking at. Disengaging, he walked across the room, turned the picture to the wall then reclined on the bed. "Finish undressing. I want to watch."

Her face burning with embarrassment, she stood paralyzed.

"Go ahead. Take everything off."

She swallowed hard as she untied her petticoats, allowing them to tumble to her feet. Down to her pantalets, shoes, and stockings, Ruby stopped again. The thin fabric provided scant protection from his hot gaze. "Everything?"

"Yes." His blue eyes danced in anticipation.

Ruby unlaced her shoes and tugged them off before loosening the cord and letting her pantalets slither down her hips. Clad only in stockings, she stood before him. Flustered, she covered her breasts with one hand, her mons with the other.

He sprang up and gathered her in his arms, swirling her to the bed. Opening his pants only enough to release his manhood, he took her. "You made me wait too long. I can't hold back."

Afterward, Ruby felt rather like she had her first time with Bismarck. D'Este had finished too quickly. She was still aroused, incomplete. Willow had never left Ruby unsatisfied. She shrugged. Maybe every man was like that the first time.

D'Este stood and rolled Ruby's stockings down her legs. When she was completely naked, he led her to the modeling stand in the center of the studio.

He circled an index finger in the air. "Turn around. Slowly." He appraised her as she rotated. "You are lovely. Perfectly proportioned." His fingers traced every curve as he moved around her. When he completed his circumnavigation, he began again with lips and tongue, nuzzling the curls beneath her arms. He ended by kneeling before her and kissing the tangled spirals only Willow had kissed before.

Everywhere he touched, Ruby's skin sparked. Her fingers struggled desperately with his buttons, seeking contact with his skin.

His clothing joined hers in a jumbled pile. She looked him over. His form was somewhere between those of her other lovers, more muscular than Willow, yet without the definition years of hard work had chiseled into Bismarck. D'Este's smooth skin was a uniform olive where Willow's was pale cream and Bismarck's either sun-browned or lily white.

Ruby and d'Este tumbled to the bed together.

* * * *

Far more experienced than either Willow or Bismarck, d'Este made frequent love to Ruby. As he caressed her, she tried not to think of how many lovers he must have had. With their explorations, she grew more comfortable with his sexuality—and her own.

With his lean, elegant fingers, he traced her bare back with his fingers, his mouth following, gently biting one shoulder blade.

She giggled. "What are you doing?"

"Nibbling away your angel's wings." His teeth moved to the opposite shoulder blade.

"Why?"

"So you can fly only by embracing me." He turned her to face him, and his lips brushed hers. "Pose for me."

"I'll live to regret it, but—" She kissed him to seal the agreement.

Often to the detriment of her own work, Ruby modeled frequently for d'Este. Before or after painting, they made love.

He first painted Ruby as a modest farm girl, her body curved to balance the weight of a basket of produce slung on her left hip. A deep green blouse draped off one shoulder, riding above a russet skirt.

"Your portrait is finished." He turned the canvas so she could see. "I call it *Still-life with Girl*."

She let out a gasp of awe. "It's beautiful, Frank."

"Only because you are. You would be even more beautiful *completamente nuda*. I have seen you without clothing many times now. There is no reason for you not to pose for me."

* * * *

After their first lovemaking, Ruby had placed Mrs. Wycke's condoms in her reticule. With no desire to start a family, d'Este willingly used them and, when those were gone, purchased more. One day Ruby was wetter than usual when he withdrew from her after making love.

He shoved her away. "*Merde!*"

Bewildered, she gaped at him.

"Clean up quickly." He tugged a tattered sheath from his shaft. "The damn thing ruptured."

* * * *

At the studio two weeks later, d'Este demanded, "Has your *flusso* started yet?"

She shook her head.

"You better pray you're not *encinta*. I told you no *bambini*."

One morning, Ruby felt queasy on rising but decided the culprit was the rich food her lover fed her the day before. When the nausea became daily, she counted days on the calendar. Six weeks since her last cycle. Those damned condoms. They were supposed to prevent pregnancy. When she held them in her hands, they seemed sturdy enough. The venerable Mrs. Wycke had never mentioned that they might fail. Agitated, Ruby paced the floor of her room at Mrs. Wheelwright's, wondering what she would do. Above all, she feared a child would affect her ability to be an artist. She could bury her relationship with Willow deep within herself, but a child would be irrefutable proof of her infidelity. Any future with Bismarck would be lost forever. Married to a wealthy man such as d'Este, she would have more options, but she feared he would not marry her. Schedules and commitments meant nothing to him. His only constant was his inconsistency.

She knew he would be angry, thus postponed telling him. At last morning sickness gave her away when she threw up for the third time during her modeling session.

"Sick again? You've been ill all week. How can I transform you into a goddess if you can't sit still? Will you ever be normal again?"

"Yes. In six months. I'm with child."

Silence filled the room. He glared at her, then fished in his pocket and withdrew his wallet. "You didn't pray hard enough." He tossed a fistful of bills at her. "Get it taken care of." He blew out of the studio, slamming the door behind him.

Ruby stared at the quivering door in disbelief, appalled at his callous attitude. He hadn't stayed to talk about the baby or getting married. Instead, he acted like their situation was all her fault.

A week passed. D'Este abandoned her, staying away from the studio completely. Ruby demeaned herself by stopping at the Art Club and inquiring as to his whereabouts. The doorman told her d'Este had gone to New York.

She sighed. He had discarded her like a worn-out shoe. She knew what he wanted her to do—women whispered of such things behind closed doors—but was uncertain she could comply. What would he—or she—do if she didn't? And if she did, would he still care for her? While reading the *Inquirer,* an advertisement in the women's section caught her attention.

Mrs. Dr. Talbott Medical Company. Positively most reliable female specialist. 27 years without failure. Safe, painless relief of female complaints or money refunded. Advice and examination free. Terms moderate.

Newspaper in hand, Ruby knocked at a row home in a shabby neighborhood. A woman in a dirty apron but a sparkling white cap answered the door and motioned Ruby inside and directed her to a chair in the parlor.

Several minutes later, Dr. Talbott appeared. She, at least, appeared clean and well-dressed. After a brief interview, she led Ruby to a bedroom at the back of the house.

"Take off your pantalets, please. Lie down. Lift your skirts. I need to examine you."

Ruby obliged, though the bed sheets were so grimy she gagged. She closed her eyes and prayed, swearing if she got through this she would never sleep with d'Este—or any man—again.

The physician pressed deeply into Ruby's belly. "Four months along. You should have come sooner. There would have been less risk."

Alarmed, Ruby opened her eyes. "What are the dangers now?"

"Bleeding, infection, inability to have further children"—Dr. Talbott turned away and began arranging instruments on a metal tray—"Death."

The word *death* hung in the air over the tinkling of medical devices. Ruby had never considered that she might die here. No one knew where she was. If anything happened, the doctor had only to toss Ruby and her baby into a dank alleyway. The authorities would chalk her up as another dead prostitute. Her parents and Willow would be doomed to never know what became of Ruby. And Bismarck? She couldn't bear thinking about him.

Dr. Talbott tied on an apron so dirty, its original color could not be discerned. "Give the money to the nurse. Take off everything from the waist down and wrap the sheeting around you. Then lie back down."

Ruby placed her hand on her stomach and felt a massive surge as the contents of her stomach spewed upward. Still retching, she ran from the doctor's office.

* * * *

Ruby hid in her room at the boarding house, growing increasingly distressed. D'Este had never addressed the issue of marriage. Perhaps he, an Italian baron, thought he could keep her as a mistress until he tired of her. She hated him. She hated the baby. Most of all, she hated herself. For being a woman. For being weak. For succumbing to his charm. For having to pay such a high price for pleasure.

Since her visit to Dr. Talbott two days before, Ruby's stomach had grumbled continually. She threw up until nothing was left. When her nausea finally eased, she lay on her bed, half dozing, her fingers splayed on her barely curved abdomen. A little twitch beneath her hand startled her. Not the violent growl of her upset stomach, but something akin to fluttering butterfly wings. In that instant she knew she and the child belonged together. She—they—would somehow get by.

On her next visit to the studio, Ruby found d'Este sketching. He immediately demanded she resume posing and allow him to complete his canvas. They fell back into an uneasy relationship that, more than once, she was tempted to terminate. But, until things were settled regarding the baby, she hesitated. Siring a bastard would have no repercussions for him. She would be left with an infant and a tarnished reputation. Hoping for marriage—and a father for her child—she repeatedly deferred the final break but pushed him toward a decision.

"Frank, we need to marry before the baby comes."

He blew out an explosive breath.

"I won't pose for you any more. I'll return to Texas and claim I'm a widow. Or give the baby up for adoption." The words left her mouth before she realized it. She hadn't thought of that before. Maybe the child would be better off with a real family.

"I will not permit it. I cannot paint without you. And my son will not be tossed away *come spazzatura*—like garbage."

"If you want me, marry me." She dumped the green velvet drape on the floor, grabbed her clothing and began dressing.

Anger flashed over his face, replaced almost immediately with his oily smile. "*Certo, madonna.*" He stepped around his easel, kissed her then returned to his painting. "You'll be my Muse for eternity."

* * * *

Ruby stretched her neck. She had stood in the same position so long she felt faint. The studio was too warm. No air moved through the open windows. "I'm exhausted, Frank. I've held this position forever."

"Don't move!"

Heavy, damp, and hot, her hair hung down her back. Perspiration glued the drape to her body. Her arms tired of supporting its weight. Droplets of moisture slithered down her bare back. No longer able to conjure the demeanor of the goddess Demeter she portrayed, she felt as limp as a tomato plant in a drought. "My back hurts. I'm hot and sweaty. I'm going to faint."

"Don't move. Just a few more minutes."

"It's past eight. I need to go."

D'Este continued painting.

Another half hour passed. Ruby shifted on her swollen feet. "Now, Frank." She stepped off the modeling stand, laid the drape on a nearby table, and stretched her stiffened limbs.

He slammed his palette on the table. "I told you not to move!" He snatched her roughly and returned the fabric to her arms before forcing her back onto the platform.

"You're hurting me." She jerked away, jarring the table. His palette and brushes clattered to the floor.

"Watch what you're doing." He raised his hand and moved closer, ready to strike her.

Frightened, she backed away, moving toward the door. "I'm leaving, Frank."

His hand paused at the apex of its arc, then slowly dropped. "*Perdonami, cara.*" He plastered a stricken look on his face. "I'm sorry. I would never hurt you. Sometimes I get involved in work and lose track of time." Arms outstretched in a placating gesture, he walked toward her.

She backed against the door jamb, hand on the knob. "I need to go. Mrs. Wheelwright will lock me out."

He grabbed her.

Her body stiffened.

With a gentle kiss, he reassured her. "Don't fret. I'll hire a cab and take you home."

* * * *

D'Este helped her from the hansom and escorted her to the front door of the rooming house. Ruby glanced at her timepiece. Five past nine. Damnation. Quietly, she turned the knob. It didn't move in her hand. She jiggled it repeatedly, growing more desperate with each attempt. Locked. No sneaking in. Ruby knocked timidly. No answer.

With a forceful hand, d'Este pounded the door. "Open up, *per piacere*!"

Heavy feet treaded the floor. Mrs. Wheelwright herself cracked the door. "You're late, Miss Schmidt." Vinegar dripped from her voice. "And with a man."

He stepped forward and bowed. "It's my fault, *signora*. *Signorina* Schmidt is blameless. I failed to watch the time."

The narrow opening widened though Mrs. Wheelwright's bulk blocked the door. "And who might you be?"

He clicked his heels together. "Barone Francesco d'Este." He extended his hand.

Mrs. Wheelwright gave a wily smile then opened the door wider to accept his hand.

He clasped her fingers and brought them to his lips. "*Gentilissima signora*, please allow *Signorina* Schmidt to enter. In the future, I shall return her to your care promptly."

The habitually dour expression returned to Mrs. Wheelwright's face.

"*Per piacere*?" He adopted a placating tone. "Surely such a handsome woman remembers the joy of being young—and in love?"

Ruby blinked in astonishment as the intimidating Mrs. Wheelwright batted her eyelashes, preened, then finally giggled in response to d'Este's attentions.

After a long pause, she relented. "Just this once, Miss Schmidt."

* * * *

D'Este laid his palette on the table, walked toward Ruby, lifted the heavy drapery from her arms, and knelt before her. His hands cupped her buttocks as he kissed her rounded belly. "*Facciamo l'amore*. Let's make love."

"Frank, I need to go. Mrs. Wheelwright will kill me if I'm late again." She tousled his unruly curls. "If we were married, I wouldn't have to go home."

He did not respond but stood and pulled her before his canvas. "*Guarda*! Look. It's finished."

Ruby's heart plummeted at the sight of the completed image, *Demeter Carrying Zeus' Child*. It was extraordinary. She was beautiful, skin radiant, hair long and wavy, breasts high and round. But she couldn't be that far along. For weeks, she had assiduously avoided looking at herself in the mirror, afraid to confirm her appearance. Yet, as she placed her hands over her abdomen, she knew d'Este's painting didn't lie. Thoughts whirled through her. Going home was impossible. Her parents would be ashamed of her. Her father would never accept an illegitimate grandchild. And Bismarck was lost to her forever.

Chapter Sixteen
Expulsion from Paradise

January 1893

Ruby stormed around the studio, fighting the urge to throw d'Este's belongings out the window into the street. Immediately upon finishing her portrait, her mercurial lover, despite swearing he'd marry her, left for Boston to meet John Singer Sargent and James McNeill Whistler. He promised to be gone only a few days. When three weeks passed without word from him, she concluded he never intended to make her his wife.

Ruby tried to paint, but her predicament swirled through her head as erratically as the wind-tossed snowflakes outside. With her tenth exasperated huff, she decided to go home. Bundled against the winter cold, she returned to the boarding house well before dark.

The second Ruby removed her coat, Mrs. Wheelwright accosted her. With a ferocious wag of her finger beneath Ruby's nose, she said, "This is your last night in this house, Miss Schmidt. Tomorrow morning you will remove your belongings. I maintain a home for Christian ladies." The wagging finger declined its angle to indicate Ruby's abdomen. "And you are scarcely that."

"But—"

"You knew the rules, girlie."

Ruby had hoped for more time to get situated but, left

with no alternative, she stayed up all night packing, her thoughts churning. That wretched d'Este had deserted her. She could not return home with a child. She had enough money in savings to see her through the pregnancy, but as soon as the baby was born, she would have to find work.

The next morning, she transported her possessions to the studio, planning to live there while searching for other lodgings. The facilities were Spartan, but with the addition of a chamber pot and forgoing bathing for sponge baths, she could manage until she found a place of her own.

She visited the Haven for Unwed Mothers and Infants on North Franklin Street. The three-story building with a picket fence was pleasant and roomy. The Lady Manager informed Ruby the home served innocent women who had been seduced but were capable of returning to decent lives. After pointed questions about Ruby's religious beliefs and whether she had any useful skills, the matron determined Ruby to be inadmissible. Her teaching certificate did not outweigh her chosen profession as an artist.

* * * *

In mid January Professor Anshutz halted Ruby as she worked and asked to speak with her in the hall. There, he advised her Mr. Coats wished to see her. She draped a sheet over her easel before walking to the administration office, her heart thumping with dread. At the president's door, she hesitated. Finally, with a deep sense of foreboding, she knocked.

A gruff voice sounded through the oak door. "Come in."

Timidly, Ruby entered and stood before the President, her fingers twisting her skirt into knots.

"Miss Schmidt," Mr. Coats began without preamble. "One of your professors has brought to my attention that you are"—he cleared his throat and looked down, avoiding her gaze—"with child."

Ruby's face burned with anger more than shame. She had hoped her voluminous artist's smock might disguise her belly a few more weeks. Anshutz had betrayed her, she was certain. The man who orchestrated the dismissal of an artist like Eakins would think nothing of ridding the Academy of a wayward female student.

Coats flipped through a file on his desk. "The Academy provides an education for students of the fine arts who aim to become professionals. A woman with children cannot hope to achieve that goal. She cannot serve both art and family but best attends her duties by providing a good home for her husband and offspring." He scribbled a few words on the file then closed it. "Your tuition for the remainder of the year is forfeit."

Ruby dashed from his office. Barely suppressing her tears, she haphazardly packed her paintings and supplies. Arms laden with her belongings, she encountered Wheatley in the hallway.

"Red? What's wrong?" He reached to help her with her things.

She held up her hand, warning him away. Her watery eyes would spill over if he offered any sympathy at all.

Wheatley stopped at her gesture. "I'll find you later, then? At Albion's?"

She nodded. Standing on the curb with her possessions, she flagged down a hansom and hauled everything to the studio.

There, nearly wearing out the wooden planks as she paced, she wondered what she would do if d'Este did not marry her. She had the teaching certificate her parents insisted she obtain, but that did little good when she was too pregnant to be hired. With careful budgeting, she could get by until she delivered, then she had to find a position. She curved her hand over her belly and felt the baby's kick. She wondered if she could give her infant up for adoption. If not, to avoid scandal, she must pose as a widow. Should she return to Truly, the options were no different, but the same lies, if told to Bismarck and her parents, somehow seemed larger.

* * * *

Three weeks later, d'Este waltzed into the studio, swirling her around as he kissed her.

She jerked away. "Where have you been?"

Unperturbed, he explained he'd extended his visit once he met Boston socialite Isabella Stewart Gardner and her coterie of artists and writers. "At a Paris auction, she purchased Vermeer's *The Concert* and just returned with the painting. The canvas was the talk of Boston. At her salon, she permitted a select few to view it."

"I thought we were getting married."

"*Non preoccuparti, bella.*"

"Are you waiting until the baby falls out?"

"*Porca madonna!* Don't worry. I gave you my word, the word of a gentleman, and you doubt me?" He gave a lazy scratch to his nose.

Ruby thought sure he'd back out at the last minute, but he showed up at the Philadelphia City Hall and only thirty minutes late. Their impersonal ceremony, witnessed by two clerks with ink-stained fingers, was unattended by friends or family. No flowers. No ring beyond the cabochon he wore on his left hand. Once he placed it on her finger, Ruby switched it to her thumb until a jeweler could size it.

Relinquishing his suite at the Art Club, d'Este arranged accommodations at the Gladstone at Pine and Eleventh. The two of them did not need such luxury, Ruby argued. He replied that nothing in America was as grand as the *palazzo* he'd grown up in. With a you-win shrug, she surrendered to her new husband's wishes. They joined children of railroad and industrial tycoons who no longer lived with their families but who required the elegant accommodations of Philadelphia's first luxury apartments. From the rounded turret of their seventh floor corner unit, the City of Philadelphia lay before Ruby, and she could watch the daylight play across its streets.

Once furniture filled their home, draperies adorned the windows, and their paintings enlivened the walls, Ruby settled into her domain. Spoiled by room service and a maid, she spent her time painting, reading, and stitching adorable baby clothes. Pleased that the capricious d'Este had abandoned his bohemian ways, she reveled in her marriage, basking in his painterly eye as he produced caring images of her growing body. They made love frequently. The best part of being with child, she decided, was being unable to get pregnant. That knowledge gave her freedom to explore her husband as she once had Willow.

Their new place supplanted the studio as a meeting place for d'Este's friends. Artists, writers, and actors dropped in most evenings paying court to art and literature. Horace's famous words, "Either to please or to educate," became the motto of d'Este's salon to the extent he painted them in bold letters on the wall of their parlor: *aut delectare aut prodesse est.*

When conversation grew ribald, when opium pipes and cheroots laced with cocaine appeared, Ruby retired to her bedroom, tugging the pillow over her head to drown out raucous male voices. "Cow patties. If they spent less time talking and more time working, they'd all be successful."

* * * *

Drowsy from an afternoon of loving, Ruby lay across

d'Este's arm. "Tell me about your family. We're married, yet I know nothing of you." She swirled a finger across his chest. "What's your family like?"

"My father poisoned my mother."

She bolted upright in shock. "How horrid. Are you certain?"

"Mother was in perfect health one day"—he snapped his fingers—"Dead the next. I was ten years old. Between Giacomo, Andrea, and me, Father had heirs aplenty. He wanted to marry his newest mistress. He didn't need Mother any longer. "

Ruby caressed his cheek. "You poor little lamb."

"*Fa niente.* Mother was beautiful but icy. *La bambinaia*, the nanny, was far more kind than my mother. Later, tutors raised us boys." He rolled on his side, gazing at Ruby. "A Titian nude hung in Mother's bedroom. A woman with red hair. Beautiful like you. We children visited Mother for half an hour each evening after our supper as she dressed to go out. Waiting my turn to be coddled, I studied that painting, memorizing every brushstroke, vowing someday I would both paint like Titian and have such a woman to love me. When Father remodeled the palazzo for his new bride, he removed everything of Mother's. So I placed the Titian in my suite." His wide grin made him look boyish. "That painting sparked my imagination for years." He leaned nearer, spiraled Ruby's curls around his fingers and drew her close for a kiss. "When I saw you at the Academy, *la signorina coi capelli rossi*, I knew my dreams had come true."

He pushed her aside and reached inside a drawer in the bedside table.

He dangled a necklace before her. "Do you like it?"

She took it from him, turning it in her hand. Light pranced off dozens of glass beads, each composed of tiny flowers. "It's beautiful."

"It's *mille fiore*. A thousand flowers. From Murano, a village outside Venice." Turning to her, he took the necklace from her and dropped it over her neck. After watching the beads tumble between her breasts, he grabbed an envelope from the nightstand. "*Tiziana*, Saint-Gaudens wrote from New York. He'll take me on as a private student."

Ruby's heart stopped. Recently, her husband, based on a sole meeting with Augustus Saint-Gaudens months before, had decided to give up painting for sculpture. The sculptor's reputation as a teacher was superb. With a wife and child, though, d'Este had responsibilities.

"You turned him down, of course?"

The pause before his reply grew too long.

"You bastard. Did you think I'd let you go if you softened me up with lovemaking and a gift?" She flung the sheets aside and stomped around the room. "What about the baby? Me?"

He stood. On her next circuit, he grabbed her and roughly shoved her on the bed, pinning her down. "*Calmati*. I'll be away only a couple of months. Anyway, I promised fellows in the New York Art Students League I'd visit again. I'll—what is it you Americans say?—kill two birds with one stone?"

"Let me go." Immobile, Ruby stared pointedly at where his thumbs pressed deeply into her flesh, her skin whitening beneath the pressure. "You're hurting me."

His gaze followed hers. Abruptly he released her.

She rubbed her arms, knowing bruises would show by morning. He never meant to hurt her, but his temper so often got the best of him. "I won't let you go." She tore Saint-Gaudens' letter to shreds and tossed the bits in the air.

D'Este backhanded her. His heavy signet ring, the one

that replaced the cabochon he'd given her at their wedding, caught her mouth, splitting her lower lip.

Ruby turned away. Her reflection in the mirror above the dresser showed a dribble of red running down her chin. Not a big wound, but somehow, because he drew blood, it felt worse than the many bruises he had caused before. She wondered how he would hurt her next, if she and the baby would be safe. The quivering of her lower lip as she fought tears made the blood flow faster. With her tongue, she wiggled her teeth to be sure they were sound. The salty flavor in her mouth drowned the sweet remnants of his taste from their earlier loving.

Behind her, he studied her reflection in the mirror, the blood trickling down her face. He gave a hoarse moan. "*Merda*. I didn't mean to—" He pulled her into his arms. "*Perdonami, cara.* I'm sorry. But I am the man. I make the decisions for my family."

Ruby nodded sullenly. "Why did we marry if we're not going to be together?"

"I *will* go to New York."

"Think of the baby. Of me."

"*Non preoccuparti, bella.* Don't worry."

"Please—" As she begged him to stay, she remembered that, to pursue her own dreams, she had abandoned Bismarck and the house he built for her. She shoved d'Este away. "Go. I don't care."

"If I remain in New York, I'll send for you. *Ti prometto.* I promise." He turned her toward him, kissing her on the lips, tasting her blood, trailing kisses down her body, leaving red smears from her mouth to her mons, making slow love to her.

A fold of the sheet rubbed Ruby's shoulder blade raw. Her head banged against the headboard with his thrusts. The elevator clanked in the background. Its doors swished open. Someone got out. Several people actually. Giggles. Voices engaged in aimless chat. Perhaps they would knock at the door and interrupt. Their heels clacked on the floor but passed. A knock sounded far down the hall. Ruby prayed d'Este would finish quickly. She didn't wish to reward him with her release, but he persisted until her body betrayed her.

* * * *

Once d'Este left for New York, Ruby halted his salons. Frankly, his bohemian buddies had come for the food and drink her husband provided with abandon. She let the maid go. It seemed foolish to pay the woman to clean up after one person. Ruby retreated into the apartment, into herself, painting in a desultory fashion, feeling too frumpy and heavy to move.

From her turret, Ruby painted a spring storm as it lashed Philadelphia. She jumped as a particularly loud clap of thunder sounded. Her water broke. After hours of increasing pains, she asked the Gladstone concierge to send for her physician, associated with Pennsylvania Hospital. At three a.m., announced by lightning and thunder, Gian-Battista Francesco d'Este entered the world. Ruby prayed the weather did not portend her son's future.

Creating art was difficult at best, and as the care of babies necessarily hampered artist expression, Ruby had been less than thrilled with her pregnancy. Willow wanted no children, but Ruby thought a reasonable number—one or two—might be nice, as long as she didn't endure a string of stillbirths like her mother.

To Ruby's surprise, the perfection of her boy's tiny fingers and toes entranced her. His little face, nuzzled against her breast, stirred tremendous emotions. She understood her mother's statement about the rewards of motherhood. When she found herself sketching pastel portraits of her sleeping baby, she laughed but promised herself she would not turn into a Mary Cassatt. She would remain a person separate from her child and would not submerge herself in her family as her mother had.

She wrote d'Este of their son's promptly birth but never knew if her husband received her letter. The World's Columbian Exposition was being held in Chicago to celebrate the four-hundredth anniversary of the discovery of America. Saint-Gaudens served as its artistic advisor. D'Este accompanied Saint-Gaudens on his travels to the Windy City, thus the two men were rarely in New York.

Wheatley called on Ruby soon after the baby's birth and immediately declared *Gian-Battista* too hard to spell. "By God, he's an American. He needs an American name. He's a Johnny if I ever saw one."

One day, when Ruby returned from walking Johnny in Washington Square, she opened her apartment to find a thick envelope slipped under her door. She slit it open with her sewing scissors to find her rent was overdue. Tucked inside, she found an itemized list of expenditures for wines, liquor, flowers, cigars, all willingly—and expensively—supplied by the building's concierge.

Furious, she stormed around their apartment. That son of a bitch. D'Este paid the lease six months in advance then took off. He left her with spending money but not enough to cover their exorbitant rent. How stupid she had been to trust him. Those first happy months of their marriage had eased her fears about him. She thought he'd changed.

If Ruby discharged the debt out of her Gran's legacy, she would use most of her savings. She tried negotiating with the management at the Gladstone, asking them to wait until her husband returned. The bastards remained unmoved by her plight. Pay up or be evicted seemed to be her only choices. So much time had passed without a word from d'Este, she could no longer rely on him. After arranging an allowance for leaving the furnishings, she paid the past due amount plus a week in advance to give her time to search for a less expensive place.

When Mrs. Wheelwright had turned Ruby out of the boarding house, she'd moved into the studio. She rejected that idea this time. Difficult to heat in winter, hot in the summer, the studio facilities were so wretched she would have trouble keeping herself clean, much less an infant. To pinch pennies, she must relinquish her workspace.

Of the original band of friends who'd rented the atelier with Ruby, Willow was in Europe. Fred was leaving for Paris in a few weeks to study at the *Académie Julian*. God alone knew where d'Este had gone. When she next saw Wheatley, the only other of the group who remained, she would talk to him about giving up the space.

Babe in arms, Ruby searched Philadelphia for a new home and ended up in the Italian section. On impulse she stopped by Farinelli's Ristorante and Bakery, an eatery that served Italian food and catered to working-class men. The wife had cooked Venetian specialities for d'Este when he grew homesick and conjured the delectable treats he brought Ruby while courting her. Occasionally, he had taken her to dinner there.

If he ever returned, d'Este would eventually visit the restaurant. *Signor* Farinelli could tell her husband she had left the Gladstone. With a heavy sigh, she entered the restaurant and explained her plight.

The husband and wife conferred briefly behind the counter.

To Ruby's surprise, they offered to rent her a third floor

walk-up. The *signora* led Ruby up two narrow flights of stairs, past the restaurant on the ground floor and the Farinelli family lodgings on the second.

As they climbed, the women chatted.

"That Frankie. He's like a son to us, but"—*Signora* Farinelli shook her head—"sometimes, like all men, he is *imprudente* and *sconsiderato*. He never thinks beyond the moment."

The third floor was divided into four tiny apartments with a shared bath down the hall. Ruby held back a sigh at the dark, gloomy suite. "I'll take it." Though ashamed to live in such squalor, she no longer had a choice.

Her problems had become so all-consuming, she could not confide in her family. On the rare occasions she corresponded with them, she wrote half-truths, reluctant to admit the fine stew she had gotten herself into. Her father's "I told you so" resounded through her head. Recent newspaper stories told of bank failures in the center of the United States but nothing yet in eastern cities. Her mother had written of tightening circumstances at the ranch. The situation back home was downright ominous if her optimistic mother even hinted at a problem. Ruby resolved to keep her situation to herself. Her ma did not need anything else to worry about.

When Ruby wrote Willow or Bismarck, she edited herself severely, unwilling to reveal how her grief and loneliness had led to infidelity to both lovers.

* * * *

After relinquishing the studio, Ruby crammed her art supplies and canvases into her three-room apartment and hung a few paintings. Back when she considered herself in love with d'Este, she had painted him. Looking at the portrait now, she had captured the glint of malice, even madness, in his ice-blue predator's eyes but failed to recognize it. Bereft of Willow and Bismarck, she had too easily fallen prey to his charms. Sorting through her paintings, throwing away the worst, keeping the best, she found she could neither discard d'Este's portrait nor hang it. Though still married to him, she couldn't bear his malevolent glare staring down at her every day. If he never returned, someday little Johnny might wish to know what his father looked like. Ruby stacked most of her canvases against the wall, hiding her portrait of him behind the others, then pushed her bed against the artworks to hold them in place. Once her paintings were stored, she barely had room to maneuver around the furniture.

Over time, *Signora* Farinelli, who had recently immigrated from Venice, told Ruby the history of the d'Este family, former rulers of the City of Bridges. For centuries, they had been infamous for hot tempers, impetuosity, exploitation, sexual predation, and general savagery, and d'Este had inherited those propensities.

After shopping for a few groceries, Ruby carried Johnny upstairs to her living quarters and tucked the sleeping baby into an over-sized basket to nap while she painted. She wondered how she would get anything done once he was mobile.

Ponderous steps on the stairs, followed by a rapping on her door, interrupted her work.

Half-hoping, half-fearing, it was her husband, she opened the door.

A depressed-looking Wheatley entered and flung himself on the settee. Its springs screeched at his weight.

Ruby placed her palette and brush on the table then sat beside him. "Is everything all right?"

He shook his head. "I'm going home at the end of the week."

"Why?"

"The stock market collapsed. In January, when

Cordage's profits were at sixteen percent, my father put everything we owned there. The company's gone belly up. My family's broke."

"I'm sorry, Ira." She patted him on the shoulder. "What will you do?"

"I have to support my family. We can't live on what I make at the *Inquirer*." He glanced over at the dozing Johnny. "What about you, Red. Any word from Frank? He's been gone months."

Ruby gritted her teeth, biting back angry words.

"That bastard." Wheatley shook his head.

She giggled. "I generally call him 'that son of a bitch.'"

He laughed. "Except for *cow patties*, I've never heard you curse before."

Her face contorted in a wry grin. "It seems only Frank can drive me to profanity."

Wheatley took out his wallet. "I'll give you what I've—"

"I can't take your money. Not under the circumstances. I have savings in the bank. At least now I don't feel guilty giving up the studio."

"Let me introduce you to the folks at the *Inquirer*. You could take over my illustration work." He thought a moment. "I'll leave the etching press, too. You can make ends meet until Frank returns."

Wheatley and friends carried the printmaking press to Ruby's apartment. It occupied most of her tiny kitchen, but knowing it might keep her from starving, she covered it with an old sheet and cooked around it, eating her meals in the parlor.

Chapter Seventeen
Ideal Marriages

June 1893

Before Wheatley left, under his tutelage, Ruby refined her engraving and etching skills. She supplemented her income, thanks to his introductions, doing wood block prints or etchings for the *Inquirer*. Once a week, the newspaper sent her home with boxwood blocks, about five inches in diameter, and copies of the ladies' stories or advertisements she was to illustrate. Her boss, a gruff man, relegated her to boring fashion illustrations for the women's section of the newspaper. Anything in the least bit manly, she submitted under her pseudonym, R. L. Carter. The pay, nine dollars a week, was abysmal, scarcely more than a shop girl's wages, but she was a mere woman, hired on a trial basis to boot. She found it infuriating men received double that. Eighty-thousand people saw her drawings daily. Perhaps one day she might find a commission for real art.

* * * *

Leaving Johnny with the Farinellis' daughter, Lidia, Ruby planned to stop at the bank then the *Inquirer* to pick up her next week's work.

To her surprise, as she stepped into her financial institution, the guard shoved her back outside, slammed the door in her face, and locked it. Ruby banged on the door hard enough to rattle the glass, causing its gold lettering to shimmer in the sunlight. "Let me in. I need to make a withdrawal."

The guard flipped the *Open* sign to *Closed* and jabbed his finger at the *Until Further Notice* handwritten beneath in large black letters.

Ruby stuck her tongue out at him, a childish gesture, but she was tired and cranky. The weather was unseasonably warm and humid, and Johnny had fussed all night. She had slept no better. They had both been sticky with sweat even with damp towels pressed against their bodies to cool them off.

Though she hammered until her fists hurt, the bank door remained locked. Every day for a week, Ruby joined others pacing in front of the financial institution trying to get in. The immediate need to retrieve her limited funds overrode her need to find employment. Without cash, she would be forced to take the first position she found rather than seek art commissions.

The people surrounding her, mostly men, wore blunted expressions. Their downcast eyes refused to meet her gaze. At first, people queued neatly. The men at the front banged on the door, just as Ruby had, as person after person tried to gain entrance.

"Open up!"

Nothing happened. The line shifted, losing its straight form. People surged forward en masse, shoving toward the door, hoping to be the first to enter should the bank unlock its doors.

"We want our money!" One by one, folks took up the refrain. "Open up!"

One man swung his fist at someone who jostled him. Others immediately joined the fight.

Ruby wiggled through the throng, sliding between people, forcing her way toward the building. There she slipped along the brick wall, dodging the crowd, until she stood on the marble steps of the bank.

A uniformed guard cracked the door and yelled through the slit, "Quiet down before we send for the police."

Ruby was close enough to force a hand into the opening. "Let me in."

"Go home. The bank's folded, lady. Gone completely under." He slammed the door, pinching her fingers. When the door didn't close, he pushed harder.

She screamed and banged on the door with her free hand.

Realizing her predicament, the guard opened the door a scant inch.

With a backwards jerk, she freed herself but lost her balance and tumbled into the crowd.

Someone roughly shoved her upright. "Watch where you're going, lady."

Damnation! Gritting her teeth to keep from screaming while shaking her hand to relieve its ache, she was unsure whether the pain or the loss of her inheritance caused her tears. Every penny that remained of Gran's legacy had vanished.

* * * *

Back at the studio, she counted her assets. The emergency money from her pa remained hidden beneath the lining of her steamer trunk along with the last of the money—forty dollars—d'Este had given her. Fourteen bucks were in her reticule plus odds and ends of coins she had tossed in a jar. One hundred fifty-four dollars and sixty-two cents. That was it. Her net worth fit into one hand. She wondered why she had ever trusted the bank. Her fellow boarders were in and out of each others' rooms at Mrs. Wheelwright's. People had popped in and out of the studio and the Gladstone apartment constantly, some were friends of friends, others strangers. Her funds would have been in greater jeopardy in her trunk than in the bank vault.

The next morning, an article in the *Inquirer* announced several local bank failures, hers among them.

Ruby sat on the settee, pencil and paper in hand, budgeting her few dollars between rent and food. She could not skimp on her own sustenance as she was breast-feeding. If she sold what little remained from her belongings from the Gladstone, she might scrape together enough money to return home but not enough to ship her possessions. Her time in Philadelphia would be wasted if she left all her paintings behind. She could not survive on the nine dollars a week the *Inquirer* paid. Every cent of that went toward rent and paying Lidia to care for Johnny. Ruby needed to supplement those earnings to save money for returning home, but companies were not hiring. Frustrated, she sank her head in her hands.

Daily, Ruby's situation grew more bleak. Finally, she decided if she did not find a job in the next week, she would write home for help. Before she could face that dreaded task, Ruby received two letters from her mother. She opened the thick one first.

> *My Dearest Ruby,*
>
> *How I have missed you these last weeks. Your sisters remain too young to understand a Lady's difficulties. Were you home, we could console each other as only womenfolk can.*
>
> *For the twelfth time, I was with child—and again lost it. I have come to hate the carrying of babies—too many of my Children lie buried in this harsh land—and I hate God for the heavy burden*

He placed on my Heart.

For days, a dust storm has plagued us. I fear for my mind. Dust composed of the bones of my Babes suffocates me. I am so disconsolate I might join the coyotes in their nightly howling. For the first time in a quarter of century, I dream of returning to Chicago, to civilization.

So many banks have failed in the Southwest, ranchers are unable to raise funds to get cattle to market. Your Father let most of the cowhands go. Under the circumstances, I could not keep Mrs. Jenkins to help around the house.

We are near losing our land. All your Pa and I have worked for, these many years, is drifting away like dust.

You are better off in Philadelphia.
Your loving,
Mother

The second letter sounded more like her optimistic mother, which only heightened Ruby's sense of dread.

My Beloved Daughter,

Please forgive my last letter. Unfortunately, before fully considering my words, I rushed to give it to your father as he rode into Truly.

When I wrote, I was peculiarly downcast. A dust storm had blown in, with days of whirling red sand followed by the inevitable cleaning of grit from every crevice.

It has rained—though not enough—and the world is green as far as the eye can see. Rest assured, Daughter, I wear my usual rosy glasses and know our Family shall endure all God places before us.

> *Your loving,*
> *Mother*

Immediately Ruby replied with encouraging words to her ma, not revealing her own predicament. She didn't wish to multiply her parents' burdens, thus neither going home nor telling her family of Johnny were options. She mailed the letter knowing it was the last time she would write. Silence seemed preferable to lies.

For days, leaving Johnny in Lidia Farinelli's care, Ruby trudged from mansion to mansion in the wealthiest sections of Philadelphia, until her feet ached and her knuckles grew bruised from knocking on doors, offering to paint portraits of the inhabitants. She gained two commissions among high society in Fairmount Park and Pennsylvania Railroad's Main Line, but not enough to make ends meet as an artist. With the tightening economy, even the wealthy spent little on luxuries.

Because she was a woman, clients assumed she would paint sweet views of mothers with children, similar to those of Violet Oakley or Mary Cassatt. Thus, if she received a commission, it was for work she loathed. Because she was female, patrons paid her less, and she was desperate enough to accept what they offered. More and more she agreed with Mrs. Wycke that a woman should be paid a man's wages if she did a man's work.

When her emotions reached their bottommost, Ruby received a long overdue letter from Willow.

> *My darling Ruby,*
> *For the past month I have been desperately ill*
> *with pneumonia. I am now well enough for Walter*
> *to take me to Lake Como to continue my recovery.*

Though lovely, Venice is simply too damp for my lungs. My parents will be returning to West Chester in September.

I hope to see you again soon, to hold you close. I miss painting with you.
Yours Always,
Willie

Willow had blacked out her postscript so thoroughly Ruby couldn't read it, but by pressing the letter against a window pane, she made out *Walter is a good man, but our marriage is scarcely what I anticipated.* In silent agreement, Ruby nodded. Like Willow, she hesitated to confide that her own union was less than ideal.

Sometimes dreams of Willow swirled through Ruby's sleep, clear blues and sparkling violets. Other nights brought visions of Bismarck's pure browns and earthy greens. More frequently, d'Este shaded her nights, deepest black with swirls of hellfire, laced with the knife-edge of violence.

* * * *

Ruby read the newspapers daily looking for work. The *Inquirer* reported that a quarter of the city's inhabitants relied on the bounty of others for survival. The bank failures quickly brought a recession to Philadelphia. She took solace in knowing she wasn't alone in being broke. Though she hadn't reached the point she needed charity, the soup kitchen was only days away.

"*Signora d'Este,*" Giuseppe Farinelli called as Ruby climbed the back stairs going to her room. "Have you gotten any new commissions?"

She shook her head. With her rent two weeks overdue, she had known this conversation was coming.

"*Merda!*" he replied. "That Frankie, he's no good. Do

you have family you can stay with until he returns?"

"No." Ruby couldn't admit that her parents were in worse straits than she was.

"One of our girls didn't show up. Help us out in the restaurant." Giuseppe waved an apron at her. "We'll take care of you until Frankie comes home."

Though her feet ached from walking all over Philadelphia searching for work, she slipped the heavy canvas over her head and began serving customers.

With her money nearly gone, she was grateful to the Farinellis for the job. She worked in their restaurant, leaving Johnny with Lidia and her three children. At least she earned a meager wage, and the Farinellis made sure she ate well. Ruby lacked time to paint for herself, spending her days in the restaurant and her evenings doing woodcuts for the newspaper.

For the first time, the *Inquirer* entrusted her with an important commission, a series of articles on the effects of the western drought. Ruby was thrilled despite knowing she got the job because she was familiar with the subject—and no one else drew animals well.

For the illustrations, she drew on her memories. The dry spell had begun before she left Truly, but recently the situation had become critical. With only rare downpours, insufficient to replenish the water table, the land was suffering. Grass dried out. Great cracks appeared in the soil. Her father's letters described neighboring ranchers selling off massive numbers of cattle. During February, March, and April 1892, over 100,000 animals were shipped from San Angelo to the Indian Territories. Over-grazing exacerbated the effects of the drought, causing further injury to already-depleted land. The combination of increased production costs, the stock-market crash, and bank failures forced many small ranchers out of business. Bigger operations, able to ride out the situation, curtailed production. Others, like her pa, caught in between, were barely holding on. During the lean days of the droughts of the 1880s, those of her childhood, her family had eaten nothing but beans and beef for months. Skin-and-bone cattle roamed the *Llano Estacado,* and coyotes grew fat as lap dogs.

Holding those harsh images in her head, she rested an etching plate on a circular sand-filled leather cushion. The pad allowed her to carve delicate undulations with minimal manipulation of her engraving burins. Wheatley, bless him, had left her a full range of tools, a square tint burin with teeth to create closely spaced fine contours, a stipple tool for small dots, V-shaped gravers for hatch marks, flat and rounded scorpers, and her favorite, the spitsticker, for fine curves.

Ruby poured her knowledge of Texas and ranching into those illustrations, populating them with folks she knew. As she carved the familiar landscape into the wooden blocks, a well of longing as deep as the Truly spring grew within her. These etchings, in the vein of *The Stillbirth*, were hard-edged and stark. Unlike her paintings, the illustrations were well received, her work acceptable as newspaper illustrations but not fine art.

* * * *

January, 1894

Christmas and New Year's Day came and went. Ruby scarcely noticed. Fortunately, Johnny was too young to know. Her workday over, Ruby sat the heavy cast iron pot of leftover soup *Signora* Fratinelli sent home with her on the floor while she let herself into her apartment. Her feet hurt. Her back ached. Her arms felt leaden. She couldn't wait to sit a few minutes. She carried the pot to the kitchen and set it outside. With winter here, her stoop was cool enough to keep the soup good until tomorrow. She was grateful for the *signora's* charity. Ruby would not have to cook on her day off and would have more time for her baby and her illustrations.

Warmth flooded her heart as she anticipated picking Johnny up from Lidia's. Once he was in her arms, she could cuddle him while resting her weary feet. She had seen her son a scant twenty minutes at her lunch break. He was growing by bounds, and she was missing most of his babyhood. His first words were in Italian. His first steps took him into another's arms. More and more she regretted the long hours she worked.

She felt for the box of safety matches on the table and prepared to light an oil lamp before running downstairs to retrieve her son.

A ghostly moan rose from the blackness. Frightened, she dropped the match before she could touch it to the wick. It fell to the floor, sputtering out. Blinded after its brilliance, she squinted her eyes peering into the gloom.

A deeper groan made her shiver.

Holding her breath, she glanced around the parlor. Nothing seemed amiss.

Another sound. A loud snort.

Ruby tiptoed to the bedroom and gingerly pushed the door open with one hand, holding the unlit lamp in the other. The rank odors of alcohol laced with unwashed man raked her nose before her eyes re-accustomed to the dimness. A dark form lurked across the white linens of her bed.

From the murkiness, another groan, then "*Tiziana, w*here have you been?"

Ruby struck a match. "Frank?" Her voice quavered.

"Aren't you glad to see me?"

She forced her lips into a smile while her heart thumped a tattoo. He had returned. Her thoughts careened from hoping that her life would improve to certainty that it'd be worse. She wasn't aware she'd been singed until the match fell. Flames flared on the carpet. She ground them out with her shoe before striking a third match and lighting the lamp.

"*Dio*! That's too bright. Put it out."

Ruby set the oil lamp on the dresser and dimmed it. "Where the hell have you been?"

"New York, Chicago, Montreal."

"You've been gone months. Didn't you think I'd worry? That I might need to know where you were? I wasn't sure you got my letters. Eventually, I didn't know where you were, so there was no point in writing."

"I knew you'd wait for me." He reached up and pulled her into his arms. "Forgive me, *cara*."

She resisted his embrace. "How did you find me?"

"The Gladstone said you'd moved out. I checked with the Farinellis. They told me you lived upstairs and let me in."

And they'd conveniently failed to mention to Ruby that her wayward husband had returned. She studied her husband. Dark circles rimmed his eyes. His face seemed haggard, no, dissolute. It wasn't worth fighting with him at this hour of the night. "You look tired." She attempted diplomacy. "Why don't you get some rest?"

His face sparked with a predator's leer. He sat up and yanked Ruby into his lap. His actions sent a half-empty bottle of rye spinning across the room. After a rough kiss, he said, "*Facciamo amore.*"

"Maybe later." Ruby wrinkled her nose and dodged away. Her usually fastidious husband reeked. "I need to get the baby from downstairs. He's beautiful. Wait until you see him."

He grabbed her arm, his fingers stabbing the soft flesh of her upper arm. "Leave him be."

"But you've never seen—"

"Forget him." He jerked his wife back to bed and silenced her with his hand, releasing her only to cover her mouth with his.

Half an hour later, while her husband snored, she ran down the stairs to gather Johnny from Lidia while apologizing profusely for her tardiness.

* * * *

"How did things go with Saint-Gaudens?" Ruby said the next morning, hoping d'Este, if not painting, was at least sculpting.

He didn't reply to her question, telling her instead about the Chicago World's Fair with its elaborate exhibition halls, the Palace of Fine Arts, and Buffalo Bill's Wild West Show located nearby. "The Fair closed October thirtieth, and I returned to you, *bella*."

Ruby rolled her eyes. "That was two months ago. Where have you been since?" Clearly, her husband made time for her only when he had nothing better to do.

"Here and there, *bella*. Here and there."

After initially refusing to talk about his time with Saint-Gaudens, Ruby's husband finally admitted the sculptor had said d'Este's eye was better suited to painting. "What does he know, anyway?"

"You're a wonderful painter. Can't you be happy with that?"

"You weren't content with what you were. You came here to study art."

"I'm trying to become what I was meant to be, not something beyond my capabilities."

He slapped her. "*Porca madonna*! Even you turn against me."

Ruby turned away, her hand clasped to a cheek already

hot from the blow. His temper was worse than ever. An innocent conversation provoked him this time. She could never
again speak freely in his presence.

Her husband took Saint-Gaudens' rejection personally
and slid into melancholy. Ruby sensed something else both-
ered him, but he wouldn't confide in her. He only left their
apartment to buy liquor—when he didn't have wine sent up
by Mr. Farinelli, the cost of which was deducted from her
wages. More frequently he used the small morocco leather pouch that held cocaine, morphine, syringes and needles,
floating in a haze for hours, too clouded to threaten her. He
frittered away his days in bed, half-dressed, content to live
in their hole-in-the-wall above the restaurant, never offering to move back to the Gladstone, never helping with the
bills, uninterested in painting. Before he spent lavishly. With
money to spare, he never considered what something cost.
Now, except for drugs and alcohol, he spent little. She wondered what had happened to the allowance from his father
but dared not inquire.

As she raced to drop off her completed illustrations
and pick up her next assignment, the brilliant colors of a
poster in the front window of the *Inquirer* caught her eye.
She backtracked to investigate a playbill advertising *Buffalo
Bill's Wild West and Congress of Rough Riders of the World.*
On the right, offset in a box with curlicued corners, Buffalo
Bill, astride his white-maned palomino, wore his signature
fringed buckskin jacket and black chaps. Men in red ban-
danas and colorful shirts, performing acrobatic tricks from
horseback, occupied the rest of the image. She peered in-
tently at the horses, realizing the artist had no concept of
equine anatomy. She could do better. Inside, a stack of the
playbills lay on the reception desk. On her way out the door,
she helped herself to one. On second thought, she twirled

and grabbed another.

When she returned to her apartment, muffled cries from little Johnny leaked through the door. Distraught, she fumbled with the key. Finally she dropped her belongings to the floor so she could manage more easily and opened the door with trembling hands.

Sprawled on the settee in the parlor, d'Este snored.

Ruby heard her son but could not see him. Finally, she localized his whimpers and found him stuffed inside the closet, frightened, cold, dirty, and hungry. She cuddled and fed him until he quieted, then placed him in his crib in the bedroom while she retrieved her things from the hall.

Stepping back into the parlor, she shook d'Este awake. "How dare you lock your son in the dark."

"He would not be quiet. I had a *mal di testa*, a headache."

"You mean you were drunk again."

D'Este stood and hit her hard, splitting her lip again, this time deeply. Then he beat her worse than Woodrow had.

When he finished, Ruby lay huddled on the worn carpet, trembling, unable to move.

Breathing hard, he swayed and fell heavily onto the settee.

A snore told her he had passed out. Ruby dragged herself from the floor. By shoving the bed in front of the door, she locked herself and Johnny in the bedroom.

The next morning, she came out of her room, praying her husband was sober. When she didn't find him, she rejoiced. Hallelujah—better than being sober, he was gone. For days, after working at Farinelli's, she hauled her bruised body up the stairs. When she opened her flour canister to add a hard-earned dollar to her egg money, the bills she had hidden there were gone. That son of a bitch.

For weeks Ruby jumped at every stray sound in the night

in constant dread of d'Este's return. Equal parts relieved and angry, she prayed he would stay gone and renewed her efforts at escaping Philadelphia.

She tacked one Buffalo Bill poster on her kitchen wall, the swirling dust and western men evoking home. The other she drew over in pen and ink, correcting the anatomy and improving the composition before mailing it, along with a request for a job, to Colonel William F. Cody.

A week later, she realized she was pregnant again—and Johnny not yet a year old. A sorry start to the Year of Our Lord 1894.

Chapter Eighteen
The Black Hand

Spring 1894

Ruby climbed the steps to her apartment two at a time, her shift at the restaurant over at last. The odor of food all day long had kept her in a perpetual state of pregnancy-induced nausea. For the moment, she bypassed retrieving Johnny from Lidia's care and raced up the narrow stairs. She'd pick him up in a minute. Before she could do anything else, she needed to throw up.

At the top of the stairs, the hall lamp was out—as usual. She had walked the hallway so often in the dark she didn't need the illumination. Oddly, a narrow beam of light spilled through the cracked door of her apartment. Certain she'd locked up before going to work, she panicked, fearing d'Este had returned. Quietly, she peeked inside and gasped.

Appalled at the damage, without thinking, she pushed the door wide open.

Every piece of furniture had been destroyed. The settee and chair cushions had been sliced open, their horsehair and cotton stuffing strewn in haphazard clumps through the parlor. Loud noises reverberated from the bedroom.

A burly man stepped from her bedroom. A snowstorm of feathers flew around the room as he tore apart her pillow.

Startled, she turned to run.

Much faster than someone his size ought to be, he raced

across the room. Grabbed her right arm. Pinned it behind her back. Spun her into her parlor.

Already near vomiting, she gagged. Stomach acid burned her throat.

"Pasquale! The *baronessa* is here."

Baronessa. She had never thought about it before but marrying d'Este had made her an instant aristocrat. Her gaze swept around her squalid apartment. She snorted. Some *palazzo*.

A second man, shorter but more powerfully built, stepped from her bedroom.

"*Signora d'Este*? Where is *il barone*?" His thick accent parodied her husband's.

"I have no idea. He left two months ago."

"Hold her, Salvatore."

The first man forced her wrist further toward her shoulder blade.

She winced.

He wrapped his other arm tightly around her throat.

She could hardly suck in enough air to remain conscious.

"*É secura*? You're certain?" Pasquale stepped toward her, whipping his arm back to strike her.

Desperately Ruby nodded her head. Bile rose in her throat, bitter and nasty. She gagged several times then, unable to stop herself, she retched. Vomit spewed on the arm of the man holding her and on the other man's shoes.

"*Merda*!" He slugged her.

The vicious punch caught her in the belly. Her head snapped forward then back. Had Salvatore not been supporting her, the blow would have knocked her over. Her dizziness flared. More nausea.

Cursing loudly, Pasquale poised to strike her again.

Her stomach erupted again with an audible grumble.

Pasquale backed up to avoid the liquid spewing from Ruby's mouth.

While Salvatore pinioned her, Pasquale finished searching her apartment, wreaking havoc on the kitchen. He upended her flour canister onto the floor. Through the swirling white powder, he waved the three dollars he found there. "This all you got?"

Still tasting stomach acid, she nodded slightly, fearing a more vigorous motion would trigger more vomiting.

He sliced open her reticule with a stiletto and dumped out its contents, claiming the few bills she had there. "No more money, *signora*? Your *sposo* is a wealthy man."

She shook her head, the effort making her feel more light-headed.

"He's in big trouble. He owes *il capo* a lot of money. If he doesn't pay up—" The man made a slicing sound through his teeth as, holding his stiletto an inch from his own throat, he indicated her husband's fate.

"He left me penniless and pregnant. You can kill the son of a bitch for all I care." The man had not been around for weeks yet still managed to disrupt her life.

Pasquale stared at her, his mouth agape, before laughing. "*Lei ha coragio, signora*. You have courage."

The thug pinning her arm behind her led her to the couch and shoved her to a seated position. "*Mi dispiace, baronessa*. I did not realize you were with child."

Pasquale returned her few dollars, shaking his head in sympathy. "Even thieves have honor." At the door, he turned back. "When you see *il barone*, tell him we look for him."

Ruby spent days cleaning her apartment, cursing her husband as she replaced the stuffing in the cushions as best she could and draped quilts and blankets over the furniture. Repair of the items would cost more than she could pay.

Even moving to a safer place wasn't feasible.

When she told Mr. Farinelli about the men, his eyes widened. "*La Mano Nera*, the Black Hand. *Tutti criminali*. You are lucky to be alive. Maybe your Frankie has been gambling?"

Though Ruby redoubled her efforts at saving money to return to Texas, she made little progress. She despised working in the restaurant, loathed having so little time to paint, and, when she did have time, detested spending precious time doing horrid illustrations of corsets and bloomers. Her bright dream of becoming an artist had become a bleak nightmare.

Johnny was so active now, keeping him out of trouble during his explorations of the apartment seemed a full-time job. Though she tried to work while he slept, many times she was forced to imprison them both in the bedroom. Ruby could not imagine coping with another child. In a desperate mood, she visited Dr. Talbott again. When she arrived at the row home, newsprint covered the windows. The office had closed.

* * * *

While Johnny napped on a drizzly spring Sunday morning, Ruby strung twine from one side of her parlor to the other from nails she hammered in the wall. She washed clothing and diapers, wringing them out with red raw hands and hanging them to dry. The heavy clouds outside made her already-dark rooms gloomy. Though she resented the expense, she lit the kerosene lamp before settling near the window. There, surrounded by her mangled furniture, she chiseled a design into a wood block for an advertisement for women's knickers.

A knock interrupted her carving. She fought her way past the dripping laundry to the door, holding her breath while listening with her ear against the door before opening it.

Men's voices came from the other side, none she recognized. Not d'Este. She exhaled in relief. A worse thought occurred to her. The Black Hand had returned for their money. Her heart raced at the thought. If she failed to open the door, they would batter it in. With a deep breath to steady her trembling hands, she turned the knob.

Two men stood before her, a third one hidden behind them, all expensively dressed. The odor of wet wool escaped their clothing. Fine droplets of rain, visible in the lamplight, spangled their shoulders and hats.

Ruby was suddenly grateful the darkness of the hallway hid the dingy paint and the tired carpet. But nothing disguised the odors of crowded living and cheap cooking.

"Is this the home of Mr. R. L. Carter?"

She nodded, her knees weak with relief. The Black Hand wouldn't know the name she painted under.

"May we speak to him?"

She stammered. "I'm Ruby d'Este. I paint under the name R. L. Carter."

The first two men looked surprised. The third man stepped forward, extending his hand. The light from the kerosene lamp in her room struck his features.

Ruby caught her breath as she recognized the most well-known face in the world. She glanced down. Dirt from her tools and oils from the wood block stained her fingers. Before greeting him, she swiped her hand against her apron. "You got my letter?"

Though he wore a dark serge suit and vest rather than the buckskin jacket she expected, he smelled of leather and the West, scents so evocative of home her heart skipped a beat. A mustache swirled above his mouth. From his chin, a narrow waterfall of a blond beard dripped with gray. Long hair fell to his shoulders, topped by a western hat a shade lighter than his curls.

"Yes, ma'am. I surely did." He lifted his hat. "May we come in?"

She nodded, turned, and mutely motioned the gentlemen inside. Aghast, she glanced around and began yanking her undergarments from the line. Removal of the laundry merely emphasized the lumpy settee cushions and the shabbiness of her home. She opened her mouth to apologize.

"Don't worry." He chuckled. "We apologize for dropping in unannounced. Won't stay but a minute."

"I'm Nate Salsbury," one of the men said. "This is Frank O'Donnell, our press agent. He forwarded your letter to Colonel Cody." He nodded toward the colonel. "I'm sure he needs no introduction."

"How do you do, Colonel Cody?" Good manners dictated that Ruby address him as Colonel, but like the rest of the world, she thought of him simply as Buffalo Bill. "It's a pleasure to meet you."

"Likewise. I'd expected a man, but no matter."

Ruby bobbed her head, still dumbfounded that Colonel William F. Cody himself stood in her parlor. "Please t-t-take a seat."

"No need." He nodded. "I was impressed with what you did on the poster you sent. Do you have other works I can see?"

"Certainly." Then, realizing where her other paintings were located, her cheeks warmed. "T-t-they're in the bedroom."

The Colonel laughed. "Lead the way." He nodded toward his companions. "We'll be well-chaperoned, Mrs. d'Este."

Ruby and the three gentlemen trouped into her tiny bedroom where the men moved her bed away from the stack of paintings. She stood on the far side of the bed and, with the help of Mr. Salsbury, handed paintings to the Colonel.

Two dozen pictures later, Buffalo Bill wiped his hands with his handkerchief. "I've seen enough." He walked through her hanging laundry to the front door. Pulling a business card from his wallet and a fountain pen from his pocket, he scribbled on the reverse and gave it to her. "My show opens tomorrow."

She nodded, having seen the posters tacked to every available surface in the city. Philadelphia was abuzz with excitement.

"Call on me tomorrow, say four o'clock? I have a business proposition for you." He tipped his hat, and the three men exited without further word.

Ruby sank into her chair and turned the card over and over in her hand, staring at the words in amazement:

Col. W. F. Cody (Buffalo Bill), President
Buffalo Bill's Wild West
and Congress of Rough Riders of the World
The Largest Arenic Exhibition known in History

Weeks ago, when she had first seen the poster advertising the Wild West Show, she had been tempted to attend just to get a glimpse of cowmen and to see how true to life such a spectacle might be. Ultimately she decided the thirty-five-cent ticket was beyond her means. Now she had an appointment with Buffalo Bill himself.

* * * *

The next afternoon Ruby took the omnibus to the Wild West show grounds at Columbia Avenue and Twenty-Ninth

Street, a few blocks from the Philadelphia and Reading Railroad line. From there she walked to the railroad. Glancing at his card, she verified the directions scrawled on the back. She passed each car, checking for the number fifty. When she found it, she took a deep breath and pulled herself up the steps of a private Pullman. No one answered her first timid rap. She knocked more loudly. A porter greeted her and led her into a plush office where Buffalo Bill sat with the men she'd met the day before.

Today he wore the expected buckskin jacket with long fringe and beadwork across the front. Ruby closed her eyes and inhaled deeply. The scent of the Wild West seemed more pronounced.

He stood, reached over his desk, and shook her hand. "I just finished the afternoon show. The next starts in two hours. Come, Mrs. d'Este. We've work to do."

Taking her elbow, he led her outside where they walked a short distance along the train tracks, Mr. Salsbury following. "Those western illustrations you did for the *Inquirer* were strong, even manly. No insult intended to such a lovely young lady."

"Thank you."

"I knew right away you were the real thing, not some dandy."

"I was raised on a ranch in Texas."

"It shows. Fine work. Good attention to detail." Buffalo Bill gave her a hand up into a railroad car. "We have two advertising cars and employ several lithographers for our posters." Buffalo Bill pointed out his employees. "But I want something different. Real art, by God, fine portraits of our top attractions. These guys wouldn't know art if it bit them in the a—pardon me—in the horse's patootie. That's where you come in."

Mr. Salsbury added, "In 1897 we're heading into Canada, and early in the next century we'll be in Europe. We need gifts suitable for heads of state like our own President and European royalty like Queen Victoria, Kaiser Wilhelm II, King Umberto of Italy, maybe even Pope Leo XIII."

"We'll set you up right here." With a sweep of his arm, Buffalo Bill indicated the lithography car they stood in. "Our stars will come to you. You can sketch while the show's in town, then do the actual artwork once we've moved on."

Before Ruby could say a word, the Colonel peeled a slab of bills from his pocket and handed them to her. "This is a one-time deal. Half now. Half when you deliver the pictures. Start tomorrow." He pointed at a man sitting at the far end of the railroad car. "Leave Joe a list of supplies you'll need." He walked away, then turned back. "And find a safer place to live."

A knock at the door interrupted Buffalo Bill. "Be right there," he said to the cowhand at the door before addressing his vice-president. "Nate, be sure she gets a front row seat in the reserved section tonight."

* * * *

Once she was dismissed, a dazed Ruby shoved her hand deep into her pocket, the still-uncounted bills clenched in her fist. She walked the few blocks to the venue on Columbia Avenue. Though she enjoyed watching the Venetian Glass Blowers, the rest of the sideshow acts—Olga, the Snake Enchantress, Millie Owen, the Long-Haired Lady, or J. McClellan and Ben Powell, the Electrograph and Mind-Readers—held no interest for her.

She wandered a small tent city, bustling with people costumed as the Rough Riders of the World: Cowhands, Indians, Union soldiers, English lancers, German cuirassiers, Cossacks, and Arabs. Stifling her nausea, she dodged animal droppings and mud puddles and made her way to her seat.

As Ruby watched the performance, she had not antici- pated the pull on her heart from the sight of the cowhands and longhorn steers and the fragrances of animals, manure, and hay. She sniffled, filled with remorse at having lost what she loved most. With trembling fingers, she removed the mon- ey from her pocket, counted it, and slumped in relief. Three hundred dollars with more to come. Enough to go home on.

The next morning, she begged Mr. Farinelli for a few days off and returned to the fairgrounds. True to his word, Buffalo Bill had organized a workspace for her in the second lithography car. He provided Ruby with photographs of his performers to supplement her sittings. Some, like Wild Bill Hickok and Sitting Bull, were now dead, and photographs were her only resource for their likenesses. Buffalo Bill did not take time from his busy schedule to pose for her.

While waiting for the sharpshooter, Annie Oakley, to arrive Ruby sketched Sitting Bull from old photographs of him taken before his death in December 1890. She'd read newspaper articles describing how he had been killed at his cabin on the Grand River.

For a week, leaving Johnny in Lidia's care, Ruby sketched in the lithography car and made over a hundred drawings of a dozen performers, making sure she caught their essence on paper, knowing she wouldn't get a second chance.

When the Wild West Show moved to the next town, she gave notice at the *Inquirer* and downstairs at the restaurant and settled down to complete her assignment. Reluctantly she continued to leave Johnny in Lidia's care while she com- pleted the artwork, promising him things would be better soon.

Ruby spent days compiling her sketches into portraits

of each Wild West star, transferring the images to etching plates, then printing them with Wheatley's press. While sitting before her window, she hand-tinted each black and white image and watched her artwork come to life—yellow buckskin beaded in bright colors, red flannel, and blue denim. Last, she wrapped the plates in soft flannel to protect the surfaces and shipped them and the etchings to Buffalo Bill.

His check came promptly by return mail, thanking her for her work and advising her that if he needed future art, he would contact her.

Ruby felt rich. Six hundred dollars total. Enough to return home *and* set up a studio for herself. Without a second thought, she bought her ticket to Truly.

At home, Ruby swung the toddling Johnny from the floor, swirling with him until they both laughed. "It won't be long, little boy, until I have more time for you. And painting. We'll ride horses. You can play outside."

Later, as he napped, she wrote her parents. She started dozens of times but crumpled page after page, tossing them to the floor. Since leaving Truly four years ago, she had changed. Her love for Willow must remain her deepest secret. Little of her failed marriage could be confided to her parents, especially her father, with his conservative views on the sanctity of wedlock. Somehow the proper words never appeared. In the end, she decided the less said the better and sent a terse telegram:

Arriving Truly July 9th. Ruby

Chapter Nineteen
Homecoming

Truly, July 1894

As the whistle announced the train's arrival in Truly, Ruby's unease grew. The days confined in the railroad car had seemed interminable. Suddenly, she'd reached her destination. Even without the heat, she would have known she was home from the herbaceous odor of grasslands mixed with the smell of manure from the nearby cattle yard. Joyful at the prospect of seeing her family, yet doleful at returning home a failure, she remained seated, fingers twisting her linen handkerchief, while everyone else disembarked. The conductor stepped into the Pullman car, counting off passengers and checking tickets.

"Need any help, ma'am?"

She shook her head.

"Then move along."

She stood and peered out the cinder-specked window. On the wooden platform below, her father paced. Eyebrows pinched together, her mother walked the length of the train, peering through the windows for her daughter.

Ruby sighed. Too late to turn back. She should have warned her family of Johnny and the baby to come. Like she should have told Bismarck. Those letters had proven too difficult to write. Now, she realized letters would have been easier than facing her loved ones in person. She swallowed, tucked her hankie up her sleeve, and wondered again if she had made the right choice.

With a gentle jiggle, she awakened Johnny. "Sweetie, we're here."

His eyes fluttered open. After a momentary frown at being disturbed, he drifted back to sleep.

Ruby smiled at his innocent face as she tied her bonnet under her chin.

"Come on, Johnny, rise and shine." She gave him another little shake then stuffed her carpetbag with the baby sweater she was knitting, her sketchpad, and their books. The tartan lap robe she draped over one arm.

Johnny yawned and blinked.

"We're home." With one hand she helped her son stand while hoisting her bag with the other.

Immediately, he started to run off.

She snatched for his hand but missed, nearly losing her grip on their belongings. "Slow down."

Looping the basket over her right forearm, she grabbed Johnny by the straps of his short-legged brownie suit to keep him close at hand as they moved single-file toward the exit. The simplest way to restrain him would be to carry him, but her arms were full of their belongings. She juggled things and took his hand at the door. Before stepping onto the platform, she hesitated.

From the wooden planks below, her father lifted his arms to assist her, his eyes level with her belly.

She glanced down. The tartan blanket hid her six-month pregnancy. With a slump of relief, she realized she could avoid the issue for another minute or two.

Noticing the boy, her father blinked. His face taut with disapproval, he bore Johnny to the ground then reached for her carpetbag, impatiently wiggling his fingers for her to give him the tartan as well.

With reluctance Ruby handed him the blanket, revealing her stomach.

Pa's eyes opened wide. His lips disappeared in a tight grimace. He placed her articles on the wooden platform before taking her elbow and helping her from the car.

Unsteady on solid ground after five days in a rocking railroad car, Ruby swayed slightly.

Her father tightened his grip.

She thanked him with a grateful half-smile.

He gave her a pat on the arm, as close to a hug as he had given her since she turned into a woman, and from the fierce expression on his face, she deemed herself lucky she got that.

Now that Johnny was no longer confined in the railroad car, Ruby feared he would bolt like a skittish colt. She grabbed her son's hand. "Ma, Pa, this is my son, Gian-Battista. Johnny for short."

Her mother snatched the boy into an exuberant hug.

He wailed with fright and broke free to bury his face in Ruby's skirts. To comfort him, she ran her hands through his sleep-tangled curls.

"Let me get a good look at you, child." Nettie stepped back a couple of paces, running her eyes down her daughter's form, stopping at the rounded abdomen. "My goodness." She blinked but quickly recovered, her arms enveloping Ruby and the boy. "Honey, I feared I'd never see you again."

Ruby withdrew slightly, pulled out her handkerchief, and patted her mother's tears away. "Ma, don't cry." Her mother looked ill, worn down. Her face held more fine lines, her hands were parched, her skin rough, like Texas dust had sucked out every drop of moisture.

"Ruby." Her father's gruff voice interrupted her thoughts.

She faced him. "Yes, Pa?" He looked older, too. Leaner, more wrinkles near his eyes, new lines of strain around his tight-lipped mouth, his hair gone completely white. The drought had been hard on both her parents.

Anger radiated off him like heat from a potbelly stove. He stared at her but avoided looking below her chin. "Your mother and I deserve an explanation."

"I know." Ruby lowered her eyes. A slow flush of shame rose on her cheeks. With so much to tell her folks, she didn't know where to start. Nor did she desire having that conversation in the middle of the train station.

Johnny's chirping voice broke the silence. "Mama, horsey?" He started to cry. "Ride horsey?"

Before she could reply, the staccato clatter of shoes on the wooden sidewalk and the call of "Ruby, Ruby!" marked the arrival of Molly Statler.

Ruby groaned. Hope faded that she would be able to slip out of Truly without having to explain why she was pregnant and husbandless. Molly had effectively announced to the whole town its wayward girl had returned.

Pretending she didn't hear, Ruby knelt beside Johnny, her handkerchief brushing away his tears. "Johnny, horses will pull the wagon today, but the riding horses are at the ranch. I'll show them to you tomorrow." She blotted her own damp eyes.

Molly embraced the kneeling Ruby from the rear.

Ruby stiffened, twisted from Molly's arms, and stood.

"You're finally back." Molly took Ruby's hands, noticing the wedding ring even before the belly. Her eyes widened. "Does he know?"

Ruby shook her head.

"Ruby, how could you? He'll be devastated."

* * * *

Her pa drove the wagon past Helles' Belles, the local brothel a half a mile outside of Truly, before he reined the wagon to a stop. "We need to talk, Ruby Louise."

Ma protested. "Now, Hermann. She's just arrived."

He turned to glare at his daughter in the rear of the buckboard. A long moment later, he filled his pipe, struck a match, and puffed a while. In the silence of the plains, the tobacco crackled as it captured the flame.

His methodical actions increased her sense of foreboding. Ruby looked at her lap. Her fingers twisted knots in the fabric of her skirt.

"She's not setting foot in my house until she explains herself. Why didn't you write? Your mother worried herself sick over you."

"I know, Pa. I'm sorry."

"Are you really married?"

"Yes, sir, I am." Ruby raised her chin and stared at her pa.

"Did you have to get married?"

She hesitated.

"Don't lie to me."

"Yes, sir." She lowered her gaze. "I did."

"You failed to live up to your name, Ruby Louise. You weren't raised to behave that way." He glanced down the road at the brothel, then back at her, scowling over his spectacles. "Your husband doesn't seem like much of a provider. What kind of work does he do?"

"He's an artist."

Her father humphed. "Doesn't he have a real job?"

"He's an Italian nobleman. A baron. He's never worked a day in his life."

With a snort, her father replied, "Any man worth a hoot works for a living. Where is he now?"

She shrugged. "Wish I knew. He left months ago. Never came back. I'd divorce the son of a bitch if I could find him."

Eyes wide, her father recoiled. "Hellion child, you'll abide by the Lord's teachings. Such language will not be tolerated in my house."

Ruby had not realized how outspoken she'd become living in Philadelphia surrounded by bohemians. "Yes, Pa." She tried to sound contrite.

"There's never been a divorce in this family. Never will be." Her father glared at her. "You've come home with your tail between your legs, without a pot to piss in, and two little ones to support. Your sisters can use their legacies to help their husbands buy land. You squandered every cent."

Ruby squared her shoulders. "I paid for my education. That money wasn't wasted. It's not my fault my bank failed." Surely God couldn't blame her for telling a half-truth. Her pa would have a fit if he learned she used most of her savings to pay overdue rent at the highfaluting Gladstone.

Her pa puffed on his pipe several minutes.

Ruby's apprehension grew with every second of his prolonged silence.

At last, he said, "You may live at home. Things are real tight around here. Everyone's got money problems, not just us. We're holding onto the land by the skin of our teeth. I sold most of the cattle for pennies on the dollar and let the hired help go."

"But I'd planned to open an art studio in town."

"Your Ma's with child again, four months along, and can use your help. She laid off her housekeeper. Pearl's getting hitched in the fall. You will live at home, and you will behave yourself. No more little bastards."

"Yes, sir."

"You'll have to come to terms with God about that boy. At least the baby you're carrying now was properly conceived."

"But, Pa—"

"No more talk of divorce. You made your bed, girl. You best lie in it." The wagon rolled forward a few feet. Pa stopped again. "And I better not see you wasting your time with a paintbrush. Near as I can tell, all it did was loosen your morals." Her father flicked the reins, and the horses started forward.

As the wagon jolted homeward, Ruby sensed reproach every time her father stole a backward glance at her. Grateful to be in the rear with her son and luggage, she avoided his accusing eyes. The cart lurched over the dusty rutted road, the jerking motion worse than the train. Exhausted, she dozed off and on. Snuggled in her skirts, Johnny drifted in and out as well.

When the wagon reached the house, a lad of ten ran alongside, his yelled welcome accompanying the excited yips of the family dogs. "Ruby! Ruby's home."

Surely this gangly stripling could not be her little brother, Jasper.

Her younger sisters Pearl and Beryl, wiping their hands on their aprons, stepped from the house. In their eagerness to hug her, they bounced on their feet. Lordy. Their eyes were level with her own. Girls no longer, they had blossomed into young ladies. Infected by their joy, for the first time Ruby thought she might survive returning home.

To make up for not greeting her at the station, Beryl and Pearl cooked her favorite foods. Ranch beans. Cornbread, crunchy and gritty on the outside, meltingly soft in the middle, laden with butter, but not sweet like Philadelphia

Yankees made it. Cobbler concocted from peaches picked this morning.

Ruby wiped her mouth with her napkin, removing the last sweet syrup of the dessert.

Pa stared at her. "What happened to your lip?"

With her tongue, Ruby rubbed the scar. Her father had made her feel so uncomfortable about her marriage she couldn't confide what really occurred. "I slipped on the ice last winter."

* * * *

Ruby climbed the stairs to the girls' second floor bedroom. Hermann and Jasper followed, carrying her trunk.

"You'll want to freshen up. I'll heat water for your bath while you unpack." Her ma's voice followed Ruby up the stairs.

Ruby would share a room with her sisters as she had before she went back East. Johnny would sleep with her until the new baby came. She removed garments from her steamer trunk, shaking out dresses to hang in the chifforobe, folding blouses, stockings, bloomers, camisoles, corsets and Johnny's clothes to fit in the two drawers her sisters had allotted.

Her father and Jasper carried in her final portmanteau and her paintings.

While making her bed, she unfolded her quilt and draped it over the footboard. Somehow, the covering seemed more at home here. With one finger, she traced the outline of the nine-patch pattern. So many tiny flowers. A thousand flowers. *Mille fiori*. D'Este had taught her those Italian words when he gave her the Murano necklace. Once, other fanciful terms of endearment, *cara* and *bella*, flowed from off his tongue, back when he swore they were dual angels sharing a pair of wings. Thrusting aside unwelcome thoughts, she decided to put this quilt, her own *mille fiori*, into a painting someday.

As a gift for her father, Ruby had framed several artists' proofs of her etchings for the Wild West show, those of Buffalo Bill himself, Sitting Bull, and Wild Bill Hickok. She removed the remainder of Buffalo Bill's money from the secret compartment in her trunk and put it in her pocket.

Downstairs, she found her father in the parlor. "Pa, I did some art work for Buffalo Bill."

He raised a doubting eyebrow.

"I thought you might like them." She gave him the images and awaited his verdict.

He glanced at the pictures and set them aside.

Disappointed in his lack of response, she continued, "I'd want you to have the rest of what Colonel Cody paid me. To help out around here."

"I'll not take what little you've got, Ruby Louise. You'd best save it for emergencies."

"Your water's ready." Her ma's voice sounded from the kitchen.

Ruby excused herself, knowing the conversation with her pa would go no further, besides, she was unable to resist sinking into the tub and soaking away a week's worth of coal dust and travel grime.

First, she bathed Johnny. Reluctant to sit long enough to get clean after days of enforced stillness on the train, he wriggled about, slippery as a soapy tadpole.

"If you settle down, I'll read to you when we're both spick and span."

With her promise, after lowering his head to the water and loudly blowing bubbles, he allowed her to scrub him.

She relished his baby-smooth olive skin. With the tangle of black ringlets inherited from his father, Johnny could have been a *putto*, a chubby little angel painted by Fra Angelico.

She tugged his nightshirt over his damp curls before sending him to her mother in the kitchen.

Once her son scampered from the water closet, Ruby slid into the tub and allowed the warm water to ease her tight muscles. When she dressed, her clean shirtwaist fit snugly in the bust. To have room for her growing breasts, she needed to let it out soon. Leftover from her first pregnancy, she had skirts with drawstrings and a corset with laces along the front bottom to accommodate her expanding waistline. In Philadelphia she had purchased a paper pattern and fabric for two Mother Hubbards, dresses with loose gathers hanging from the bust. Early in her confinement, a woman belted the dress around her waist. Later, she cinched it beneath her breasts.

Ruby collected Johnny from the kitchen where her sisters were spoiling him with sugar cookies and led him upstairs. Together, they sank onto her bed. Johnny, with his thumb in his mouth leafed through a book of nursery rhymes. He'd always had to be good, to be quiet while she painted, and, living in the city, he never had the opportunity to run wild outdoors.

"I promise things will be different here, sweetie." With a quick wiggle of her fingers, she tousled his hair. "Tomorrow you can feed the chickens."

He rewarded her with a rare view of his tiny toddler's teeth. "Horsies?"

"Tomorrow we can ride horsies." It was good to make a promise she could keep. With a laugh, she pulled him into her lap to read nursery rhymes before tucking him into bed.

* * * *

That night, joining Johnny in her childhood bed, Ruby tossed and turned. The light pouring in from the full moon and occasional soft snores of her son and sisters were not the trouble. After the noise of the city, the interminable chugging of the train, and the chatter of her family as they became reacquainted, the silence deafened her. Careful not to disturb her son, she slipped out of bed and stared out the window. Home. As far as she could see, the land belonged to her father. Cooing mourning doves settled for the night in the cedar elm near the front porch. Closest to the house lay the yard and garden. Further out were the stock pond and windmill. Beyond that lay what she had missed most while living back East, the wildness of the plains separated from the homestead by a barbed wire fence. Tonight, moonlight silver-plated puffy clouds strewn across a cobalt sky and gave an argent shimmer to the grasses below.

She pulled her sketchbook from beneath her bed. To test her memory, she had painted a watercolor of the scene before she left Philadelphia. Flipping to the page, she held the image at arm's length. Back East, the pigments she used seemed right. Here, even by moonlight, they were wrong. Life in the city had changed her palette, grayed her colors, shading them with the perpetual coal dust that coated everything. The same cold gray had enveloped her heart.

With her quilt draped around her shoulders, she eased down the stairs and out the back door, closing it gently behind her to avoid waking her family. Making her way to the pond, she dropped to the ground, propping her back and head against the windmill tower, wrapping herself in a thousand flowers. As a young girl, she sat toward the plains, dreaming of riding in the company of conquistadores or Indians. When a teenager, in her dreams she shared a horse with Bismarck, relishing the hardness of his muscles and the warmth of his body. Their ride always ending with them sprawled in the grass, their limbs wound around each other.

Tonight she faced the house, changes settling in her soul, wondering if her parents' home would prove a refuge or a prison. Above her, the steel blades of the windmill creaked as they rotated the crankshaft, transmitting their slow vibrations down the frame into her body like the heartbeat of the earth itself.

In the distance a coyote howled. Seconds later its pack replied in a raucous caterwaul. Her face contorted with tangled emotions, she threw back her head and wailed with them.

Ruby was nearly asleep when warm arms gathered her tight. Recognizing Bismarck's scent of leather, horse, and Prince Albert tobacco, she smiled. He slid between her and the windmill leg, his denim thighs wrapping outside of hers. Her back rested against his chest. The thump of his heartbeat was as reassuring as that of the earth. She sank into him like the past had never happened. When she realized what she had done, she sat up quickly and swallowed hard, clearing a sudden lump from her throat. "I'm sorry. So sorry."

"Hush, little one. Molly told me you were back." Rough hands stroked her hair. "I knew I'd find you here."

When he pulled her back against his chest, she sighed. Her home was in his arms. But, because of her own stupidity, she no longer belonged there. Surely, just this once, it would not hurt to seek comfort.

Silence stretched between them.

"Tell me what happened." The stubble of his whiskers scratched her cheek as he whispered in her ear.

"I was lonely. Stupid. Naive." She told him the parts of Philadelphia she found herself unable to write him or her family—at least most of them. "Do you hate me?"

"For a while. Not any more."

A wail from the house shattered the quiet. "Mama? Mama!"

Ruby's heart beat faster. She pulled herself from

Bismarck's arms. "I need to go. My son needs me." She stood and faced him. The quilt slid off her shoulders. Her thin summer gown revealed what she hadn't told him.

He stared at her belly.

Ashamed, she hung her head and turned to go into the house.

Bismarck grabbed her left hand. "I decided if the Lord brought you back, I could live with anything you'd done." He twirled the gold ring on her finger and sucked in a deep breath. "I just never thought—" He backed away from her like she was the rattlesnake that bit him as a child. "God damn you to hell, Ruby."

Chapter Twenty
The Wedding

August 1894

As plans progressed for Pearl's wedding to Willem Buskirk, Ruby's giddy sisters devoured *Godey's Lady's Book*, exclaiming over piquant *toreador* jackets, adorable Leghorn *chapeau* trimmed with taffeta ribbons and blush roses, and clever kidskin ankle-high shoes fastened with tiny buttons. Cowpatties, just a different kind. What really mattered was that Willem was a stolid young man, nothing at all like d'Este. Pearl would be safe.

Ruby and her ma had been married in civil ceremonies. Ma wanted something more elaborate for Pearl, but their financial circumstances constrained her. The Schmidt women scrimped where they could, making the wedding dress themselves, embroidering, sewing, and knitting zealously to prepare Pearl's trousseau, including several dresses that could be left unbelted or easily altered to accommodate future pregnancies. The church ladies volunteered a covered dish supper. Pearl's wedding would be the biggest celebration in town since the Fourth of July.

The Friday before the Sunday wedding, the family drove into Truly. Years before, Hermann built a little shotgun house for Nettie and the girls to live in during the ninety-nine day school year. Most of the time, the family drove into town on Saturday morning, stayed overnight, attended

Sunday morning church services then returned to the ranch. Now, they would stay several days to put the final touches on wedding plans and to decorate the church with ribbons and flowers from neighboring yards.

Once Pearl walked down the aisle on the blessed day, Ruby joined several other women at the serving line handing out punch and wedding cake.

Like most men, Ruby's father considered the public display of a pregnancy inappropriate. Children could be seen, if not heard, but pregnant women were expected to be silent *and* invisible. Thus, Ruby and her mother hid behind the serving table. Over her meadow green dress with leg of mutton sleeves, Ruby tied a white apron beneath her breasts in a vain attempt to disguise her form. Several old biddies peered at her from behind fans of Chinese silk, their speculative eyes quickly hidden when she glanced their way. Certain she provided grist for the rumor mill, she shrugged, knowing there was nothing she could do about it.

An hour later, the cake was gone. Silver flasks appeared, and men drizzled amber liquid into punch cups. Ruby and the other ladies pretended not to notice.

Tired herself, she knew her mother must be as well. Ruby wiped her hands on her apron, excused herself from the serving line, and led her mother to an unoccupied chair. Unable to find another for herself, she leaned against a tree in the churchyard, lost in shadows, shifting her weight from swollen foot to swollen foot, wiggling her toes within her shoes.

The festivities surged around her. Longingly she watched the dancing townsfolk. Had she stayed in Truly, she and Bismarck would have shared a similar joyous union, surrounded by family and friends. Instead, she and d'Este had been joined in a five-minute ceremony mumbled by a half-drunk clerk in the Philadelphia City Hall. She twirled the heavy family ring that served as her wedding band then patted her seven-month abdomen. Act in haste, repent at leisure. She'd had plenty of time to regret marrying that son of a bitch.

Bismarck claimed his dance with the bride then whirled Hortense, Molly, and Hortense again, through square dances and waltzes.

Envy flared within Ruby. She tried to vanquish it from her heart, knowing she had no right to begrudge his interactions with other women. The bobbing rhythm of the polkas made his limp less noticeable. Around the floor, he guided the ladies, handling them as naturally as the horses he broke, with the same ease he'd ridden her bucking hips long ago. No longer a youth, he was a man in his prime. His face held the improbable combination of a Roman nose and denim blue eyes. A perpetual halo from his Stetson dented his unruly brown hair. The droopy handlebar mustache was new and added to his appeal. Recalling Mrs. Wheelwright's words, Ruby acknowledged that he was dangerous, very dangerous indeed.

When he disappeared from view, she sighed, filled with an indefinable sense of loss.

Minutes later, from behind, a hand touched her shoulder.

Ruby jumped.

"Hush, little one." Bismarck's breath tickled her ear. "Don't turn around."

She exhaled in relief.

"Your pa's doing his darndest to keep me from you."

She nodded.

Bismarck drew her deeper into the shadows then turned her toward him, pulling her as close as her rounded abdomen would allow. "What is it about you, Ruby, that gets me so riled up?" He released her. "I cain't live with you. Cain't live without you. And knowing another man's laid with you pert near drives me crazy." He ran his hand over his face. "I reckon it's partly my fault. I should have written more. Should have given you the time you needed to study. But it irked me you loved art more than me." He clasped her chin, forcing her to look at him. "Do you love this feller?"

She closed her eyes and whispered, "It doesn't matter if I love him. I'm married to him." Tears gathered in her eyes.

"Do you love him? I need to know."

"I despise him." Jealousy stabbed her as she remembered Bismarck's repeated dances with the blonde. She poked a finger at his chest. "What about you and Hortense?"

He shook his head. "She puts more stock in me than I do in her." His voice caught. "I've waited for you this long. I figure I can wait until you're free again. Just let me know I'm not wasting my time."

"Pa won't let me divorce."

"If your husband stays gone long enough, Judge Willis can declare him dead."

Her lips curved weakly. "Really?"

Bismarck nodded. "I checked. Wanted to be sure we could plan for our future." He wiped the moisture from her cheeks with his thumb then kissed her.

His new mustache tickled her lips. The aroma of the wax that held the bristles at stiff attention filled her nostrils, mixing with the horse and leather scents that never left him. She inhaled deeply before pulling him closer, running her tongue across his lips, then slipping her tongue inside his mouth, moaning as she tasted him.

At her response, he gave a resonant chuckle. "I reckon I'll keep waiting."

"What about my children?"

"They're a part of you. I reckon they'll become a part—"

"Ruby? Where are you?" Beryl called from the serving line.

Bismarck kissed her again. "I'll never marry unless I marry you, Ruby Louise. Kids and all."

* * * *

On a long, hot, dry September day, Ruby went into labor. Ruby's own mother, now six months pregnant herself, delivered her granddaughter.

"I swear I will never lie with a man again." Ruby moaned as her mother passed a damp cloth over her face.

Her mother laughed. "That will pass, child. Never you fear."

Other than interminable morning sickness, the pregnancy had not been difficult. The arduous twenty-six hour birthing, confined to the stifling attic bedroom where a white-hot sun baked the tin roof and not a shred of air stirred the flour-sack curtains, left Ruby drained for weeks.

Like her brother, little Sophie had her father's dark hair, icy eyes, and olive skin. Ruby had not given a single physical characteristic to either child. She prayed they had not inherited her husband's personality.

Johnny had latched on with ease. Breast-feeding him had been joyous. A colicky baby, Sophie was fussy and inconsolable, constantly crying. She mangled Ruby's nipples, suckled intermittently, lost interest, took forever to nurse, never became a fat happy baby. Because she ate poorly, she awakened every hour or two to feed. Ruby despaired of getting a full night's sleep or completing a task without interruption. Some days she thought her failed relationship with d'Este colored her feelings for his child. Others she questioned her ability to mother. Still others, she blamed the child.

While tucking them in bed, Ruby gazed upon her

children. No longer a baby, Johnny was growing up too fast. She should paint his portrait but knew she wouldn't follow through with her desire. She contented herself with drawing in a tiny sketchbook she stowed in her pocket, filling it in stolen moments when certain her father wouldn't catch her. If she unpacked her brushes and paints, she would incur his wrath, a battle she lacked the energy to fight. *The Stillbirth* and other paintings remained crated, tucked under her bed, too painful to look upon. Some, Este's *Still-life with Girl* for instance, were too intimate to share with her family. The desire to paint dried into the hard knot of a rose hip.

Every few weeks a packet of letters arrived from Willow, gushing about her travels. Soirées in Paris. Meeting Edgar Degas. Watching the sunrise on the Venetian lagoon. Looking at Titian's paintings, the ones which obsessed d'Este and on which he patterned his work.

> *My darling Ruby,*
>
> *In the past, I could not say what I wanted to say, do what I wanted to do. Having broken entirely with my parents, I feel free. I am no longer enslaved by their ideas of what women ought to do. I no longer tolerate others pontificating on what my art should be. Now I listen only to myself and paint what I wish, how I wish. To fill my canvas in a beautiful way, I simplify, simplify, simplify, often making only the most lovely of shapes.*
>
> *Walter supports me in all I do, but he is not you. I miss our talks and painting together more than you can imagine.*
>
> *My dearest friend, how I long to see you again...*

* * * *

In her cradle in the parlor, two-week old Sophie

screamed with hunger. Almost finished with cleaning the kitchen after supper, Ruby rushed through the dishes trying to finish the task before beginning the tedious breastfeeding of her child. Behind her at the kitchen table, pencil in hand, her father balanced the books for the ranch.

A plate slipped through her wet fingers and fell to the floor, breaking into countless shards. "Damnation."

"Ruby Louise, I heard that."

"Yes, Pa." She bent to pick up the largest chunks of broken porcelain before sweeping up the bitlets with the broom and dustpan.

Jasper's voice, yelling from the yard, broke the evening quiet. "Pa! Someone's coming."

Her father stood and strode to the row of pegs above the kitchen door. Reaching for his firearms, he strapped the holster with his pistols around his hips and loaded the ten-gauge shotgun before heading to the front porch. The ranch was isolated, so visitors were rare and could be neighbors or desperadoes like the infamous Doolin-Dalton gang.

Curious, Ruby wiped her hands on her apron, planning to follow him outside and see who was coming. It would be helpful to know if she needed to prepare a plate of food for someone before she got everything put away.

"It's only Nokoni," came Jasper's follow-up call. "With somebody else."

Ruby plunged her hands back into the soapy dishwater. Without a doubt, that someone was Bismarck. Since Pearl's wedding, she and Bismarck had not spoken. Not that her pa had anything against the young cowhand, but Hermann feared Ruby would further tarnish the family reputation with a divorce or another ill-gotten child. He barely allowed her room to breathe, much less converse with the bachelor.

Though she strained to hear, the mens' voices were too

low to understand. Only Jasper's boyish pitch had penetrated the walls of the house. Ruby tuned out the murmurings and returned to her chores.

The words "I'll surprise her" preceded the opening of the kitchen door. Ruby's shoulders tightened in response to the oily voice. The pine floor creaked with a familiar tread. She did not turn around.

He placed a kiss on her right ear.

Her whole body tensed. His breath against her neck burned hotter than the evening sun piercing the window. She shivered.

"*Tiziana*, why'd you run away?"

She let out an exasperated huff and evaded his arms. "You took off, Frank. Never came back. Never wrote. I feared you were dead."

"You should have remained in Philadelphia. The Farinellis told me where you were, but a man should not have to search for his wife."

Before Ruby could reply, her mother rushed in, breathing heavily from the exertion. A basket of tomatoes rocked dangerously on her arm. She wiped her face and hands on her apron as she looked d'Este over.

"Ma, you should be taking it easy." Ruby took the vegetables from her mother, concerned at her shortness of breath and overly red cheeks.

"Jasper just informed me we had a guest." Nettie's smile said she was withholding judgment until she got to know the newcomer better. "Pardon me for not greeting you earlier."

Ruby's husband stepped towards Nettie, clicked his heels together and gave an attenuated bow. "Barone Francesco d'Este." He extended his hand. When Nettie stretched hers toward him, he brought it to his lips. "*Gentilissima signora.*"

That son of a bitch and his damned charm.

"My goodness." Nettie fluttered into a half-curtsey. "I'm Nettie, uh, Antoinette Schmidt."

Ruby cringed and helped her mother up. "You don't have to do that, Ma. He's not a king."

"It's late. I'm sure you haven't eaten." Nettie turned to her daughter, accusation in her voice. "Why haven't you fixed a plate for your husband?"

"Perhaps I could freshen myself first?" he said. "I had no idea your Wild West was so dirty."

"Certainly. I'll fetch you clean towels." Nettie stepped from the kitchen and arduously climbed the stairs to the attic. She returned with snowy linens draped over her arms, and while passing them to d'Este, directed him to the water closet just off the kitchen.

"Ma, those are from my hope chest."

"Who are you hoping for? Your husband's right here." Her mother paused, thinking. "For now, I'll move you and Mr. d'Este into Jasper's room. The boy can sleep with the hired hands."

"Let Frank sleep in the bunkhouse." Ruby's skirts swirled as she turned to the kitchen cabinets, slamming doors and drawers as she pulled out utensils to serve him.

"He's your husband. Men have needs—"

"Long-lost husband. And I'm sure Frank's needs haven't gone unfulfilled!"

"Ruby Louise!"

The water closet door opened. D'Este stepped out. "*Signora* Schmidt, I couldn't help but overhear. I am happy to sleep in the barn. Perhaps Ruby and I need time to become reacquainted." He gave a self-effacing shrug before sitting at the table.

Ruby dropped a plate of food before him while looking

beseechingly over his head at her mother.

"If you insist, Mr. d'Este," her mother conceded. "But you'll sleep in Jasper's room. No guest of mine bunks with the hired hands." Nettie excused herself to see to Frank's bedding.

Her husband ate heartily. Once Ruby cleared the dishes, he pulled her into his lap, caressing her. She endured his pawing but did not respond.

"What's wrong, *gioia*, don't you love me anymore?"

Ruby jerked free and stood.

He grabbed her arm, tightening his grip until she winced. "I asked you a question."

"You left and never came back."

"I got into a little gambling trouble." He shrugged. "I returned to Venezia."

"You left me penniless. And pregnant. I had to face the Black Hand alone." She struggled to control the quaver in her voice, the sudden rush of tears to her eyes, hating that they revealed her weakness.

"It was better you not know where I was." He waved his hands reassuringly. "*Non preoccuparti*. My father straightened things out with *La Mano Nera*. He paid them off."

"And you couldn't write? Not a word for months." Ruby blew out a huff of air. "How long was I to wait before you remembered you had a wife and children?"

D'Este blinked at her words. "Children?"

Dismayed, she gaped at him. He truly appeared to have forgotten Johnny and, of course, had no idea Sophie existed.

He shook his head, "Where is my son?"

The scurry of feet interrupted them. Nettie entered carrying Sophie, her screams even more indignant as her dinner had been delayed by d'Este's arrival. Johnny toddled behind his grandmother.

"Sit down, Ma. You're doing too much." Ruby pulled out a kitchen chair for her mother, then knelt and put an arm around her son, directing his gaze to her husband. "This is your papa."

Johnny hid his face in his mother's skirts.

D'Este scowled at the child and yanked the boy from Ruby's arms. "Don't be a baby."

The toddler burst into tears.

"Why are you frightened? I'm your papa."

Johnny squirmed from his father's hand and ran from the room.

Ruby stood and took the baby from her mother and passed the infant to d'Este. "You have a daughter as well."

"What's wrong with her?" He recoiled from his screaming daughter, nearly dropping her in his haste to return her to Ruby. "And the boy?"

"He doesn't remember you, that's all. And she's hungry. I'll feed her and put them to bed."

When Ruby joined the others in the parlor, she found her husband regaling her family with a story of falling into a Venetian canal during a mock sword fight with his brothers.

At bedtime, d'Este followed Ruby upstairs. He pinned her against the wall. "Aren't you glad to see me, *cara*?"

She shook her head.

"You were supposed to be my Muse. Instead you abandoned me." He pinned her against the wall, one leg shoved between her thighs, kissing her hard, making it clear what he expected.

"Frank, I just had a baby. It's too soon."

He squeezed her milk-hard breast, twisting her already-tender nipple until she squirmed. "I can be patient—to a point." He stormed into Jasper's room, slamming the door behind him, its thunder rattling the window at the top of the stairs.

* * * *

After breakfast one morning, her pa lingered over a rare third cup of coffee. He glared at Ruby. "No wonder you call him a son of a bitch. He drinks too much. He cheats the cowhands at cards, fleecing them of hard-earned wages. He's been slouching around here two weeks. Better get off his lazy rear-end and earn his keep."

"What can he do, Pa? He can't rope, brand, shoe horses. He can't even ride worth a d—"

"Watch your language, Ruby Louise. He can slop hogs, muck stalls, weed the garden. Either he starts earning his keep, or he moves on." He tilted his cup back and downed the last of his coffee. "And a wife belongs with her husband."

The blood drained from Ruby's face at the thought of following d'Este anywhere. "Don't make me go with him, Pa."

"You made your bed, girl." Hermann scowled. "If you don't talk to him, I will."

The next morning, Ruby slammed a plate of eggs and ham before d'Este then sat down across the table. "Frank, we need to talk."

Lazily, he rearranged the utensils.

She looked down as she drew little circles on the table-top with one finger. "We're hard-working people. Everyone in the family has chores." With a glance up at him, she added, "You're family, not a guest. It's time you accepted some responsibilities."

He forked a chunk of meat and lifted it to his mouth, chewing with an insolence that maddened her.

"Times have been hard for my folks the last few years. There's been a horrible drought. Pa's let most of the cowhands go. We could use your help. You're not cut out to be a ranch hand, but you might clean the barn, polish tack, or help with the gardening."

He dropped his knife and fork. "You expect me to work?" He snickered as he wiggled his elegant fingers before him.

With her own well-calloused ones, Ruby slammed his soft hands to the table, rattling the cutlery. "Yes, damn it, I do."

Chapter Twenty-One
Rape and Plunder

October 1894

To Ruby's surprise, d'Este began working. The first day, after weeding the fall garden without gloves, he came to her, saying, "There's something wrong with my hands."

She took a clean cloth and wiped the dirt from his fingers exposing fluid-filled bumps on his palms. "Haven't you had a blister before?" With a glance at his scarlet face, she choked down her laughter.

"Don't laugh at me. Make them go away."

"They'll go away on their own eventually. Wait here." She retrieved a needle from her sewing kit and flamed it in a match before using it to deflate the bubbles. "From now on, wear gloves from the tack room to protect your hands."

For two weeks, d'Este took over the garden, hauling water each morning to see the plants through the day, proudly carrying in baskets with the last of the summer vegetables and the fall crops of peas, pumpkins, and cabbages. To avoid losing the last of the tomatoes to frost, they were picked green, wrapped in newspaper, and set in the cellar to ripen.

D'Este had not struck her since he arrived at the ranch. He worked hard at what jobs he was capable of performing around the house. One morning, when he touched Ruby to give her a chaste kiss, his palms had been calloused. Conceding she might have been wrong about him, she returned his kiss with one equally chaste.

He continued to press for relations, but she had not fully recovered from Sophie's birth. She wondered how much longer she could delay his demands. Another month at most. At that point, she would have exhausted that excuse. Frankly, every time she looked at her mother, Ruby grew more convinced she wouldn't risk carrying another child.

While dusting the parlor one morning, Ruby glanced out the window. With an egg basket dangling off one arm, Beryl clutched d'Este's arm in a proprietary grasp with the other as they headed toward the barn.

"Stupid little chit!" Ruby raced to the henhouse, finding Beryl with her hand in a nest box searching for eggs while d'Este's hand fondled her sister's derrière.

"Keep your hands off my sister, Frank." Ruby pushed him aside and snatched Beryl by the ear.

Eggs tumbled out of Beryl's basket and broke. The dogs leapt eagerly for the free meal, lapping up the yellow yolks that polka-dotted the red dirt.

Ruby towed her sister back to the house and shoved her through the back door. "Stay away from Frank if you know what's good for you!"

"Why? He's charming, handsome, amusing. And a real baron. You don't love him. You don't even try to make him happy," Beryl whined, rubbing her ear. "But you won't let anyone else have him."

"You're too young to understand." Ruby gritted her teeth.

Beryl raised her chin high in the air, her voice defiant. "I'm old enough to know you're a bitch."

"Hellion child!" All the rage Ruby felt at her husband accompanied the slap she gave her sister. "Trust me, Frank is no good. Stay away from him."

The blow stunned her sister into utter silence.

Ruby stared at the red mark on her sister's cheek then at her own hot, stinging hand. Horrified, she realized she was no better than Frank. "Beryl, I'm sorry."

But her sister raced out the door.

* * * *

Ruby pulled her mother to a chair, lifted her feet and slid a needlepoint ottoman beneath them. "Ma, you're doing too much. Your feet are all swollen again." She stepped back and looked closely at her mother. "Even your face and hands are swollen. Maybe we should send for Doc Granger?"

"I'm fine, honey. Really." Her mother gave a wan smile and patted her daughter's hand. "Just getting too old for this. As much as I love babies, in a way, I'd hoped I go through the change of life early and be spared further childbearing."

Less than a week later, only seven months into her pregnancy, Nettie began having contractions. Doc Granger put her at bed rest. Exhausted by her thirteenth pregnancy in twenty-two years, she sank into bed and rarely roused herself, growing weaker by the day.

In the hallway between the attic bedrooms, D'Este again approached Ruby at bedtime. "I'm your husband. You can't put me off forever."

"I just had a baby, and I'm doing the work of three women." She paced before her bedroom. "Look at Ma. Seeing her so sick scares me. With the next child, I might be in the same condition."

"I grow impatient, *cara*. I can't hold out forever." His eyebrows drew together, his displeasure at her refusal evident. "Your sister seems willing enough."

The malevolent edge in his voice made her legs wobble. "Leave Beryl alone. She's too young."

"I can take what you refuse to give." He shoved Ruby to

her knees, twisted his hands tightly into her hair, and forced her to take him in her mouth.

Despite working from dawn to dusk, Ruby found herself unable to sleep after the encounter with her husband. Lying alone in her childhood bed, applying cool compresses to the bruises he left on her arms and breasts, trying to erase his vile taste from her mouth, she was frightened. Scared of d'Este. Scared of being crushed under the responsibility of caring for an invalid mother, a toddler, two infants—her own and her mother's—plus two younger siblings, and her father. Scared of losing herself between all the household chores and feeding her family plus six cowhands. Ruby wished Frank dead and almost hoped her mother would lose this child. She asked God's forgiveness for her wicked thoughts but refused to take them back, though she was scared of going to hell.

* * * *

Ruby's pa and several local ranchers scheduled their annual cattle round-up, sorting the animals by brands, separating the calves from their mothers, branding and ear marking the youngsters, and castrating the bull calves. Ordinarily, Nettie would have gone, cooking beans and sourdough bread over a campfire and helping with the branding, but she remained at bed rest. Ruby would have gone, her hands better at wielding a gelding knife than most men, but she couldn't leave Ma with her flibbertigibbet fourteen-year-old sister. And her husband, not merely useless, was downright dangerous. She dared not leave her baby sister alone with him.

So Ruby packed lunches for her pa, Jasper, and the ranch hands, stowing food into wooden crates, a Dutch oven filled with pinto beans, a bowl of coleslaw, biscuits, lemonade, bread and butter pickles, several pies, and a pound cake.

The men would roast *cabrito*, a young goat, over a spit as they worked.

With the men out of the house, Ruby finished the breakfast dishes then checked on her mother. In the past week, her mother had rarely risen from bed. Bloated and ill-appearing, she bled off and on but resolutely held onto the baby.

As Ruby helped her to the chamber pot, her mother clutched her hand. "Honey, if I don't make it through this, promise me you'll take care of your pa."

"Don't say such things. You'll be fine."

"Promise me, Ruby."

"He's my pa. You know—"

A scream from the direction of the barn interrupted Ruby.

Worry flashed over her mother's face. "Go. I'll be all right."

"You sure?" At her mother's nod, Ruby ran to the kitchen and pulled the shotgun from the rack above the door. Jamming two cartridges in place, she flew to the barn.

She entered the building as silently as a hunting owl, stopping every few steps to listen. With a few blinks, her eyes adjusted to the darkness. Rather than comforting her, the familiar smells of manure, hay, horses, and leather compressed the air, weighing heavily on her lungs, causing them to feel tight. Narrow shafts of brilliant sunlight sifted through cracks in the barn walls, making seeing into the shadows difficult. Hunting for the rat she knew was here somewhere, Ruby methodically checked every stall. Each was empty. Her apprehension rose.

The hay rustled at her feet.

She froze, held her breath, prayed it wasn't a rattlesnake. Instead, a mouse scurried by. Swallowing her sigh of relief, she tiptoed on, planting each foot noiselessly on the cushion of dried grasses.

The last stall. A sharp snap. A hand striking flesh. Cloth ripping. He was there. With Beryl. Ruby sucked in a silent breath to steady her nerves then, shotgun aimed before her, peered into the enclosure.

"Stop!" Beryl, her dress ripped open at the bodice, fought d'Este.

"You've been begging for this."

Ruby, refusing to give up the element of surprise, silenced the howl that leapt into her throat. Her gaze caught Beryl's. Ruby mouthed "Sh-h-h."

Eyes wide, her sister complied, backing further into the corner of the stall.

D'Este followed her, holding her throat by one hand while fumbling with his pants with the other, focused only on his lust.

Unnoticed, Ruby entered the stall. She raised the shotgun to her shoulder. With a deep inhalation, she cranked the lever of the shotgun.

The sharp, metallic click caught his attention. He released Beryl. Snarling, he whirled to face Ruby.

"Run, Beryl!"

Her sister wasted no time dodging between d'Este and the grazing box, fleeing toward the barn door.

"*Cara*, don't shoot." He held his hands in a placating gesture. "Put the gun down." He edged toward her.

"Don't come any closer."

"You wouldn't harm your own husband." His lips curved into the winning smile that had once charmed her.

The clatter of hooves distracted Ruby. Her aim wavered as her gaze darted to the right. Beryl, bareback on an old pinto pony, galloped away.

He rushed at her, forcing the shotgun to the side.

Surprised, she screeched. Inadvertently, she pulled both triggers, firing the barrels into the barn wall. The double recoil reeled her backwards, nearly knocking her over.

He threw himself at her, wrenching the firearm away and tossing it into a nearby stall. His first blow, a hard backhand across her face, split her lip.

She staggered backwards. "How could you?" Salty blood followed the words from her mouth.

"That little *puta* was begging for it."

"She's a child!"

Fists raised, he advanced.

She drew up her hands to protect her face and edged backwards.

He followed, beating her with every step.

"Don't, please. Think of our children." She tried to sound soothing, submissive, sweet. Tried to reach through his anger, reach for any love for her that might remain. But he'd gone to some dark place where she couldn't reach him.

When Ruby lowered her hands to protect her chest and abdomen, he grabbed her neck, choking her.

Her fingers lacked the strength to pry his from her throat. Her vision began to fade. The world grayed.

He threw her to the ground.

Her airway free, Ruby gasped and coughed as she curled into a protective ball. A brutal kick knocked the wind from her. She heard more than felt her ribs crack. Pain ripped through her with every inhalation. She lay still, panting.

"Frank, stop!" She uncurled her body. Tried to crabwalk away.

His body vibrated with rage. He stepped on her. One booted foot between her breasts pinned her in place. He unfastened the remaining buttons of his trousers, released himself, and dropped onto her.

His weight on her ribs made her cry out. She scratched him with her fingernails. Then she flailed at him with both fists.

D'Este pulled her head up by her hair and slammed a fist into her chin.

Bright lights exploded behind her eyelids. Her head swam. He'd never gone this far before. This time he would surely kill her. No one was at the ranch to help her. She had to fight him alone.

He threw her skirt and petticoats above her head and twisted them around her, immobilizing her arms, before ripping her pantaloons open and forcing himself inside.

She struggled, trying to claw her way out of her clothing but was wrapped too tightly.

After two rapid thrusts, he lifted her buttocks high, dragged her closer, yanking her legs apart, plunging in more deeply.

His actions loosened her clothing. She wiggled one arm out of her straitjacket.

Scuttling her fingers through the hay and dirt of the barn floor, she searched frantically for something—anything—to use as a weapon. She lost track of time. She didn't taste the blood filling her mouth. She didn't feel him sliding in and out. She didn't hear his piglike grunts faster—faster—faster—as he neared release.

An eternity later, her fingers closed around something hard. A bent nail.

Arched above her, stroke by stroke, he pounded the air from her. With a loud groan, he emptied himself into her, his eyes shuttered with the intensity of his climax.

With the nail fisted in her hand, Ruby slashed his face with all her might.

"*Putana!*" His next punch snapped her head against a

pole supporting the roof.

* * * *

A noxious odor irritated Ruby's nose and made her gasp for breath. Recoiling from the scent, she turned her head. The movement precipitated a wave of nausea. Stomach acid burned her throat. She tried to swallow, but an iron band squeezed her neck so tightly nothing could pass down her esophagus. Every part of her body ached. Her fingers fluttered in an effort to touch her mouth.

A deep voice penetrated the fog surrounding her.

"She's coming around."

Ruby swam through the darkness, finally cracking her eyes to see old Doc Granger wafting smelling salts under her nose. She recoiled at the noxious odor.

"Ruby? Ruby!" A hand slapped her cheek. "Wake up now. How many fingers do you see?"

She tried to focus. The doctor was cheating. He wasn't holding his fingers steady. With feeble hands, she pushed his big paw from before her face and tried to sit up. She groaned with the effort and sank back into the pillows.

"Good girl. You've got some spunk left in you." Granger patted her shoulder then lifted her head. "Take it easy." He forced her mouth open and spooned in a bitter liquid. "A little laudanum will ease your pain."

She frowned at the nasty taste.

He pinched her lips closed so she couldn't spit it out.

For a moment she struggled to remember what had happened, but her world swirled, and she retreated into darkness.

* * * *

Wet fabric touched Ruby's lips. She opened her mouth and ran her tongue across her lips. They felt twice their normal size, cracked and dry. With her tongue she sought the moist towel. Her eyelids fluttered but wouldn't remain open.

"Good afternoon." A disembodied voice penetrated her consciousness. "You've been out the better part of two days."

Ruby opened her eyes. She looked around, but things wouldn't come into focus. Unsure of where she was, she reasoned she was floating in Purgatory. She hurt too much to be in Heaven yet was not burning in Hell. A shadow appeared across her vision. Surely Death himself hovered over her.

"Sugar, could you get a few sips of water down?"

The voice was familiar. Not the Devil, after all. Her vision cleared. Cornelia Granger, the doctor's wife, looked down at her.

Ruby nodded. She tried to speak. Her throat was too dry for words. She raised her hands to her neck and felt deep bruises along her windpipe. With every breath, a knife slid between her ribs. Her breath stifled in her chest.

"Beryl?" The word creaked from her mouth.

"She's fine."

Ruby's eyes widened. Her heart raced and her breathing accelerated as disjointed bits of memory hurtled into her consciousness. "Frank?"

Miz Granger put her hand on Ruby's shoulder, preventing her from sitting up. "Don't worry about him. Your ma shot him. He's locked up in the Truly jail."

"Ma got out of bed? She shot him?" Alarmed, Ruby tried to sit up.

Before Ruby could ask more questions, Cornelia held a cup to Ruby's lips and allowed her a few sips of water followed by a dose of laudanum before pressing her into the bed. "If you keep that down, we'll try a bit of broth. You need to get your strength back."

* * * *

Ruby awakened, her head somewhat clear at last. A glance around the room sent her head spinning. Judging from the light coming through her bedroom window, it was mid morning.

She had no idea how much time had lapsed since she'd been injured. Her children and family had vanished. The only person she recalled seeing was Cornelia Granger. Flashes of what had happened whirled through her head. Beryl. Frank. She nearly fainted from the violence of the memories. And Miz Granger said her mother shot Frank.

"Ma?" Her voice sounded scratchy and hoarse.

No answer.

Though dressed in a flannel gown with a quilt covering her, her feet and hands were frozen. Goosebumps covered her arms. If a part of her did not hurt, she could not find it. A bone-deep ache had established permanent residence in her neck and shoulders. Movement in any direction caused an agony worse than she had ever experienced. She wiggled her fingers, then her toes. They worked. The effort of lifting her arms and legs, one at a time, made her gasp from a searing pain in her chest. Reaching for the headboard, she grabbed it and pulled herself up, panting with the exertion.

Ruby stood, almost dropping to the floor as pain burst from her ribs. The room gyrated unevenly. She suppressed the urge to vomit. Using the edge of the bed, the nightstand, the dresser, then the chair to support herself, she worked her away across the room.

Her reflection in the dresser mirror trapped her gaze.

My God. She cringed at her own image. Deep purple outlined both eyes. One cheekbone, so swollen the skin was taut and shiny, had turned indigo. Half of one eyeball was blood red. A thick black scab perched prominently on her lower lip. Purple fingerprints encircled her neck. Jagged edges sprang from broken fingernails. Scrapes and scratches adorned both hands. She pulled back her sleeves. Bruises covered both forearms. Trembling, she leaned against the dresser and lifted her gown. Strips torn from old sheeting swathed her chest from armpit to waist, wrapped as tightly as a corset. When she ran her hands over her torso, the unraveled edges tickled. She winced as her fingers found the broken ribs. Her breasts, engorged and tender, rose above the bindings. Her right shoulder was black and blue from the kick of the shotgun. She hadn't seated it well against her shoulder before it went off.

Images of what had happened whirled through her head. By rights, she should have shot Frank the second Beryl was out of the way. Because Ruby's attention had wandered, that son of a bitch had damned near killed her.

Exhaling slowly, Ruby reached for the back of the chair and sank on its rawhide seat. The significance of the deep ache between her legs registered. Never had she thought he would go this far. Ruby started to cry. Wracking sobs aggravated her broken ribs. She held her breath, forcing her tears to subside. Crying was too easy. She would never waste another tear over that monster.

For a minute she rested, summoning strength to continue, knowing she could not sit there forever. She had to find her family and feed her baby. From the chair, she stretched for the doorknob and pulled herself to her feet.

Chapter Twenty-Two
Crime and Punishment

October 1894

Ruby opened the bedroom door. "Ma?" Her raw dry throat croaked the word.

Voices, men arguing, floated up from the kitchen. Leaning heavily on the railing, Ruby eavesdropped as she crept down the stairs.

"Now, Hermann, I can't hang a man just for beating his wife. Hell, I'd have to string up half the town."

Ruby recognized the squeaky voice of Judge Everett Willis. His voice, like his pince-nez spectacles, was too small for his tall lanky frame.

"Everett, you saw Ruby. That bastard beat her half to death then raped her." Her father slurred his words.

"A man can do whatever he wants to his wife. May not be moral, but it's legal."

Ruby wobbled, her legs unable to support her any longer. She dropped to the next-to-last stair and peered around the corner, clinging to the railing to keep from keeling over.

A handful of men circled the kitchen table. Doctor Granger, Judge Willis, Sheriff Tuttle, and Deputy Booker kept her pa company. Thick tobacco smoke filled the air surrounding them. An empty whiskey bottle, glasses with fingers of whiskey, and coffee mugs sat before them. Miz Granger poured the judge a fresh cup and replaced the pot on the stove.

Ruby's pa looked tired. And drunk. He cracked the seal on a fresh bottle of whiskey then slammed it on the table, jostling nearby glasses. "He killed Nettie and the baby." He brushed a hand over watery eyes.

Ma dead? When Ruby opened her mouth, spasm in her ravaged throat snatched her scream. Tears cascaded from her eyes. Silently she rocked back and forth, arms clutched across her chest. This was all Frank's fault. No, all her fault.

Doc Granger spoke next. "Hermann, you know as well as I do that Nettie was barely hanging onto that child. Whether in her own bed or out in the barn defending Ruby, she'd have lost that baby."

"She might have lived."

Doc Granger shook his head. "I'm sorry. She lost too much blood."

"And Beryl?" Hermann said. "What about my baby girl?"

The judge cleared his throat. "The most we can charge d'Este with is attempted rape of a girl he swears up and down was willing."

"He'll get away with destroying my family?"

"I wouldn't say that. Nettie shot him. Ruby sliced up his face. Bismarck damned near beat the bastard to death when the posse found him. D'Este will carry those scars forever." The judge, his voice oozing with solicitude, looked at Hermann. "I'd hate to put your little gals through the horrors of a trial. Their reputations would be ruined. You know how folks talk."

Doc Granger added, "Ruby's not going to be in any shape to testify for a while anyway."

The judge continued, "Your best bet may be to offer him a ticket back to Italy in exchange for a divorce."

"Damn it!" Hermann choked on his whiskey. "There's never been a divorce—"

"Think of what's best for your daughter." Judge Willis jabbed his gavel toward Hermann.

Rocking backwards, Ruby sucked in such a deep breath that her broken ribs grated against each other. Her vision hazed red with pain. Judge Willis was right. If that son of a bitch went to jail, she would still be married to him. As soon as he got out, he would find her, just as he did when she escaped Philadelphia. She would suffer even more then. The lily-livered judge clearly could not—or would not—hang her husband, the fate that son of a bitch deserved. On the other hand, if either Pa or Bismarck killed d'Este, they *would* go to jail. Divorce and deportation remained the only logical answer to her dilemma.

She stood and whirled around the corner.

Her father scowled at seeing her clad in only her night-gown. "Clothe yourself, Ruby."

"Pa, listen. I want a divorce. I tried to tell you before, but you wouldn't listen. I fear for my children and myself when Frank's around. I can't bear to be with him." She start-ed meekly then, determined that a handful of men would not determine her fate, she instilled her voice with a persuasive authority. "He'll kill me next time. You know he will."

"Now, Ruby—" the judge sputtered.

She opened her mouth to respond. Too late. The walls swirled. Her vision blurred. Trying to focus, she opened her eyes wide. The kitchen floor moved nearer and nearer.

She regained consciousness long enough to recognize Bismarck's scent and knew he carried her up the stairs. If only she could stay in his arms forever.

* * * *

Over the next few days, in bits and pieces, Miz Granger

told Ruby what had happened. "Pearl and Willem took in your two little ones, plus Jasper and Beryl. My Clarence brought me here to nurse you."

Memories surfaced of Bismarck's callused hands wiping her face and his soft words, "Hang on, little one. You'll pull through this."

"And Ma?" Ruby croaked out the words, her voice still hoarse.

"I'm sorry, honey." Miz Granger took Ruby's hand, squeezing it gently. "She shot Mr. d'Este to save you. But it cost her the baby—and her life."

Sobs tore through Ruby. She deserved the pain. No punishment God inflicted on her would suffice for what she had done to her loved ones by bringing d'Este into their lives.

Doc Granger had ridden from town to check on her. "How're you holding up, Ruby?"

"Better," she lied. She still ached like a herd of stampeding longhorns had trampled her. Any sudden movement made the room orbit around her, and a constant headache befuddled her. But being confined to her bedroom made her feel she, rather than d'Este, was in jail.

After she counted the appropriate number of fingers, Granger deemed her well enough to taper off the laudanum and walk around with assistance.

* * * *

Judge Willis, rather than have Ruby and Beryl endure a full trial in town, planned a hearing at the Schmidt homestead after the Christmas holidays.

Willem escorted Beryl from his ranch. Jasper, Johnny, and Sophie stayed behind with Pearl.

Pa, Doc Granger, Judge Willis, Sheriff Tuttle, and Deputy Booker again gathered around the kitchen table with two additions—d'Este, handcuffed and chained to a chair, and

Luther Eddleston, the lawyer he had hired for himself, all the way from Dallas.

Ruby took grim delight in the fact her husband looked worse than she did. A sling supported his right arm. Across his left cheek, a deep puckered slash held the railroad tracks of Doc Granger's stitching. She rejoiced mirthlessly, pleased she had so thoroughly marred his handsome face. Perhaps the scar would deter the next woman.

Judge Willis led Beryl, Ruby, and Doc Granger through their testimony. Ruby broke down as Beryl described how she had ridden for help. Hermann and Bismarck told how, when they arrived at the Schmidt homestead, they had found Ruby unconscious and Nettie bleeding to death in her night-gown, her pearl-handled derringer still in her hand. A horse, saddle, and bridle were missing from the barn.

Hermann and a cowhand carried the two women into the house. Jasper rode into town to get the doc and the sheriff. Bismarck organized an impromptu posse of cattlemen and tracked the stolen horse. Every man present testified they had come upon d'Este a few miles away, struggling to his feet after being bucked off, and that Bismarck had severely beaten the Italian.

After a brief recess, the judge said, "Mr. d'Este, you may now give your version of the facts."

"*Cara, ti amo alla follia*—I love you to distraction." Facing Ruby rather than the judge, d'Este attempted a smile, but the wound on his face twisted his mouth into a cock-eyed snarl.

Ruby rotated her head to avoid his gaze. The rapid motion made her head spin. She swallowed her nausea.

"I'm sorry, Ruby. I didn't mean to hurt you. *Una pazzia*, a terrible madness, overcame me. I could not help myself."

Eddleston grabbed his client's shoulder and shook him.

"Don't admit anything."

Hermann leapt to his feet, his chair clattering to the ground behind him. "You're one crazy bastard if you think that excuses your actions."

Bismarck grabbed Hermann's hand before he drew his Colt.

"Enough, Hermann!" Judge Willis hammered his gavel on the kitchen table. "Truly is a civilized town. We shall abide by the letter of the law." He glowered at Bismarck and Ruby's father.

Bismarck nodded abruptly.

Hermann provided an even more grudging dip of his head.

They resumed their seats.

Judge Willis cleared his throat. "Mr. d'Este, this court is inclined to release you on three conditions. First, you provide Miz Ruby a divorce. Second, you have no further contact with her or your children. Third, you never return to Texas."

"But I am *un barone*—"

"And you're in the United States of America. Them fancy titles don't mean a goddamn thing here." The judge slammed his gavel on the kitchen table. "Accept this offer. We're being downright generous. Twenty years ago, when frontier justice prevailed, you'd already be strung up from the nearest tree."

D'Este gulped, then looked at Ruby. "*Tiziana, perdonami. Per piacere?*"

Ruby held up a warning hand. "Don't, Frank. You're not sorry at all. You don't deserve my forgiveness."

"I wish to speak with my attorney—privately."

While d'Este, chained to his chair, conferred with Eddleston, everyone else filed to the front porch. Ruby's father filled his pipe with shaking fingers. The judge puffed on a cigarillo with one hand and held a glass of whiskey in the other.

Ten minutes later, d'Este's lawyer approached the judge. "My client has agreed to your terms."

D'Este signed the divorce papers the judge had drawn up and laid down the pen.

Bismarck drew his Bowie knife from its scabbard and held it against the Italian's throat. "You sorry bastard, if you ever come back, I'll stake you out on the plains and gut you. The coyotes will eat your intestines while you're still alive."

Beneath his olive skin, d'Este blanched. His Adam's apple bobbled against Bismarck's knife blade.

"Biz—" Judge Willis warned. "Sign here, Ruby." With an *X*, he indicated the space for her signature. "You have to wait a year for it to be final." He jerked his head toward d'Este. "We'll put him on the next train out of town. Booker will accompany him to New York and release him on a ship bound for Europe."

* * * *

Ruby's milk had dried up by the time her children returned from Pearl's. Torn between relief and a sense of failure as a mother, she rationalized it was for the best. Sophie, bottle-fed goat milk for weeks, had gained weight. With the return of her monthlies, Ruby thanked God the son of a bitch had not impregnated her again.

For the sake of Johnny and Sophie, Ruby moved mechanically through the day, though she had a constant headache and sudden movements still made the world spin.

Her pa repaired the hole Ruby had shot into the barn wall. Every time she entered the barn, though, the pale new boards mocked her. She should have shot her husband instead of the weathered gray siding. Though the bloody straw had been removed and burned and fresh dirt tamped down, if she dug deeply with her toe, she could find the dark stain of her mother's blood.

Beyond the barn, she practiced shooting tin cans. If d'Este returned, she wouldn't hesitate this time. She stitched slits into the sides of her skirts so she could reach her mother's pearl-handled derringer holstered on her thigh. She'd stick the pistol in his belly and pull the trigger. Hell, she'd fire through her skirt if she had to. In her apron pocket, she carried a gelding knife. If d'Este returned, not only would she shoot him, she'd emasculate the son of a bitch.

She slept with the derringer beneath her pillow. Though she cleaned her weapon after target practice, the pungent odor of gunpowder lingered, filling her dreams. Most nights she woke with a jerk, heart pounding. Driven by a compulsion to protect her family and children, she roamed the house, pistol in hand.

Other nights she awakened with the scent of turpentine and oil paint wafting past her nose, the smooth of a brush still present between her fingers, hearing the soft sigh of the bristles kissing the canvas, but the images, the images always faded first, leaving her aching with need, never able to recall her heart's desire.

With the first rooster crow, she rose and made her way downstairs where she awakened her father by pulling the whiskey bottle from his hands. After that, the endless chores of the day stretched before her. First, a massive breakfast for her family and the hired hands. Then house work until it was time to begin lunch. Daily tasks followed a long-established routine. At times she swore she knew the day of the week only by the chore she was doing. Wash on Monday, iron on Tuesday, mend on Wednesday…rest on Sunday—though her day of rest involved cooking three meals and cleaning up afterwards. Somehow she squeezed in knitting, sewing, doctoring injured cowhands, making soap. Planting and weeding, hauling water by hand to saturate the dry soil of the garden. Canning meat and vegetables, filling the root cellar, setting aside seeds for next year's garden. Not a moment remained in the day to call her own.

Along with rearing her own children, she assumed her mother's role with Jasper and Beryl, giving them lessons after everyone had finished their chores. Ruby had hoped Beryl would become more amenable with time. Despite Ruby's efforts, her sister withdrew, not communicating except to scream at Ruby. Jasper moved to the bunkhouse with the cowhands to escape the chaos in the house and, at thirteen, assumed a man's tasks on the ranch.

"Beryl, can you sweep the kitchen floor, please?" Ruby said as she finished the breakfast dishes. "The men tracked in a bunch of dirt."

"You're not my mother!" Her sister roused herself to scream. "This is all your fault."

Beryl's words invariably brought Ruby's guilt from a slow simmer to a rapid boil. She didn't need Beryl's latest taunt to know everything was her fault. As her sister stomped away, Ruby suppressed her anger and swept up the dirt.

Sunday afternoons brought her only respite—Bismarck's weekly visit. Her stress diffused with his arrival. His calm floated like oil on water, relieving strain, soothing tempers.

Johnny's excited voice usually announced Bismarck's arrival. From wherever she was, kitchen or yard, Ruby followed the boy's shouts and watched the man she loved ride up. Ruby was unsure how much Johnny remembered of his real father. Bismarck, as he did with animals, had created a quiet energy between himself and the boy, winning him with patience, affection, and horses.

Eager for attention, Johnny raced to the road, arms waving in the air. "Ride horsie."

"You been a good boy?"

Thumb in his mouth, Johnny replied with a slow nod. After a full day on horseback, Bismarck hoisted the boy to the saddle horn and rode another mile or so. When they dismounted, Johnny wrapped himself around the man's legs, hobbling him, until Bismarck dropped his hat on the boy's head, raised Johnny to his shoulders, and gave him another ride.

Even the colicky Sophie, held in Bismarck's arms like a delicate changeling, gurgled and cooed.

Ruby alone did not seek Bismarck's touch. She was grateful that he sensed how skittish she felt around men and kept his distance. He approached her as he would a wild horse, moving as close as she would allow then backing away before she grew agitated.

* * * *

With warmer weather, still unable to sleep, Ruby resumed her childhood habit of sitting by the windmill wrapped in her *mille fiore* quilt, listening to the steel blades creak, feeling the vibrations of the vanes and the steady heartbeat of the earth itself, pulling her to become part of the land. Taut neck muscles rebelled when she leaned her head backwards to rest on the frame. Tears running down her cheeks, she closed her eyes. Though she tried to still its voice, her heart called for Bismarck.

"You don't have to do this alone, Ruby Louise," the wind whispered.

With a start, she opened her eyes.

Somehow, as he had so many times before, Bismarck found her at the windmill. He sat near her, close, but not touching, his body angled ninety degrees from hers. Only their feet were inches apart.

She did not think he would touch her first, but she was not yet ready to reach for him. "How do you know I'm out here?"

He shrugged. "Just do. Always have."

"Could you have found me in Philadelphia?"

"I did, once, remember? But lost you anyway." His leg stretched across on the grass until his foot touched hers, his boot rubbing her bare little toe in a comforting circular motion.

She breathed in relief. Close, but not too close.

"Sometimes I wish I could blindfold you like a horse, to calm you and lead you out of danger."

"I fear blinders wouldn't help." Her mouth twisted. "Horses don't have much imagination. Every time I close my eyes, I relive that day."

"Want to talk about it?" He hesitated. "Or him?"

She shook her head, shuddering.

"Talk about other things then. I need to hear your voice."

She leaned back against the windmill frame. "What do you want to know?"

"Everything."

After a long silence, her fingers twisting her nightgown, she started. "I had talent and drive. I thought being an artist would be easy. But I didn't count on how difficult being a *woman* artist would be. Struggling every day to paint my way. Never fitting in." Her voice trailed off. "Later, I was too poor to leave. Trapped in an existence I couldn't escape. I'd hurt my family—and you. I was too ashamed of what I'd become to come home."

He reached for her but pulled back. "I want to hold you, but I fear the minute I do, you'll start sun-fishing or crow-hopping like a bucking bronco." His words were light but his eyes dead serious.

"I probably would."

"What happened with that bastard wasn't your fault."

"Then whose was it?" She let out a long sigh, accepting that responsibility anyway.

He shook his head. "D'Este was a bad apple, born and bred." Bismarck paused, cleared his throat. "The problem with you being back East was you were looking for yourself. I didn't figure I could help you with that." His voice tightened. "All I could do was wait here, praying you'd come back. It took a while, but God answered my prayers. You're here now. I'll help anyway I can, Ruby Louise. I'm counting days until you're free."

Night after night he met her beneath the windmill. "You're plumb tuckered out." He appraised her by moonlight. "Beryl still not helping?"

"The more I ask, the less she does. I'm tired of her whining. It's easier to do things myself."

"I reckon if she didn't have you to hate, she'd have to hate herself. That's a heavy burden for a child." He gazed at Ruby a long while. "Her body's telling her she's a woman, but her mind ain't grown into it yet."

With a wan smile, she acknowledged that he was right. She looked at him. "You're worn out, too. Stay home. Get some sleep."

"I couldn't sleep knowing you're here all alone."

She dug into the earth with her toes.

He reached slowly, so slowly she was unsure when he claimed her foot, only becoming aware when he ran his thumbs over her arch, starting softly, then digging in deep, releasing knots she hadn't known were present.

She moaned.

He laughed, low and warm. "One way or another, I can make you sing."

Over several nights, his touch grew more intimate, moving from her feet and calves, up to her hands and arms, massaging, soothing, until he stood behind her, hands on her shoulders, kneading her rigid muscles.

She squirmed at his touch, squeezing her shoulders toward her ears, trying to escape his probing fingers. "Let me go."

"No." Bismarck stretched her muscles, wringing them with strong fingers. "Your muscles are too tight, partly from hitting your head but mostly from trying to hold your whole family together, for taking the blame for what that bastard did. It wasn't your fault."

He lapsed into a silence that stretched forever, his fingers working the whole time, his thumbs digging in, not letting her escape, driving the tension from her neck and shoulders.

When he finally spoke, his voice was hoarse. "That—that day—there wasn't a spot on your body that wasn't—you were too battered, I couldn't—Jesus Christ, I thought you were dead." He paused. "I've never been so scared or so angry in my life. Something in me snapped. I beat that bastard until he was as bloody as you were. I wanted to kill him. Damn near did. It took four men to pull me off him. I'm not proud of that. I'm not that kind of man. Hell, Ruby, I cain't live with that, but I cain't let go until you do."

His taut emotions transmitted themselves to his fingers. He dug more deeply into her neck, pressing harder on her tender muscles.

She struggled to escape his grip.

"Stop fighting me."

"I can't."

He dropped behind her, pinning her between his legs,

still digging deep into her tense neck. "Let go. Please? Just let go."

At last she moaned in defeat, allowing her shoulders to slump.

"Easy now. That's a good girl," he whispered into her curls. "Easy, little one. Easy."

Her skin warmed under his touch. Iron bands around her muscles began to relax.

Taking her head between his hands, he snapped her neck sharply from one side to the other.

A sound exploded in her ears like dominos falling. She screeched as her vertebrae realigned themselves. The release was instantaneous, so intense she broke into loud sobs.

Bismarck gathered her in his arms, rocking her, until she was empty of tears. Exhausted, she hiccoughed and sniffled into the bandana he handed her. He pulled the quilt around them. They slept bound by a thousand flowers.

Chapter Twenty-Three
A New Life

April 1896

Ruby knitted on the front porch, keeping a watchful eye on her children playing in the yard. Sunday dinner dishes were done. The Schmidt family digested their Sunday dinner on the front porch. Pa smoked his pipe and rocked. Jasper read. Beryl embroidered pillowcases for her hope chest.

A distant cloud of dust heralded a visitor. Before long, Bismarck pulled his buckboard to a stop before the gate. Jumping down, he nodded a howdy to Ruby's pa and the rest of the family then addressed her. "Would you ride with me?"

Her father gave a warning *humph*. "Ruby Louise, you're in an awfully big hurry to jump from the frying pan back into the fire." His disapproval shone bright and hard on his face.

"I'm a grown woman, Pa. Let me be." She stared at her father, daring him to stop her.

His eyes veered to the yard, back to her, then dropped.

Though she'd won the encounter, Ruby didn't feel victorious. Despite her best efforts, she had been unable to fill the sinkhole left by her ma's death. In his grief, her pa had abandoned his family. Though he had liked Bismarck in the past, if Ruby remarried, her pa would lose the woman who held his fractured home together. In her mind she apologized to her ma for not fulfilling the promise to care for her pa. If she didn't marry Bismarck, she would lose her last chance at happiness—and her sanity.

She turned to Bismarck. "Would you like a slice of pie? Coffee?"

"All I need is you." With a slight bow, he offered her his arm.

She hesitated then glanced at her sister, hoping Beryl would volunteer to watch Johnny and Sophie.

Beryl bent her head and paid inordinate attention to her stitchery.

Jasper looked up from his dime novel. "Go ahead, Sis. I'll keep an eye on your kids."

She smiled at her brother. "Thanks." She set her knitting down and placed her hand, damp from her jitters, in the crook of Bismarck's elbow. Beneath her fingers, his body felt fiery. Talc and bay rum scented the air. His blue eyes twinkled in a freshly shaved face, and his waxed mustache swirled across his cheeks. She took another deep breath. Lordy, he was definitely a dangerous man.

With a firm grip on her arm, he helped her into the buckboard.

Knowing what was coming, her lunch sat heavily in her stomach. Judging from his fancy duds and his demeanor, Bismarck deemed a decent amount of time—fifteen months— had passed since the incident with d'Este. Her divorce was finalized. He was going to ask for her hand. She wasn't sure she was ready.

In silence, they rode toward Stonecrop Ranch, named for the sedum that grew among its many rocks. He reined to a stop before the house he'd built for her five years earlier.

Bismarck showed her their home, the siding gleaming with fresh white paint, the shutters sparkling in sky blue. In front of the house, a picket fence had replaced the barbed wire. Nokoni and Magdalena had built their own house fifty yards away. Bismarck had added a bunkhouse, a tack room to the barn, a henhouse with a double wall of chicken wire to keep out coyotes, and had fenced the corrals with cedar. He saved money capturing wild mustangs rather than buying horses, how many horses he ran, how many were due to foal, how many he'd sold, how many cattle he kept to offset a slow year in the horse business, how much money he made the year before. Contracts to supply the army with horses kept him solvent when cattlemen around him went broke. He intended to reassure her of his worthiness.

"Ruby Louise, I'm all set to make you mine. If you're ready, that is. But I want you to see what I've got—I mean, what we'll have together—before you decide."

She swallowed hard. "You going to show me the inside of the house?"

Bismarck hesitated. "I reckon." He opened the front door and led her in. Like the exterior, the interior was spotless. "I've been mostly living in the kitchen. Less to heat. Easier for an old bachelor to keep up with."

Meager furniture stood clumped in patterns comprehensible only by a man to whom interiors were less important than the outdoors. Beneath the sparseness laid an emptiness, a sense he had built the home but did not deserve to live there.

He shifted on his feet. "Will you have me, Ruby Louise?"

Behind a tight smile, she hid her disappointment. No words of love passed his lips, yet all her life she'd known he cared for her. Once she had foolishly placed too much emphasis on a man's charming words. Bismarck's actions spoke far more eloquently. After a moment's indecision, she clasped his waist and pulled him outdoors, heading toward the barn. "Let's save the bed for our wedding night."

In the hayloft, they stood apart. He seemed as uncertain

as she did. She scuffed her toe on the floor, sending bits of grass drifting into the barn below.

"You sure, Ruby?"

She nodded.

He mounded hay to form a comfortable bed and laid horse blankets on top. "Take your clothes off then."

Ruby closed her eyes. Her breath hitched in her chest as she reached for the buttons of her shirtwaist.

Bismarck took each article of clothing from her, folded it, and set it aside.

When she was nude, the cool air tightening her nipples, he walked around her slowly, inspecting her. She clenched and stretched her hands over and over, growing anxious under his gaze. In the tiny mirror in her bedroom, she had checked herself, finding stretch marks from bearing two children but few outward signs of her ordeal with d'Este. Bismarck was sure to find scars she could not see. Defects that would brand her, leave her too ugly for him to bear.

When he finished his circuit, Bismarck continued to stare at her.

"I'm no filly at auction."

"I know." After swallowing several times, he started to speak but stopped.

"What?" She grew more nervous with his delay.

He sank to his knees before her, burying his face in her belly. "To have you before me, whole and beautiful, is a miracle."

Moisture trickled down her abdomen. She settled to her knees, wiping his eyes before unfastening his buttons with damp, trembling fingers.

When he entered her, he whispered, "I'll be easy, little one." And for the first few minutes he loved her tenderly, taking her to the brink, but holding himself back.

She locked her legs around him to pull him deeper, spurring him on.

Above her, his face grew fierce. "Tell me when I've driven him away forever."

"Now, Biz!"

Together they cried out, disturbing the barn swallows nesting along the roof, sending them spiraling upwards in flight.

Afterwards, he led her to the buckboard to take her home. "I'm a simple man. I can build houses, fences, barns. I can turn the meanest horse into a lap dog. I can repair anything that's broken. But I cain't spin the flowery words you want to hear." He nodded toward the barn. "But every time I walk through that door, I think about the hayloft. What we done up there. I want to love you, make you sing, for the rest of our lives."

He turned and stretched his arm across the horizon, indicating the open prairie carpeted by wild flowers. "My feelings for you are all mixed up with the land. I cain't separate the two. Your hair is in every sunset. Your eyes in every blade of new grass. And every primrose is the pink of your breasts after I've loved you."

In the corral, a couple of mares nursed their little ones. "Every foal, every calf, every little chick makes me want our child quickening in your belly." His Adam's apple slid up and down several times. "I need you, Ruby Louise. Pick a date."

* * * *

The ever-righteous Reverend Magruder wouldn't allow Bismarck and Ruby to marry in the church as she was tainted by her divorce. So, two weeks later, Ruby and Bismarck stood before Judge Willis. Ruby's pa refused to attend the civil service because it would not receive God's blessing.

Bismarck's brother, Christoff, and Molly stood as witnesses. Otherwise, the ceremony was as meager as Ruby's first marriage in the Philadelphia City Hall.

Ten minutes after slipping a gold band on her finger, Bismarck helped her into his buckboard. "Let's go home, Ruby Louise."

Chapter Twenty-Four
Little Bird

May 1897

"Biz?" Ruby poured Bismarck a cup of coffee, then sat beside him on the porch. He sipped then leaned back, propping his feet on the porch railing, his eyes focused on Johnny and Sophie playing in the yard.

"Willie wants to stop here on her way home from San Francisco. Do you mind?" Ruby pulled a letter from her apron pocket. "You wouldn't have to put up with her for long, only two weeks. Please? She's my dearest friend, and we haven't seen each other in years."

"That woman gets you all riled up. You're as ornery as a rattler for days after one of her letters. I cain't imagine what you'd be like if she was here."

"I don't have anyone else to talk to about art. Her letters remind me how much I miss her. How much I miss painting."

"But you act like I've hogtied you to this place, and you can't escape."

"It's not that. It's just—"

"What?"

"Willie and I painted together every day. Now, there's always something more important to do—canning, cooking, cleaning. Part of me is missing."

He turned his eyes back to the children and spoke without looking at her. "Bring me another slice of that peach pie, would you, honey?"

She glanced at her husband, suddenly aware he feared a visit from Willow might pull Ruby back to art, to Philadelphia. She sighed and went inside, folding the letter and slipping it into her pocket as she walked. When she returned with the pie, she rested it on the porch railing and patted his arm. "Never mind. I have too much to do before the baby comes. Don't have time for a guest."

He raised an eyebrow.

She saw the question in his eyes but kept her face carefully expressionless, hiding her disappointment. Only the bobble in her tight throat gave away her emotion.

The muscles in his jaw clenched. He pulled her into his lap.

She placed his hand on her belly. "Can you feel our child kicking?"

His words were muffled as he buried his face in her hair. "We cain't let those damned Yankees think us Texans are inhospitable, can we?"

* * * *

"Willie!" Ruby waved at the familiar figure stepping off the train at the far end of the Truly station. She gave Willow a hug before pulling back to get a good look at her friend's face.

Despite days traveling, the other woman appeared immaculate, understated, and expensive. Though a plain woman, Willow looked happy, at least as happy as Ruby had ever seen her. Her eyes were warmer and her smile less tight.

Beside her slender, bird-like friend, Ruby felt gauche, her pregnant body draped in drab, dusty, out-of-date clothing. When Willow took her hand, Ruby's eyes watered at the differences in their entwined fingers. Ruby's own hands, browned from the sun, had calloused from ranch work. How she envied the alizarin crimson and Prussian blue paint that dotted Willow's smooth hands like speckles on a fanciful bird's egg. Ruby quickly pulled her hand away. "Nearly seven years, and you haven't changed a bit."

"You have. You're positively rotund." Willow patted Ruby's belly. "When's the baby due?"

"July." She groaned. "Two more months in this heat."

"You're more beautiful than I remembered." Willow leaned forward and kissed Ruby's cheek. "My dear, I have missed you so." She clasped Ruby's hand again, squeezing it.

"How's Walter?"

"He's opening a gallery in San Francisco. He was too enthralled to return to New York with me."

Before either woman could say anything else, Bismarck appeared with Willow's trunk, set it down, and placed his arm around Ruby.

Under his appraising gaze, Willow released Ruby's hand.

Suddenly self-conscious and tongue-tied, Ruby failed to introduce her own husband.

An awkward silence arose.

Damnation. Ruby was surprised her feelings for Willow had not burnt out with time. Desperate to see her friend, Ruby had not fully considered how difficult it would be having both lovers around.

Finally, Bismarck lifted his hat and broke the silence. "Howdy, ma'am." He stuck out his hand. "Bismarck Behrens. You must be Miz Wycke."

On the way back to Polecat Draw, Bismarck drove the wagon while the women sat in the back and chatted, two magpies, catching up on each other's lives and those of Philadelphia colleagues.

"On our last trip to Europe, Walter bought art for his new gallery in San Francisco. We saw an interesting show in Italy. And spoke with the artist." Willow's voice dropped to a conspiratorial whisper. She hesitated a minute before adding, "Someone you know."

Ruby was afraid to ask who.

Willow replied anyway. "D'Este's in Venice."

The blood drained from Ruby's face. For a moment she feared she'd swoon.

"Are you all right, dear?"

With a deep breath, Ruby pulled herself together. She shook her head. "We're divorced. He's out of my life forever."

"You're not out of his. Imagine my surprise when I entered the salon and found paintings of my dearest friend and lov—"

Ruby shook her head in desperate warning.

"Anyway, the entire show consisted of paintings of you."

"All resembling Old Masters, I suppose?"

"His technique rivaled Titian's. In the early portraits, you were positively luminous. The newer ones depicted you as Medusa or a Harpie, lovely but hideous. Those paintings were exquisite but far darker than anything we saw from him at the Academy."

Ruby shivered.

"Critics said d'Este had found his own Angela del Moro, that Venetian courtesan who was Titian's companion and model."

"People think I'm a—" Ruby's eyes popped open.

"Don't worry. He refused to tell anyone who his model was." Willow shrugged. "He's changed. Not aging well at all. An underlying malevolence lurks in his eyes. And he has this scar." With her index finger, she drew a slash across her left cheek. "Rather than mar his looks, it makes him more dashing. Venetian ladies certainly found him attractive."

Ruby closed her eyes, reliving how she'd fought him. "Did he say how he got it?"

"In a duel. Defending some woman's honor."

Ruby ran her tongue over the bump on her lower lip.

* * * *

Back at the ranch house, Ruby introduced Willow to her children, four-year-old Johnny and two-year-old Sophie, both hiding shyly behind Ruby's skirts.

"Sorry." Ruby shrugged. "We don't get a lot of company out here."

Willow retreated slightly as if she didn't know how to approach youngsters.

To break the uneasy moment, Ruby said, "Would you care to clean up? We can visit while I heat water." She lit a fire in the stove, pumped water into two large cauldrons, poured Willow a glass of tea, and laid out a plate of cookies.

Two little vultures, her children circled her skirts. They knew better than to beg for treats, but their eagerness betrayed their knowledge that she would give them one.

Willow excused herself to the water closet.

After pumping a couple of buckets of cold water, Ruby lugged them to the door. She knocked and said, "I have your water."

On the inside, the lock clicked. The handle rotated beneath Ruby's hand. The door cracked then opened more fully. Ruby passed the water through the door, relieved Willow wore a robe.

Returning to her stove, Ruby passed her hand above the kettles and deemed them still not hot enough. A watched pot definitely never boiled. Her thoughts turned to Bismarck out in the barn. As soon as they had arrived home, he put the wagon away, curried the horse, and returned to work. He would not come in until dark, a good two hours away. She then thought of Willow bathing in the adjacent room, her slim body covered with soap bubbles. Lordy, those lustful feelings had not died out. Again Ruby wondered if what two women did together was adultery. Whatever it was called, she would not commit it. Perhaps Willow no longer found Ruby attractive. After all, Willow had called her rotund. Ruby forced away those thoughts. Her children were here. The child she carried was due soon. Her husband worked not fifty yards away. She simply could not carry on in this fashion.

When the water was warm, Ruby lugged a kettle to the door and knocked. "Hot water."

Willow opened the door.

Careful to respect Willow's privacy, Ruby averted her eyes as she poured the steaming water into the tin tub, adding a little cold before bending to stir it with her hand.

Willow placed her hands on Ruby's waist and pulled her erect.

Ruby turned. Her chest trapped her breath. Willow was naked. As slim and fair as ever, her dark hair flowed over her shoulders. Longing welled inside Ruby for the friend and lover she had missed for years. She lifted Willow's long hair, exposing small breasts with hazelnut nipples already hardened.

Their mouths met in a gentle, inquiring, longing kiss.

Ruby sighed and shoved Willow's hands away. "Bismarck is in the barn—"

"My love," Willow whispered. "So much time has passed. Yet nothing has changed." Her fingers fumbled with the buttons of Ruby's shirtwaist.

"Mama! Mama? Sophie hit me." Johnny's voice rang out as his feet stomped on the kitchen floor.

Ruby shook her head. "Everything has changed." Disengaging from Willow's arms, she refastened her buttons. "I'll be right there, Johnny." She opened the water closet door and stepped into the kitchen to mediate her children's quarrel.

* * * *

That night, after moving Johnny into Sophie's room in the attic, Ruby settled Willow into her son's room, rushing away to avoid the other woman's touch.

Downstairs, Bismarck stretched over the bed while Ruby brushed her hair the requisite hundred strokes before sitting opposite him.

Bismarck's hands settled on her shoulders, pulling her toward him. "You sure you didn't lose count? Seemed more like two hundred tonight. Took you an awful long time to get here."

She sank into the mattress, her hair tumbling across the linens.

"Willow mentioned d'Este. What's that sorry bastard up to?"

"He's in Venice. Just had a big art show." Ruby's shoulders tightened.

Bismarck sat up, pulling her chest against his, breathing reassurance in her ear. "Little one, you're safe. I won't let anything happen to you."

"I know." She pressed herself more tightly to him and shuddered. "He told Willow he got the scar on his face in a duel."

Bismarck snorted. "You didn't expect him to admit a little Texas gal got the best of him, did you?"

Ruby giggled. "Guess not."

Bismarck looked into her eyes. "Ever think about him?"

"It's hard not to—Johnny and Sophie resemble him. I worry they'll be like him inside, too. Especially Sophie. She was a difficult baby and already has a terrible temper." Haunted by memories, Ruby looked down.

Bismarck wrapped his fingers around her curls, tugging slightly. "Don't let that bastard come between us again."

Ruby lifted her face and kissed him gently. "You're the man I want."

Before Ruby could cover herself with the sheet, he raised her cotton gown, burying his nose between her legs. "Just smelling you, I get as hot as a July day."

She rolled away, thinking of Willow directly above them.

"You're mine, Ruby Louise. He doesn't belong in our bed." Relentlessly, Bismarck pursued her, touching her until she responded. "Come." He pulled her on top, guiding their joining. "Sing for me, little bird." In his ferocious ardor, the bed banged the walls. The breeze carried their cries out the open window.

Chapter Twenty-Five
A Quick, Clean Cut

After breakfast the next morning, Ruby toured the ranch with Willow, a slow walk through the garden, barn, chicken coop, and immediate vicinity of the house.

"In Philadelphia you told me Texas was flat and dry. Remember?" Willow reminisced as she looked across the plains. "I didn't realize how literally you meant that."

"I also said there is a beauty here found nowhere else."

"You're right." Willow turned in a slow circle, her eyes on the distant horizon. "There's certainly nothing extraneous to clutter your faculties." She took Ruby's hand. Linked, they walked on. "How can you bear living in the middle of nowhere? Last year Walter and I visited Monterrey, California. Other than the sound of the surf and wind, there was utter silence. Since my brain was not filled with noise, I felt compelled to fill it with art. Every day I painted the same view of the coast. Every image was different." Willow closed her eyes, conjuring the scene, choosing words that would bring it to life in Ruby's eyes. "Amazing light! The greens of the pines, the azure of the sea, the red of succulents on the beach. At sunset the sea turns a rose doré with mauve shadows. Breathtaking. But after two weeks—my God, I was bored to tears. After three weeks, I was insane. I left Walter there and returned to New York, to civilization."

"The last time I picked up a brush, I painted the shutters."

A bitter tinge colored Ruby's reply.

"You haven't painted at all since returning home? I would have thought the land—and Bismarck—would have restored your equilibrium."

"I've done sketches of the children here and there but never seem to have time to translate them to paintings. Ranching is hard work. Raising children harder. After…after Ma's death, I didn't have the energy. Maybe in a few years,"

"Do you miss it?"

Ruby nodded, not adding that she dreamed of art in the same way she dreamed of making love, awakening with the smell of turpentine and linseed oil in her nostrils, as rich and intoxicating as a lover's scent. The texture of the oil paints on her fingers, each color with a different feel, the coolness of blues, the muddiness of browns, the warmth of yellows. She missed how painting transported her to a place where nothing existed but herself and her canvas, where time stood still, where she felt complete.

Abruptly she changed the subject. "You can't imagine how distraught I was when you disappeared after Woodrow caught us. You didn't write. I didn't know what had happened to you."

"It wasn't my fault, my love. Father and Woodrow held me prisoner. I wrote, but they destroyed the letters before I could mail them. And beat me after every one." Willow shook her head. "I grew to hate those two. And my parents, for all their liberal leanings, denied their daughter the very rights they promoted. I expected more of them, especially Mother."

"Poor Willie. I didn't know." Ruby gathered Willow in her arms. "But you married Walter and escaped your parents. But that letter—the one in which you told me you'd married—ripped my heart out. Learning you loved someone else."

"I wouldn't call it *love*. By then I would have married the devil himself to escape my family." Willow stepped back a moment, though she retained Ruby's hand.

"And how is Walter?"

Willow hesitated. "He's fine."

"What aren't you telling me?"

"Our relationship is"—Willow searched for the word—"interesting? Complicated? When I first arrived in Europe, deprived of you, my heart was shattered. In my despair, I fear I mistook Walter's kindness for true love. It didn't take long to realize I loved him no more than he loved me."

"Poor thing." Ruby put her arm around Willow's waist and leaned against her shoulder while thanking God she and Bismarck had a true bond.

"In truth, Walter is a lavender man." At Ruby's questioning gaze, Willow added, "He prefers other men to his wife. We have a white marriage—one without conjugal interaction."

Ruby blinked in astonishment. "I suspected something. There was so much you didn't say in your letters. At times you seemed so circumspect, I couldn't even read between the lines." She recalled the line Willow had blacked out in that letter long ago.

In silence, the women walked side by side.

Eventually, Willow continued. "I suppose my relationship with Walter works oddly well. He is what Mamá would call a 'suffrage husband.' He doesn't hinder me or my career in any way. Children hold no appeal for either of us. Other than occasional companionship or appearances at art openings, he makes no demands. With him, I am as independent as a modern woman can be." She kicked at a patch of dry grass, sending grasshoppers flying. "Walter and I have become dear friends. We love and respect each other, drive each other to new creative pinnacles, just as you and I did at the Academy—"

"But what about"—Ruby swallowed— "passion?"

Willow raised her chin to a defiant tilt. "I believe women—and men—have a right to love whomever we choose, for as long as we wish. To change lovers as often as we please." Willow turned away. "Walter feels the same way. We turn blind eyes to each other's current whim."

Shocked, Ruby released Willow's arm, backed up several steps, then whirled to confront her friend. "You've taken lovers?"

"Many." Willow dodged Ruby's gaze. "During a painting jag, I isolate myself for weeks, scarcely speaking to anyone, not even Walter. Afterwards, the drive that had gone into painting becomes…sexual. I need to fuck someone."

Ruby blinked at Willow's use of the obscenity. "Men?" She swallowed. "Or women?"

"Mostly women. An occasional extraordinary man." Willow pulled Ruby toward her and kissed her deeply. "Jealous?"

"No…perhaps…yes." Ruby moaned. Her cheeks flamed as unbidden images of Willow with others appeared in her mind.

"Montmartre is a modern Mount Olympus. Young gods and goddesses abound, all eager to pose for, and perhaps become the companion of, a wealthy *Americaine*. I have my choice of Adonis or Aphrodite, a new one daily if I choose. Things are different in Paris, Ruby. Wilder, more open. I often think the French completely amoral."

Ruby sighed as she turned her back to Willow. "I'm less hurt now that I understand about Walter." She dodged a cow patty. "Have you found another 'special' friend?"

Stepping behind her friend, Willow wrapped her arms around Ruby and sensuously rubbed her pregnant belly, one hand moving to curve beneath a rounded breast. "No one recently. You remain my true love. Everyone else is merely an attempt to replace you."

Ruby leaned back, resting her head beneath Willow's chin, feeling the flutter of the other woman's pulse.

"You and Bismarck seem compatible enough."

Ruby pulled away. "Jealous?"

Willow nodded. "No—and yes. I hoped you and I might share one of those infamous Boston marriages between two women. All along I feared—I knew—you were truly Bismarck's. I never dreamed seeing you with him would hurt this much." She paused and stared at Ruby. "I was truly surprised you married d'Este. He seemed too mercurial to appeal to you. I remember you saying you'd not fall prey to his charms."

Ruby sighed. "He can be quite charming—when he chooses."

The women walked a few steps. Willow shot a glance at Ruby. "When you found Bismarck again, I was even more surprised. You have yet to tell me, my dear, what happened in the years between those two men." She reached for Ruby's hand and kissed it.

Ruby, growing uncomfortable under Willow's amorous gaze, shifted to a more decorous line of conversation. "Shown anything recently?"

* * * *

Ruby brought out her colors in response to Willow's order to do so.

"While I'm here we shall paint together just as we used to."

Stored in the attic closet for years, the pigments proved unusable. Tubes of oils had dried up. Brushes shed bristles like molting animals. Ruby dumped them into the waste bin to be burned later.

"Never you mind," Willow said. "We'll share mine."

Minutes later, Willow galvanized Ruby into action, dragged her outdoors, and commandeered Bismarck to model. Sophie and Johnny chased each other through the grass, laughing.

Ruby worked on a portrait of Bismarck, his face shaded by his Stetson, his mouth clamped tightly against the stem of a pipe, his chambray shirt the same blue as his amused eyes, all outlined by the brilliant gold from the sunset.

Ruby sketched, erased, sketched, becoming more frustrated with each attempt. "I've lost my skills. All that time at the Academy wasted."

"Quite nice, Ruby." Willow's voice came from behind Ruby's shoulder. "There's more there than meets the eye." Willow looked at the man, then back at the painting. "Bismarck's stoicism shows in his eyes. He's uncompromising yet not unkind." She hesitated, as though hating to admit her next sentiment. "A good man."

"Sit still, Biz! I can't sketch you if you keep moving." Ruby blamed him for her failed attempts to capture his features.

"You're making it more difficult than it is." Willow placed her hand over Ruby's, guiding the pencil. "You must not *think* the lines, Miss Schmidt—"

"—you must *feel* them." Ruby rolled her eyes as she finished the quote. "But it's all wrong." Ruby gritted her teeth. She tore the painting from the easel and ripped the paper into bits, releasing them into the breeze. Johnny and Sophie raced after the fragments, chasing them like butterflies.

"You simply need to get your fingers on a paint brush more often."

A flash of anger raced through Ruby. That was easy for Willow to say. She'd never done a day's work in her life.

Willow returned to her own work, and Ruby peeked at her friend's easel. The other woman had filled her watercolor paper with a single over-sized desert poppy, its six translucent petals crinkled like old tissue paper. White, but not white. Against the stark purity of the paper, Willow traced meandering lines with a near-calligraphic hand. Each wrinkle in the delicate petals had a shadow of lavender with a highlight of gold from the setting sun. Yellow prickles adorned the pale green stem.

"Exquisite. A strong image, Willow. The flower looks too beautiful to be poisonous."

Side by side in the evenings, the women applied brush to paper as the clouds turned scarlet and yellow against the cobalt sky, lavender cenisa bloomed after a recent rain, and tall grasses waved as far as they could see.

Despite her initial frustration at the loss of her skills—and feeling that her work was inadequate compared to Willow's—Ruby regained confidence quickly. A growing joy filled her. She had her hands on a paintbrush, her dearest friend beside her, an indulgent husband watching, two healthy children playing nearby, and another growing inside her. Surrounded by everything she had ever wanted or loved, she felt satisfied. Women, if lucky, *could* have everything they desired.

With Willow's arrival, Bismarck became quite attentive. Ruby was unsure if his behavior was due to Willow or the baby. He made sure Ruby was comfortable and even washed dishes one night so she and Willow could visit on the porch. Another night, as she stood before the mirror, he brushed her curls until they gleamed. When he lifted her nightgown over her head, her hair, crackling with electricity, formed a nimbus around her, glowing golden in the lamplight. Kneeling before her, his lips brushed her lower curls until she moaned. He stood slowly, his head rising between the pale moons of her breasts. His mouth found her nipples, large and dark from pregnancy. By the time he turned off the lantern and carried her to bed, she was already singing.

In the pitch black, long after he made love to her, he stroked her rounded belly. "Our son's growing like a weed."

"Don't count your roosters before they hatch, Biz. This little chick might be a hen." She moved his hand to her breast.

He gave a deep laugh as he stroked her nipple. "Being with child must agree with you."

"What makes you say that?"

"You're more"—he paused to kiss her shoulder—"obliging."

Once Bismarck had made love to Ruby the second time that night, he fell asleep straightaway, lying on his side, an arm and a leg flung possessively over her.

With a sigh, she thought that it was easier to be amenable if one were not preoccupied by pregnancy. Already expectant, she would be free from worry for several more months. Lying awake afterwards, as she curled against Bismarck's back, Ruby's forehead rested in the hollow between his shoulder blades. Her hand laid claim to his hip, a rise in the familiar landscape of his body. God must have placed men's bones for just such a purpose, for women to cling to when they needed reassurance, when they sought an anchor.

* * * *

"Anyone need a refill? I'll get the coffee pot." Ruby carried their dessert plates to the kitchen, leaving Willow and Bismarck together on the porch. On her return, coffee pot in hand, Ruby stopped just inside the front door, watching her husband and dearest friend, listening to their near-whispers.

"I can see it, Mr. Behrens. Why can't you? Ruby is shriveling up inside."

"She's doing just fine." Bismarck sipped his coffee, his throat working long after he swallowed.

"A man does only a man's work. A female artist must be a superwoman, someone of two selves. One performs the work she is called by God to do while the other fulfills the womanly obligations our culture sets upon her." Willow waved her hands expansively emphasizing a woman's duties. "With all Ruby does now, she doesn't have time to paint. With a new baby, she'll be more overworked."

"Ruby knew how hard ranch life was when she signed on."

The conversation fell into dense silence.

"Hire someone to help her. If money is a problem, I'll pay for it."

"Goddamn it! I can support my own wife." Bismarck started to rise. With his sudden movement, the cup clattered precariously on its saucer.

Quickly, Ruby pushed open the door, letting its screech announce her return. "More coffee?" She should have brought a knife to cut the tension.

The uneasy truce between Bismarck and Willow ended with that conversation. Ruby didn't believe the two had said a word to each other since. This time around Ruby was not the one as ornery as a rattler. Bismarck spent more time out of the house. He wolfed his meals quickly then headed back to the barn. She wondered if he sensed the feelings between her and Willow, if he was jealous. At night he went to bed early and fell asleep facing away from her, a gap between them. Willow's weight lay between them, pressing into a space that seemed far wider than the few inches it measured. During the night, Bismarck rolled over and spooned with her. Out of habit, she supposed, a need that could not be denied in his sleep. His curls tickled her where his warmth pressed against her buttocks. If she reached behind her, a few strokes of her fingers would rouse him. She imagined the feel of him, hard, needy, heavy in her hand. When he was too drunk with sleep to resist, she could get what she desired.

A kick from the baby disturbed her thoughts. Always more active when Ruby wanted to sleep, the baby seemed determined to remain awake, no matter which position Ruby settled into or how much she rubbed her belly. Unable to rest, she sighed. She was as restless as her child. Easing Bismarck's arm from her waist, she rose, poked her feet into the *huaraches* she used as slippers, and draped a shawl around her shoulders. Her feet moved toward the attic without conscious thought. At the creak of the first stair, she stopped, knowing Willow would want far more than talk, and Ruby found herself unable to break her wedding vows.

Instead, she went outside and sat by the stock pond. The moon rose high, its reflection oscillating with the ripples in the black water. Around her, crickets chirped and frogs croaked, echoing the creak of the windmill twirling in constant subjugation to the wind. She plucked a blade of broad grass and ran her fingers over it, soothing herself with the repetitive motion. On this vast expanse of prairie, she felt trapped. She had seen spring-coil animal traps in which a single paw remained clamped between the steel teeth, where a coyote had chewed off a leg rather than be captured. No matter which leg she chewed off, she would hurt someone and she herself would be devastated.

As she sat there, the indigo sky lightened to heliotrope. Against that not-color, not-purple, not-pink, not-blue, the morning star rose. The baby stopped his frolicking at last. Ruby drifted off. In that moment between sleep and wake, she became part of the sunrise, floating among the colors and the stars, painting a dream canvas. As she lifted her paintbrush to splash color across the sunrise, grasses stirred behind her, dragging her back to earth. She recognized the footsteps and turned.

Bismarck walked toward her leading a horse and a pack mule, the uneven turf disguising his limp.

When they'd gone to bed last night, he hadn't mentioned riding out this morning.

He dropped the reins, walked behind her, and sat, engulfing her in his legs. The rough denim of his pants rubbed her thighs as he pulled her against his chest. His hands ran up and down her arms, warming her.

"You've been out here a while. You're cold. And damp."

"Couldn't sleep. The baby's been a Mexican jumping bean."

"You smell good, like fresh water." He buried his face in her hair, sniffing the dewdrops, his breath hot against her neck. "What have you been doing?"

"Thinking."

"Trouble always brews when women think." He tried to make it a joke, but his voice cracked.

She didn't laugh but jabbed him in the ribs with her elbow.

He held her tighter. Neither spoke. The silence grew long, tense.

Bismarck's rough hand brushed her hair from her neck. His kiss was so soft she thought she dreamed it, so light she almost couldn't bear it.

She leaned further into him.

He retreated a hair's breadth. "Ruby, you been all stirred

up since Willow got here. You barely give me the time of day."

She opened her mouth to protest, thinking of all the loving she and Bismarck had enjoyed recently. The current shortage was all his doing. At his irritated *tsk*, she refrained. "Willie and I have a lot of catching up to do. I haven't seen her in years. Haven't had a conversation about art in ages."

Bismarck gave an another *tsk*. "You two talk a language I don't understand. Words like lizard crimson and rose do-re-mi. Pwontilism."

Amazed that he had paid attention to her conversations with Willow and struck by his mispronunciations, Ruby laughed. "You speak a language she doesn't. Bronco, latigo, cayuse, grulla."

He ignored her response and continued, "All my life, I've loved you. Since we were little kids, I've tried to tie you to me. You've always been the better part of my heart." He rubbed her belly with his rough hands. "I thought sure this baby would do the trick. Make you completely mine. Not his any more."

His forehead rested against the back of her head, his breath damp and warm on her neck. "Now she's pulling you away from me. I cain't compete with no rich city-lady. I cain't compete with art. Hell, I cain't fight something I cain't see or touch. At night I try to show you where you belong, but you're still slipping away. I don't know what else to do." He stood. His hand rested on her shoulder a few seconds before giving a slight squeeze.

He rose, strode to his stallion, and gathered the reins. "I'm heading to the drift line south of San Angelo looking for strays. I'll be back when she's gone." He swung into the saddle, his spurs reflecting the first red light of dawn. "If you leave me, Ruby Louise, don't drag it out. When she leaves, go with her. Make a quick, clean cut."

Chapter Twenty-Six
Wages of Sin

June 1897

Though Willow's train was not due until Thursday, Ruby had Nokoni hitch the buggy on Wednesday. Seven months pregnant, she feared making the round-trip journey in one day would be too fatiguing. She planned to stay in her parents' house in Truly. With Nettie's death and since the younger children no longer attended school, her family used it only on weekends. The hired hand loaded Willow's trunks in the back while Johnny and Sophie bounced in glee with the novelty of staying overnight with Magdalena and eating fresh tortillas rather than cornbread, while Ruby was gone.

As soon as the women crossed the threshold of the little house, Willow grabbed Ruby and kissed her. "We're alone at last." She unbuttoned her own shirtwaist with glee.

"Willie, stop!"

Instead Willow, with every article of her clothing that hit the floor, pulled Ruby closer to the bedroom.

Ruby pushed Willow away.

"We have precious little time." Willow gathered Ruby's hand in her own.

"But you've married. And taken lovers."

"I simply search for someone to ensnare my heart as you have. But you married as well, my dear. Twice. Bismarck, I can understand. You always loved him. But d'Este?"

"That son of a bitch—"

"Sh-h-h, love." Willow ran a finger over the thick scar on Ruby's lip. "Did Bismarck do this?"

"No! Of course not." Ruby jerked back. "He's such a gentle soul, he refuses to whip horses."

"Then d'Este?"

Ruby nodded. A sudden rush of tears betrayed the sink-hole of her emotions.

Willow stared at Ruby then took her arm. "Something happened?"

Again, Ruby nodded.

"And you didn't tell me?" Willow sounded hurt.

"I couldn't." Ruby began. A few steps took her beyond Willow's reach. When she turned to face her old lover, her voice quavered. "Willie, believe me, living through it once was enough. I couldn't write it. And, had I put the events on paper, I would have had to acknowledge my own culpability."

"I'm here now. Tell me." Willow pulled Ruby to her bosom and dropped them both to the bed.

After days of tiptoeing around their feelings, their past, in the safety of Willow's arms, Ruby spilled the story of her mother's death, the shattering of her relationship with Beryl and her father, and her sense of failure at her divorce, wretched though that marriage had been, and last, the rape.

"Oh, my dear." Willow soothed Ruby with soft kisses and delicate caresses. "I sensed your withdrawal. Your letters lacked their usual sparkle. But I never imagined anything so horrible. I thought perhaps you were unhappy with Bismarck. If so, I thought to rescue you, to steal you away, and free you from the bondage of marriage."

Ruby stared at Willow. "You have changed."

Willow nodded emphatically. "Leaving my parents was for the best. As much as Mamá considered herself a modern woman, she never stood up to Father and Woodrow. Not once did she defend me—or my right to love whom I chose. Despite all her preaching about Free Love and a woman's right to control her own body, she refused me ownership of myself.

"While I might miss a *passion amoureuse* with Walter, he has given me something I never expected, something infinitely more precious than a physical relationship. He has given me freedom. No longer must I be meek. I am a pliant willow changed to staunch oak. I grasp what I want from life. I no longer permit others to bunt me around like chattel."

Ruby laughed. "Nonetheless, I believe your mother would be proud of her daughter. I am."

"What about you and Bismarck? Are you happy?"

"Bismarck is the best man I know. We have a good life together."

"But are you *happy*?"

"For the most part." Ruby gave a diffident shrug. "Some days I am discontent. Others I think I'm a fool for wanting more. But, God, I miss painting like my life's blood." Ruby ran her thumb along the side of her index finger. "In dreams, I feel the delicate weight of a brush. My fingers run its length, feeling the smoothness of the wood, its roundness, its taper. I long for those moments when I commune with my canvas, when I lose myself in my painting, when it tells me where it wants to go. I awaken, realize I've been dreaming, and feel a part of me has been amputated."

Willow took her hand. "And this baby?"

"Bismarck has taken Frank's children to raise as his own, but he needed his own child." Ruby rubbed her stomach. "This one will bind us more tightly."

Willow slowly removed Ruby's clothing. "You are beautiful."

"But you called me 'rotund'." Ruby's lips curled into a pout.

Willow laughed. "Perhaps I was jealous. You are all aglow with this child. I want to see you—all of you—and paint you." She led Ruby to the bed, removed her clothing and began sketching all the while regaling her lover with tales of Parisian *maisons closes* where any variety of sexual satisfaction could be found—for a price.

Ruby found herself blushing at Willow's tales, yet the telltale shimmering she had felt when they read *Fanny Hill* rose between her thighs.

When Willow finished, she carried her sketches to show Ruby, sat beside her, and stroked her shoulder as they looked at the images. Soon Willow's mouth found Ruby's lips. "I want to make you forget how you got this." She caressed Ruby's lip with her tongue before pulling the scar into her mouth and sucking gently on it as her fingers meandered to Ruby's tender nipples.

After a few kisses, Ruby stilled Willow's hands. "I can't do this, Willie. Not to Bismarck. Not to our baby."

"Give me tonight. Just tonight. Please? I beg you. I'll never ask you again."

"But—"

"Every nerve in my body delights at your voice, begs for your touch, desires you. Please. It's been so long." Willow's fingers and mouth persisted, wearing down Ruby's resistance.

At last, the passion that had simmered beneath the surface during Willow's visit boiled over.

After their loving, as Ruby lay curled in Willow's arms, the baby kicked for a few minutes then settled down. Ruby slept better than she had in a month.

The next morning, Ruby and Willow walked in Nettie's

garden, snipping new rose buds before they opened, forming tight nosegays for each other, wrapping the stems in satin ribbons and tying them with bows like little wedding bouquets for a love that died on the vine.

"Come with me, Ruby. We can go to Paris. Women like us are free there."

"Women like us?"

"Women who love one another. Destiny made us women at a time when only the law of men is recognized. Yet all over Europe and America, women live together without men being the wiser. Our sole sin was getting caught. In Paris we can live openly."

"I love you, but—" Ruby twirled her bouquet in her hand, unable to continue.

"I gather you still love Bismarck as well?" Willow closed her eyes, her face pinched.

"Yes." Ruby gave a helpless shrug. "Willie, if a magician could conjure a spell to combine you and Bismarck into one, I would be complete. As it stands, if I love you, I hurt him. By loving him, I hurt you. Loving you both, I am torn asunder." She paused and looked closely at Willow. "How do you and Walter manage? Surely you must care for each other—at least a little?"

"We care deeply—on some levels. We built a two-winged house joined by common rooms. He resides on one side, I on the other. By mutual agreement, we occasionally meet in the middle."

"How would I fit in there?"

"You will live with me. Walter would understand."

"You sound quite certain."

"The arrangement has worked since we first married. We simply ask no questions about what happens in the other's space."

"And Johnny and Sophie?"

Willow recoiled. "I suppose you might bring them."

"Oh, Willie, I do love you. But I could never forsake Bismarck or my children."

As they exchanged nosegays, tears glimmered in Willow's eyes. "Our days as lovers are over, aren't they?"

Ruby nodded. "I'm sorry."

"However many paramours I take, Ruby, you remain my true love."

Before leaving to catch the train, Willow gave Ruby a farewell gift, a mahogany box a foot wide, six inches deep and three inches high. Ruby turned the key in the lock, opened the box, and found a Winsor and Newton watercolor paint set. Inside, thirty-six colors imprinted with a winged sea-lion lay in four rows along the rear of the box. In front sat two twelve-sided glasses to hold water. A shallow drawer held a porcelain tray to mix paints and storage space for pencils and brushes. Elegant and understated, the box must have been terribly expensive. Ruby was speechless.

A folded piece of paper lay on top. Ruby reached for it. The cubes of pigments had stained the page.

"Read it later." Willow's hand stopped Ruby before she opened the sheet. "You need to paint, my love. Above being a wife and mother, you are an artist. You've lost sight of the real you. Claim yourself again. Otherwise you'll never be truly happy."

"Someday I will resume painting." If there were no more children for a while. If she and Bismarck ever reached the point they could hire someone to help with the housework. If he came home in a better mood.

"But how empty you shall be until then. If nothing else, paint your babies. How can one live without making a grand effort all the time?" Willow kissed Ruby gently on the cheek. "Do not give up. Become ruthless. You can succeed as a woman artist."

Though Ruby did not voice her thoughts, it occurred to her that success as a female artist must be infinitely easier if one were wealthy and had no household duties. Immediately she berated herself for her jealousy and thanked Willow again for the lovely paintbox.

* * * *

After Willow boarded the train, Ruby pulled the buckboard in front of Statler's Mercantile. As long as she was in town, she would stock up on necessities and a bit of hard candy for her children. She pulled out her list. The usual staples, Liberty Brand coffee, Bismarck's Prince Albert tobacco, and a bottle of whisky. Moderate in all things, once he finished supper, he puffed his pipe and sipped two fingers of whiskey as he read.

Jack Statler bagged nails for a rancher. Molly, now Mrs. Thomas Stephenson, stepped from the storeroom just as Ruby walked in.

Molly smiled in greeting, then said, "Turn around, Ruby."

Ruby pivoted. An advertisement for Martin Seeds was tacked to the wall, featuring a red-haired farm girl, breasts as ripe as Early Elberta peaches, her body sensuously curved to counterbalance the weight of a basket of produce slung on her left hip. Draped off one shoulder, a deep green blouse rode above a russet skirt.

"Damn him!"

Molly recoiled at Ruby's profanity. "I thought you'd be excited. She looks just like you."

"She is me." Ruby snatched the poster of *Still-life with Girl* off the wall and crumpled it before tossing it in the waste can.

"That won't do much good." Molly's eyes twinkled. "Your picture is on every seed packet."

"Damn him!" Years before, d'Este had framed his first portrait of Ruby and given it to her as a wedding gift. Unable to bear looking at it, she had crated it when she returned to Texas and had not viewed it since. That sorry son of a bitch had repainted the image, then sold it—sold her—to the Martin Seed company. Ruby supposed she should count herself lucky that, unlike other paintings he had done of her, she was not pregnant and, at least in this particular portrait, wore clothing. She found it ironic that rather than achieving fame as an artist, she would be infamous as the face of Martin Seeds.

Her head was still spinning from Bismarck leaving and Willow's farewell, and now d'Este had invaded her life again. Two years after he raped her, Ruby still had nightmares and feared she might never escape his grasp. Willow had said he was in Venice, thousands of miles away. Even from that distance he wreaked havoc on her life.

The door of the mercantile opened. Ruby turned. Doc Granger stuck his head in.

"Saw your wagon out front, Ruby. How's the baby?"

"No problems."

The doctor eyeballed her belly. "I need to examine you soon. You look farther along than I thought. With your ma's history, I want to keep a close eye on you. I'd do it now, but I'm heading up to the Carsons' place. Their youngest broke his leg." Granger looked around. "Where's Bismarck?"

"Gathering strays down by San Angelo."

"Don't worry. He'll have plenty of time to get back before you drop that foal."

* * * *

Dejected, yet somewhat relieved, to have sent Willow

on her way, Ruby started home. With the jarring of the wagon over the rutted road, an ache started in her back. The closer she got to the ranch, the more anxious she became, her foot tapping on the floorboard of the wagon, as she wondered what she would find when she got home. Bismarck was gone. He'd said more the night he'd left than in all the years she had known him. She had never realized she could measure her husband's despair by the number of words he strung together. The guilt she felt for being with Willow spiraled in slow circles in time with the turning wagon wheels.

Ruby had not intended to be unfaithful. She had loved her husband, really loved him, since childhood. A good, kind man, he represented everything a woman should want. But she and Willow had been torn apart, separated against their will. Somehow they'd needed to touch, to reconnect, to release the stored-up longing, to heal the jagged wound between them. Ruby vowed it would never happen again. Bismarck had forgiven her d'Este. That absolution, she knew, would not stretch to include her loving another woman.

In many ways, Bismarck was a hard man, shaped by the harshness of Texas, used to spending time alone. When he spoke, his sentences were picked clean by buzzards, but he could telegraph his meaning with the cock of an eyebrow or stubbing of a boot toe in the dirt. Arms that broke horses and wrestled cattle and delivered puppies also loved her. Once a year, her husband took off with a bunch of local ranchers and cowhands, rounding up the herd, getting ready for branding. Hard work, but also an excuse for manly camaraderie, drinking, tall tales around a campfire. This time, he ran off to sulk in isolation. Two days ago, when she and Sophie had gathered eggs, a dozen cows with calves circled in the corral. Bismarck had driven them in and ridden out again without a word. Instead of waiting for her to leave him and go back east, returning to art and Willow, in a preemptive strike, he'd left.

In the near distance, low hills rose from the smooth belly of the *Llano Estacado*. Basalt spires above limestone hills marked the location of the only permanent groundwater for miles. Bismarck had not returned from chasing strays. Johnny and Sophie were safe with Magdalena and Nokoni. With no need to rush home, Ruby turned the wagon toward the springs. For the first time since she married, hell, for the first time since returning to Texas, she could steal time for herself, time alone to work through her conflict. Perhaps a walk would ease the discomfort in her back, and painting, as it had in the past, would relieve the disquiet in her soul.

Close to the springs, Ruby set the wagon brake, grabbed Willow's watercolor box, and hiked the few yards to the waterhole. Stepping through a cleft in the limestone walls that surrounded the water, she slipped inside. Above her head, monoliths rose like bell towers. The white rocks glowed. Green leaves filtered the sunlight. The dust and heat didn't penetrate the oasis. As tranquil as a cathedral, the spot was her favorite place on the prairie.

In the past, Ruby's family had picnicked here. She and her siblings had learned to swim in the pool. Bismarck brought her here to court and spark.

She set the paintbox on a large flat rock overlooking the spring and seated herself beside it. There, she ran her fingers over figures carved into the stone, *BB + RS* surrounded by a heart. Bismarck had gouged their initials into the slab when they were youngsters. When her fingertip grew raw from repetitive tracing of the letters, she popped it in her mouth and sucked gently, allowing her thoughts to join the wind-whispered prayers of the oaks and cottonwoods.

Refusing to surrender to her unease, Ruby pushed herself

to paint, to not waste the rare freedom from chores—and from Willow's recent disapproval that Ruby was neglecting her talent. She opened the box, saw Willow's note, and immediately closed the lid. It was best that she and Willow part, but she could not bring yet herself to read the farewell letter. She would be forced to admit their relationship was truly over.

With Willow gone, Ruby hoped that she and Bismarck might return to their former ease. Her feelings for him were as deep as those she had for Willow. Surely loving two people was not a sin, but breaking her marriage vows had been. Thinking on the enormity of her actions, she grew too agitated to put pencil to paper. She tried to sketch, but her body absorbed her brain's disquiet. Again and again, she shifted her position, seeking relief from the vague, but worsening, low back pain. Surely the jostling from the wagon caused the aching.

Soon the pain moved to her abdomen. Cramps settled into her womb. She moved her hand from place to place, trying desperately to remember the last time she felt the baby kick. Her heart plummeted. She had no clear memory of any baby movement after Willow had slipped that *thing* inside her. "It's a *godemiché*. It will make you feel you've been loved by a man," Willow had explained moments before bringing Ruby to that astounding release.

Ruby and Bismarck had loved each other only days before. That object could be no different from having her husband inside. Nonetheless she feared it had injured her baby. Her self-loathing grew. What kind of mother lost track of her child?

Leaving her box of paints on the rock, Ruby stood, paced a few steps, stretched backwards, bent at the waist, paced a few more steps, trying to relieve the ache in her back and belly.

She should go home. After taking a few strides toward the wagon, her pain intensified. A rip deep inside dropped her to her knees. Her bloomers and petticoats grew heavy and wet. She lifted her skirt. Dark red stained her linen undergarments, the same color as the Dragon's Blood pigment, as yet untouched by a brush, in her new paint box.

No! It was too soon. Ruby clutched her belly and staggered to the wagon. "Don't come. Not yet."

Chapter Twenty-Seven
Loss

Hoisting herself into the wagon, Ruby whipped the horse to a trot. Another contraction doubled her over. The reins slipped from her fingers. She curled on the floorboard, rocking herself back and forth, and allowed the mare to wend her way home. Somewhere along the way, she realized she'd abandoned her paintbox. No matter. Someone could retrieve it later.

The horse, pacing herself, slowed to a walk but continued toward the ranch.

Breathing slowly, Ruby tried to remain calm. Johnny had come after eight hours of labor, Sophie after twenty-six. This one was coming too soon, too fast, with too much blood. Ruby feared she would be like her mother, producing a string of stillbirths, all to be buried in the cemetery on the ridge behind the house. She remembered how high her mother's hopes had risen with each pregnancy and how low her spirits had sunk with each loss.

The windmill. Ruby sagged with relief when she glimpsed the sunlight reflected off its steel blades. Before long, the metallic creaking of its gears reached her ears. Almost home. "Hold on, little one." She prayed, fully aware her prayers came too late.

As the wagon neared the homestead, the dogs announced her arrival. The mare slowed to a stop.

Nokoni stepped from the barn. "*Señora* Ruby." He lifted his battered hat in greeting.

Ruby tried to rise but sank back to the floorboard. "Get Magdalena. The baby—"

Nokoni raced to the wagon.

"Mama, Mama!" Johnny ran towards the wagon, the barn dogs followed him, yipping and dancing in circles around the boy.

"Not now, sweetie. Stay away." Ruby held up her hands and cautioned her son, afraid he'd be frightened by her blood-soaked clothing.

Nokoni lifted her from the wagon and carried her to the house. Along the way he sent Johnny to find Magdalena.

Within an hour, the baby arrived.

No lusty cry broke from her son's new lungs.

"*¡Madre de Dios!*"

"What's wrong?" Ruby demanded.

"*Nada, Señora.*" Magdalena cleaned the infant, wrapped him in a linen towel, and passed him to his mother. "*Que lástima. Señora, él es muerto.*"

Ruby beheld a tiny, perfectly formed baby boy, his hands smaller than a quarter. Not a normal healthy pink or the blue of a babe who hadn't drawn a breath, but a baby as white as the linen that swaddled him. Eyes wide with panic, she shook his little arms and legs trying to force a breath, a cry, from his still lungs.

Magdalena tried to pry the baby from Ruby's arms.

"Send Nokoni for the doctor." Ruby clenched the babe to her breasts, tears streaking her cheeks. "And someone to find Bismarck."

When Magdalena left for the night, Ruby lit a lantern. Though the other woman had bathed him, Ruby gently cleaned him herself and dressed him in a white gown. She shook her head. The garment was far too big. For hours, by flickering lantern light, she trimmed and stitched, sizing the frock to fit her little one.

When her boy was perfectly garbed, she cradled his skull and, with her hand, fixed its geometry in her brain. Her thumb inscribed the arc of his brow in her memory. Her nose imprinted the scent from the crook of his neck on her dreams. The pad of a finger applied the burnished new-penny color of his hair to her mind's palette. Her arms held him, awed by how his tiny body made her soul feel so heavy. Finally she sketched her son so she would never forget his innocent face.

* * * *

Thousands of square miles of land lay between Truly and San Angelo with Bismarck the proverbial needle in the haystack. Ruby waited three days for her husband's return. With the weather uncomfortably warm, the baby's burial could not be postponed. She sobbed as Nokoni slipped a tiny wooden coffin into the hard dry ground. Children weren't supposed to regard their parents from Heaven. She sensed the babe looking down in both accusation and pity.

The wind, though it carried the scent of distant rain, stirred dust into the cloudless sky and whipped her skirts behind her. She held her other two children tightly against her side. They whispered to each other and fidgeted, untouched by the solemnity of the moment. Magdalena and Nokoni stood nearby praying in Spanish. After she read from the Bible, Nokoni hammered a filigreed wrought iron cross at the head of the little grave.

When everyone else went inside, Ruby remained at the site. Her baby's resting place, sheltered by the Italian stone pine windbreak Bismarck had planted when they first built their house, was visible from her kitchen window. But she was not ready to let go yet.

When she needed him most, Bismarck could not be found. If only she had him—or Willow—to talk to, maybe the rip in her soul would not seem as deep. She thought of the little bony hand she and Willow had thoughtlessly sketched at the Academy, never considering the pain experienced by the child's mother.

The sky in the west darkened. Sheet lightning slashed the sky, its brilliant light unable to penetrate the blackness surrounding Ruby's heart. She had lost Willow. She had lost Bismarck. She had lost her babe. She wondered how long it would be before she lost her mind.

* * * *

In the wee hours, while the rest of the ranch slept, a nightgowned Ruby returned to her baby's grave. By moon-light she wandered the nearby landscape, gathering stones and arranging them in concentric ovals on the freshly turned earth, as neatly as pecans atop her pies.

Distant thunder sounded. She looked up. The sky was clear in the east, but from the west thunderheads roiled toward her. Only in Texas was the firmament big enough to contain such contradictions. The first teardrops of rain touched her cheek. Moments later, the sky opened. Rain lashed her. An irrational fear that a torrent would wash her baby away filled her.

The wind whipped her wet hair. Wet clothing clung to her. Iron-red pigment from the earth stained her gown to mid thigh. The same bloody color coated her arms.

By daybreak, as the storm dwindled to sprinkles, she finished the stone cairn covering the grave. She drew no comfort from the rosy dawn that promised a sky as blue as Bismarck's eyes. A day that by its very clarity seemed hell-bent on erasing the fact of her child's death. Crying was too easy. Three days of tears had not relieved the ache in her womb. She threw herself across the stones, welcoming the pain of tender breasts crushed against rock, breasts filled with milk that would never nourish. At some point, exhausted, she slept.

A shadow crossed her face, waking her. On the opposite side of the grave, Bismarck sat atop his horse, water still dripping from the brim of his hat.

Ruby couldn't tell if tears or rain fell from the tips of his mustache. She stood and reached for him.

He danced his horse away from her. "I rode as fast as I could to get here." Bismarck turned, unbuckled his saddlebag, pulled something from it. "I found this when I stopped for water at the spring."

Ruby recognized her paint box. She stood, raising her arms to take it.

He held it beyond her grasp. "What were you thinking? Two women out there alone? Something might have happened."

She pinched her lips together, trying not to look down at her now-flat abdomen.

"Jesus Christ." Comprehension lit his face. "You lost the baby there, didn't you?" His jaw muscles clenched. "And you couldn't hold off burying him? You didn't think I'd want to see my son?"

"I tried. We tried. We couldn't find you. We couldn't wait any longer." She reached again for him, both seeking and offering comfort.

His face distorted by anger, he raised the box above his head.

"Biz, no—" She stretched on her tiptoes to stop him. Realizing there was no use, she dropped to the balls of her feet. Seeing the hardness in his face, she curled into a ball in the mud and steeled herself. The blow never came. At last, she glanced up.

He held the box high in trembling hands. He looked down at her, hesitated then dumped the contents of the box over the grave. The glass water cups and porcelain palette shattered on the rocks. Cubes of paints scattered, sinking into puddles of water between the stones.

With all his strength, he slammed the empty case on the cairn. The wood splintered on the stones, shards flying.

A fragment flew through the air, sliced her temple, narrowly missed her eye. Her hand darted to her face.

"You let that son of a bitch's bastards live, but by traipsing around, being someplace you oughtn't, you killed my boy." He kicked his mount and rode off, turning back only to say, "God damn you to hell, Ruby."

Too stunned to call after him, Ruby tried to gather the precious cubes of paint. Her hands bled with greens and blues as the colors melted between her fingers. Red from her face joined the other hues.

Two days later she realized that, though she had tried to save the paints, she hadn't retrieved the farewell note from Willow. Returning to the baby's grave, she searched for the folded square of paper, but the wind must have whisked it away.

* * * *

Leaving her children in Magdalena's care, Ruby helped Nokoni exercise horses and gentle yearlings. Magdalena and Nokoni fussed at Ruby for doing too much, but she pushed on. Inordinately fatigued, she worked past the point of exhaustion.

On his last trip to the ranch, Doc Granger had pinched her fingernail hard. He released his grasp and counted off the seconds needed for the blood flow to pink her skin. "You're anemic. You lost too much blood along with the baby. Eat liver every day for a couple of months, and we'll see how you do."

Ruby ate liver until it turned her stomach. Her stamina seemed in no hurry to return. An hour on horseback still exhausted her.

Having ridden before she could walk, Ruby handled horses well but had never ridden a bucking bronco and lacked Bismarck's facility with animals. One morning as she rode a filly, the clatter of hoof beats drew her to the barn to investigate. Wild horses stirred up a cloud of dust as they trotted into the corral. Nokoni spoke to a still-mounted cowhand. Though his face was covered with a full beard, she recognized Bismarck. He glanced at her just long enough to freeze her heart with his glare. He spurred his stallion and galloped away.

"*Señor* Biz brought *los caballos* from the Davis Mountains," Nokoni told her. "He's gone back for the rest of the herd."

Damn him. He took off without speaking a word to her.

With two dozen horses to break and more on the way, the ranch needed her husband. Without his abilities, the place didn't stand a chance of making a profit. Ruby was superfluous. If Bismarck stayed away only because she was there, her leaving would permit his return.

Her decision made, Ruby packed. She emptied her egg money from the Mason jar in the pantry and gathered the remainder of the cash from Buffalo Bill, now grateful that Bismarck—like her pa—made her set it aside. She had earned it, he'd said. It was hers. No self-respecting man would take money from his wife.

She visited the baby's grave one last time. With shaking fingers, she removed her wedding ring and placed it on a filigreed arm of the cross.

"I have buried a son and a marriage here." She remained dry eyed. With two little ones to care for and a new life to start, she couldn't afford the luxury of tears.

The next morning, Nokoni drove Ruby into town, dropping her and her children at her family's house. She had a few days to situate herself before her father's arrival for Saturday shopping and Sunday church. She wouldn't be welcome to live there permanently. Her pa would have a conniption fit when he learned she'd left Bismarck. He'd never support a second divorce and would never allow her, a doubly tarnished woman, to live at home. Ruby was on her own and damned near broke.

The next day, Ruby rented a tiny furnished shotgun cottage and moved her belongings into it. Once she and the children were settled, she bought a sheaf of high quality paper and envelopes from Statler's and ordered fresh art supplies. She would support herself and her children as an artist. No more waiting tables. No more life-sucking, soul-destroying ranch work. No more denying her true calling. That night, as her children slept, she wrote letters to the *Philadelphia Inquirer*, *Century*, *Life*, *Harper's*, and *Collier's Weekly*, and the publishers of western dime novels seeking illustration work. Even Buffalo Bill, reminding him she had done etchings for him. Illustrations of this sort, while not fine art, beat the dickens out of drawing lingerie ads for the *Philadelphia Inquirer*. When her fingers and eyes ached from writing, she blew out the kerosene lantern.

Curled against Johnny and Sophie, Ruby tried to sleep. Restless Sophie kicked constantly, moving the way her baby brother had not. Ruby rolled on her back and placed one hand on her empty womb, still feeling her soul had been torn from her body. God was punishing her. Her many sins had caught up with her at last—lying with Bismarck before marriage, loving Willow, lusting after d'Este, fearing being trapped into caring for her ill mother and that poor unborn child.

* * * *

With her self-reproach over losing the baby so tightly bound with remorse for loving Willow, Ruby postponed telling her lover the news. When Willow wrote asking what baby gift she might mail her, Ruby could no longer avoid the inevitable.

> *Though a walk might do my spirits good, today I feel too puny to go out. To avoid upsetting the children, I blame my tears on the sniffling and sneezing, and watery eyes of a terrible cold. This physical misery comes hard upon the most terrible, most heartbreaking event of my life. I lost my baby. A beautiful boy. I named him Bismarck Johannes. Oh, Willie, I wish you were here...*

Willow replied:

> *My dearest Ruby,*
> *I know how much the child meant to you—and Bismarck. I share your sorrow in the loss of your babe. I have enclosed the sketches I made that last day we were together. Your breasts so round, your belly full of life.*
> *When I put pen to paper now, I feel your emptiness. After all, we are one, you and I. If with our love, we together create and recreate each other, then also must we suffer together. What breaks your heart also breaks mine. How I wish I could hold and comfort you, my beloved.*

* * * *

Since the baby's grave was on the ranch, Ruby's only remembrances were her sketch of the baby and Willow's drawings. She placed these images in her Bible marking Psalms 139.

> *...you knit me together in my mother's womb...*
> *Your eyes saw my unformed body; all the days or-*
> *dained for me were written in your book before one*
> *of them came to be...*

* * * *

Seated in her family's usual pew, Ruby felt the judgmental eyes of the church members. Word quickly spread through Truly that she had left Bismarck and reverted to the wayward girl who'd come home penniless and pregnant. When she caught men staring at her, most regarded her with brows raised in speculation. Only a few dropped their gaze, abashed. Women, the second she noticed them glaring at her, looked away.

Ruby scooted down the pew to make room for her father and siblings. Her pa avoided looking at her and strode past. Jasper and Beryl veered to chat with their sister. Before they could speak, Pa backtracked, grabbed the napes of their necks, and hurried them to a front pew.

After the last hymn, as she carried the dozing Sophie, Ruby passed Hortense and her sister, holding court with several men just beyond the front door. Ruby started to speak to the women but stopped in mid hello when Hortense pointedly pulled her sister away. They turned their backs on Ruby, took the arms of the gentlemen beside them, and walked off.

Midweek a knock sounded on Ruby's door. She peeked out her front window. Elmer Magruder, the pastor of her church, shifted from foot to foot on her front porch. The widower had undoubtedly arrived near lunchtime hoping for a free meal.

After wiping her hands on her apron, she invited him in, indicating a chair in the parlor. "Have a seat, Reverend. Can I get you something to drink?"

"No, thanks, ma'am." He remained standing. Sweat mixed with grease dripped from his hair and found its way to his white clerical collar, staining its edges a waxy brown. His pink, sausage-fingered hands twisted the brim of his black bowler. "Miz Behrens, the women of our congregation are a tad concerned about having a grass widow, a divorcée, in their midst."

"And why might that be?"

He refused to meet Ruby's gaze. "You living alone and all."

"No man to protect me?"

"You chewed up and spit out two men already." With spite in his eyes, he glanced at her. "The ladies in the congregation fear you might start in on their husbands, especially since you've been hanging around Helles Belles."

"I'm painting Miz Majors' portrait." Ruby pinched her lips together. The local madame had commissioned a fancy portrait of herself *au naturel*—though discretely draped with velvet and lace—to hang above the bar of her establishment. Every morning, Ruby and her children walked to the brothel, half a mile outside of town, and the whores entertained Johnny and Sophie while Ruby painted.

Recognizing the righteous gleam on the pastor's face, Ruby strode to her front door, opened it, and motioned for him to leave. Hell would freeze over before she fed him lunch. "Thank you for dropping by, Reverend. You've made the church's position quite clear."

"I would advise you to return to Bismarck, beg his

forgiveness, and submit to his will. Legally, and more importantly, spiritually, a woman's place—and that of her children—is with her husband. I postulate that a good beating would strengthen your moral fiber."

Ruby's lips twitched in a bitter smile. "I've already been beaten half to death, and it didn't do me a damned bit of good."

* * * *

Molly apprised Ruby of circulating rumors, how talk had spread around Truly about her abandonment of Bismarck. "Hortense thinks Bismarck will divorce you. When that happens, she plans to snatch him up."

Ruby let out an exasperated breath, picturing the short, gap-toothed blonde. Elaborate hats as wide as her broad hips overshadowed Hortense's pudgy face with its pasty bread-dough skin. Bismarck made fun of her "war bonnets" as often as her butt. Hortense didn't stand a chance, at least she hadn't in the past.

Molly continued, "Miz Johnson says you lost the baby because of your sins…" At the gleam of tears in Ruby's eyes, Molly patted Ruby's hand. "He's an angel now."

Ruby placed a hand over Molly's mouth. "Don't say anything. My child died. Just be my friend until it doesn't hurt so much."

Molly, like the few folks who still spoke to Ruby, didn't know what to say about the stillbirth. Most acted as though nothing had happened, assuming, because the child had been born early, Ruby had not yet grown to love him and would not feel the loss. Most simply seeded the furrows of their conversation with platitudes.

"He's in a better place."

"Time heals all wounds."

"Everything happens for a reason."

Ruby grew so weary of the hackneyed responses she nearly screamed. With new understanding, she reread the desperate letter her mother had written her in Philadelphia. Now, Ruby feared for her own sanity and felt the same urge to howl with the coyotes, to howl with sorrow, to howl with rage.

Intellectually, she knew loving Willow had not caused the baby's death nor had her trip to the Truly hills, any more than having relations with Bismarck had, yet her guilt persisted even after Doc Granger reassured her that the baby's death was not her fault.

"I've never seen a 'ghost baby' before. They're real rare. They look white because they don't have any blood inside. Medical science isn't certain what causes them to hemorrhage out." He patted Ruby's shoulder. "Nothing would have prevented it. Just one of them things. God's will, so to speak."

How Ruby hated the God that had stolen her child.

Chapter Twenty-Eight
Stations of the Cross

Autumn, 1897

Ruby, when she wrote Willow of the death of her baby, deliberately omitted the demise of her marriage. She simply could not write those words. If Willow knew, their relationship would become infinitely more complicated. When it became clear Bismarck was not coming after Ruby, and she could not bring herself to return to the ranch, she told Willow of the change in her circumstances.

By return mail, both Willow and Walter wrote offering Ruby a home. She considered their proposal, but Willow's aversion to children combined with the goings-on in a bohemian household couldn't be healthy for Sophie and Johnny. Since Willow spent months abroad, Ruby either would have to chase her lover around the world, dragging her children behind her, or remain in New York without Willow. As Ruby could not maintain such a lavish lifestyle, both options required reliance on someone else's financial support.

> *While I thank you and Walter most whole-heartedly for your kind offer, I must decline. If the Texas plains could not withstand the forces of our love triangle, a mere building would implode.*
> *Too, the East is tainted with memories of Frank, of my many failures as artist, mother, wife.*

And the thought of living in a big city is abhorrent.
I need open space in which to create...

Though Ruby knew the whole situation was more her fault than Willow's, it was easier to blame the other woman. She found herself unable to respond to Willow's declarations of love. In self-defense, her letters became matter of fact, full of her daily routine. Willow's letters became as prosaic. Time and distance muted all passion between them, and their repressed emotions were never proclaimed on paper.

Though Ruby and Walter had never met, he acted as her agent, advising her to continue painting under the name R. L. Carter to disguise her gender. He advertised her work under that pseudonym through New York publishers. In Philadelphia, Ruby barely had made ends meet. Now, thanks to Walter and his vast connections, her illustration business blossomed.

Illustrating changed how she looked at the world. Except for the covers she did for dime novels, everything was black and white, life reduced to simple lines. When she sketched a horny toad, jagged lines represented its scales and horns, dots of graduated sizes captured both highlight and shadow yet could not project the subtle tans and browns nor the rainbow-shimmer of sunlight on its reptilian scales. Sometimes, she thought how difficult capturing these subtleties of nature was in black and white but conceded that a faithful color rendition would be equally difficult.

As she did her household books, calculating income versus expenses, she realized her income had reached the unbelievable sum of four hundred dollars a month, enough for a house and a servant. With great pride, she purchased her cottage and added a studio and a second bedroom. Since she didn't maintain a horse and buggy, she converted the stable at the rear of the property into a room she rented to Truly's newest deputy. It wouldn't hurt to have a man, especially a lawman, around the place, though at a discreet distance.

She hired the youngest Statler girl, sixteen-year-old Jeanette, to help around the house. With the girl's assistance, Ruby achieved a balance in her life between painting and caring for a home and children. Housework was not so odious, she discovered, if done in dribs and drabs. She made breakfast and dressed her youngsters each morning. Jeanette arrived at eight. While Ruby painted, her hired girl did the cleaning and cooking while keeping an eye on Sophie and Johnny. At five, Jeanette went home. Ruby had several hours to share with her children, serving an already-made dinner, washing those few dishes, helping Johnny with his counting and teaching Sophie her alphabet. Once the children were abed, Ruby worked on her illustrations until midnight.

Two or three times a week, she walked to Statler's to mail woodblocks or etching plates back east.

"Why don't you go back to Bismarck?" Molly's face puckered in disgust as she licked a stamp and stuck it to Ruby's package. "It's been months. He still cares. Every time he comes in, he asks about you."

Ruby sighed, unable to confide in Molly what transpired between her and Bismarck. "It seems I can be an artist or a wife, but not both." She refrained from adding that women, like dogs, were trained to be obedient, to come when called, to sit, to stay, to fetch. Her marriage with Bismarck failed because she had not adhered to the principle that women are not to be alone, not to go far from home, nor stay away for long. They must always rush back to their cages ready to tend their husband and litters of children.

Johnny started school in the same brick building Ruby had attended as a girl. She walked him to and from class along a route that led past Our Lady of Guadalupe. One morning she paused, somehow drawn to enter the chapel. She hesitated, ultimately turning away, fearing the reception a white woman might receive in a Mexican church.

Before she had gone ten steps, a wizened woman with a gravelly voice took her by the elbow. "*Venga, Señora.*"

Inside, the woman stood on tiptoe and draped her *rebozo* between Ruby's head and her own, dipped a gnarled finger into holy water, genuflected, then crossed herself and Ruby. Next, she tugged Ruby to a pew. The woman's hands gathered Ruby's and placed them on a worn rosary, moving their fingers along the beads, one by one. Her kind touch eased Ruby's heart. She realized how isolated she had become living in town, more alone than she had ever felt on the ranch.

Though they shared nothing beyond a need for solace, Ruby soon met the *señora* daily before the church. Ruby learned the rosary in Spanish by rote. She didn't understand the words but found she didn't need to. The soothing rhythm of the murmured prayers was enough. The quiet of the sanctuary calmed her spirit. Her heart felt naked before God, and she sought His forgiveness.

After prayers and Mass each day, the old *señora* scrubbed the floors of the entire church on her hands and knees. Ruby, wanting to thank the old woman for her kindness, decided to help her. The next day she tucked a scrub brush in her pocket. She knelt and began working alongside the *señora*, but the ancient woman screeched and flew at Ruby, arms flailing.

Ruby stood and backed away, surprised at the reaction. "I only wished to—"

"Miz Behrens?"

Turning, Ruby found an elderly priest approaching

her, his white hair giving him a silvered halo. "I'm Father Damiano."

He took her elbow and led her to his office. "Sit, please." He indicated a chair before he took a seat behind his desk. "*Señora* Romero seems to have adopted you, ma'am. I suspect it's because, like you, she lost a baby."

Ruby gave a sympathetic murmur.

"Many years ago, she and her husband crossed the *Llano Estacado* in a wagon with their firstborn, a boy of two. One evening, the child disappeared while she cooked their dinner. Despite searching for days, they never found a trace. No one knew if Indians kidnapped him, if he wandered away, if coyotes devoured him."

The padre stood and stared out the window, gesturing at the harsh landscape. "*Señora* Romero went *loca*, a little crazy, back then. Probably still is a bit. She raised another ten children, but some days she wanders the plains looking for that baby. Her self-imposed atonement for misplacing her child is scrubbing our floors."

Ruby nodded her understanding.

Father Damiano placed a hand on Ruby's shoulder. "Reverend Magruder cast you from his flock?"

She nodded, blinking back tears.

The Father's expression acknowledged his own shortcomings as well as those of the Protestant pastor. "Doubtlessly, Magruder deems himself sinless enough to cast the first stone." The priest raised his eyes to the ceiling. "Holy Father, forgive me, but you know it's true." Returning his gaze to Ruby, the priest continued, "Miz Behrens, all God's children may enter here. You're welcome for as long as you need or wish to come. When you're ready, I'll be happy to hear your confession and absolve you of your sins. But find your own penance. Leave *Señora* Romero to hers."

* * * *

In the middle of the night, Ruby rose from bed, unable to sleep, her hands itching to draw. She struck a match, lit the kerosene lamp then settled down with pencil and paper. Her western illustrations, designed to illustrate lurid potboiler dime novels, were sensational and superficial, characterized by broad streaks of color that reproduced well but lacked subtlety. The works supported her family but did not relieve her desire to produce fine art. Tonight, she would create what lay in her heart.

She leafed through her art books, studying pictures of European cathedrals and mentally comparing them with Our Lady of Guadalupe. In the tiny Mexican church, only a hand-painted frieze at waist level decorated the walls. The windows held the simplest of stained glass. Other than a primitive crucifix and a *santo*, an image of the Virgin of the Guadalupe on a wooden panel, no paintings hung on the walls. The severity of the whitewashed adobe cried out for artwork.

Scarcely aware of what she was doing, Ruby drew the men and women of the mission. Eventually, she fell asleep at the table, her face buried in her arms, until sunbeams crept between the curtains and struck her face. She stirred. Her pencil rolled to the floor. Beneath her forearms, she found a well-developed drawing of the first Station of the Cross, *Christ Condemned to Death*, and, beneath it, rough sketches of others.

For weeks, Ruby painted by daylight when colors appeared more intense, creating in a mad rush. Compelled to complete the full set of Stations of the Cross for Our Lady of the Guadalupe, she worked nonstop, understanding at last what Willow called a "painting frenzy." During the evenings, she worked on black and white illustrations for which good lighting was less critical. At night, crucifixes and crowns of thorns, Roman gladiators and apostles swirled through her dreams, only rarely allowing a ghost baby to invade.

Before Ruby finished the first painting, she started the second, transferring the cartoon to a gessoed canvas and laying on the *imprimatura* to establish light and dark values. While the under-coats of the second painting dried, she glazed the first, applying successive layers of transparent and semi-transparent colors. In the completed painting, the white ground of the gesso would reflect the light through the glazed layers, creating the illusion of dimension. To move more quickly to the next layer of glazing, Ruby placed her canvases outdoors in the summer heat to speed the drying. Soon fourteen images in various stages of completion leaned against the walls of her house.

* * * *

For a year Ruby painted like a mad woman. The week before Christmas, she finished the first painting.

"Done!" She voiced her exaltation. "If I keep going, I'll ruin it. Better stop now."

Loading a thin sable brush with lamp black paint, she prepared to sign her name, but an inner voice stilled her hand. With a sigh of acceptance, she cleaned her brush with turpentine, wiped it dry, and placed it in a paint-speckled Mason jar. She had not created this painting to promote herself as an artist. Instead, like *Señora* Romero's mopping, it was her penance. For infidelity. For doubting God's wisdom in taking her baby. For not using the Gift of art He had given her. For loving neither Willow or Bismarck enough to choose between them. Or perhaps loving both too much to give either up.

On Christmas Eve, Ruby wrapped *Christ being Condemned to Death* in flannel sheeting and carried it with her to midnight Mass. When everyone else filed from the mission, she leaned the wrapped canvas against the altar and slipped away.

Over the next several weeks she went to Mass with *Señora* Romero, expecting to see her painting hanging at the place marked with a small wooden crucifix above the number *1* to the right of the front entrance. But the space remained empty.

At home, she paced before the remaining thirteen paintings, muttering to herself. Remembering the horrible reviews *The Stillbirth* had received, Ruby again questioned her own talent. "Father Damiano hasn't hung my painting. What does that mean? Doesn't he like it? What happens if he doesn't like the others? I can't stand not knowing."

At last she conceded that by only losing herself in those paintings had she found relief from the loss of her baby and husband. "To save my own sanity, I must finish the series. Father Damiano might not care for my paintings, but that does not mean God is unappreciative."

She delivered the second, *Christ Carries His Cross*, in February. The second painting, like the first, was never hung. It simply vanished. Ruby buried her disappointment and kept painting.

By November, she carried the last of the series of fourteen Stations, *Jesus is Laid in his Tomb*, to the altar. She held little hope for this final image. It might meet the same fate as the others. But, she reminded herself, she had chosen her penance. Whether God accepted her atonement—or not—remained beyond her control.

Three weeks later, Father Damiano stopped her on her way out of church. "May I speak with you, *Señora* Behrens?"

She nodded. Her mind raced to figure out what he wanted, fearing she was no longer welcome in the church or that her images had truly been rejected.

He led her to his office. The full complement of her pictures, each bordered by a hand-carved gold-leafed frame, leaned against every inch of wall space.

"Lordy!" Ruby swallowed hard, attempting to contain her emotions. Oh, God. They were beautiful. Real paintings. With elegant frames. They could hang in any museum and not be out of place. She closed her eyes tightly to dam her tears.

He smiled. "You chose your penance well, *Señora*, using the gift God gave you to give a gift in return."

"Thank you." Her face flushed with pleasure.

Father Damiano clasped her hands between his in a fervent gesture. "I never dreamed my little mission would house such magnificence." He released her hands and looked at her paintings. "I carried them by wagon to the Diocese in Dallas for the Bishop's approval." He gave a small laugh. "When he saw them, I half-feared he would keep them. In the end, he donated the gold leaf for the frames." Overcome, Father Damiano allowed tears to trickle down his lined face.

Ruby handed him her handkerchief.

He accepted it with thanks. "Forgive me for testing your commitment. I did not want my flock to be disappointed if you only painted one. Once it became apparent you planned a series, I chose to wait and display them all at once."

"I feared you didn't care for them."

He sniffed then continued, "I pray the Lord will forgive me, but while waiting for you to finish, I most selfishly enjoyed your paintings as if I had a private gallery. I'll hang them soon. By Christmas Eve, Our Lady of the Guadalupe will shine with their glory."

"I want to do one more—with your permission, of course."

* * * *

Ruby started preparing the front wall of Our Lady of Guadalupe for a fresco of the Ascension of Christ. Though untrained artisans had built the church, the wall somehow attained the divine proportion, the golden ratio of 1 to 1.618, laid out by the Greek sculptor, Phidius, two thousand years earlier. Twenty-three feet wide and fourteen feet high, the wall was by far the largest "canvas" on which she had worked, even bigger than the *Dead Man restored to Life by touching the Bones of the Prophet Elisha* she had seen on her first day at the Academy.

Father Damiano organized local men, and with their help, she plastered, sanded, and gessoed the entire back wall of the church. She came home every night so covered with white dust that a giggling Johnny pronounced her a ghost. The skin of her hands cracked from the constant exposure to plaster, but at last, when she ran her fingers over it, the adobe wall was eggshell smooth.

Ruby had never envisioned herself as Michelangelo painting the Sistine Chapel, but sitting on scaffolding high in the air, she felt a kinship with the Old Master. For propriety's sake, she wore trousers beneath her skirt. For safety's sake, she eschewed her petticoats and tucked her skirts into her waistband as she climbed up and down the ladders.

Once she transferred her cartoon to the wall, she started painting in the upper left corner, working her way to the lower right. Along with their eagerness to model for her, daily comments from the parishioners and their heartfelt appreciation of her work encouraged her, unlike her days at the Academy when her work pleased no one.

Chapter Twenty-Nine
The New Millennium

At midnight Mass on Christmas Eve, Ruby and her children followed *Señora* Romero into the chapel. When the old woman stopped suddenly, they nearly fell atop her.

Ruby looked around. Her paintings hung as she had envisioned. She clamped her lips together to keep from laughing aloud in pleasure and admonished herself not to skip to her pew and leave the *Señora* behind.

"*Qué hermosa.*" The *señora* joined the crowds of people walking looking at the Stations. "*Es un milagro.*"

As Ruby followed the old woman around the chapel, countless people greeted Ruby, shook her hand, or kissed her cheek in thanks for her gift. Unaccustomed to such heartfelt approval of her work, Ruby's face flushed until she thought her cheeks might permanently redden.

Midnight Mass finished. Church bells all over Truly announced Christ's birth and united the little town for one brief moment. Ruby looked around the mission, sniffling. A tear or two escaped. In that simple setting, just as she had foreseen, her paintings glowed like vibrant jewels.

"These are your pictures, Mama. Why are you crying?" Johnny's sweet voice broke her reverie.

She tousled his curls. "Sometimes people cry from joy, sweetie."

Ruby glanced around one more time, emotionally

distancing herself from her work, and decided her paintings were good, as good as any she had ever seen. Although Willow and Walter had helped to establish Ruby as an illustrator, this body of work was hers alone. Against all odds, she had become a real painter.

She gathered the sleeping Sophie in her arms for the short walk home, stopped behind the last pew, and looked at the front wall of the church. The scaffolding for her new painting had been removed for the Christmas holidays, but the backbones of her fresco filled the wall between the two hand-carved wooden doors. The ascending Jesus, suspended between clouds, regarded a flock of Our Lady of Guadalupe parishioners. The white of his shroud hovered, a holy ghost above the prairie. When completed, the painting would reproduce the Truly hills beyond, making the thick adobe seem like glass.

"You have changed, *Señora*." Father Damiano stepped beside her. "Though it's unfinished, I see hope in this painting."

Ruby studied her fresco. The priest was right. Her palette, the subject of the Resurrection, the awed faces of the crowd watching Christ ascend, all seemed brighter. "Me, too."

"*Feliz Navidad*, Miz Behrens."

"Merry Christmas, *Padre*."

"Your New Year will be brighter. I can tell. So can He." The padre pointed at the ceiling.

She stepped outside into the winter air. Nestled against her breast, Sophie snored softly. Johnny, drowsy at her side, clutched her skirt for support. Behind her, the church darkened slowly as Father Damiano blew out candles.

Around her, families moved toward home, warmth, and meals of homemade tamales, beans and rice. Ruby was left alone in the dark with her children. The plains sparkled with frost. In the distance, the Milky Way frosted the sky. Somewhere in between, lay the Truly hills, a deeper black against the black sky. A black that sucked out all light, like the velvet ribbon holding her mother's cameo around her neck. Her own heart no longer seemed dark. A surge of happiness flew through her joining the coyotes' exultant song to the heavens. Though she had been unaware of the changes as they occurred, she realized that for the first time in a long time, if not happy, she was at least content. She had survived the loss of her baby and her marriage, emerging from that darkness a stronger, more self-contained woman—and a damned fine artist.

* * * *

Ruby watched Sophie and Johnny open their gifts before their little feather Christmas tree. Ruby bought Sophie a set of wooden alphabet blocks and stitched a dress for her doll. For herself, Ruby ordered several new tubes of paint from the latest Winsor and Newton catalog—Italian Purple, Violet Carmine, and Field's Orange Vermillion—and three new brushes, a squirrel's hair for mopping in large areas and two Series Seven sables for fine details. Within seconds she regretted buying Johnny the whistle she placed in his stocking along with a dozen lead soldiers, an orange, walnuts, pecans, and a few pieces of candy. Watching her serious son laughing too hard to tootle, she didn't have the heart to restrain him. In self-defense she closed the kitchen door behind her to block the noise.

While preparing a holiday dinner for the three of them, a momentary loss filled her, a counterpoint to her elation the night before. Sniffing the air, redolent with cinnamon and spices and the yeasty tang of sourdough bread, she remembered large family gatherings with a roasted wild turkey, cornbread stuffing, fruitcake, and eggnog. All that food would be too much for the three of them. Instead, she baked gingerbread men with the children, helping them cut the figures and place currants for lopsided eyes and buttons, before putting a small pot roast on the stove. As she cooked, she realized she missed her family. Her father, Beryl, Jasper would join Pearl, Willem, and their two children for Christmas Day. Her pa had not spoken to Ruby since she married Bismarck and refused to allow Beryl and Jasper any contact with her, fearing the headstrong spirit of his eldest daughter would rub off on his other offspring.

Molly had told Ruby that Bismarck had spent the last two holidays alone. This year, Ruby supposed, he would go to his parents if he celebrated at all. She thought of Christmases in happier times. If Johnny and Sophie had been his own, Bismarck could not have delighted more in her children's joy. Too young to remember the man, Sophie's memories of Bismarck were those of Johnny, his idolization of the horseman planted in her head by her brother's childish ramblings. Ruby felt guilty, depriving the boy of the only father he remembered, but with time, the boy quit asking for Bismarck.

Tears hovered in Ruby's eyes, blinding her before dripping onto her sourdough bread. Wrist-deep in kneading, her hands stilled. She prayed for her husband. In that moment, she realized that her anger toward him had vanished. Somehow she had forgiven him. She understood that, grief-stricken by the loss of their child, he had lashed out. In the nearly three decades she had known him, Bismarck had lost control only twice—when he beat d'Este and when he destroyed her paint box. For two and a half years, she and Bismarck had been apart. She hoped that he, too, had found a measure of peace. The time had come to release the past. They had

meant too much to each other for too long to remain ene-
mies. Whether they divorced or resumed their marriage, she
wished for accord between them. Before the New Year, the
new Century, and the new Millennium arrived, she vowed to
set things right.

With the children abed, she wrote Bismarck. She wavered back and forth about the greeting. Maybe she should
do a rough draft.

My darling Bismarck,

She crossed out that line. Too possessive.

Bismarck alone seemed cold and impersonal, denying
their relationship.

The closing proved difficult as well. *Your loving wife*
seemed presumptive, yet anything less repudiated the love
they once shared. At last she wrote

> *Biz,*
> *Please forgive me for the pain I caused you*
> *when last we saw each other. I do not know if we*
> *can repair what happened, if we can ever be close*
> *again, but perhaps with the new Millennium we*
> *might make peace.*
> *Ruby*

The next morning, she placed the note in the general
delivery mailbox at Statler's.

* * * *

New Year's Day, Ruby turned a pound cake onto a towel
to cool on the kitchen table and checked the hen roasting in
the oven. Black-eyed peas simmered on the stove. A day of
good fortune for every pea you ate on New Year's Day. To
fix things with Bismarck, she'd need all the luck she could
get.

Standing over a pan of hot potatoes, she mashed them with milk and butter while counting the days—six—since she had taken Bismarck's letter to Statler's. She might not be the best of Christians, but at this most holy time of the year, she had taken the first step toward reconciliation. She took comfort in that fact while praying he'd received the note and wondering how he would react.

Merry sounds from the parlor brought her back to the moment. The noise level was deafening. She gave a low laugh. Johnny had not tired of his Christmas whistle, and Sophie screeched in harmony with his tooting. Ruby hoped that someday soon he would lose the whistle. Or perhaps, she thought with a grin, she could lose it for him. Even with the kitchen door closed, the noise was barely tolerable, but it was a holiday. Let them rejoice and play.

The shrill whee-e-e-e-e halted abruptly, followed by a scream.

Potato masher still in hand, Ruby ran to the kitchen door, flinging it open to see what was going on. In her shock, she dropped the utensil.

A cowman knelt on one knee, crushing her son in his arms. Johnny wrapped his arms around his neck. Sophie peeked from behind the curtains, her eyes wide with uncertainty.

A Stetson hid the fellow's face and an oilskin duster covered his frame, but Ruby recognized him immediately. She'd just been praying to God, and the Devil himself arrived. Not the Devil himself, but a man just as dangerous to her well-being. She clutched the doorframe to steady her wobbly legs. Despite her best efforts, her voice shook. "What are you doing here?"

Without saying a word, Bismarck stood, removed his hat, and dropped it on Johnny's head. The boy spun in giddy circles sounding his whistle. Sensing all was well, Sophie slipped from her hiding place and joined her brother in frolic.

With a deep breath, Ruby returned to the kitchen and closed the door behind her. She sank into a chair and, with shaking fingers, picked bits of mashed potato from her skirt, letting her heart rate slow, pulling herself together before facing her husband.

Damn him. She wondered why he had chosen New Year's Day to come. Only recently had she realized her anger had dissipated. Perhaps he came to reconcile. Hope flared in her heart that they could resolve their hostility. Then, unbidden, the alternative thrust her optimism aside. He came to divorce her.

The front door opened then closed. With equal measures of relief and disappointment, Ruby sighed. Bismarck had gone.

Then footsteps, too heavy to be those of her children and laced with the jingle of spurs, crossed the parlor toward the kitchen.

She held her breath and twisted her fingers in her skirt.

The door opened. Bismarck entered, the potato masher in his hand. He laid it on the table. Bits of potato dropped onto the kitchen table like blobs of thick white paint.

"I sent the kids out to play. Figured they didn't need to hear grown-up talk."

Unable to get a word out, she nodded. When she wrote the letter, she'd never thought beyond the original impulse, never visualized the moment of confrontation, never figured out what she'd say.

"I got your letter." The muscles in his jaw tightened. His voice was gruff.

Ruby's throat constricted in apprehension. This was it. She tried to swallow, but her mouth had grown cotton. She hoped Bismarck's next words would be *I've come to take you home, Ruby Louise, the* words he'd spoken in Philadelphia years before. But he didn't speak. Not a word. Never raised his eyes, just stood, watching his own hands thumb the brim of his Stetson.

Ruby wasn't ready for this moment, for the imminent demise of her marriage. She and Bismarck had shared many memories, but the death of their baby had destroyed their love. Before harsh words were spoken, before the situation spiraled out of control, she wanted to reach him.

"I'll be right back." Her long skirts swished against his legs.

Bismarck reached for her, putting a hand on her waist to stop her. "Ruby—"

Though his touch seared her, she sidestepped to avoid him and left the room.

Moments later she returned. "I want you to have this." She handed him the sketch of their baby, its edges softened by repetitive touching, its surface speckled with tear stains.

Bismarck sank into the nearest kitchen chair. His Stetson tumbled unheeded from the edge of the table. He stared at the image, his hands trembling. He swallowed hard, but his voice still quavered. "He had the dimple in your chin."

"And your jug-handles." With one finger she traced the curve of his ear.

He covered her hand with his, pressing her against his head.

She bent and placed her forehead atop his head, inhaling the scent she had known since childhood. Behind tears, her vision blurred. She straightened and pulled her hand away before her emotions overwhelmed her. Might as well get the reason for his visit out in the open. "Why are you here?"

He tucked the sketch into his shirt pocket, stood, fished

in the watch pocket of his trousers, and pulled out something. He dropped it on the table where it spiraled a few times before landing with a ping. Her wedding ring.

"I found this at the baby's grave. Figured you'd ask for a divorce. But you never did nothing about it." He paced the kitchen. "As long as I'd waited for you to be my wife, I figured we'd be together forever. After what happened, I lost sight of *us*. I couldn't see us together anymore. But I couldn't bear thinking of us apart neither."

His feet stopped, but his fingers picked up his nervous actions, roughly scrubbing his scalp with his fingers.

"I reckon I've only been that angry one other time in my life. Since then, I've beat myself up over what happened. Then I got your letter. Realized there was hope. Before the New Year, I wanted to round up the last of my strays. If I apologized, if I courted you again, I thought I might win my wife back."

Elation raced through Ruby. She opened her mouth to speak, but he held up a hand to hush her.

"Let me finish. I've got to spit this out all at once." He resumed pacing. "I came in for church this morning. I headed to ours but heard you was going to the Mexican one, so I went there instead. The service was over, the place emptying out. While I looked around for you, I saw those pictures on the walls." Again, he turned to face her. "You painted them."

Ruby nodded. He must have really wanted to see her if he'd gone to Our Lady of Guadalupe. Then she wondered what he thought of her images, if he had liked them. Probably not. His voice carried an accusation of some unknown sin.

"Until I saw them, I didn't understand. Now I do. The folks in your pictures looked alive. You ought to be famous like Willow—or that bastard d'Este. You belong back

East." Bismarck put his hand on the door, turned the knob then twisted to look back at her. "I reckon I was meant to be yours, Ruby, but you weren't meant to be mine. I'll stop by Judge Willis' on Monday and set you free."

Before Ruby could speak, he was gone. Her shoes were nailed to the floor. She ran after him the second she pried her feet free. By the time she reached the porch, he was halfway out of town, head down, spurring his horse to a gallop. She returned to her kitchen, mentally churning over the unexpected turn of events.

If she had wanted to, on her comfortable five thousand dollars a year, she could have moved back east any time. Apparently, Bismarck never realized that she chose to remain here.

Though he stated there was hope, since he had ridden away again without looking back, she was no longer certain peace between them was possible. Her head cradled on one forearm, she sat at the table, twirling her wedding ring in circles on the table until the odor of burnt chicken filled the air.

* * * *

January 1900

The next morning, Ruby left her children in Jeanette's care. Instead of painting on her fresco, Ruby walked to the judge's office. A hand-lettered sign read *Closed until Tuesday, January 3rd*. She exhaled in relief. She had time to talk to Bismarck before he took any action. Returning home, she put on riding clothes, hired a horse from Mueller's livery stable then rode toward Stonecrop Ranch.

Brisk winter air burned Ruby's cheeks as she followed the familiar road. All she had to do was walk to the edge of Truly and she could see the plains, but since she left Bismarck, she had not been further from town than the half-mile to Helles' Belles. She galloped with a wild exhilaration at being on horseback then reined to a walk responding to a growing anxiety about seeing her husband.

As she approached the homestead, sunlight winked off the windmill. She hesitated, pulling back on the reins to slow the horse. Perhaps she was not quite ready to see Bismarck after all. As always, she had acted impetuously, without thinking matters through. Now she needed a moment to organize her thoughts. With a tug on her reins, she turned her mount off the road and headed toward the Italian stone pines north of the house.

"Whoa." She patted the mare's neck and dismounted. After running a hand over the wrought-iron cross, she knelt beside her baby's grave. The white stone cairn was barely visible. Fat-leaved succulents nestled between the rocks. Bismarck's doing. In the springtime, the grave would be covered by a soft quilt with a thousand flowers. *Mille fiori.* She fingered one leaf. Her shoulders shook.

A hand clasped her shoulder.

She jumped at the touch then turned to see Bismarck.

"He was my child, too." He relaxed his hand, retreated a step. "I was at the barn. Saw you ride up."

"I named him after you. Bismarck Johannes Behrens." She sniffed.

He pulled his hat further over his eyes blocking her from reading his expression, but he couldn't hide the rhythmic clenching of his jaw.

"I curled the baby up like he was still in me and planted him facing the house so he could always see us." With a small flutter of her hand, she indicated the grave. "I like what you did here. No fancy flowers to shrivel up and die, just wild things that will bloom forever."

"Your rocks seemed too rough a blanket for our baby boy. You must have had a reason for putting them there, so

I left them."

"It rained so hard that night." Memories stabbed her. The downpour. Her irrational fears. Her wild grief. She choked down a sob. "I was afraid he'd be washed away. Afraid he'd be lost forever out on the prairie, all alone. And I'd never know where to find him."

Bismarck shook his head. "You were out here in your nightgown, soaked to the bone, covered with mud, your hair writhing like drowning snakes." He ran his hand through his hair. "God, I was angry." He swallowed hard—once, twice, three times. "I came so close to hurting you. I cain't forget the sight of you, cowering on the ground, all scared—scared of me. I thought smashing that box would relieve the urge to strike you. When I saw blood on your face, I knew I'd hurt you, even though I'd tried not to. I was no better than *him*. But I was too damned angry to care. I took off. Didn't stay to comfort you." He covered his eyes with a hand, turned away.

She placed a tentative hand on his arm. "Or let me ease you."

He turned back. "Christ, Ruby, you looked like a mad woman. It took everything I had to heal you when that bastard tore you apart. I feared I didn't have the strength to mourn my boy and fix you again." He squatted beside her.

She ran her hand over his cheek. "We should have comforted each other, instead we let his death tear us apart."

"That we did." Tears shimmered in his eyes, the reflection of the northern sky turning them a deeper blue. "What do we do now?"

"I don't know. We can't undo this, can't go back."

"No." He leaned forward and whispered, "Maybe we can move forward?"

Ruby didn't trust her voice so nodded silently.

His arms closed around her, wrapping her in his warmth,

burying her face in his chest. His shoulders shook.

She looked up.

He placed his cheek against hers.

Their tears merged.

She thought the bitter wind might freeze their faces together.

He broke the silence. "You're cold. Head to the house. I'll put your horse in the barn."

She watched him cross the barnyard, trying to decide if his steps held a new jauntiness. Entering the kitchen through the back door, she found pinto beans simmering on the back of the stove. Sourdough starter bubbled in its crockery. Two links of sausage and several rock-hard biscuits sat on a plate on the chopping board. A little giggle burst from her. His biscuits never rose high and fluffy like her own, but as he was fond of saying, his "squatted to rise and baked on the squat."

She might as well get busy. It was almost lunchtime. Busy hands would keep her mind out of the Devil's workshop while she waited for Bismarck. She draped her coat over a kitchen chair, opened a drawer, pulled an apron from its depths, and pulled it over her head. A musty smell drifted past her nose, telling her the ruffled pinafore hadn't been used since she left. Mixing flour with the starter, she kneaded and shaped a pan of rolls and laid them to rise on the back of the stove.

That done, she anxiously twisted her fingers together. Bismarck had not returned from the barn. He must have gotten bogged down with chores. Or maybe, he too was ill at ease and avoiding coming inside.

As she waited, she wandered through her former home, feeling strange in the familiar setting. Things were the same, yet not. In the parlor, a fine coating of dust covered everything but the chair Bismarck sat in. She swatted a lone cobweb from a corner, noticing her house was clean enough for a man but not up to her own standards. No longer mistress here, she was reluctant to start cleaning.

The door to the bedroom they had shared was closed. She hesitated before opening it, fearing what she might find.

Chapter Thirty
Horse Trading

January 1900

With trembling fingers, Ruby turned the doorknob and entered her old bedroom. When she found no evidence of another woman, she sighed with relief. Across the room, a picture was stuck in the frame of the mirror—one of the seed packets from Martin Seeds printed with *Still-life with Girl*. She picked it up, looked at it then compared it with her reflection. Never had she believed she was as comely as d'Este painted her.

Motion in the mirror caught her attention. Bismarck stepped behind her. He studied her likeness cast back by the silvered surface. "You've lost all your baby fat."

She glared into his reflected eyes. "I've never been fat in my life."

"Sweet Jesus, you're beautiful. Your face is honed to its essence. Nothing's left but eyes, cheekbones, that stubborn little chin." He turned her toward him, and his callused thumb traversed the planes of her face.

She had forgotten how perfectly his thumb rested in the dimple in her chin while his index finger tilted her head to meet his mouth. But he didn't kiss her.

"You've a woman's face now." He traced her temple with his fingers.

She knew what he was looking for. "You can barely see

it."

"I feared I'd done as much damage to you as he did." His thumb edged toward her mouth, caressing, until his hand dropped like he had been burnt by the scar on her lip. But he didn't kiss her.

Her lips tingled from his caress. Now that he stopped, she wanted his touch back.

He looked down and pulled the seed packet from her fingers. "Everywhere I go in town, you're hanging on the wall. I cain't escape you. My wife. Painted by another man. Every man in town can hold my wife in his hands. I hate it. But it's the only picture I have."

"I'm sorry. That was Frank's doing. Another way to hurt me."

"I know. But you're mine. Not his." His voice tightened. He stared down at the paper, gripping it so hard it fluttered in his hand. Then he looked at her image in the mirror, not at her. "Leastwise, you used to be."

She took the seed packet from him and laid it face down on the dresser. Unable to face him any more than he could her, she turned away. And saw their bed. She staggered backwards, recoiling when their bodies collided. Memories of what they had shared on that bed crowded out other thoughts.

He drew her toward his chest.

Since that distant night with Willow, Ruby had been celibate. Warmth feathered over her face. Her nipples puckered. Shame at her infidelity warred with the desire that shot through her. The sharp intake of his breath, the sudden tautness of his body, and the tightening of his hands on her waist told her his passion echoed her own.

"Ruby." His warm breath danced across her ear.

Lordy, she wanted him. But their truce was too fragile to risk lovemaking. Not once today had he called her *Ruby*

Louise in that loving tone. In his mind things were not back to normal. He must be as apprehensive as she was about starting over. She could not deny her attraction to him. He wanted her. She wanted him. But she wanted her current life, too. With careful negotiation and compromise, perhaps she might have both. Reluctantly, she pulled away.

He held tightly to her arms, seemed loath to release her.

"I should get home to the children." She moved more forcefully.

His hands dropped to his sides, flat palms slapping his thighs. "What do we do now, Ruby?"

She shook her head. "I don't know."

He shrugged. "Me, neither."

"Come to Sunday dinner. We'll talk."

* * * *

On Sunday Ruby sent her children to Molly's. Johnny had talked incessantly of Bismarck, horses, and the ranch since seeing the man he called Papa. She didn't want her son to get his hopes up should things not work out.

After frying chicken, baking bread, and making Bismarck's favorite pie, Ruby dressed, changing clothes three times before settling on a simple skirt and blouse and twisting her hair into a tight matronly knot low on the back of her head, all the wildness flattened from her curls. At last she was satisfied her appearance did not suggest that she had dressed to please him.

Fifteen minutes before noon, three faint raps sounded on Ruby's door. Before answering Bismarck's knock, she pulled a clean apron over her head. With a peek through the window, she looked him over. Freshly shaved, his mustache no longer swirled like handlebars but hung from the corners of his mouth, like the tusks of a virile animal. A dark gray coat partly covered a shirt that matched his blue eyes. Damn him. He had groomed himself to please her. Definitely a dangerous man.

After motioning him inside, she stood silently by the door. Afraid to go forward. Afraid to retreat. More afraid of standing still. She twisted the strings of the apron between nervous fingers. As on the day he began courting her after her divorce, he smelled of talc and bay rum. Unsure where to start, she closed her eyes and wound the apron strings more tightly around her fingers, vowing she wouldn't cry.

Bismarck placed his hands on her waist. His breath, soft against her cheek, smelled of whiskey. On a Sunday morning! Lordy. He'd found it necessary to fortify himself before coming to see her.

"Ruby Louise," he whispered. "I need you. Now." He drew her tightly against his chest.

Her voice thickened with her own need, but she pulled back. "I won't risk a child until we've sorted things out."

He dropped his hands. His voice sank to a growl. "So what are we going to do?"

"I can't—won't—be a plain old ranch wife anymore. I have to paint."

A year ago, Bismarck and his hands had driven hundreds of mules and horses into Truly to be shipped to the British Army to use in the Boer War. Rumor had it that the deal had made him a well-to-do man. He had taken that money to Kansas City and bought prime horseflesh to improve his *remuda*.

Ruby wanted to prove herself his equal. These days made a good living painting. Recalling Bismark's litany of material things when he asked her to marry him, she wondered if her own list would impress him.

"I own this house." She gave a huff of annoyance. "Actually it's in your name since the courthouse wouldn't issue a property title to a mere woman. I converted the stable in back to a room I rent out. To have time to paint, I hired Jeanette Statler to take care of the children and the house."

"You saying you don't need me?"

"Not financially." She tangled her fingers so tightly in her apron strings she couldn't move them. "That doesn't mean I don't need you in other ways." She glanced down. Lordy, he was as ready as she was.

"So we're dickering about our marriage?"

"You're a good horse-trader, Biz. I'm sure we can come to terms that'll satisfy us both."

Ruby was disappointed, but not surprised, when he spun on his heels and walked out. At least she had tried to mend things.

* * * *

Long before daybreak two days later, a pounding awakened her. She lit an oil lamp and, half alert, answered the front door. The lift of a brow above a sleepy eye was the only greeting she gave Bismarck.

"Couldn't sleep." Winter followed him. He strode past her into the parlor, his face lighting up the way it used to when he first laid eyes on her first thing in the morning and when they lay together at the end of the day, like he couldn't believe she was his.

"It's awfully early." She yawned and ran a hand through her disheveled hair, smoothing errant locks. "I'll put on some coffee."

He followed her to the kitchen. His hands on her waist, he pushed her against the table, kissing her hard. "You're beautiful." He nuzzled his cold cheek against hers, kissing where her neck joined her collarbone. "You're warm."

"Not as warm as I used to be." She shivered. "You're freezing." Leaning her head against his cheek, she relished the rasp of his stubble against her skin.

"Spit out your terms, woman. Let's get down to horse trading." He untied her robe. Reaching between it and her gown, he cupped one hand around her bottom, pulling her closer.

Heart pounding, she buried her nose in his chest, inhaling bay rum. "If I move to the ranch, I need to paint."

"What do I get out of this deal?" His other hand clutched her breast.

Her nipple tightened, her breast engorged with desire. Her need was so great she thought she'd faint. "A happy wife."

"You sound pretty happy right now." He dropped his head. Right through her gown, he suckled her breast.

"You have a ways to go before I'm really happy." She tangled her hands in his hair.

He came up spitting. "I hate flannel. All those fuzzy little hairs."

She laughed. "I need a studio like the one I built here. But bigger."

"What do I get in exchange?"

"A happy wife."

"You already played that card." He chuckled then nibbled her ear lobe.

"With the money I make, we can pay off the land, weather a drought, not go under." She unbuckled his holster, let it slide to the ground, and began unbuttoning his coat.

"What else?"

"A housekeeper. Someone to tutor the kids."

"Who'll pay for all that?"

"If the housekeeper only works for me, I'll pay her wages. If you want her to cook for the cowhands, too, you should pay part."

"You did all that before—for free."

She pulled away, glaring at him. "How would you feel if you couldn't ranch?"

"I'd roll over and die."

"You were born to be a horseman. You love it. Yet you're denying me the right to be what I was meant to be."

"So you were never happy out there with me?" Lips twisted, he turned away.

She reached for him, but at the sight of his tight shoulders, she withdrew her hand. "I didn't say that. I wasn't unhappy. Not with you. Something was lacking in me. I've built a life here in Truly. But something's missing. You."

"You don't know what it's like, crawling into that bed every night. I roll over, hard as a crowbar, certain you're there, smelling you, feeling your hair against my chest. Then I wake up—" He turned to face her.

"I know exactly how that feels." She rubbed her forehead against his chest as she slid his coat down his arms, dropping it on the floor.

He tugged at his shirt, helping her remove it. "What else you offering?"

"We can rent out this house, a steady little income."

He tugged her gown up, slipping his hand between her legs. "Sweet Jesus, you're slicker'n cow slobber already."

"Thanks—I guess." Distracted by his touch, she fumbled with the buttons on his pants placket. When the last one surrendered, she yanked his trousers to his ankles and reached through his long johns. Her hand cupped his sac. "What else you got?"

With her touch, he inhaled sharply. "I'll pay for anything related to ranching."

She knelt before him, freeing him from the constraints of his underclothes. Her hand curved around his length.

"Jesus Christ." He placed his hand on hers, tightening her grip. Barely able to gasp out the words, he said, "You pay for anything related to art. We split the cost of the house and any children."

"Including Johnny and Sophie?"

He nodded, his trembling hands knotted in her hair. "We make big decisions together, no matter whose money we're spending."

Ruby thought a minute. "A business meeting after Sunday dinner sound all right to you?"

When he nodded, she took him in her mouth.

He pulled away. "Christ, not that way. Not the first time."

Still in his long johns, he lifted her to the kitchen table and tossed her gown to her chin.

She retreated slightly. "You have to pull out. I don't want a child yet."

"The second we touched last time, I knew our bodies still hankered for each other, but I didn't want to risk a young'un 'til our minds were tied to the same hitching post. I came prepared."

Ruby laughed and pulled him closer.

Now he backed away. He withdrew a condom from his pocket, placed it, then entered her so hard she yelped.

She didn't hear the table screech across the floor or pound against the wall. All that reached her ears was the squelching sound of Bismarck moving within her, his chanted "Sweet Jesus Sweet Jesus Sweet Jesus," and the acceleration of her own moans. Minutes later, she was ready, whether he was or not, understanding for the first time a man's need for immediate release. "Now! God, now."

"Sh-h-h, don't wake the kids." He swallowed her sounds with kisses.

Sheened with sweat despite the cold, they finished together, hard, fast, intense.

Between slowing breaths, Ruby said, "You got yourself a deal, mister. We can start right after Easter."

Bismarck stood up. "Easter? That's three months away."

"I need to stay in town until I complete the fresco."

He groaned. "The one that's barely started?"

"Yes. And Johnny needs to finish school."

"But I need you now. I cain't hold out that long."

"Come to bed. We'll work something out."

When he stripped, his familiar legs, as white and prickly as a Chihuahuan poppy, contrasted with the deep tobacco of his face, chest, and hands. His slim feet and long toes were unchanged. Slight atrophy of his right leg and an X-shaped scar on his calf were the only reminders of the snakebite. Overall he was thinner, his muscles were incised more deeply. He'd been working too hard and not eating well. A long scar, still pink and new, trailed down one arm. She followed it with her finger, raising a questioning eyebrow.

"Barbed wire."

He whisked her gown over her head, cackling at the crackle of electricity in her hair, and led her to the bedroom. "Lie down, little one." He covered her with himself and the quilt.

* * * *

While Ruby painted on her fresco, Bismarck supervised the building of the studio she designed. Weekends, she and the children rode a buggy to visit Bismarck and inspect the progress on her workspace. They had tried to explain the situation to the two children. Johnny, faced with interminable months until Easter, offered to leave school and live at the ranch with Bismarck. The dogs and chickens held Sophie spellbound. At every visit she begged to take them home.

Ruby waltzed when she entered the completed studio. Her space shared the back porch of the house so she could dash from one building to the other without facing the elements. An expanse of windows twelve feet high ran along the northern exposure. Heavy draperies would soften summer heat or stave off winter chill. A potbelly stove sat smack in the middle of the room. Beneath the windows, low shelves held supplies and art books. She moved her big steamer trunk, all her paintings, many still unpacked from Philadelphia, a wingback chair and a rocker, plus a stool and her easel into the space before deciding she had entered heaven.

The week before Easter, Ruby climbed off the scaffolding the last time. Leaning against the back pew of Our Lady of Guadalupe, she waited impatiently for the framework to be removed. Father Damiano and *Señora* Romero stood on either side of her. When Ruby saw the painting for the first time in its entirety, without its lines being interrupted by boards and ladders, she caught her breath. Her *Resurrection* filled the wall between the two main doors of the chapel. An emaciated Christ floated above the landscape, one hand pointing aloft, the other carrying a lily. Blood dripped from Jesus's wounds. In contrast to her *Stations of the Cross*, this painting was filled with light and hope. The shifting morning light from the mission windows glanced off the minute flecks of gold leaf that surrounded Christ, forming a nimbus rather than the more traditional solid-appearing halo. Vaqueros in sombreros, women in *rebozos*, half-naked children, longhorn cattle, sheep, and goats joined coyotes, pronghorn antelope, and jackrabbits in worship.

The door on the right opened. Bismarck entered with Sophie and Johnny and came to stand beside her. "You all right?"

Pointing to the finished painting, she nodded, too

overcome to speak.

Bismarck turned toward her artwork. For a long time he stood in silence before giving a low whistle of appreciation. "It's beautiful." He took her hand. "Show me the others."

"But you saw them at Christmas."

"Not with my wife." His warm eyes revealed his pride in her and in her work.

They walked slowly around the church, hand in hand, stopping at each Station before finding their way back to the *Resurrection*. He lifted her hand to his lips and kissed her fingers. "Before, I couldn't grasp what you meant about needing to paint." He stopped, swallowed hard. "All these years, I never realized you had this in you. I never meant to hold you back."

She closed her eyes, relieved he finally understood. Her throat too tight to reply, she nodded.

"The wagon's out front. Let's go home, Ruby Louise."

Chapter Thirty-One
A Fence with One Post

January 1926, twenty-six years later

Clang! Clang! Clang! The chow bell on the back porch rang, three urgent sets of three. The ranch signal for an emergency.

Ruby, working in her studio, started at the sound. She flung her brush to the table, not bothering to clean it, and raced through the kitchen. On her way out the door, she glanced at the thermometer. Twenty-eight degrees. She shivered. *As she dashed to the barn*, frost dampened her *huaraches.* The warm socks she wore beneath didn't begin to protect her toes.

In the brittle sunlight, cowhands ran awkwardly toward her.

Cold air—and fear—halted Ruby's breath. Her husband dangled between three men, one at each shoulder and another between Bismarck's splayed legs, supporting his knees. Like the town drunk being hauled to jail, his head lolled backwards.

She raced back to the house, threw the door open, and dashed into the kitchen. From a cupboard she drew out an old sheet, tossing it over the well-polished oak. "Put him on the table. What happened?"

"Diablo bucked him off." Nokoni grunted as he and the men lifted Bismarck to the table. "Hit his back on the fence by the barn, took down the whole section."

"Put him face down then. Let me take a look." She fished a knife from a drawer then filled a basin from a kettle on the stove, its water still warm from breakfast.

As she looked him over, slow blood oozed from Bismarck's scalp. "He hurt his back? Not his head?"

"Both, *Señora*. When the fence went down, he hit his head real hard on a cedar post."

"Biz, you awake?" She patted his shoulder. When he didn't respond, she lifted his lids. Pure white glared back at her. His eyes had rolled backwards in their sockets. She shot a glance at Nokoni.

The foreman continued, "Diablo was *un bruto* today, gave everyone the *mal de ojo. Señor* rode him anyway, but his mind—it was not on Diablo." He waved his hand vaguely in the air. "*Señor* Biz was someplace else."

Her eyes closed briefly then snapped open. No time for stray thoughts. She jerked her mind to her task and sliced off Bismarck's shirt. Between his shoulder blades, dark blood had pooled beneath the skin. Her index finger traced the bones of his spine, confirming what her eyes told her, but she refused to believe. Instead of lining up in a neat row, the bones had shifted to one side. She lifted and released one arm, then the other. They plopped down like no muscle remained in them. Her heart dropped into her belly as she realized Bismarck's back was broken. "Send someone for Doc Granger. The young one, not the old man."

"Shall we move him to the bed, *Señora*?"

"Wait 'til Doc Granger sees him. No point in hurting him any more than we have to." She studied each cowhand's face. "Nothing you all can do in here." She made a shooing motion with her hands. "Best get back to work. I'll let you know what Doc Granger says."

The subdued ranch hands nodded and shuffled outside.

Ruby wiped blood from Bismarck's hair, cleaned his face, bandaged his head and his upper back. Time and again she patted his cheek. "Biz? You awake?"

His silence persisted.

Time slowed, then stopped, while she waited for the doctor. She cleaned an already-spotless kitchen in an attempt to settle jangled nerves.

If Bismarck died, she'd shoot Diablo herself. More than once she glared out the window at that goddamned stallion. More than once her gaze turned to the gun rack just out of her reach above the kitchen door. More than once she scooted a chair toward the door. More than once she returned the chair to the table and sat by Bismarck, clutching his hand, one that failed to grasp hers in return.

Bismarck moaned.

Ruby tightened her grip on his hand. "Biz, honey, how're you feeling?"

He screamed. "Let me loose! I'm all tied up."

"Calm down. Doc Granger's on his way." She took his hand. "Move your fingers for me."

"I cain't move a goddamn thing." He flailed his head from side to side then passed out again.

Her husband couldn't move. Her worst fear was confirmed.

Rage surged through Ruby. She shoved the chair to the door and climbed up so fast she had to grab the doorknob to keep from losing her balance. She wrapped her hand around the gunstock, lifted the rifle from its rack, and jumped to the floor. Her heart racing, she threw the back door open and ran outside, making for the corral. There, she raised the gunstock to her shoulder.

Diablo dangled his head hangdog over the upper fence

rail.

Ignoring his nicker of greeting, she aimed between those brown eyes. Damnation. Tears blurred her vision. Her hands shook so badly she'd surely miss the animal and blow a hole in the barn. She sank to her knees, screaming with frustration and anger and fear until Nokoni confiscated the firearm and led her back to the house.

Inside she strode the kitchen, agitated, unable to calm herself. A dumb animal hadn't caused Bismarck's accident. The fault lay in her obstinance. She'd gotten him all riled up at breakfast this morning.

Since their reunion twenty-six years earlier, their marriage had withstood the inevitable ups and downs. Overall, marital disagreements had been rare and—until recently. And this current batch was all her doing. The older she got, the more susceptible to cold she became. Tired of traipsing across the yard to the outhouse in the dead of winter, cringing as she placed warm buttocks on an icy wooden seat, she wanted indoor plumbing. A few folks in town had already dug cesspools and installed the toilets in little rooms tacked to the rear of their homes. Every time she brought up the subject, Bismarck, convinced the modern convenience was a fad, refused her request. This morning, he stormed out of the house, yelling behind him, "No one's going to *shit* in my house."

* * * *

On his seventh visit to the ranch in seven days, young Doc Granger said, "Bismarck's doing as well as can be expected, Miz Behrens. You might want to get a nurse."

"I'll think about it."

"He's a strong man. Could linger indefinitely. He's paralyzed. Can't help you. Or himself."

"But his hands move from time to time." A quaver in her

voice betrayed her hope.

"It's involuntary. Muscle spasms. *He's* not doing it consciously." The doctor patted Ruby's arm. "Get someone to help you out." For emphasis, he snapped the catch on his black bag. "You don't need to be doing all that heavy lifting."

Ruby's eyes narrowed. "I said I'd think about it."

"Let me know. I'll track down someone for you." He doffed his hat. "I'll drop in again day after tomorrow."

She let the doctor out then returned to her post in a rocking chair by their bed where her husband now slept alone.

She should write Willow, but Ruby could not pull herself from Bismarck's side long enough to locate paper and pen. Maybe later, when Ruby knew more, when she had an idea if Bismarck would recover. Not *if*—she refused to give up on him—*when* he recovered.

* * * *

The children came daily to help lift Bismarck. Matteus, the son born after Ruby's stillbirth, rode over first thing in the morning from the house he'd built a couple of miles away when he married. The youngest, Lucinda, and her husband, Parker, came before supper. All stole time from busy schedules to help her out.

Lucinda, a born mother hen, said, "Doc Granger is right, Ma. You don't need to be caring for Pa all by yourself. You're not a spring chicken any more."

"I told Granger I'd think about getting a nurse. It's bad enough you and Parker have to help him."

Ruby couldn't imagine anyone else caring for her husband. The doctor taught her to empty Bismarck's urine by passing a rubber tube into his bladder every six hours and to clear his rectum of stool every few days. The first day she gagged repeatedly. She soon realized cleaning him was no different from changing a baby. Bismarck found it humiliating that she cared for him so intimately. He'd be mortified if anyone else performed those duties, even Gertrudis, the housekeeper who had been with the family for years.

Weeks passed. His sun-browned skin faded to waxy white. His cheekbones and hawk nose protruded above slack hollow cheeks. Blue veins mapped his blood flow. Like hard ivory, the bones of his arms and legs showed beneath lax muscles and sickroom pallor. Already his firm muscles had wasted, his abdomen softened. Even his manhood shrunk.

"Make me hard, Ruby," he demanded one morning as she bathed him.

She tried. Lordy, she tried, performing familiar motions to something that no longer seemed part of the man she loved, working long past the point of despair. His privates rose, erect enough to tempt her but too soft to do much with. With a sigh, she released him.

"You're not doing it right."

She sucked in a deep breath, swallowing the spiteful remark she was about to make. "You need more time to heal. That's all."

While Bismarck slept that night, Ruby pulled off her gown and stood before the mirror. The last weeks had been hard on her, too. Though her reflection looked thin, she felt flabby. Since that fateful day, she'd been too afraid to leave the house to ride. Dark circles hung beneath exhausted eyes. Her skin looked dry and pasty. Her shoulders drooped in a new slump. No wonder he didn't desire her. Even if he were capable of making love, she wasn't. Not from lack of desire. From fear of hastening his death.

He moaned in pleasure at night, so things worked in his dreams. Just not when he—or she—wanted. Tension rose between them, the difference between their desires and their capabilities. He couldn't caress her or hold her. She wasn't woman enough to stir him while he was awake and wouldn't ride a sickly man anyway.

After her unsuccessful attempt to stimulate him, Bismarck muttered about no longer being a man and retreated into silence, shutting her out, not wanting to talk about what happened or plan for their future. So many questions needed to be settled, but for weeks, he rarely spoke.

She stayed by his side, babbling to fill the silence. At times, she ran out of words to say aloud, but that didn't stop thoughts from whipping through her head like the wind across the prairie. One moment, knowing he would never accept being an invalid, she hoped for his death, his freedom from his affliction. The next she prayed—though Doc Granger assured her she was overly optimistic—he'd recover. Mostly she dreaded being alone, being without the man she loved.

Finally, the dam broke. More words poured from Bismarck than in all the years she'd known him. As though everything he ever wanted to say to her, he had to get out. Not a word of complaint or regret about his current state but a reliving of their years together.

Ruby was so relieved he'd come back to her, she no longer pressed him about ranch-related issues but let him ramble like a free-range chicken.

"Remember the snake bite?" He gave a faint chuckle. "I still cain't figure out how such a scrawny gal got me on her pony."

Ruby managed a smile as twisted as her heart. She remembered her panic back then. After forty-two years, the fear of losing him hadn't lessened. That terror still made her heart race and her hands tremble.

"The best part was you waiting on me hand and foot."

She snorted. "You were a pistol." Even then she had been aware of his body, already tall and lean, every muscle as well-defined as an anatomical drawing. The taste of him. The soft feel of his lips on hers. The hardness that tented his linens. And the desire to unpin her hair, so they could cocoon themselves in it and shut out the world.

After each spell of reminiscence, Bismarck dozed. The effort of speaking wore him out. Slowly the periods of sleep exceeded those of nostalgia.

* * * *

At every visit, Doc Granger expressed surprise that Bismarck still lived. "He could linger indefinitely. If pneumonia doesn't take him."

Ruby closed her eyes, shutting out Doc Granger's kind face. If he offered to find her a nurse or gave that sympathetic little pat to her arm one more time, she'd scream. She wasn't ready to relinquish care of her husband to another but wondered how long she could hold up without help. Years before, she'd feared being stuck caring for an ailing mother, never once thinking the same might hold true for her husband.

Though Bismarck couldn't feel her touch, pain jolted through him where no injury existed. His nerves misfired, causing suffering that wasn't really there. He required more and more laudanum to be comfortable. Sometimes he didn't rouse for hours. According to the doctor, the opium slowed his breathing. The paralysis kept him from clearing his lungs.

Every two hours, following the doctor's instructions, she shifted Bismarck's weight to prevent bedsores and thumped his back with her fists, avoiding his broken ribs, to loosen congestion in his chest. At least, if he went, he would go of his own choosing, not from her neglect.

Despite her constant care, pneumonia set in. His

breathing grew more ragged until gurgles sounded in his chest with every exhalation.

Ruby sat close by, half-afraid to eat or go to the outhouse—one of those indoor toilets would be real convenient right now—fearing he might pass without her knowing.

She had finally drifted off when a shift in Bismarck's breathing woke her. More shallow, more labored, his rapid panting was inaudible beneath the murmur of sleet against the window. Beneath the covers, his chest rose and fell in near-imperceptible motions.

A glance at the window showed the faintest brightening of the eastern sky through the curtains. Her shoulders drooped. The doctor told her many folks live through the night, only to die at dawn, unable to summon the energy to sustain them another day. This would be his last dawn. And her first day without him. She wasn't ready. Not yet.

With a shuddering breath, she lit a lamp then felt Bismarck's forehead. No fever, yet a sheen of perspiration sparkled under the lamplight. His skin felt clammy and chilled.

His eyes, the new-denim blue now turned to faded chambray, opened and looked at her. By kerosene light, his skin looked yellow. The color of life giving way to death.

He tried to smile but achieved only a faint twist of his lips. "Ruby Louise." His voice grated in his throat, like he was pumping a dry well.

She lifted his head and gave him a sip of water.

He dropped his head back with a deep sigh, opened his mouth, started to say something, but stopped.

Ruby's right hand covered his where it had fallen outside the quilts. She had tucked him in less than an hour ago, but spasms had driven his hand from the warm covers. His fingertips were blue and cold. After stroking them back to warmth, she kissed each finger and tucked his hand beneath the quilts. Then, knowing he couldn't feel anything below his chest, she lifted her hand to his face, caressing him softly, feeling the stubble that had rasped her body so often. He could no longer control his bodily functions, yet his hair grew relentlessly. More gray had infiltrated the chestnut in the past weeks than in the decade before, making him look nearer seventy than fifty-six.

"I cain't live like this...all cut off from the land." His voice caught, and he swallowed hard. "I'll never ride a horse again."

"I know." With her free hand, she wiped her eyes, then his. When she reached over him to straighten his pillow, her breast brushed his face.

Somehow, through her flannel gown, his mouth found her nipple. He sucked once before drawing back, sputtering. "I hate flannel."

She gave a soft laugh. "You always have." Knowing this was the only way he could touch her, she unbuttoned her nightgown, allowing the only pleasure left him. His attentions stirred her. She tightened her muscles, hoping he wouldn't feel her shoulders shake. An involuntary moan escaped her, pleasure mixed with sorrow. She clenched her teeth to keep from crying. This would be the last time she felt him love her.

He suckled briefly then turned away. "I'd give any-thing...to hear you sing...one more time..."

"Me, too." Her voice shook.

"I'm like one of them sandhill cranes." He gave a faint chuckle. "I always knew...you were...the only woman...I'd ever love." His lungs gurgled. "Fifty years...good enough run...for any man."

Not wanting to impair the movement of his lungs, she laid her head lightly on his chest. Certain she felt his hands in her hair, she looked up, but only his breath had stirred her curls. Lordy, she needed his arms around her. "What will I do without you?"

"I was…meant to be yours, Ruby Louise, but you weren't…meant…to be mine. Leastwise…not forever."

He took a deep rasping breath then coughed. "I've lied to you…for years…and I am…sorry…for that."

Ruby's eyes widened in surprise. She lifted herself from his chest and stared down at him. "What are you talking about?"

"Though I damned myself to hell…worth it. Couldn't… lose…you…again."

He shuddered. His breathing stopped. His eyes dimmed. His face slackened.

Her pulse beat double-time, like his heart had moved in with hers. Her chest felt corset-tight. She patted his face and hands trying to revive him. Air. Bismarck needed fresh air. She dashed across the room and threw open the window. Cold slammed her face.

A glance back at him showed no change. He was truly gone.

In the bitter draft, she stood, staring outside. An eerie landscape, painted with more colors of gray than she had known existed, lay before her. Frost covered the ground, muting the tan of dead grasses to tarnished silver. Branches of the peach and pecan trees bowed to the ground under heavy winter coats of ice. The tin barn roof reflected the sky like worn pewter. Too overcast to give the sun purchase, the sky was iridescent with sleet, sheer curtains blown before the wind.

The sound of her own teeth chattering brought her back. Shivers wracked her body. She lowered the window. Returning to Bismarck, she closed his eyes. Her fingers explored his drawn face one last time, stroked his hair, caressed each finger, every inch of his familiar, yet now unfamiliar body. Her hands shook so badly she dropped the sheet and blanket twice before getting them pulled over his head.

"I was the sinful one, Lord. You should have taken me. He was a good man. Hold him tight in your bosom." Maybe, like her miscarriage, losing Bismarck was her punishment for being wicked. A clawing sprang in her gut. A wild beast trying to escape. Again she felt a kinship with that three-legged coyote.

For weeks, her sleep had been constantly interrupted by Bismarck's dreaming, by listening for his breathing, by the need to turn him, by the desire to spend every last minute she had with him. Now she felt like a rope stretched until no give was left, but sleep wouldn't happen in the house. Not with him here.

At the back door she pulled on boots and slipped Bismarck's oilskin duster over her nightgown. She held the sleeve to her nose and inhaled. Buried within the garment, a trace of bay rum remained.

Outside, the wind flapped the coat, slit to drape over a saddle, and plastered the hem of her gown to her ankles. The icy grass crackled under her feet. She slipped and slid across the yard, bypassing the bunkhouse. There was no point in telling the cowhands yet. The ground was too slick for safe travel anyway, the weather too severe to even advise her children. Matteus, strong and resilient like his father, she could handle, but Lucinda, her youngest, would require more energy than Ruby had.

In the barn, the horses nickered in greeting, their breath steaming the air. Unheeding, she walked past them. She had her studio. Bismarck had his own domain, an office tacked to the far end of the barn. The moment she opened the door, his scent assailed her, nearly dropping her to her knees. Her breath hung hazy in the frigid air as she looked around. The room held a run-down settee, retired long ago from their parlor, now draped with horse blankets. *The Stillbirth* and a handful of her paintings hung on the walls. His oak roll-top desk, shelves filled with reference books on veterinary medicine and western dime novels, bottles of liniment, his pipe, and a pouch of tobacco. An old stirrup he found at the Truly springs served as a paperweight. He swore some conquistador lost it while riding the *Llano Estacado* centuries before.

She built a fire before wrapping herself in horse blankets and curling up on the lumpy settee. The golden light flickering through the grate of the Franklin stove swirled like stars in an impressionist painting. She thought of the coming days. The coming years. Her life without him. It had taken a long time for them to let go of their pride and stubbornness and come together as a couple, to build not merely a marriage, but a true partnership. She thought he'd been as happy as she had been.

She studied his last words, unable to imagine what he might have lied to her about. Perhaps, as he approached death, his mind had simply wandered. He chose to go. He chose to leave her. She knew that. For weeks they had been bound in the same prison. He chose to escape and release her at the same time.

* * * *

Three days later, the weather warmed enough to melt the sleet. The sun came out, thawing the ground enough for the ranch hands to dig a grave on the hill behind the house. Except for the frigid air, it was a good day for a funeral, windless and sunny. Never one to refuse a favor or fail to lend a hand, Bismarck had been well thought of. People came from miles around to pay their respects.

After burying Bismarck, Ruby settled in the parlor. Folks formed a loose line before her, offering their condolences. She patiently shook every hand offered, kissed every proffered cheek, and thanked those who uttered hackneyed platitudes about Bismarck being "in a better place". Here to pay respects to her husband, few offered her, the town's wayward daughter, any substantial support.

Ruby restrained her impulse to chase them away so she could be alone with her memories. She refused to provide such an absurd display. She wanted Bismarck to be remembered for his kind nature, not his wife's hysteria. It was enough Hortense had made a spectacle of herself by swooning when the pallbearers lowered Bismarck into the ground. The old biddy had nearly fallen in on top of the casket, and Nate Greene wrenched his back jerking her out.

To her relief, the cold prevented people from lingering. Molly and other town ladies cleaned up the leftovers from the wake, dried, and put away the dishes, then bundled their families in winter coats and bustled them out the door. Dozens of slower moving wagons and buggies followed the spirals of dust thrown up by the first two automobiles in the county. Ruby shooed her children out the door, too. Despite their protests, they became the final wagons in a long caravan of folks heading home.

After waving everyone off, Ruby sat coatless on the porch in the rump-sprung chair Bismarck had preferred, rocking in the last remnants of a cold sunlight. Bismarck's scent wafted from the horse blanket draped over it, and a red wraith of dust swirled around her before setting on her black dress, a reminder of his presence, of times they'd spent evenings on the porch in the comfortable silence of the long-married. Her eyes clouded with tears, but she did not need to see the little cemetery beyond the Italian stone pines to visualize the graves. Her kids had not wanted her to be alone today. But she was not. Death and memories kept her company.

Lost in the past, she sat on the porch until she grew so cold she might never thaw. As she stirred, his scent again brushed her nose, reassuring her. With stiff movements, feeling far older than her fifty-four years, she rose and entered her empty home.

Having shed enough tears to irrigate half of Texas, Ruby realized crying was too easy. She had to go on. Alone. She did not have to survive the rest of her life. She needed only to make it through the next minute. Then the next. And the only way to do that was to paint, to allow her work to transport her to that sacred place where time did not exist, where only she and her canvas dwelled, where she felt complete—even without her Bismarck.

Chapter Thirty-Two
Life After Death

March 1926

In her studio, two dozen incarnations of Bismarck surrounded Ruby. Since the funeral, she had remained in the studio, working around the clock, sleeping in an old chair when she could no longer hold her head erect, starting painting after painting. For fifty-four years, she had known the man. For over half that time, she'd shared his bed. Yet his features already were slipping away, memories of his hard muscles diluted by those of his infirmity. Driven by a powerful need to capture him before he faded completely, she drew directly on the canvases, not bothering with sketches on paper. No sooner had she started one portrait, she recalled a facet of Bismarck she had yet to capture. She painted, painted, painted—yet the essence of the man, his soul, eluded her brushwork.

At night she awakened from dreams in which Bismarck's face shifted and moved, turned liquid, and ran down her canvas. If she could just catch the fluid, she could put it back and all would be well. She couldn't find a cup anywhere in the studio, so she used her hands. His face leaked through her fingers and dripped to the floor below.

* * * *

A banging on the studio door interrupted Ruby.

Lucinda erupted through the door. "Ma! Didn't you hear

me? You haven't touched the food leftover from the funeral. You're not taking care of yourself."

"Luce, I am a grown woman. If I were hungry, I'd eat."

"You sure you don't want me to stay with you? Or come to my house?" Lucinda, apron on, broom in one hand, dust pan in the other, appeared to be on a cleaning tear. "How about moving to town? You could sell the ranch. With your income, you'd be real comfortable."

Ruby snorted. "I like where I am. I'm not in my dotage—yet. Quit trying to run my life."

Lucinda clucked as she walked around the studio, looking for things to scrub. "Do you need Parker or Matteus to organize the hired hands?"

Ruby glared at her daughter. "I can run this ranch blindfolded. What I can't handle, Nokoni can. I don't need your help. Nor do I need to be mother-henned."

Lucinda swished the broom back and forth, stirring up cloudlets of dust.

With a wave of her hand before her face, Ruby coughed. "Don't you dare sweep in here. Paint's too wet."

Lucinda stilled her broom. "Have you written Willow?"

Ruby shook her head. Not that it was any of Lucinda's business. "Not yet."

"You better. How about staying with her awhile?"

"She's in Europe." It would be weeks before Willow got the news, longer before Ruby got a response. Time enough for Ruby to sort things out.

"I'll never understand how you two could be friends all those years but never visit."

Ruby ignored her daughter and dabbed at her palette, reloading her brush, half aware of Lucinda across the room, staring at the portrait of Bismarck at thirty. Tall. Lean. All man. His work shirt barely disguised muscles chiseled by hard work. His grin was sheepish, a little self-conscious. His eyes were amused and full of desire for the woman he regarded. Thumbs hooked in his pants pockets, his curled fingers, together with leather chaps, emphasized his groin. She remembered peeling off his clothing after each painting session, their laughing mouths eager for contact. Riding him as he wore only his chaps. Her womb gave a powerful lurch.

"Aw, Ma. Pa never looked like that."

Ruby glanced at her daughter, conceived on one of those wild rides, and chuckled at her daughter's words. "Maybe not to you, Luce. But all that—and more—to me." She rose, moved to her daughter's side, and tweaked her cheek. "Don't tell me Parker doesn't look that good to you."

Suddenly overcome, she sidestepped her daughter, dropped to her desk, pressed her hands against her eyes, remembered Bismarck's hands twisting her curls into tighter knots, pulling her close, whispering, "Sing to me, Ruby Louise." She sighed. To have regained that love after losing each other... Now he was gone, but she was still bound, oh-so-tightly, to the man. Her body might survive, but her heart—never.

The ebb and flow of footsteps told Ruby her daughter was wandering the studio.

"Are all these of Pa? All you've been doing these past few days is painting him?" A gasp. Then "M-M-Ma!"

Ruby raised her head at her daughter's outrage. Unable to bear remembering Bismarck with his manhood limp and shrunken, Ruby painted him nude, from her point of view between his thighs. He leaned back on his elbows, legs spread, eyes hooded with pleasure, awaiting her mouth.

"M-M-Ma! How could you paint Pa like that?" Lucinda's face turned dawn red, her mouth hung open in shock. "It's nasty. Sinful. I can't believe you did that with him!"

She turned the painting around, slammed it against the wall.

Still sputtering over the first and second paintings, Lucinda found a third, Bismarck as *Christ in the Sepulcher,* the painting Ruby had been working on when Lucinda entered. Its basic structure was fleshed out but the details not yet filled in. The grays of the morning he died predominated. His body rested on a stone slab, a coarsely woven shroud draped over his groin. The intimacy of working with Bismarck's frail body had given Ruby new insight into that Biblical scene, the blue-gray of lips no longer warmed by blood, the greenish cast to the face, the way white flesh hung slackly from bone when unsupported by functioning muscle.

Lucinda whirled and ran screaming from the studio.

With a sigh, Ruby slipped her stockinged feet into her *huaraches* and followed her daughter to the porch. Standing in the cold, she held the girl until her tears subsided then led her to the warmth of the kitchen. "Let's clean out the icebox. I could use a cup of coffee and a piece of pecan pie."

Her daughter wailed. "I can't believe he's dead, Ma."

"Me, either. But under the circumstances…" Ruby's voice shrank. "Find the pie, would you, Luce?"

"I know. But I still miss him."

Lucinda searched through the icebox, her motions agitated and sharp. She slammed the pie on the table, slammed slices on plates, slammed forks on napkins.

Ruby made and poured coffee in silence, knowing her daughter's anger disguised grief.

"I can't believe you'd paint Pa like that. He's dead. Let him rest in peace."

Ruby patted her daughter's hand. "Sweetie—"

Lucinda jerked her hand from beneath her mother's. Using both hands to support her cup, she sipped the hot liquid and grimaced. "Sacrilege *and* pornography?"

Eyeballing the pecan pie, Ruby helped herself to another piece. Without the distraction of painting, she realized she had not eaten in days and was famished. "Don't be ridiculous, Lucinda. That painting is not pornography."

"But he's my *father*!"

"Every marriage, even yours and Parker's, is a mixture of sacred and profane. I wanted to remember my husband as he was…before."

"You're too old to be thinking about such nasty things."

"Your pa and I loved each other. We enjoyed touching each other." Ruby's insides clenched at the memory of their caresses. "We might have been old, honey, but we were nowhere near dead." In fact, with her change of life, no fear of pregnancy, and no children left at home, she and Bismarck had surpassed the passion of their youth.

"What about the other one?" Lucinda sniffled, tears threatening again.

"That was the most difficult painting I've ever done. But I wanted to remember him that way, too, though it broke my heart." She flicked a bit of pie crust from a finger before passing a hand over damp eyes. "It was all my fault."

"What was?"

"His accident. We had an argument. Your pa stormed outside all mad. Right after that he got thrown. Nokoni said his mind wasn't on the horse…"

"But you two never argue. At least not the way Parker and I do."

"Our arguments were rare, but when we had one, it was usually a doozy."

"What'd you fight about?"

Ruby made an unladylike sound. "Indoor plumbing."

"You're kidding." Lucinda suppressed a smile, but her shoulders shook. "I can hear him now, 'Nobody's going to *shit* in my house'."

Sniffling, Ruby tried not to giggle, but laughter won. Soon she and Lucinda were regaling each other with remembrances of Bismarck's old-fashioned notions.

Lucinda stroked her mother's hand. "Ma, it wasn't you. It was Diablo. Even Pa called him Satan's own steed." With a few more grumbles, she stood, then in a dust devil of activity, swept and mopped a kitchen unused since the funeral, then moved into the parlor, trailing broom and mop behind her.

Ruby resisted the urge to still Lucinda's activity, realizing that her daughter needed to organize her space—even if it was her mother's home—to order her emotions.

When the house gleamed, Lucinda, holding forth less vociferously, on her mother's need for companionship, returned to her own home.

Relieved at being alone again, Ruby returned to the desk in her studio. Bismarck's passing changed everything. Though she wished she could postpone the task perhaps for a year—or two—or perhaps forever—until she came to terms with Bismarck's death, she began a letter to Willow.

> *My dearest Willie,*
> *Eight long, long, long weeks ago, Bismarck broke his neck when thrown from a horse. He was paralyzed. In the doctor's opinion, moving Biz into the Truly Clinic would do more harm than good. I cared for him here until he passed...*

Since the year Ruby lost the baby, the two women had not seen each other. They continued to write, though their expressions of love had long since been reduced to chatty tidbits shared by women who'd been friends forever. Ruby shared every letter with Bismarck, often leaving them out where he could read them if he chose, proof she had nothing to hide. As far as she could tell, he never violated those pages. He had always seemed more jealous of d'Este.

Night after night, after wakening from dreams of Bismarck rolling over in bed and spooning against her, reaching for her in his sleep, Ruby slept in her workspace, sitting in an old rocking chair upholstered with worn buffalo hide. Eventually, tired of rising stiff and unrefreshed, she had Matteus and Parker move a bed from the attic to her studio. Even there, even dead, Bismarck made her cry out in pleasure as she slept.

Every day Ruby wondered about Bismarck's last words. He had loved her when she had been unable to love herself, had taken her back after d'Este, had forgiven her every pain she caused him. She could not imagine what he, the most honest person she knew, might have concealed. Ruby struggled with his confession, searching memories for clues, never reaching a conclusion. She breathed in relief that he had never learned her own dark secret.

* * * *

A simple man with simple tastes, Bismarck had few belongings, yet Ruby could not bear going through his things. Because he accumulated so little, every item carried correspondingly more significance. She shared his clothing with the hired hands, after checking every pocket for a clue to his secret, searching. Before she divided his books between their children, she leafed through each, searching. She emptied his rolltop desk and poured over the ranch finances, searching.

His Bible still sat on the table next to his favorite chair, his spectacles on top. Since his death, she had dusted around the little still-life, somehow hoping if she left it undisturbed he might return. Now, she sat in his chair, set aside his glasses, and though her eyes were too watery to make out the words *HOLY BIBLE*, she opened it. She knew what caused the lump in the front cover—the tip of the braid he had stolen from her forty years earlier.

His mother had given them this Bible as a wedding gift, and he had dutifully recorded the event on the frontispiece. Ruby ran her finger over the words.

> *Married this day, June 16, 1896*
> *Bismarck Gustav Behrens to Ruby Louise Schmidt*
> *d'Este*
> *I am my Beloved's, and my Beloved is Mine.*

She didn't think she could keep going, but her eyes had already scanned the next line. *Bismarck Gustav Behrens, Truly, Texas, July 23, 1870—*. She sucked in a deep breath before wiping her eyes with her sleeve. With cautious fingers to ensure her trembling didn't foul her script, she added *February 26, 1926*, blowing on the ink to hasten its drying. Somehow, the black words on ivory paper made his death more final.

As if knowing her heart could not bear the sight of the round loops of her handwriting contrasting with Bismarck's angular script, her gaze turned outside and meandered among the tombstones set in the stone pines. Never had she thought her dead would outnumber her living. Three children and a husband *there*; only she remained *here* in this house.

Composing herself, she regarded the Bible and moved her finger, name by name, down the page.

Ruby Louise Schmidt Behrens, Truly, Texas, October 19, 1872—. Herself. Still alive. But, heart shattered, barely surviving.

Bismarck Johannes Behrens, Truly, May 31, 1897—. Here, the straight line of Bismarck's writing had wavered as he wrote "Stillborn." Her breath caught in her throat. A vision of the black curlicued wrought iron cross that marked the baby's grave danced over the page. The death that tore her and Bismarck apart.

After several moments lost in remembrance, her heart still heavy, Ruby resumed reading.

Gian-Battista d'Este Behrens, Philadelphia, Pennsylvania, March 4, 1893—France, June 1918. A black granite obelisk marked where Johnny's bones ought to be. Unlike her stillborn son, tucked snugly beneath those pines, her firstborn lay lost and alone somewhere in French soil, one of a thousand American soldiers missing after the Battle of Belleau Woods.

Sophie Marie d'Este Behrens, Truly, September 29, 1894—January 14, 1918. Of pneumonia. A passing cowhand brought influenza to the ranch. Everyone got sick. Only Sophie succumbed.

Ruby remembered her sorrow at losing Sophie and Johnny. And her relief. Relief at losing a daughter destined to be as mercurial as her father. And, when Ruby wrote d'Este of the deaths of their two children, relief that her ties to him were finally and utterly severed.

Matteus Bismarck Behrens, Truly, April 19 1903. An exact copy of his father. A delight in his mother's eye for that reason alone.

Lucinda Estelle Behrens, Truly, July 29, 1906. The features of Ruby's mother with Bismarck's coloring. Born to be a wife, not an artist. And, Lordy, how much simpler Lucinda's life would be for that.

Wondering how many more names and dates she would add, she idly leafed through Bismarck's Bible. He had tucked her sketch of the baby in the *Book of Matthew* and underlined the verse, Matthew 5:4, "Blessed are those who mourn, for they shall be comforted."

The page shimmered before her eyes. She looked outside again. She no longer had Bismarck to anchor her. How would she manage?

With a sigh, Ruby returned her attention to the Good Book, aimlessly flipping pages, reading passages Bismarck had annotated. Just before she closed the cover, she noticed the back end-sheet, which should have been pasted down, was loose. She ran her fingers over it, feeling something inside. With a knitting needle, she carefully lifted the end-sheet. Tucked beneath, she found a folded page. She extracted the paper and turned it over. The reverse had faint colored squares, as though the sheet had rubbed against some kind of pigment. Her heart stopped even before she opened it.

> *My beloved,*
> *I can't bear causing you pain.*
> *Go with Bismarck. Be happy.*
> *Let my love no longer trouble you, but know I*
> *shall wait for you—for your love—forever, if need-*
> *ed. Every night until we are reunited I will dream*
> *of your skin, your breasts, your kisses…*
> *Your ever-devoted lover,*
> *Willie*

Ruby gasped. Bismarck knew. Had known all along. Seconds later, rage flashed through her. She threw his Bible across the room then read and reread Willow's letter.

Hours later, once Ruby calmed down, she reexamined her memories of the morning Bismarck had broken the paint box. He had not only blamed her for the loss of their child but for loving Willow. No wonder he had been so hell-fired angry. No wonder he had smashed the box, destroying Willow *in absentia*. Fear that his wife would leave him forced an honest man to lie. No wonder he had hated Ruby.

Now, though, Ruby would never know why he let go of that wrath, what made him forgive her, what let him love her again.

* * * *

June 1927

Ruby reread Willow's most recent letter. The woman had invited herself to the ranch on short notice, her arrival a mere five days away.

> *My dearest,*
>
> *I will be arriving in Truly on June 15th on my way to San Francisco.*
>
> *For the first time in years, I returned to Philadelphia. In Villanova, I visited three women artists who live together most harmoniously, Violet Oakley, Elizabeth Shippen Green, and Jessie Wilcox Smith. They attended the Academy shortly after we did. The Red Rose Girls, as they are called, are dear friends and successful illustrators.*
>
> *I came away from their home hoping we might similarly become companions, sharing our lives as artists—and as lovers—once again...*

Damnation. There was not enough time for a reply to reach Willow, though Ruby was unsure whether she would have told her lover to come or stay away.

Fifteen months had not been long enough to erase Bismarck's presence. She needed more time. Willow would want to resume their affair, but, when Ruby thought of sharing coffee on the porch, Willow sitting in Bismarck's chair, his image overrode hers. Making love in the bed she had shared with Bismarck was unthinkable. In fact, she could not envision sharing any room, any bed, with Willow. Yet she could not deny the reemergence of her long-suppressed attraction to the other woman.

* * * *

At the Truly station, while wondering if her fellow artist had missed a connection along the way, Ruby chatted with Molly, who was checking stock against a bill of lading while her oldest son unloaded barrels and boxes for the mercantile.

"Look at that." Molly jerked her chin toward a woman who had just stepped out of the station. Dressed in startling attire, an arrow-straight, long-waisted black dress with the hem riding just below the knee, she was clearly not a local.

After a glance their way, the woman looked around, then paused to light a cigarette before walking toward them.

Ruby recognized her friend at last. Her pulse hammered in her ears. "Willie?"

"Darling, you haven't changed a bit." Willow blew out a stream of smoke, kissed Ruby on each cheek in the European fashion then looked around. With a smile as dry as her voice, she added, "Neither has Truly."

Ruby clenched her tongue between teeth. After thirty years, change could be expected. Willow looked different, but Ruby didn't want to mention it. She stepped back to get a good look. The other woman wore her hair in a sophisticated chin-length dyed-black bob. An emerald brooch adorned her felt cloche, the only color in her somber attire. Ruby felt frumpy in her long skirt and sunbonnet. She shifted from one foot to another, unable to put together a coherent thought or say a word of welcome.

After an awkward moment, her brain began to work.

She introduced Willow to Molly and left instructions with the porter for the baggage to be loaded in the buckboard. She led her friend a few doors down from the station, to Edith Ann's Cafe, a brick building with a big front window with bright red geraniums dancing in flower boxes. In mid afternoon, the two women were the only customers.

Before the doorbell finished its clang, the woman scrubbing tables greeted them. "Howdy, Ruby. Be right with you."

"Take your time, Edith." Sitting at a table covered by oilcloth, Ruby, unable to think of anything to say, just looked at Willow.

Willow, appearing equally ill at ease, glanced around. Over the cash register, a Martin Seed calendar of *Still-life with Girl* hung beside a schoolhouse clock. "D'Este?" She jerked her chin toward the image. "It looks like his work."

Ruby nodded. "That son of a bitch. I can't escape him— or the picture. Used to make me mad. I'd rip them down. I finally realized it was useless. Everyone in town has one of the calendars or posters or seed packets. Nowadays, fewer people realize it's me." She gave a rueful laugh. "I guess there are advantages to getting old."

"You were lovely then." Willow caressed Ruby's hand. "You still are." Willow's voice sounded like she had thirty years before, springlike and eager.

Flustered, Ruby jerked her hand from beneath Willow's and lifted her coffee cup to disguise her action.

After they finished their coffee and cake, Willow said, "Are your *Stations* and *Resurrection* nearby? I've never seen them."

"We can walk. It's not far." Ruby led Willow the few blocks to Our Lady of Guadalupe at the edge of town. She hadn't been there for years. After she moved back to the ranch, she stopped going to the Mexican church except on holidays. Her ties to the place died completely with the deaths of Father Damiano and *Señora* Romero.

"I'd forgotten you lived in the heart of nowhere." Willow stared at the Truly hills in the distance. "God, it's bleak. There's nothing for miles."

"There's plenty out there, Willie, just open your eyes. All that openness frees me to paint. There are no distractions. No buildings to cage my thoughts. Subtleties of light and hue become more apparent. In Paris or Venice, all the people, the prettiness, the profuse colors, would distract me."

Inside the mission, Ruby led Willow on a tour of her paintings. After viewing the fourteen Stations of the Cross, they sat in the last pew together.

Willow didn't say a word about Ruby's paintings. Quiet stretched between them, filling the chapel.

Ruby could stand the silence no longer. "Well? What do you think?" Her voice tightened. "You're the only one who's seen them that knows anything about art."

"They're strong, powerful. You've taken traditional images and made them modern. In every one, I see God questioning whether the sacrifice of His Son will save His Creation." Willow patted Ruby's hand. "And I see your sorrow at the loss of your babe."

"If I hadn't painted, I would have gone insane. Painting kept me from dwelling on losing the baby—and Biz." Ruby wiped tears away with the back of her wrist then placed her hand on Willow's arm.

Willow lifted Ruby's hand and kissed the dampness away.

Ruby withdrew her hand and twisted her body to look behind her. "Turn around. I knew I was better when I painted that." She indicated the *Resurrection.*

Willow looked behind her and caught her breath. "It's

magnificent."

The fresco, nestled between the two front doors, filled the front wall of the chapel. Christ holding a lily floated above the Texas landscape. Filled with light and hope, the image stood in sharp contrast to the darkness of the Stations.

"You're wasted here, Ruby. In Paris or New York, you'd be recognized as the extraordinary artist you are."

Ruby shook her head. "I'd be lost, like I was in Philadelphia. Other people's expectations, their criticism, their work would crowd my paintings right out of my head."

* * * *

After arriving at the ranch, Ruby said, "Nokoni put your things in the girls' bedroom upstairs."

"Will we not be sleeping together?"

Ruby's face heated. "I don't know if I'm ready."

"It's been over a year." Willow sighed.

During the night, Ruby awakened to gentle kisses. Her drowsy body responded. With a jolt, she realized who was with her. "What are you doing here?" She shoved Willow away. She thought she had made things clear the prior afternoon. "I can't do *that*. Not here. Not in this bed."

"Upstairs?"

"In my child's bed?" Ruby clenched her hair in her hands. "I don't know if I can do it at all in this house."

"I don't mean to press you, but it has been a long time." Willow settled on the far side of the bed as far from Ruby as she could get. "Better?" Wringing her fingers together, she cleared her throat. "Are you no longer attracted to me?"

"It's not that." Tears filled Ruby's eyes. "I miss him every single minute."

"Damn you, Ruby. I know you do. But I've missed you for years." Willow's voice caught. "What happened between us was no accident. You deny your true self if you won't admit your attraction to other women."

"I can't deny Bismarck either."

"We were such innocents back then. We slept together, made love, vowed eternal devotion, declared ourselves sisters, not knowing we were far more than that. We never grasped the fact that we were not unique, never knew others like us existed, never knew the word *lesbian*. We're not the only two women to have fallen in love. There are thousands of us in the world."

"But I'm not like that. I love you, but I'm not attracted to other women."

Willow tilted her head. "Really?"

"It's true. My love for you has nothing to do with what's on the outside and everything to do with what's in here"—she touched Willow's forehead, then her chest—"and here." She kissed Willow's hand. "And in these fingers." Willow's soft hands were as paint-speckled as Ruby's own.

In silence, they sat on the bed. Unfulfilled desire weighted the air.

Finally, Willow stood. Her gown swished softly as she walked away. "Good night, my love."

Chapter Thirty-Three
Overcoming Paralysis

June 1927

After breakfast the next morning, Ruby led Willow to her studio adjoining the back porch.

Willow followed eagerly. "Except for yesterday at the church, I haven't seen your work in years."

"Nor I yours," Ruby reminded her.

In the studio, floor to ceiling windows like in a French atelier faced the northern sky. The room overflowed with art—hung on walls, propped on easels, stacked against each other along the baseboards. Images of Bismarck, some finished, some not, surrounded Ruby's easel. The blatant nude of her husband popped into her head, and not wanting to hurt Willow's feelings, Ruby rushed ahead and turned the painting toward the wall.

"What are you hiding from me?" Following behind her, Willow flipped the image and discovered Bismarck. She raised an eyebrow. "My, you paint the most interesting things."

Ruby's face heated. "I'm sorry."

Willow sighed. "Don't apologize. You two clearly enjoyed one another—unlike Walter and I." She wandered around the studio, "I had hoped, here, surrounded by art as we were at the Academy, that we might—"

With a rapid inspection of her workspace, Ruby shook

her head. "No, not here either."

"I didn't think so. Too much Bismarck." Willow moved from image to image, taking time to study each. "How many times have you painted him?"

Ruby shrugged, wondering if Willow was jealous. "Since he died? Three dozen. Maybe more."

"You really are good, you know. Have you done anything at all with your work? Have you had a show?"

Ruby shook her head. "Not since *The Stillbirth* at the Academy. Those horrible reviews devastated me. I haven't opened myself up to that sort of criticism since."

"Styles, expectations, techniques have all changed since we were in school. Your work would be more favorably received now. Women aren't expected to produce 'pretty' paintings any more."

"What about your work?"

"I still simplify, seeking the perfect line, the perfect form."

Ruby laughed. "You spend your time taking out details I slave to put in. Maybe you seek the perfect form to avoid revealing your heart."

"And because you don't show your work, you have the luxury of bleeding all over your canvases."

Her words shot a barb into Ruby's heart.

"I'm sorry, dear, but in these last portraits of Bismarck, your pain is so raw, people will be uncomfortable looking at them."

At Willow's words, tears welled in Ruby's eyes.

Willow took her hand. "But we could all use a good jolt to push us from our complacency. Walter could arrange a show for you, I'm sure. All your works of Bismarck, shown together, would be interesting. Similar to d'Este's show, years ago, where every painting was of you."

Ruby shook her head. "Just what I need—comparison with my former husband."

"You have a unique vision. I'm sure Walter could sell your work."

"I don't know. Illustration gives me a steady income. Long ago, I learned I don't make art to sell. I paint to save myself."

Willow chuckled. "What a romantic notion, my dear."

* * * *

Early the next morning, the two walked the prairie. Crickets and grasshoppers hopped away at their approach. Mourning doves sounded their coo-ah-coo-coo-coos, already lamenting the passage of the cool night. Moisture from the night's rain clung lovingly to the earth. With the brilliant red sunrise, the dew flared like ruby dust thrown down by the hand of God.

"Ruby, come away with me."

"I can't leave." Ruby bent and picked a blade of grass. "Not just because of Biz, but because this is my home." She stroked the grass with her fingers and sniffed. "Smell the rain, the earth, the grass. Look at the sky. Those puffy clouds floating like piles of cotton. The sound of the wind in the grass. I need all that."

Willow touched Ruby's arm, tracing a slow path. "I love you. I always have. But I've also waited for you a long time."

"Waited?" Ruby snorted. "How many lovers have you taken while you've waited?"

"Leave the past where it belongs." Willow's voice snapped like tree branches in an icy wind. "This is the first time we've both been free—"

"You're not free. What about Walter? Do you not care an iota for him?"

"Walter and I have worked together well all these years,

even developed a true affection. But never desire. Never lust. I lack what he seeks—a cock." Willow shrugged. "If it would make you happy, I would divorce him in a heartbeat and take you as my only love."

Ruby's mouth popped open in shock. "But the marriage suits you both. Why leave him?"

"Because like a swan, my dear, you have archaic ideas of fidelity." Her elegant fingers stroked Ruby's jaw before pulling her close and kissing her fiercely. "Come with me to Paris. Natalie Barney, an American expatriate there, holds weekly salons where women like us—celebrities, artists, writers—congregate. We talk for hours on women's issues. Nat recreates the atmosphere of Sappho's school at Lesbos where women learned from other women."

Ruby wrinkled her nose. "That holds no appeal to me." Her hands fluttered, reflecting her agitation. "I couldn't work with all that socializing going on. I learned that in Philadelphia."

Willow clutched Ruby's arm. "But in Paris we could live together openly. Unlike the laws of marriage, we don't have to own each other. There are no regulations for women in love. We can do whatever we want, make our own way, shape our own rules. We'll build a house where we both can be comfortable."

Ruby pulled away. As often as she had rebelled against the rules women were supposed to follow, she could not envision a life completely outside the boundaries of decency. "I can't imagine living in Paris. Living *that* way."

"We could visit the Louvre, Versailles, Sainte Chapelle, the Pont Neuf. I could introduce you to influential artists—Picasso, Matisse, Braque."

"Even with the art, Willie, I couldn't live there. This is my home."

"How about New York or San Francisco?"

"You're pushing too hard." Ruby's face flushed with anger. She shoved Willow away. "How can I deny Bismarck? I loved him. Truly loved him. What we had was real, Willie."

Willow touched Ruby's shoulder. "I'm sorry, beloved. I know it was. I never meant to imply otherwise. What we had was genuine, too—at least for me."

"For me, too." Ruby wrapped her arm about Willow's waist. "I've missed you every day we've been apart."

The two women walked by the corrals. Horses nickered at them. Ruby reached into her apron pocket for carrots and gave each animal a treat as she rubbed their noses. "Be realistic, Willie. A place that combines high society and open grasslands doesn't exist. As much as we wish to be together, one of us would always be miserable."

"Is there no hope?"

Ruby gave a helpless shrug.

"There's no time limit on my love. I've waited this long. I can wait longer." Willow turned and strode quickly back to the house. She turned back. "But, please, don't make me wait forever."

* * * *

That night, after tossing and turning for hours, Ruby carried her *mille fiore* quilt to the windmill. After her children's deaths, Ruby often sat by their graves to think and read. Since Bismarck's death, she found comfort in his office. Now, it seemed inappropriate to visit either place to consider loving Willow.

Here, surrounded by the constant soft whir of the windmill's vanes, the slow deep clunk of the water pump, the whispering wind waving the prairie grasses, the chirp of insects and frogs, she found a measure of stillness. She sat, thinking, until dew settled on the grass between her toes and deep purple clouds pinked with dawn. After giving an explosive huff of air that emphasized nothing was settled, she stood. Returning to her room, she fell into an exhausted sleep.

When Ruby rose, it was noon. Disoriented and out of sorts, she couldn't remember if she had ever slept so late. After dressing, she walked through a silent house. Her breakfast lay on the kitchen table, covered by a towel. She looked outside. Gertrudis, the housekeeper, was working in the garden. Even Willow should be up by now, but there was no sign of her.

Ruby hesitated before climbing to the attic. Each creak of the steps urged her to return downstairs. Willow, assuming Ruby had changed her mind, would expect the unthinkable. The bedroom door stood slightly ajar. Ruby tapped lightly. When there was no answer, she opened the door a bit and peeked in. Willow's bed was made. An envelope lay on the pillow. Her hands shaking, Ruby opened it.

> *My dearest Love,*
> *I won't pressure you further. Nokoni is driving me to the station. If ever you are ready, know I still wait...*

With Willow's departure, things remained the same except for the addition of indoor plumbing. Yet the ranch itself shrank. Ruby's workspace seemed small and empty. Her studio, the sanctuary she had so carefully constructed and meticulously filled with small comforts, became oppressive. Though she painted, she thought her work sterile and lifeless. She felt stiff, old, and faded, like all color had been squeezed from her life. No longer did the black shade of d'Este hover over her, but a gray shroud of her own making.

After Bismarck's death, Ruby felt fragmented. Now missing him and Willow both, she realized part of her had been asleep. Through her own doing, her contact with other artists had been limited. She read avidly and kept past issues of the *Art Journal*, *Colliers*, and *The Century Illustrated Monthly Magazine* for reference. Except for letters from Willow and rare notes from Wheatley and Ames, Ruby had not been in contact with another artist since leaving Philadelphia.

With a heave, Ruby removed the paints, books, and tablecloth that covered the steamer trunk she had taken to the Academy. For years, she'd used it as a table. The last time she remembered opening it, she placed Johnny's documents and war medals inside. Bismarck's death certificate still sat on her desk as she couldn't bear locking him away completely.

She fished in the back of her desk drawer for the key. Damnation. It was not there. With her fingers, she tugged at the lock, slammed at it with her fist, but it wouldn't budge. She removed everything from her desk, upended every drawer, and still could not find the key. Finally, she strode to the barn and grabbed the crowbar. Back in the studio, it took all her strength to pry the lock open. The wood of the trunk cracked with her efforts.

With a shove, she lifted the lid. Inside she found mementos: Buffalo Bill's business card, her marriage licenses, her wedding ring, the *mille fiore* necklace, and divorce papers from d'Este. And far too many death certificates.

After reviewing these, she lifted the false bottom, revealing stacks of dollar bills wrapped in lace handkerchiefs and tied with ribbons, money she dared not entrust to a bank. Beneath those were other treasures. Her first drawing of Bismarck's most intimate parts. *Fanny Hill*, its pages foxed with age. Willow's pastel of Ruby wearing the red kimono. The drawings Willow had made of a pregnant Ruby. And the sketchbook in which she and Willow had documented their love.

* * * *

A letter arrived from Willow late in April the following year.

> *My beloved Ruby,*
>
> *I am in Taos, New Mexico, at the invitation of a remarkable woman, Mabel Dodge Luhan. She reigns over an artists' colony in town with luminaries such as D. H. Lawrence, Willa Cather, and Leopold Stokowski drawn to her flame. Ira and Nan have bought a small place here, and Fred visits from Paris from time to time. If you were here, it will be like the old days at the Academy.*
>
> *The Taos Valley has mountains curving around one side and desert on the other. Colors are vibrant. Textures rich. Like your Texas, Taos has a remote beauty all its own.*
>
> *You could be happy painting this landscape and the Pueblo Indians who inhabit it. A place that combines intellectual pursuits and open grasslands exists after all.*
>
> *Please meet me in Paradise for a month? A week? A day?*

Ruby studied the letter, holding it in quavering hands for what seemed like hours, weighing her options. Texas bred three types of men, married and content, married and discontent, or unmarried and tetchy. While someone in the latter two groups might consider rolling in the hay with her—and there'd been offers—she wasn't sure that would be enough for her. She wanted—needed—an *affaire de cœur*. She could think of no man who could understand her, excite her, or love her as much as Willow, the woman she'd denied for so long.

* * * *

New Mexico, May 1928

The Atchison, Topeka and Santa Fe hauled Ruby west toward New Mexico's Sangre de Cristo Mountains. Coward that she was, she had not written Willow she was coming. Ruby needed to feel she could escape, could return to Truly if her nerve failed.

As the train climbed toward Santa Fe, the landscape blazed with spring color. Sometimes a single color washed over the hillsides like spilled paint. Sometimes multiple colors sprinkled mountains as randomly as confetti.

Ruby had started to pack her oils but at the last minute chose watercolors and pastels. A new life meant an opportunity to reinvent herself, to vanquish the staleness from her work, to free herself from Venetian oil painting techniques and her obsession with detail, to conquer new painting techniques.

New Mexico was different from anywhere Ruby had been. Compared to Texas, the days were warm but the nights downright chilly. At an altitude of seven thousand feet, a mile higher than Truly, the air was thin and crystal clear, so attenuated she could not catch her breath.

She spent two days in Santa Fe, paralyzed, unable to move forward or back. Though she walked for hours, her thoughts churned so wildly she couldn't enjoy her surroundings.

At the Cathedral Basilica of Saint Francis of Assisi, she pulled a scarf over her head and entered. Out of deference to *Señora* Romero, she genuflected and crossed herself. She wandered through the church, comparing her own paintings at Our Lady of Guadalupe with those in the larger, more ornate cathedral. Her works were as good, if not better, but any painting would show to best advantage in the simple setting of Our Lady. She knelt and tried to remember the rosary the old woman had taught her but mangled the prayers. Surely God would accept their imperfections.

Later, Ruby blinked as she walked from beneath the portico of the Governor's Palace. With little atmosphere to filter the sun, New Mexican light blazed intense and harsh, blinding her. The effect was strangely unsettling. Brilliant daylight bleached important details. Dense shade obscured others. Salient information got lost in those extremes. The narrow range of mid-tones didn't tell the full story.

For most of her life, like those middle tones, she was caught between loving Bismarck and Willow. In truth, without light, there could be no shadow. Without shadow, no mid-tones, no highlights. There was no contradiction in loving both. Her mind made anxious circles around her unresolved relationship with Willow. Bismarck, always present, had given her unconditional love even when she could not love herself, forgiven every transgression, and shared her connection to the land. Yet Willow, absent for years, understood Ruby and her art in a way Bismarck never had. She loved both deeply, passionately, yet by loving both, had been unable to love either fully. She had short-changed them both. Perhaps she'd short-changed herself as well.

That night Ruby leafed again through the old sketchbook. In the mirror in her hotel room, she catalogued her flaws, compared her body then and now. Crow's feet. The scar on her lip. Five pregnancies and the change of life irrevocably altered a woman. Her breasts sagged. The pooch of her belly, barely noticeable in clothing, seemed magnified in her reflection. Her bottom and thighs remained firm from riding every day. Little gray had invaded her hair, though its red had softened to strawberry blonde. Not bad for a woman nearly fifty-five. Would her body—would she—be enough?

Ruby settled on the bed and, opening the book of figure studies, relived every encounter captured there. She traced the beloved curves, her heart supplying the dimensions her eyes and fingers could not, the exquisite textures of milk-smooth skin, the hard nipples, the silk of waist-length hair, and the intoxicating scent of *English Fern*. That night, for the first time in years, Willow—rather than Bismarck—came to her in her dreams.

The next morning, before she could change her mind, Ruby telegraphed Willow.

* * * *

The closer the train came to Taos, the faster Ruby's heart thumped, a rhythm loud enough to fill her head entirely, drowning out the clattering of the wheels on the tracks. When the engine pulled into the station, while everyone else disembarked, she remained seated, shoulders slumped, fingers twisting her wedding ring. Since Bismarck had placed it on her finger the second time, Ruby had not removed the band. It became more precious the thinner and more scratched it had become.

Ruby thought back to the long weeks after his accident when they talked for hours, reliving their marriage. Overall, despite its ups and downs, the relationship had been a good one, sensual and earthy. She still found herself unable to let go.

The young conductor stepped into the car, counting off passengers and checking tickets. "Need any help, ma'am?"

Ruby shook her head.

"Best move along then."

She nodded then rose stiffly, slowly. With a stretch, she stood and looked out the cinder-specked window. Willow was not there. Ruby glanced at her watch. The train was seven minutes early. She clapped a wide-brimmed straw hat on her head then stepped from the Pullman car. The heels of her shoes clicked against the platform as she claimed her baggage.

Dust swirled around her. Cool air darted up her skirt. Above, clouds turned a cobalt blue darker than the sky. Cold, hard drops of rain splattered her head. She dashed for shelter in the station. Inside, the raindrops crashing on the tin roof sounded louder than thunder. Minutes later, as suddenly as it had arrived, the shower departed. Ruby stepped outside as rays of sunlight splayed from scattering clouds and a double rainbow appeared against the still-dark sky. Awed, she stared at the unearthly vision of a Jacob's ladder ascending to the heavens.

Behind her, a clattering of feet at the other end of the station drew her attention from the spectacular sky. She turned to see if it was Willow.

"Ruby!" A tall red-headed man and a petite gray-haired woman waved from the end of the platform.

Ruby blinked in slow recognition. Wheatley and his Nan. With a return wave, Ruby started toward them. How delightful to see them after all these years. A thought popped into her head. Willow must have been anxious enough about their reunion to need reinforcements. Ruby slowed her steps. Perhaps they were bearers of bad news. Wondering where her lover was, she looked around the station then returned her gaze to Wheatley. Movement behind him caught her attention. A third person, a thin figure in black trousers and a bolero jacket embroidered in silver, stepped from behind Wheatley's bulky frame.

It was Willow, running her hands around the brim of a black hat.

Ruby's breath hitched in her chest. The gesture was so evocative of Bismarck, it brought Ruby to a halt, leaving her uncertain she was truly ready to move on. She glanced down at her wedding ring. He remained with her, but, unless she pledged faithfulness to a ghost, there could be no infidelity. Loving Willow now would not erase his love or their marriage. No contradiction remained.

Ruby looked up at Willow and took a deep breath. She twisted her wedding ring one last time, then willed her feet to move forward and close the distance between them. Willow's scent reached her first. No longer *English Fern*, but a fancy fragrance that hung heavier and sweeter in the desert air than the delectable smell of rain.

Two thin creases between Willow's eyebrows revealed her tension. Her lips couldn't decide whether to smile or not. Instead, she took a deep breath. Hesitating just a moment, she reached for Ruby's shoulders, kissing her formally, once on each cheek.

Rather than responding in kind, Ruby clasped the other woman's head between her palms, placed her lips full on Willow's sensuous mouth and kissed her. As their moist tongues sparked, Ruby ignited with a different kind of fire. "Take me. I'm yours."

Author Bio

Suanne Schafer, born in West Texas at the height of the Cold War, finds it ironic that grade school drills for tornadoes and nuclear war were the same: hide beneath your desk and kiss your rear-end goodbye. Now a retired family-practice physician whose only child has fledged the nest, her pioneer ancestors and world travels fuel her imagination. She originally planned to write romances, but either as a consequence of a series of failed relationships or a genetic distrust of *happily ever-after*, her heroines are strong women who battle tough environments and intersect with men who might—or might not—love them.

Suanne completed the Stanford University Creative Writing Certificate program. Her short works have been featured in print and on-line Suanne's next book explores the heartbreak and healing of an American physician caught up in the 1994 Rwandan genocide.

Book Club Discussion Questions for
A Different Kind of Fire

1. Throughout the novel, Ruby is the stay-at-home while Willow is the traveler. How do the two live vicariously through one another? What about their differing personalities make their relationship credible? Which woman, if either, do you most easily identify with?

2. Ruby has a single-minded love of the vast prairies and skies of Texas where Willow is unsettled, moving between Paris, San Francisco, and Philadelphia. How do these environments define each woman?

3. Willow was a ground-breaking artist while Ruby became enamored of the centuries-old technique of Venetian oil painting. How do you think their choices of media influenced their careers?

4. At the time these two women painted, the art world was dominated by men: male artists, critics, and gallery owners. Willow navigated this world, even married a gallery owner/photographer, while Ruby married a cowboy and fought simply for the right to paint. Discuss how the challenges and the risks these two women took as women and artists. Do those feel relevant to women today?

5. While in Philadelphia, Ruby is exposed to new ideas about the place of women in America. She meets suffragettes like Willow's mother, reads pamphlets advocating Free Love, and learns about birth control. How do these new ideas influence her? What new ideas have influenced your life?

6. Why is Ruby so invested in her education? Is it a means to an end, or an end unto itself? If a means to an end, what end? Is she being realistic, or is she fooling herself?

7. What are the abiding characteristics of Ruby's relationship with her mother? Who do you think suffers the

most—mother or daughter?

8. Bismarck is Ruby's devoted, long-suffering love. What "wobble" does his personality have? What incidents set him off his usual course?

9. Desire is a powerful force for Ruby: desire for art, desire for place, connection to the land, to solitude. There's also the desire between two people. Compare and contrast her desire for Bismarck, d'Este, and Willow. Which do you think was more vital to Ruby?

10. *A Different Kind of Fire* is not a romance, but it is a love story on many levels. It is also full of love triangles such as Ruby-Bismarck-art and Ruby-Bismarck-d'Este. How many other triangles can you identify? Ruby, at one point, notes that she had seen "spring-coil animal traps in which a single paw remained clamped between the steel teeth, where a coyote had chewed off a leg rather than be captured. No matter which leg she chewed off, she would hurt someone and she herself would be devastated." Which leg of these triangles, if chewed off, would most devastate Ruby?

9 781641 368650